PRAISE FOR MARTIN SHANNON

"…it's like Dean Koontz and Terry Pratchett had a baby with a Mission Impossible film…"

— FAERA LANE, SCIENCE FICTION AND
FANTASY ILLUSTRATOR

…a breath of fresh air in the urban fantasy genre.

— EDISON T. CRUX - AUTHOR OF THE ENOC
TALES

Martin hits the weirdness that is Florida right on the nose. The magick is clever, the laughs are big, and these people are my neighbors.

— G. MICHAEL REYNOLDS

TALES OF WEIRD FLORIDA SHORT STORIES

VOLUME 1-15

MARTIN SHANNON

FREE STORIES

Pixies, Shades, and tribal Magick—having a baby is hard enough, but having a Magician's baby is in a league all of its own...

Sign up at www.martin-shannon.com to get "Danderous Delivery," the Tales of Weird Florida short story only available to newsletter subscribers.

For my fans...

HOOK, LINE, AND SLINKER
BY MARTIN SHANNON

*P*elting rain smeared grime across the Dad Wagon's windshield. I kicked the wipers up a notch, but that only angered the muddy dirt more. The light turned green, and I coaxed my Mazda through the particularly large puddle that filled the intersection. There was a moment's hesitation by both me and the car when the water came dangerously close to the door seam, but thankfully we inched through without stalling.

There's a first time for everything.

The Dad Wagon lurched along, sliding through deeper puddles and doing whatever it could to flirt with automotive disaster.

My phone chirped, and I hazarded a glance at it, knowing full well I was in direct violation of my own family rules.

Don't text and drive—well, it's more like boating in this storm.

There was no picture to go along with the message, but there didn't have to be. I knew who it was from the words alone.

It's happening again, are you close?!

A brilliant flash of lightning lit up the sky and pulled my

attention away from the phone—none too soon as the stop light directly in front of me was now red. I slammed on the Mazda's brakes and it groaned in frustration, skidding along the last twenty feet or so of wet road.

Only an idiot drives around in this...

The wind picked up and Tropical Storm Florence sent rain at me sideways, pressure washing a few weeks of yellow-green pollen off the driver's side. I took that moment to fire off a response.

I'm trying.

The light turned green, and I gunned the engine. The Dad Wagon only grunted, before lurching forward and down the flooded road toward Lifeway Hospice. Together the old car and I hadn't made it more than a hundred feet before Florence shifted direction. Her whipping wind sent us skidding off the road and into the wet grass. I pulled back hard and just missed depositing the Dad Wagon in a swollen ditch.

My phone chirped again, but I didn't risk grabbing it.

I already knew what I was dealing with—Umbralings.

I flicked the wipers up to full blast and pushed my car into the heart of the storm. High winds be damned—I had a job to do.

My name is Eugene Law, and I'm a professional Magician.

I don't pull rabbits out of hats, nor do I saw women in half. I deal with the supernatural forces of evil hell-bent on our shared destruction, and the occasional Magickal item that has worked its way into the Sunshine State. I've been doing this since high school—that's when most Magicians figure out they've got some talent, and in doing so either find a willing teacher, or get consumed by the dark things that love to snack on the innocent.

Isn't Magick great?

Another text lit up the tiny phone screen, but the Dad

Wagon chose that moment to fishtail around the next turn. The net effect sent my phone tumbling into that damnable crease between the seat and the center console.

That's going to be a bitch to find later.

I wasn't far now, just a few more turns.

The bright lights of Lifeway Hospice cut through the rain and I followed that glow into the parking lot. Above me, hundred-year-old oaks swung with the wind. Not willing to press my luck further, I found one of the few spaces not covered by those hulking monstrosities and parked the Dad Wagon—it just happened to be the farthest spot from the door.

The rain picked up, slamming the Mazda like a firehose and making it difficult to see the golden-orange glow spilling out the automatic doors of the main building.

I pulled a small duffle out of the back seat and set it in my lap.

The bag contained an assortment of items I might need for a situation like this. I unzipped the duffel and found Betty's horn-rimmed glasses lying gently in their soft floral-patterned pouch on top. I'd picked them up at the Sponge Docks in Dunedin—an old, sweet-as-pie librarian had been willing to part with them after I'd exorcised the poltergeist screwing with her expert filing system.

Don't mess with the Dewey Decimal system—Dewey's got friends in high places.

They weren't quite my size, meaning they pinched my nose something fierce, but that wasn't what made them valuable.

Gloom Glasses...

The Gloom existed in the same space as our own, a duplicate reality that was chock full of dark and evil things. Seeing the Gloom was a neat trick, but visiting the Gloom was borderline crazy. Home to Deep Magick and forever-hungry creatures that would like nothing more than to chew on your face—a trip to the Gloom was sort of like visiting my wife's family. I pushed Betty's glasses on and turned the car over just long enough to get the wipers to clear the windshield.

Oh, hell.

The rain-soaked building lay covered in thick, web-like strands of threaded darkness. Macabre party streamers done at full scale, the swollen lines dangled beneath the narrow legs of bulbous, spider-like Gloom vampires, better known as Umbralings. These weren't the Bela Lugosi style monsters of the silver screen, these were supernatural ticks, big as golden retrievers with an appetite to match.

I took off Betty's glasses and shoved them in my jacket pocket—sometimes it was better when you couldn't see the evil—then beat a path for the entrance, tucking the bag under my arm and trying to forget about the spindly Gloom ticks dangling just above my head.

The automatic doors whisked open and ushered me in to the sterile reception area of Lifeway Hospice. While they'd tried to brighten it up with cheerful colors and inviting paintings, the lobby still had its gray tile floor and harsh overhead lighting, both of which put the screws to any joyful energy still hanging about.

I found Axel behind the main reception counter, sliding over a banker's box of knick-knacks to Rob, my favorite mechanic. Given the spit and duct tape state of the Dad Wagon, I'd gone through a few car guys over the years, but my current grease monkey was the best by far. Short and stocky, with close-cropped ginger hair and a talent for keeping engines running far beyond their expected life, Rob was quite the catch—mechanically speaking of course.

Next to Rob, Axel made quite the sight. He was a mountain of a man, easily six feet tall, and with tattoos that had their own tattoos. I'd met Axel during a diving expedition gone bad—really bad. Did you know the Blue Holes in the Bahamas doubled as a portal to a frightening plane of alien Magick? Not I, and—as luck would have it—not Axel either. Still, we saved each other's bacon more than once during that trip, and since then the big man was always quick to call me in when things got weird, and in Florida that was pretty damn often.

"Is this everything?" Rob asked, turning a few items over in the cardboard box.

"Yeah. Listen man, I'm really sorry for your loss."

"Rob," I said, running a hand over my soaked head. "What are you doing here?"

The mechanic turned his tired eyes toward me. "Hey, Gene. My aunt passed away this morning. I was just coming by to collect her things."

"Oh, wow. I'm sorry. I had no idea—"

"It's all right, she was in a lot of pain."

Axel was busy trying to get my attention from behind the red-haired mechanic, but I wasn't about to interrupt Rob. He looked bad, but then again, his aunt had just died. Still, I couldn't shake the feeling this was more. The bags under his eyes had their own carry-on luggage, and his typically straight shoulders had drooped noticeably.

It might just be the death in the family. You moron, the building is crawling with Umbralings, and suddenly you are believing in coincidences?

I took a deep breath and slipped Betty's Gloom glasses back on my face. The thick strands of woven midnight glittered across the lobby, dangling from the ceiling and hanging in graceful curves like flowing tapestries. While he didn't have an Umbraling on him, Rob was covered in festering bites—the poor guy must have been fed on for weeks.

Wait. That's not an Umbraling bite... what is that?

Past the festering sores of invisible Umbraling fangs, was something else, a bright red and pulsing spot along his neck.

Gloom beasts like Umbralings love negative energy: sadness, pain, and the depression that come along with loss. Lifeway Hospice must have been dinner buffet for them. It didn't help that the building also appeared to be right smack in the middle of a low-grade Thinning.

The Sunshine State was known for many things: retirees, golf, beaches, and—among Magicians—Thinnings, thread-bare spots in the veil between the real world and the supernatural. No one really understood why, but Florida seemed to exist at that geometric focal point of weird that made it ground zero for easy passage between here and the great beyond.

Location, location, location.

The lights flickered, then cut off completely, plunging the three of us into an inky darkness. It didn't take long before the telltale prickle of Umbraling feelers danced across my face.

Bold.

These weren't your standard run-of-the-mill Gloom-beasts, like Axel had indicated in his text; these were different. They were aggressive, plentiful, and—worst of all—very hungry. A fang grazed my skin and sent my heart racing. Unexpected physical contact in the dark can do that to a guy, even a Magician.

I pulled Betty's glasses off and ripped my bag open, but before I could dig into it, the lights popped back on, this time accompanied by the hum of a backup generator. The automatic doors whisked open and a young woman raced in, holding up a jacket against the driving rain. She flipped her hood back and shook out gorgeous blond ringlets, letting them fall in soft curls around a model-like face.

Neither Axel nor I looked away—we couldn't. This girl was beyond stunning. Thankfully Rob clued us in.

"Gene, this is Cordelia, my girlfriend."

* * *

"ROBBIE, we've got to go. The storm is really picking up steam."

Cordelia wasn't kidding. From the looks of things outside the wind had shifted direction yet again. Large oak branches swayed precariously above the parking lot.

"Yeah, Rob. It was good seeing you, but your girlfriend's right. You two should get out of here before it gets worse."

Judging by the number of Umbralings here, it's going to get a lot worse.

Rob hoisted his aunt's box of things, and together with Cordelia he headed for the parking lot.

My favorite mechanic hadn't made it much past the automatic doors before Axel came around the reception desk to meet me. "Thanks for coming, Gene. I know we talked about this before, but I think it's getting worse."

I nodded. "I know it is."

Crash!

One of the large oak limbs gave way. A combination of the rain and wind must have been too much for that old branch. It broke from its mooring and crashed into the Lifeway Hospice sign. The fallen branch crushed the sign and bounced into the driveway, blocking any path to getting a car out of the lot.

Rob and Cordelia ran back into the lobby, shaking the rain off their clothes. "So much for leaving now, I guess we're stuck here for a bit."

Crap.

The lights flickered again. Bulbs buzzed in the lower power mode but didn't go out.

"How long do the backup generators hold?" I asked, keeping an eye on the flickering lights.

Axel cocked his head to one side. "Typically a lot longer than that."

"How many staff are on the clock today?"

"Just me. We've got most of the patients moved thanks to the storm and all. Florence's hitting too hard now to move the last one. I'm waiting for a break in the rain bands."

I slipped Betty's glasses back on my face and immediately pulled them back off. "I think you need to risk it; these things are acting a lot more aggressive than I would like."

"What are you talking about, Gene?" Rob asked, setting his aunt's box against the counter.

"Just a small—"

"Pest problem," Axel said, finishing my sentence. I didn't like lying to Rob, but the fewer people that knew about what I do, the easier it was to do it.

"Ah."

"Robbie, let them be," Cordelia said, unzipping her rain coat and *inadvertently* giving us an eyeful of her tanned, toned physique. "Sit with me, I'm cold."

One of the monitors flashed behind Axel, throwing a bright red light against the wall. "Shit! Hold on, Gene."

The big man returned to the reception desk and checked the display. The screen flashed again, this time a decidedly angrier red.

"Not good!"

The nurse cleared the reception desk and bolted down the hall. I turned to Rob and Cordelia. "Stay here," I said, fishing a small metal lantern out of my bag and placing it on one of the magazine-laden tables in the reception area. It was an old and boxy design, with cheerful cutouts of frolicking animals on each of the sidewalls.

"What's that?" Cordelia asked, frowning at the small toy.

"It's a shadow box lantern," Rob said, leaning forward in his chair. "My aunt used to have a few of these."

Cordelia didn't appear convinced. "Why do you carry around a shadow box lantern?"

"I'm eccentric," I said, placing a small battery-operated tea-light inside. "Just leave this on for me and sit near it."

Bright horses and leaping rabbits danced across the walls. The tiny light cast fun shapes from the cut-out metal and filled the dreary reception area with something other than depressing gray.

Rob didn't seem to mind, but Cordelia wanted nothing to do with my miniature light show and turned up her nose at it. "Why?"

Because it'll channel a little positive energy into this place— hopefully enough to keep the Umbralings in this room from snacking on you.

"I just don't want it to get broken," I said, removing Betty's glasses from my pocket. "Just keep an eye on it for me and don't go anywhere."

"Whatever."

That's the ticket.

I carried my bag into the hallway and started counting doors while I looked for Axel. Umbralings were rarely this plentiful, or this aggressive. I'd had a few direct confrontations over the years, but like most pests, the easiest solution was almost always environmental modification. It was no different than when we had roof rats in our attic after we'd moved in. Back then, I'd tried all manner of solutions, both the Magickal and the mundane, but those damn rats kept getting back in. In the end, the best option had turned out to be the easiest—removing the fruit tree. We'd had an old orange tree in the yard that the rats loved to snack on, and with their food source gone, they promptly moved on.

The Mildred's Mellowing Lantern wasn't perfect, and it sure wasn't doing anything for Rob's girlfriend, but the Magick it possessed was sound. It *should* elicit feelings of happiness, joy, and love—at least that's what it was supposed to do. Umbralings weren't much for any of those things. So, just like with the roof rats, I was banking on removing their food source as going a long way in improving our situation.

I found Axel, along with what I assumed was the last patient to be moved. His room was piled high with complex machinery, apparently doing its damndest to keep the elderly man comfortable in his final days. A lone chair on the far side of the room was occupied by a tired-eyed middle-aged woman. Her head was tucked up against the chair back, long and draping hair making it impossible to see her face.

I pushed Betty's glasses on and immediately wished I hadn't.

Black threads hung from the ceiling like sticky streamers. They dangled from dense knots of nest-like strands that pockmarked the walls. Umbralings dripped from those strands like cold syrup, their feelers gently tasting the air.

"Axel, don't move!"

The man-mountain stopped cold.

Bulbous and spider-like, at least half a dozen Gloom beasts had settled on the poor woman. Long and invisible fangs held their prey pinned, while beneath them, tiny mandibles gorged themselves on her life essence.

"Is it... them?" Axel asked, his eyes wide.

More Umbralings poked out of the corners of the room, their feelers dancing softly in the Gloom's eternal twilight. Hungry faces peeked out from the edges of those midnight threads, their silent fangs quivering in anticipation.

"Yes," I said, pulling the glasses down to look the large man in the eyes.

Axel took a tentative step. "What can I do?"

"Nothing yet."

I unzipped my bag and placed it on the floor. One of the things I'd tried on the roof rats was poison. Being rodent geniuses, though, they got smart to that rather quickly.

Still, I took out more than a few of them in the process.

Sadly, they didn't sell Umbraling pellets at the corner store.

An untapped market if ever there was one.

But being a Magician, I had a few other options available to me.

"Is this like the blue hole?" Axel asked, keeping a wary eye on the woman.

"Sort of. Just be happy you can't see them—"

"Just so long as they aren't spiders—I frigging hate spiders, man."

"Ah, nope, nothing like spiders," I lied.

"What are you going to do?"

"I'm going to give them something more exciting to chew on."

I removed an old clam-shell corsage box and placed it on the floor. The flowers inside had long since dried to faded husks of their former glory.

"What is that?"

Pop.

I opened the dusty plastic and let the room fill with the faint smell of cloves and incense.

"This is the corsage of a young man who died in a car accident before he could deliver it to his prom date."

"Damn, man. That's terrible, I mean... wow."

"Tristitia," I whispered, willing Magick into the decaying flower. I hated to lie to him, but it was all part of the process.

I needed real emotions, and something told me big Axel wouldn't have mustered the same sort of military-grade sadness if I'd told him the truth—I'd bought the corsage on discount and let it sit in the hot garage a few weeks.

"Yes, it is terrible, depressing, and gut wrenching—premium-grade Umbraling feed."

Come on, you little bastards, take the bait...

One of the feasting monsters paused, its feelers tickling the air. It appeared to have found something more enticing.

Oh yeah... come to papa.

Umbraling fangs retracted, leaving an angry and festering sore on the woman's skin before crawling slowly down her leg. The other creatures took notice, pulling away one at a time.

"That's it…"

"What? Do you see something? What's happening?"

I'd forgotten the big man didn't have a set of Gloom-vision librarian glasses. "They're letting her go. Just a few more seconds and you'll be clear to—"

White light filled the window, followed by a booming crack of thunder.

Beep! Pop! Whizz!

The impressive wall of electronics flickered in and out, the facility's backup generator thumping angrily at the surge of electricity.

No, no, no!

Beep!

A shrill warning beep cut the tension in the room, and a flat line graph splashed across one of the many screens.

"What in the Sam Hell is going on here?"

I spun around to find the spiritual form of the bed's current occupant floating above his withered body.

"Stop, don't say anything—"

It was too late. There was one thing Umbralings enjoyed

more than Magickally induced sadness and depression—fresh meat.

* * *

AXEL PUSHED past me and checked the displays, hitting buttons and turning dials. "Hold on there, Mr. Wagner…"

The spirit of Mr. Wagner drifted gently between the black streamers of Umbraling thread, an impressively groomed mustache giving him an almost regal appearance. His translucent hospital gown ruffled in the Gloom's eternal breeze. I was immensely thankful it didn't blow up much above his knees, though. There were things I didn't want to see, translucent or not.

"What the hell are those things?" the spirit asked, swimming desperately toward his body.

"Umbralings…"

"Umma-What?"

"Gloom ticks. Now listen, I need you to focus—"

At the word 'ticks' Mr. Wagner broke into a fit of crazed scrambling, his arms and legs flailing in all directions. Being a spirit and armed with no understanding of the unique dynamics of the Gloom, he flopped around like a fish out of water—lots of activity, zero motion. To make matters worse, all this gyrating was really only accomplishing one thing—sending out vibrations along the Umbraling webs throughout the building and beyond.

"Would you stop ringing that damn dinner bell for one second?"

The bulbous bodies of no less than a dozen Gloom beasts crawled up the edge of the bed. Feelers out and positively twitching with excitement, their spindly arms pulled at the thin sheet. Mr. Wagner's flailing spirit was putting out more than enough activity to overpower whatever the garage corsage could muster.

Axel, blissfully unaware of the Umbralings and their fangs, joined them at Mr. Wagner's bed side. "What's happening?"

"Well, he's jiggling like a caught fish, which in turn is bringing in more Umbralings than I can handle."

"What can I do?"

"Yes, what can he do?" the suddenly stiff-as-a-board Wagner said, his eyes darting between the dozen hungry sets of fangs just below his feet.

"Nothing. If it's his time, it's his time. He should get a ride shortly."

"Huh?" they both said in unison.

"His ride," I said pointing to the window. "If Mr. Wagner's dead, then someone will pick him up shortly for his trip to the other side."

"You mean... Heaven?" the floating spirit said, pulling his legs in to avoid the sweeping feelers of hungry Gloom ticks.

"Not necessarily..."

Axel shook his head and checked the displays. "I know we aren't supposed to say this, but he really wasn't a very good person."

"What!?" The disembodied spirit shouted, the sudden outburst enough to put him on a collision course with a large patch of black webbing.

"I don't think he wants to hear that."

"Well that's just too bad. I was with him and his wife during those first visits. He's a cantankerous old bastard. He made her feel terrible—insulting, rude, demeaning. I'd say he's not up for the husband of the year by any stretch."

"Bah," the mustached spirit shook his hand at the nurse. "What do you know? Why, I'm a wonderful husband..."

Long and spindly legs emerged from the inky threads of

an oversized Umbraling nest behind the drifting man. Silent as a church mouse, milky white eyes and glistening fangs shined in the cranky spirit's reflection.

"He disagrees with you, Axel."

The muscular nurse shook his head. "I'm sure he does. Has his ride appeared yet? I'm guessing he's on the bullet train to you know where."

Whichever way he was headed, there's wasn't a ride in sight—had I been wrong?

Mr. Wagner had just spun back around to give Axel a verbal lashing, when a faint and razor-thin silvery thread leading back to his body drifted into view. That thread was his connection back to his living body, provided he didn't get it snapped by Umbraling fangs.

Ariadne's Thread—he's still alive!

The Gloom wasn't just home to Umbralings and newly departed souls, it was also somewhere you could visit—although I'm quite sure Mr. Wagner hadn't wanted to.

"We have a problem," I said, digging through my bag.

"What?"

I tossed aside unnecessary items. "He's not dead."

The angry spirit slapped a hand against his glowing face. "That's what I've been trying to tell you! I'm not de—"

Piercing fangs cut short Mr. Wagner's words, the Umbraling's barbs stabbing deep into his fragile shoulder.

"Ah! So cold..." The old man's angry spirit slumped forward, the monster's venom coursing into his translucent form.

Shit!

I grabbed the old man's shoulder, his body cold beneath the scratchy sheets. "Can you bring him back?"

"What?" Axel asked, pulling open drawers and looking for something.

"Bring him back—can you bring him back? This wasn't

his time. He got zapped right out of his body, and now he's about to become Umbraling feed."

Axel pulled an AED out of the drawer and set it on the table next the bed. "I can try. It might kill him, though."

Seeing the limp form of Mr. Wagner slowly fade under the hungry fangs of a massive Gloom beast made me think he wouldn't mind us trying.

I stepped back, pulling my hands away. "Do it."

Axel slapped the sticky contacts against the old man's chest, then hit a button on the machine. The tiny box let out a high-pitched whine. "Clear."

Whump!

Power roared through the silver thread. Like Benjamin Franklin and his majestic key, the AED's spark shot up the shimmering cord only to vanish into the fading spirit of Mr. Wagner.

"Do it again," I cried.

"Clear!"

Whump!

Another arc of current raced through Ariadne's Thread and into the drifting Wagner. The second charge knocked the Umbraling's fangs from the cantankerous spirit's back.

"Gah!" he cried, coming to his senses just in time to see the monstrous Gloom tick fall to the ground beneath him. "What.. I… Oh my God, help me!" The poor spirit scrambled end over end, twirling in the air like a child's lost balloon.

All of this activity had done the one thing I hadn't wanted to do: invite the rest of the family to dinner.

Pale white eyes and Umbralings feelers appeared in all corners of the room. Large or small, it didn't matter, they were coming for the feast. In the hungry twilight of the eternal Gloom, Mr. Wagner didn't stand a chance.

Axel pointed to the monitor. "His heart's beating!"

The frayed end of Ariadne's Thread drifted past like the

torn end of a kite's tail. Mr. Wagner, no longer tethered, was now a free-floating morsel in a burgeoning sea of hungry Umbralings.

Crap.

More beasts poured into the room, crawling out of nests and dancing across twisted webs.

"Not for long it's not," I cried, leaving the old man's body to grab my bag.

Slippery's Pole.

I dug a small freshwater reel and handle out of the duffel. It was just the sort of thing you'd take fishing, except you'd need a pole to go along with it. This one had a pole and a line, they just happened to only exist in the Gloom. It was a handy bit of Magick I'd found at a yard sale just outside of Weeki Wachee—that old merman hadn't known what he had.

"We've got one shot at this!" I shouted, pressing down on the line release and whipping my arm back for the cast. "I'm going to pull him back to his body."

"Yes," the twirling spirit cried. "Do that—fast, fast!"

I placed one hand on the frail man's bedridden body, and with the other I cast a whipping line out into the Gloom. The shimmering thread shot out with a rainbow arc into the space between us, looping around the cranky spirit.

"Fish on," I cried, giving the Magickal reel a quick tug to secure the line.

"Nice work, young man. Now reel me in!"

"Thanks, it's really all in the wrist, you have to—"

Spindly legs and the bulbous body of an overzealous Umbraling crashed into Mr. Wagner, its impact sending the hooked spirit spinning like a top.

"Get it off of me," he cried, his turns sucking up line faster than I could pull it back.

"I'm trying, damn it. Stop squirming around!"

He didn't; instead, the quarrelsome spirit only flailed

harder, wrapping himself and the Umbraling tighter together. Like a cocoon of unpleasantness or the world's least appetizing burrito, the truculent spirit twisted the Gloom-dwelling parasite fast to his fading spirit.

"Do it again, Axel," I cried, tightening my grip on Mr. Wagner's barely breathing body.

"Huh?"

"Shock him."

"What?!" both the nurse and the rapidly mummifying Mr. Wagner shouted in unison.

"Gene, you've got a hand on him—"

"Right," I said, Slippery's Pole giving out almost all its line, and the trapped Umbraling's fangs dangerously close to breaking free. "Trust me, I've got a plan."

"Does it involve me getting eaten?" the old man yelled.

Axel hesitated, his finger hovering above the button. "But, you can't—"

"Just do it," I cried, closing my eyes. "Now!"

"Clear!"

Whump!

The smell of burning ozone hit my nose, and with it came a body-wracking arc of electricity. My fingers dug deep into Wagner's pale skin, while electrons raced back up them and into Slippery's Reel. Magick and electricity danced along the silvery fishing line and directly into the twirling jelly roll of translucent terrible that was the floating spirit.

Note to self, don't do that again. Ever.

The shocking jolt came to an abrupt end, and I tumbled backward, the tangled mess of Slippery's line, Mr. Wagner, and the Umbraling blurring in a wave of furious energy.

Come on, damn you.

The old man and a newly cooked Gloom beast drifted softly back into his body. I wish I could have said the same for myself, instead, I hit the vinyl floor hard, the impact knocking the air out of my lungs, and something else with it.

"Gene!" The big man crouched next to me and pressed his fingers against my neck. "No, no, no." Axel readied himself for chest compressions as I floated gently next to him.

Okay, okay, okay, not a problem, I can handle this...

I wasn't dead, I had Ariadne's Thread to prove it. The silvery cord floated just outside my body and kept me tethered, but I must have been looking pretty bad, because tattoo mountain was already deep into CPR.

Sightless white eyes and glistening fangs clamored out of their nests and down the hanging streamers around me like hungry rats with a whiff of fine cheese. There was a fresh morsel to be had, and it was big enough to form a proper meal.

Oh, hell.

I wrapped my translucent hands around Ariadne's Thread and gave it a tug. Typically the fastest way to get back to your body, a quick pull on my cord should have done the trick.

It didn't.

I yanked the line a dozen more times in rapid-fire succession like I was pull-starting the world's least effective lawn mower, and just like that bastard grass-rending machine, nothing happened.

Okay, now that's a problem...

* * *

Bang!

The commotion had brought my favorite mechanic, the compact redhead, throwing open the door and running into the narrow room.

"Gene," he said, dropping down next to Axel. "What happened to him?"

The tattooed nurse pointed to the AED wires still attached to Wagner's chest. "That."

"What can I do?"

"Sub in," Axel said, handing over the chest compression duties to the stocky mechanic.

I'm so going to feel this in the morning—provided I survive that long.

Umbraling fangs and pupilless white eyes shined in the dim glow of the AED machine, while all around me long legs skittered along the drifting strands, clicking in the quiet of the Gloom.

Think, Gene.

"Easy, guys…" I drifted backward, scooping up my silvery thread like spent line. "You don't want to eat Magician, we're terrible for your digestion."

With a hiss, one of the Umbralings launched at me, its fangs hungry for my translucent flesh. I shot up and out of the way, the Gloom tick missing my feet by mere inches. Fangs that had been pointed at my chest missed the tasty spirit of Eugene Law and ended up crashing into the hallway.

"Ho, ho, ho! You gotta get up pretty early in the timeless eternal twilight to catch a Magician like me, you stupi—"

Yeah, sometimes you really need to stop when you are ahead—or at least refrain from taunting.

I'd shot out of the lunging grasp of one Umbraling, only to land myself right in the shimmering web of another, and this new challenger made the one on the floor look like a wee babe by comparison.

You're a damn professional, Gene. You know the Gloom, it's your bag. You come here all the time… oh, those fangs are really big—stop, that's not helping. Focus on the problem; you have nothing with you and no way to draw power from the—wow, I think those are the sharpest fangs I've ever—power! That's it.

"Rob," I cried, trying not to move in the sticky strands. "I need the juice. You've gotta hit me again."

The mechanic ignored me and continued blasting his palms into my chest.

He can't hear me.

"He can't hear you, you idiot."

Spindly legs poked at me like they were testing the quality of a fresh steak. "Who said that?"

"I did."

"Wagner?"

"Yeah." The old man's spirit peeked out from his prone body, careful to avoid alerting the nearby Gloom beasts.

The Umbraling fangs were now practically on top of me, and I'd now learned they had a thin sheen of slime—who knew?

Dear Diary, did you know there's slime on Umbraling fangs?

The body below me twitched ever so slightly.

"Well if you can hear me, tell them," I cried, again trying desperately to move without moving.

The old man's spirit peeked out again. "I can't."

The fangs glistened, sliding back and forth over each other like self-sharpening kitchen cutlery.

"Why not!"

"Because," he poked his head out briefly, "I have no interest in being eaten. I'm not your puppet thank you very much."

Wagner's pale fingers wiggled, but neither Rob nor Axel noticed.

Puppet!

I kicked my silver cord like a lasso, looping it over Wagner's hand.

"Hey," the octogenarian said. "What the heck are you doing? That's my hand."

Umbraling feelers brushed across my shoulders as if searching for the juiciest part to consume first.

I gave the thread a gentle tug and Wagner's hand swung off the bed, but still neither Rob nor Axel noticed, they were too busy keeping me alive, or giving me the single largest bruise in the history of subdermal hematoma.

Come on, guys. Look over here.

The Umbraling's fangs dripped newly discovered slime across my neck.

Oh, hell no. This is not how I go out.

I pulled my legs up hard and swung them to the side, slamming Wagner's hand into the AED and knocking the entire box onto the floor next to Axel.

"What the hell?" he said, rubbing his shoulder and finding the toppled machine.

"Should we hit him?" Rob asked.

Sharp fangs grazed my translucent skin.

Yes! Yes you should.

Axel alternated between me and the monitors. "I don't know…"

"Wagner," I shouted, "Give them a sign!"

"What do you want me to do? I can't move and I can't speak."

Narrow legs wrapped around my mid-section, effectively signaling the impending end of my time in the Gloom—or anywhere else, for that matter.

"Do something, damn it. 'Cause those Umbralings aren't going to stop with me. Where do you think they'll go next? You can hide all you want, but they'll find you. I promise you that."

The room was silent—even Rob had stopped his pounding.

Frrrrpppppppptttt!

Mr. Wagner let out a long, loud, and perfectly musical toot.

The two men froze, then looked at each other.

"Ah… do you think that's a sign?" Rob asked, his hands hesitating over my severely bruised chest.

Axel fingered the AED's pads. "Uh… I don't know."

Frrpt!

"That's it, that's all I've got," the cantankerous spirit said, somewhat out of breath.

"Thanks, Wagner. I hope they—aargh!"

White-hot pain erupted in my shoulder. Umbraling fangs pierced my translucent flesh and sent chilling venom flooding into my tired spirit.

"I say do it," Rob said, pulling back his hands.

Legs, feelers, and fangs filled my fading vision.

"Works for me." Axel turned up the dial and charged the pads. "Clear!"

Darkness settled in on me like a dentist's lead blanket, the numbing cold of the Umbraling's venom making it impossible to move. One second the AED was charging, and in the next the pads were on my chest.

Come on… guys… you can…

Boom!

For the second time today I got a hint at what the iron key felt like when Benjamin Franklin discovered electricity.

My silver cord looked more like a strand of Christmas lights than Ariadne's Thread. A blinding hot stream of electrons roared up the line, crashing into my fading spirit with enough force to light up the Umbraling attached to me like a tiny flood lamp.

Pop! Pow! Bang!

Bulbous creatures flailed in the webs, dropping off in blackened husks like bugs hitting a porch zapper. My whole body shook from the contractions, but I was able to focus just long enough to pull the cord.

There's no place like home...

I opened my eyes and took a deep breath, only to be greeted by my favorite mechanic and nurse kilowatt.

"Gene?" Rob asked, his hands hovering above my swollen chest.

"Yeah," I said, pushing myself up with weak arms. "Ugh, that hurts like a mothe—"

"You're alive!"

I had to push back from the crushing mechanic hug. "Whoa there, buddy, easy on the sternum..."

"Gene, are we okay?" Axel asked, keeping an eye on Wagner and his wife. "I mean, are there any more?"

Shit. He's right.

In the fall my glasses had landed on the ground and slid under the bed. Without them, I couldn't navigate a way out. "I need my glasses—"

"Robbie?"

Cordelia's husky voice broke the tension in the room. "Are you in here?"

"Yeah—"

"Don't come in!" Axel shouted, crawling under the bed to get my glasses. "It's not safe."

"Whatever..." the young woman said, pushing her way into the tiny hospital room. "Ugh, it's so... icky in here."

Axel placed the glasses in my hand. "Here you go. Can you get us a way out?"

Betty's horn-rimmed glasses once again revealed the room, with its flowing black threads and quickly encroaching brood of Umbralings. One of them broke rank and closed in on the leggy blond.

"Yes," I lied, not sure if there was a way out. "Uh, Cordelia, if you would step over—"

The young woman gently placed a hand on Rob's neck, her fingers digging into his skin. Cordelia's pleasant features melted away; gone were the beautiful ringlets, angelic face, and buxom chest. Black claws formed from her narrow fingers, while leathery wings unfolded from the deformed skin of her back. The young woman's trim and toned physique vanished beneath a pot-bellied gut and oversized sagging breasts.

Succubus!

Succubus were demonic residents of one of the middle layers of Hell. They made their bread and butter sucking the life essence from unsuspecting men and women through weaponized sexuality—fatal lovers of the worst sort, and in my current state, way the heck out of my league.

Cordelia fingers dug into the same red spot I'd found earlier, and did what Succubi did best, she drained more of his life force while giving him a pleasant sensation to the man bits.

Okay, so his girlfriend's a Demon—where does he find these women?

"Videre..." I whispered, placing a hand on both Axel and Rob. There was no way they were going to believe this without seeing it.

"Oh my God!" Rob pulled away from Cordelia, but not before she'd powered up with a decent amount of his life's essence.

"If you want to get anything done, sometimes you just have to do it yourself," the young-girl-turned-Succubus said, grabbing the Umbraling and crushing its face like papier-mâché.

Succubi and Umbralings don't get along, the former having a healthy disdain for the latter, and for good reason. You don't want anything else competing for your meal ticket.

It didn't take Cordelia more than a minute to tear apart

or eviscerate the remaining Gloom ticks and stir up enough shock waves in the eternal twilight to send the rest of them packing.

Finally, the whirling monster came to a stop and dragged a chair over to place herself in front of us.

"So, Magician," she said, wiping the gore from her claws. "What are we going to do now?"

"I can't have you hurting my friends," I said, feigning bravado. I was too weak to banish her, but she didn't necessarily know that.

"You're too weak to banish me."

Damn...

"What the—" Rob said, backing away from the black-winged Demon.

"Oh, Robbie. I wasn't going to kill you. You're just too... you. I don't know. It's hard to describe."

My mechanic didn't appear to know what to do. "Gene?"

Axel couldn't tear his eyes away from what remained of the fading Umbralings. "They looked *just* like spiders, you bastard."

"Well... I guess, sort of. If you squint really hard, and—"

Axel shook his head in apparent disbelief. "And she just destroyed every single one of them."

"Yeah, but—"

"Well." The nurse rubbed his angled jaw. "I might be in the minority here, as she is completely terrifying—"

"Why thank you!" A claw-admiring Cordelia said, with genuine appreciation in her voice.

"—but could you do that again?"

Cordelia smiled like the cat that ate the canary. "Anytime."

The strongman looked at me. "She won't eat us... right?"

"She lives on sexual energy."

Rob blushed. "That explains a lot."

Axel addressed Cordelia directly. "Do you need to... you know... do it?"

The Succubus admired her nails. "Oh, sweetheart, no. I can get what I need just from a touch."

"And that touch won't kill us, right?"

"She could very well kill you, that's what Demons do—" I said, still trying to get a full breath into my bruised and battered chest.

"No, in fact, I leave my victims feeling like they've just had the lap dance of a lifetime."

Rob nodded. "It's true."

"Axel, don't even think about it!"

The big man ignored me. "So, just little bits at a time, right?"

Cordelia's wings folded away, vanishing against her back. "Of course."

"Well, Mr. Wagner, can she stay and take little bits in exchange for keeping those monsters away?"

"Axel," I said, rubbing my very sore chest. "Let me put this in simple terms. This is a no-bueno idea, bro. I mean, she's a—"

Frrrpppptttt!

"Cordelia, right?" Axel asked, extending a hand.

"Yes."

"You're hired."

BALLROOM AND CHAIN
BY MARTIN SHANNON

*M*oorish minarets scraped at a darkening sky, their muted steel catching the last rays of a setting sun. The Old Tampa Hotel's towers glowed like hot embers in the advancing twilight. Far below the impressive spires, sprawling gardens and brick-laid paths separated the hotel from the Hillsborough river. At present, much of the building's beautiful facade lay hidden behind an erector-set of scaffolding. Soon the ancient structure would be home to my employer's latest reconstruction project, but tonight, it had a more important function.

Charity ball, ugh.

I guided the Dad Wagon into the valet lane, slowing to a stop and taking the opportunity to tug at an overly constricting tuxedo collar.

"Stop doing that." My wife brushed at a piece of lint on her little black dress. "You're going to stretch it out, and you have to return it in the morning."

I don't care how many times they say they've cleaned them, rental clothes have all the trappings of a community toothbrush.

A young man motioned us forward. He did little to hide

the disappointment on his face at seeing the Dad Wagon rumble along the curbside. The old Mazda had been my constant companion since the earliest days of my marriage. She was a good car, no matter what that kid thought.

"Valet?" Porter said, raising an eyebrow. "Since when do we do valet?"

"If you must know," I said, giving the teen valet a stern look, then pulling on the collar one more time out of spite, "I'm checking in on a friend."

The driver door popped open, and I was greeted by a new young man's smiling face. "Mr. Law! It's great to see you."

Yep, not even a hint of Bridge Troll—well, maybe a little. Still, nice work, Mr. Magician.

"It's great to *see* you too, Tommy. Any relapses?"

The skinny young man gave the other valets a quick sideways glance to make sure no one was paying attention. "Not really," he whispered. "There's still a few things—like sometimes I feel like eating rocks… is that normal?"

I placed a hand on the young man's skinny shoulder. "Completely. You were transmogrified into a Bridge Troll—stuff like that takes time to recover from."

Tommy let go of my door handle, his fingers leaving a bent metal impression in the shiny steel. "I see you still have the grip strength…"

He sighed. "I'm sorry. There's that, and I lose my temper in seconds—"

"Hey, they're starting to back up," one of the other valets said, smacking Tommy upside the head. "Get a move on, dipshit."

Uh oh.

The recently un-trolled car hop's eyes turned red and his fingers crushed what remained of my door handle.

I liked that handle, it went so well with the rest of the car.

"Tommy…"

The young man's skin took on a very granite-like hue—a very Bridge Troll shade of gray. With Bridge Trolls, the angrier they got, the harder their skin became. Get them mad enough and you might as well be playing tag with a wrecking ball.

"Tommy..." I placed a hand on the young man's quickly hardening arm. "Just breathe. Let the Magick work."

Tommy's nostrils flared. "I'll show him..."

Just keep it together, let the Magick do its thing.

"Let me see the sigil," I said, directing his attention back to me and away from any other distractions.

Tommy pushed up his jacket sleeve. The swirling lines and interlocking angles of Weavelick's True Form danced across his forearm in stark black ink, the sigil shimmering in the bright street lights. The men in Tommy's family had been turning into Bridge Trolls since the thirties, but thanks to a bit of Magickal research and some excellent ink work that was all about to change.

My name is Eugene Law, and I'm a Magician.

I don't pull rabbits out of hats, nor do I saw women in half. I deal with the supernatural forces of evil hell-bent on our shared destruction, and the occasional Magickal item that has worked its way into the Sunshine State. I've been doing this since high school—that's when most Magicians figure out they've got some talent, and in doing so either find a willing teacher, or get consumed by the dark things that love to snack on the innocent.

Isn't Magick great?

Tommy puffed like a locomotive, his face flattening out and features distorting.

"Deep breath," I said, inspecting the young man's quickly hardening arm. "It looks good, but it's a little inflamed. Have you been putting the cream on it like Xander said?"

Troll-boy Tommy tilted his head at me, those bright red

eyes letting me know whatever I was going to do I better do it fast or risk having my spine removed through my throat.

"That would be a no. Quiescis..." I whispered, pouring a bit of Magick into the already powerful tattoo, and giving it just enough to get the inflammation down.

Tommy's eyes reverted to their normal blue-green color, and his skin returned to a healthy pink. He was Tommy-the-gangly once again.

"Thanks..."

I handed him back his arm. "The ink work looks good, you just need to put that anti-inflammation stuff on it."

"I forgot."

I don't do tattoos, but Xander and the guys in Ybor City worked wonders, and they'd done exactly that with Weavelick's True Form.

"It happens, but just promise me you'll baby it for a while. We need it nice and solid, right?"

"Yeah... but, I still—"

"It's not going to go away overnight, we've got a multi-generational curse we are working against."

The young man's face fell.

"Don't worry, I think it's just your body getting used to it. Listen, take good care of it for at least a few more days, okay?"

The young man nodded.

"If after that time it still needs work, I'll meet you at Xander's and we'll tighten up the edges."

"You'd do that?"

"Of course I would. Trust me, it just needs a few days to heal, then it'll be permanent."

"And no more... you know?" The young man feigned monster claws with his fingers.

"Nope."

I sure hope not. If your curse overpowers that tattoo then we're in the deep water without a paddle.

Porter joined me at the driver's side. Her flowing black dress hugged at all the right curves. No matter what happened tonight, she'd already made me the luckiest man at the ball.

"Oh my God. Is that you, Tommy Tiller? Little TT? Wow, you've gotten so tall, and handsome too. I bet you have to keep the girls away with a stick."

Porter had known Tommy from my days as a little league coach. He'd always been sweet on my wife, even at the ripe old age of five.

"Hi, Mrs. Law," Tommy said, blushing.

My wife tucked a clutch under her arm. "How's your mom?"

The young valet slipped past Porter and into the car. "She's good. Said she owes you guys a pumpkin cake, for... you know."

Now that's a proper reward. I remember receiving one of those cakes after the first season of little league, and I don't believe I've ever been the same.

Tommy didn't know I'd filled Porter in on his problem. I'd learned years ago that secrets in a marriage rarely work, unless it was who left the seat up.

That will forever remain a mystery.

"Tell her thanks, but it's not necessary," Porter said, crushing my hopes.

Wait, what? It's not? Goodbye, sweet cake of goodness.

Tommy carefully climbed into the Dad Wagon, trying very hard to not bend, crush, or break anything else in the process. The car groaned, and its struts shuddered—he might not look like a Bridge Troll anymore, but he still weighed as much as one.

"He's a good kid," Porter said, slipping her arm inside mine. "Even if his family is a little weird."

Unhealthy fascination with bridges if you ask me.

"Why did you turn down Mrs. Tiller's Pumpkin cake?" I asked, guiding her up the hotel steps. "I love everything his mom makes. I have ever since I coached him in little league."

My wife patted my belly gently. "I know."

Half-way up the stairs I froze, the cold tickling of Wild Magick prickling at my skin.

Thinning...

A threadbare spot in the veil between the supernatural world and the real world, Thinnings were like watering holes for all manner of dark and frightening monsters, and we were walking right into one.

"You okay?" my wife asked, already a few steps ahead of me.

"Honey, I'm getting a bad feeling, are you sure you don't want to just bag it and go get beers?"

Porter laughed and pulled me up to the steps. "Bad feeling? You must have figured out my true motive for bringing you here."

"Which is?"

"Porter!"

Shelley's shrill voice split the air like a harpy, and if there was a Shelley, there'd be...

"Yo, Genie!"

Jeff—God help me.

"That," my wife whispered, waving to the most annoying of her old sorority sisters. "Be careful, Gene Law... You just might have fun."

Cold tendrils of Wild Magick snaked between the pant legs of my community formal wear.

Yeah, among other things.

* * *

I LET the cold water splash over my hands before punching the soap dispenser a few times. It made me feel better imagining that dispenser was Jeff's smug face, but the joy it provided was fleeting—Shelley's husband had decided to follow me into the bathroom.

"Yeah, so like I said, I got this sweetheart deal on a new boat. You should come out with us sometime. I'm telling you, Genie, Shelley loves to invite some of those sexy little babes from her promotions team."

"Uh, huh."

It really didn't matter what I said, Jeff would keep talking indefinitely. The wealthy real estate mogul really didn't need an audience; he was like one of those dolls with the pull cord, except he pulled it himself—again and again.

Jeff adjusted his stance in front of the urinal. "Ah… Shelley's been doing great with this new gig. She runs a team of foxes pushing high-end spirits at different…"

"Uh, huh."

Spirits—I was far more concerned with the disembodied kind than whatever Shelley's perky team of junior-college hotties were peddling. The Old Tampa Hotel had a reputation, and there were plenty of stories surrounding floating women, unhappy souls from ages past, and even a confused soldier that wandered the grounds. Most of the time I would have dismissed these stories, but when you coupled them with the Thinning…

Danger, Gene Law… Danger.

"Porter's looking hot—"

Jeff's words shook me out of my thoughts. "Excuse me?"

The gregarious man zipped up his pants and joined me at the sinks, slapping an unwashed hand on my shoulder.

I'm sorry, community tuxedo…

34

"Don't be a jerk, Gene. Your wife is smoking hot, and that's after like what? Three kids?"

"Two."

Jeff blanched, then shoved his hands under the water. "Wow, two kids—better you than me."

I would weep for the world if you had progeny.

Jeff ignored the soap, much to my disappointment. "Don't get me wrong, Shelley'd be a great mom and all, but let's be honest. Once they squeeze out kids, it's all downhill from there. Nothing fits quite the same anymore, am I right?"

Must resist the urge to smash his jerk face...

Jeff flicked his wet fingers at the sink, spraying them with man-slime.

"Oh. Damn, man, I forgot to tell you. I got word you guys are going to win the remodel here."

"What?" For the first time that evening I was actually interested in what the jerk had to say. "Kinder Construction is going to win the bid for the Old Tampa Hotel remodel?"

Jeff's smug face nodded. "Yeah, that's what I'm saying."

"How do you know that? That's supposed to be sealed until the—"

"Shelley's not the only girl I can sweet talk into giving things up."

Come on, Gene—karma would totally forgive you if you belted him.

"You got the family to tell you who won?"

Jeff held up his wrist. "Yeah, and that's not all. I mean look at this. I got this girl to give up her family heirlooms and your project details for a little slice of the Jeff pie—I bet it's worth a mint."

Jeff shoved the bracelet's intricate details in my face. This wasn't your run-of-the-mill men's bracelet, there was something more to the detailed design etched into the recently polished silver.

It looks almost Magickal...

"Where did you get that?" I asked, light sparkling along the shiny metal.

"Like I said, Genie, she gave it to me."

"Who?"

"You already guessed," Jeff said, pointing at the ceiling. "I've got connections."

"Can I see that again?"

Jeff shoved the band in my face. "Sure—it's a sexy bitch isn't it?"

"Revelare…" I whispered, letting the tiniest bit of Magick slip out of my body and into the bracelet. The silvery band sucked up that cosmic power like a shammy, twisting it around before dissipating it into the stuffy bathroom air. "Odd…"

"Whatever, you're just jealous. I'm telling you, bro, you need to get out on the boat with Shelley and me, and bring that hot momma with you. I bet she still looks great in a bikini."

Jeff slammed his hand down on the paper towel dispenser a few times, ejecting enough paper for three pairs of hands before tearing off the wad. "Anyway, let's get back to the party. I don't want to wait too long—these hands need to grab a little Shelley-backside before they get to wandering." Jeff tossed the wadded-up paper towel on the floor. "Come on."

The jerk hadn't yet made it to the door before the lights flickered. "What the hell? You guys need to get in here and get this renovation going asap." Jeff pulled on the door handle, but it didn't budge.

Thunk.

Something shifted in the cold of the Thinning, while the faint sound of a hunting horn drifted over my ears.

The Hounds of Helvet.

The bracelet was a tracker, a Magickal dog whistle, that had just turned the crushing maws of the Helvet's spectral hounds loose on a very unsuspecting Jeff Masterson.

"Jeff, I need you to take that bracelet off right now."

"Very funny, Gene. Whoever locked us in here, you're gonna open this door right now or I'll—" Jeff dropped to his knees, unable to finish his hollow threat, his fingers clutching the bracelet.

"Aargh! Shit, shit, shit. It's too tight!"

The silver bracelet cut into his skin, sending a thin trail of blood streaming down Jeff's arm and onto the bathroom tile.

"Take it off," I cried, grabbing his wrist.

"I'm trying." He dug at the ever-shrinking band. "It won't come off!"

His fingers shifted from fleshy pink to a bright red—at this rate they weren't going to be around for much longer.

The baying of the Hounds of Helvet echoed through the tight confines of the bathroom—Jeff might not have been able to hear their chilling cries, but that didn't mean they weren't coming for him.

"I can't get it off, damn it. Gene, help me!"

The once smug real estate mogul kicked his feet out like a tantrum-wracked toddler on the bathroom floor, but for all of his fighting the bracelet only tightened down harder.

The faint wisps of Helvet's Hounds faded in and out around Jeff, and just like trained attack dogs, they had the bracelet's scent and weren't letting go.

"The water," I said, yanking Jeff to his feet. "Put it under the water."

Jeff struggled to his feet, tears welling up in his eyes. Together we shoved the rapidly suffocating hand, bracelet and all, into one of the sinks.

I turned on the cold water faucet and held Jeff's hand under it. Real world dogs had trouble chasing a scent across running water. I figured a few seconds under the faucet's running water might buy me some time.

Ghostly hounds pawed at the mirror's glass, their snarling jaws hungry for Masterson's soul.

So much for that.

"Gene, I can't feel my fingers..." The real estate mogul's hand was turning black. Getting the bracelet off in a few minutes wouldn't be a problem, because he wouldn't have a hand anymore.

"Where did you get this?" I cried, smearing my hand across the steam-covered glass and pushing back at Helvet's attack dogs.

Jeff's eyes rolled back in his head and he slumped forward against the sink. "I... I told you, she gave it to me."

"Damn it, Jeff. You want to keep your hand? Tell me where you got this!"

"I stole it."

There it is.

"From where?"

The faucet water was now red with Jeff's blood. I wasn't sure how much more he could lose before it was too late.

"The... estate... I stole *them* from the estate."

"Them?"

Jeff's legs buckled, and I had to fight to keep the asshole from collapsing onto the tile.

"What do you mean *them*?"

"I took a... a... necklace for Shelley."

Aw Hell!

The jerk chose that moment to lose consciousness and drop to the tile floor, his blood covering my hands and the cuff edges of my community tuxedo.

"Damn it, Jeff!"

Helvet's hounds circled, their translucent paws sweeping over the dirty tile.

Think, Gene...

I placed a hand on Jeff's chest and reached for my Magick. The cosmic power swirled and danced in my chest, but the ghostly beasts' incessant baying wrecked my concentration and sent the Magick slipping out of my grasp. Sharp teeth and smoky eyes, the spirits paced a tight circle around Masterson and the calling bracelet.

Too many...

I needed to focus, but for that I'd need a totem, something to help me push past the powerful cries of the circling hounds. The countertop was a cornucopia of individually wrapped trinkets: soaps, colognes, towels, condoms, and packages of gum.

Blackberry gum!

Blackberry leaves were rumored to be an effective defense against evil spirits, but the books hadn't said anything about blackberry-flavored gum.

After taking another look at Jeff's wrist and the circling dogs of damnation, I figured it was worth a try—it was either that or call the jerk Captain Hook the rest of his life.

Tempting...

I left Masterson on the floor and grabbed the open purple package off the counter.

One piece left? You've got to be kidding me.

I contemplated washing my hands, but one look at Jeff's rapidly blackening digits and the hungry eyes of those circling hounds convinced me otherwise.

Ugh. The things I do for people.

I crushed the stale gum and worked it into a malleable piece, then slipped between the pacing hounds and grabbed Jeff's wrist.

"Jeff, you colossal asshole, wake up!"

Nothing. So much for that legendary Masterson toughness.

Strong like string cheese.

Jeff's wrist bones shifted under my fingers, telling me all I needed to know—chew faster or he kisses that hand goodbye.

"God damn it. Okay, this is the best I've got. Here goes nothing."

I spit the purplish gum into my hand and pressed the sticky wad against the rapidly vanishing clasp.

"Patentibus," I cried, willing the Magick out of my chest and into the partially masticated blackberry-flavoring. The power I'd spent vanished into the Thinning. I was going to need to put more into this if I wanted to stop the spirit from crushing my friend's hand.

Friend is a really strong word.

"This might sting a little."

I turned the Magickal faucet up to full blast. It was sort of like trying to open the cereal bag without tearing it—sometimes it worked, and sometimes you ended up with a confetti spray of bran flakes.

"Aargh!" Jeff screamed, his eyes popping open long enough to scare the crap out of me and lend just enough emotional energy to the blackberry spirit-stopper.

The bracelet popped open like a dying star—a bright flash of light signaled the end of Helvet's Hounds dog whistle, but that wasn't the only thing that tore open; the Thinning wasn't trickling Wild Magick anymore. Now it was flowing like a firehose and bringing with it a torrent of unpredictable energy.

Yep, confetti spray of bran flakes.

I took off my jacket and tied it around the end of Jeff's arm, effectively stemming the flow of blood for now, and guaranteeing the loss of my security deposit.

Look at the bright side, it's not a community tuxedo any more... it's yours.

I scooped up the gummy remains of the bracelet, but not before Helvet's Hounds tore out of the bathroom.

I didn't have to guess at where they were headed, I already knew.

Shelley.

* * *

MISSING MY JACKET, and with a good bit of blood on my sleeves, I drew looks the instant I burst from the bathroom. I rolled up those sleeves to hide what I could of the blood and beat a path toward the ballroom.

Jeff was sorely in need of emergency medical attention, but right now I had to get to Shelley before her necklace collapsed like a bear-trap and removed the vapid woman's head from her body.

I reached the ballroom to find the charity event in full effect.

Classical music rained down from a stage occupied by at least half the string section of the Florida Orchestra, but even they struggled to overpower the noise of the crowd. The fire marshal's plaque indicated this room would max out at two hundred and fifty, and at first glance it would appear we were just about there. Couples spun and twirled across the dance floor, their intricate moves far exceeding my meager talents. My wife was sure to know that, but would have made certain to find a seat close to the dance floor—if only to make it easier for her to drag me onto it like a captured caveman.

Trays of food and champagne whisked between the tables, guided by expertly dressed waitstaff. One of those trays stopped long enough to block my view.

"Champagne, sir?"

"No, I—Tommy?"

The gangly valet had changed his clothes and was now sporting a somewhat crumpled tuxedo.

"Hey, yeah. Whoa, Gene, are you okay?" the young man asked, seeing the red edges of my rolled-up sleeves. "What happened to—"

I grabbed the young man's arm and guided him toward the edge of the room. The first calls of Helvet's Hounds were already echoing in my ears. I didn't need a Bridge Troll to join them.

"Tommy, have you seen Porter?"

"Uh… Yeah, I think so—"

"Where? Where did you see her?"

"I saw her over…" The young man scanned the room. "Yeah, that's right, she's over there," he said, pointing toward the far end of the ballroom, not far from the orchestra.

I followed Tommy's eyes and found my wife at a table just off the dance floor. A silver chain flashed from her neck. Its twin was resting in my pocket.

Son of a…

"Tommy," I said, pulling the waiter's attention back to me. "I need you to listen to me."

Just like animals can feel the pressure drop before a storm, I knew Tommy was experiencing the sudden change in Wild Magick brought on by Helvet's Hounds and the Thinning. Weavelick's True Form might have been holding for now, but I wasn't sure how long that would last—I didn't want him in a crowded space when we found out.

"You have to get out of here. Now."

The young man placed a hand on his covered sleeve. "Oh my God, it's not going to happen again, is it?"

"Not if you get out of here," I said, trying to keep tabs on Porter and Shelley's silver necklace, but losing them again in the crowd of revelers. "I don't have time to argue with you, just leave now before it gets any—"

The lights flickered and the sudden outpouring of Wild Magick prickled my skin. Porter's scream cut through my confusion like a clarion bell. Helvet's Hounds were upon us.

"Go, Tommy," I cried, not hanging around to find out if he understood me or not. I beat a path through the confused crowd toward my wife's table. I wasn't halfway across the room before the lights dropped out and plunged us into darkness.

Great—this is just what we need to keep people from panicking...

In the dark an unexpected elbow to the gut knocked me to the ground. All around me, high-heels clacked on the hard floor like hammer blows as party-goers beat a path for the door—so much for orderly departures. I scrambled to my feet, but not before taking a silky-smooth knee to the cheek for my efforts

"Porter," I cried, rubbing at my face in the darkness.

"Over here!"

I stumbled over chairs trying to follow the sound of her voice. The baying of Helvet's Hounds echoed in my ears. "Are you okay?"

"Gene, it's Shelley, she's choking," my wife cried, panic in her voice.

Damn it, Masterson.

I clawed my way around a table. "I'm coming! Stay calm, I've got a plan."

Oh yeah, you got more gum in your pocket?

The flashing lights of fire alarms lit up the room in staccato pulses, their shrieking sirens cutting over the chaotic crowd.

Porter!

I found my wife in the angry red light, hovering over her prone sorority sister. The petite blond woman clutched at her husband's stolen necklace, the silvery dog whistle giving her neck a death-hug.

"Do something!" my wife shouted, digging her fingers beneath the tightening chain and trying desperately to pull it off.

I needed focus, but in the maelstrom of the ballroom, focus was in short supply.

If only there were a way to tattoo some focus on my arm... That's it!

"I need something to write with," I said, fishing through my pockets to no avail.

"What?" my wife yelled over the wailing siren. "Help me get the necklace off her."

"I am—but there's too much Wild Magick in the room. Helvet's Hounds are soaking it up like premium paper towels. It's everywhere. Anything I try to do will be like striking a match in a hurricane. I need to focus."

Shelley's eyes bulged in her head and her tongue lolled to one side. Translucent dogs prowled the surrounding air, their snarling jaws snapping in anticipation.

"Gene!"

I tore Porter's clutch open—the lipstick.

There was too much energy in the room to think straight, let alone work Magick. I needed some way to get that necklace detached from whatever was powering it. I needed to cut Shelley off from the Helvet's debt collectors before the necklace removed her head from her neck.

Eldero's Fifth? No. The Pervellick Juncture? No! Think, Gene...

Shelley's arms twitched, while the rest of her neck took on a lovely shade of purple.

"Can't you hurry?" my wife shouted, the hounds circling tighter.

"This is like underwater geometry with imaginary numbers, can you please give me half a second?"

44

Ollie's Outsider, yes!

"Gene!" Porter screamed, causing me to smudge a symbol in the complex pattern with my arm.

Shit.

I wiped the smear away. "Just a second, I'm going as fast as I—"

Bang!

A steak knife embedded itself in the wooden floor by my arm, narrowly missing the important arteries by inches.

"What the—"

I didn't have time to contemplate the situation before a salad fork impaled itself in my calf.

"Aargh! Porter, table."

"On it."

This wasn't my wife's first Magickal rodeo, although it was the first one in formal wear—we didn't get out much.

Porter flipped the table like she'd seen *Road House* more than once—she had—and gave us a makeshift shield from flying cutlery, while all around us, Helvet's circling hounds pulled in Wild Magick from the Thinning.

"Gene, she's not going to make it," Porter cried, her sorority sister jerking violently on the hard ground.

Let's go out—we never go anywhere. I got us tickets to a charity ball. It'll be fun...

"I just need a few more seconds—"

"She doesn't have any left!"

I traced the last curve of Ollie's Outsider with my wife's lipstick and leaned in to will a little Magick into the symbol, but before I could I was jerked back hard. The ballroom became a blur moments before I crashed into another table— this one being upright, of course.

Ugh, I'm so going to feel that in the morning.

I landed with my face pointed up to the ceiling, giving me a view of the colorful dome above the ballroom. That was my visual, at least until Tommy's Bridge Troll face replaced it.

"Stupid Magician."

Oh, crap.

* * *

I ROLLED to my side mere seconds before Tommy shattered the table with his fists. It takes a lot of power to reduce pressboard to splinters, but the young man's troll half had that in spades now.

"Whoa, Tommy," I shouted, falling off the table edge and onto my feet. "It's me. You know, Gene?"

The rapidly growing Bridge Troll tossed what remained of the table aside like a frisbee.

"I remember."

I dodged a chair. "Good, you remember. So you can stop—"

"You try to hurt Tommy," the Bridge Troll said, holding up his tattooed forearm. Weavelick's True Form was in tatters, most likely sliced up by errant cutlery.

Son of a...

The young man's red eyes practically glowed in the flashing lights of the fire alarm.

"No," I said, ducking another piece of furniture. I had to get back to Porter and Shelley. Ollie Outsider was done, and Shelley was inside it, but without any Magick it was about as useful as a TV remote with no batteries.

"Gene!" Porter shouted, pulling at the necklace. "She's not going to make it! Do something!"

"I'm trying!"

Bridge Troll Tommy increased in size again, now easily pushing seven feet—and to make matters worse, he was getting pretty damn mad.

"Try harder!"

My wife, ever the comedian.

I grabbed one of the chairs like a prime-time wrestler, but Tommy was faster, and much more up to date on his wrestling moves. He yanked the chair and sent me flopping onto the abandoned dance floor like an under-sized snapper.

"I can't get my hands free!" Porter yelled, her fingers now trapped beneath the chain's crushing grip.

"I'll think of something, just give me a—"

Crash!

A large crystal sliver from the ballroom's previously impressive chandelier hit the ground next to me, exploding in all directions and taking with it a chunk of dance floor as well as at least one of my nine lives.

"Whatever you are going to do you need to hurry," my wife cried, pulling against the chain while Helvet's Hounds circled ever closer.

Stone-cold bratwurst-sized fingers wrapped around my calf and squeezed more than a little blood out of the already painful salad-fork holes.

Or was it a cake fork?

I flipped over to find Tommy's slate gray face hanging over me. His nose had flattened, and his ears had disappeared into a now all-but-bald skull. He puffed out air like a freight train, causing his chest to tear apart the tuxedo shirt.

"Thomas Michael Tiller, you stop right this instant!" my wife yelled, her voice cutting through the wailing fire alarm. "What would your mother think? You let him go right this instant."

Mom tone...

The troll-boy hesitated, his fingers loosening slightly. There was a power in words delivered at just the right tone— you didn't need to be a Magician to know that.

"Good. Now, let him go so he can save our friend."

A tableau of emotions played across the young man's face —was it working? Had my wife just talked down a Bridge Troll with what amounted to maternal nagging?

Tommy's fingers slipped off my leg.

"It's working, Porter. Keep it up!"

"And another thing—"

My wife didn't get to finish her motherly mojo before another ballroom crystal crashed into Tommy's head.

Boom!

The troll's granite-like skull took the blast without flinching, but his once again bright-red eyes told me all I needed to know.

"Run!" Porter screamed.

Another chandelier crystal shattered next to me, sending up a cloud of splinters and dust, and leaving me with a few bits of the sparkly stone embedded in my arm.

Crystal!

"You want me, block head?" I shouted, not exactly sure if this was going to work, but knowing I really didn't have much else in the way of options.

Bad plan beats no plan every time.

"What are you doing?" my wife yelled, the snarling jaws of Helvet's Hounds now only inches from her.

"Change the seal!" I shouted, getting to my feet and dodging a haymaker from Tommy.

"My hands are stuck, you idiot!"

Damn you and your logic, woman.

I narrowly avoided a left cross from the Bridge Troll that would have cleanly separated my head from my body. "Just wipe off that part."

"What part?!"

"The part that looks like a sideways four," I shouted, before taking a back fist to the mid-section.

Porter kicked off her shoe and reached out with a hose-covered toe toward the lipstick sigil.

"No!"

"What!" She stopped, her foot just inches away from the red seal edge.

"Not that one," I shouted, dodging Tommy's fists and flying cutlery propelled by Wild Magick. "The *other* part that looks like a sideways four."

My wife moved her foot. "This?"

"Yes!"

Porter swiped her foot over the symbol, removing the lipstick and giving us a chance—even if it was bat-shit crazy.

"Now what?"

"Now," I said, ducking a particularly fast-moving left jab. "You need to hold on, because this is about to get crazy."

I scooped up a large piece of chandelier crystal and ran toward my wife. The air was thick with flying debris, and I knew I took more than a couple forks to my side, but that was the least of my worries with Tommy crashing through the tables behind me.

Just a few more feet!

Shelley twitched again, then stopped moving—and breathing.

"Gene!"

"Here goes nothing," I yelled, falling to my knees and sliding the last few feet up to the sigil. I slammed the crystal shard onto the open spot in the seal, then placed one hand on Shelley's limp form. The other hand I extended out behind me in the perfect 'stop' pose.

True to form, Bridge-Troll-Tommy did no such thing, and instead his face ended up right smack in the middle of my palm.

"Cutis Artis!"

Thanks to the crystal, Magick coursed through me. Crystals weren't just for new-age yogis and fancy light fixtures, they were a focusing force, and one I desperately needed in the middle of this insanity.

Shelley stirred and Tommy collapsed at my feet, no longer a troll, and now looking the part of a teenager again.

"You did it!" my wife yelled, still trying to free her fingers.

I did something, all right.

Shelley's pale white skin darkened.

"What did you do, Gene?"

The necklace snapped, freeing Shelley to enjoy her new Bridge-Troll-bikini bod, and sending the spectral hounds packing.

"What did you do to her?" my wife yelled, shaking out her swollen fingers.

"I'm working on that…"

"What are you working on?"

Shelley's face flattened, her features rapidly trolling by the second.

"Just give me a second, I'll figure something out."

"So help me God, Eugene Law, if you turned my sorority sister into a Bridge Troll I'm going to… Well, damn it. I don't know what I'm going to do, but it's going to be bad."

"Amen."

Wild Magick continued to swirl around us while Shelley's previously petite form filled out in massive detail.

"She's trolling up fast—it's got to be the Thinning."

Porter grabbed the lipstick. "Draw something! Isn't there a doodle, or whatever you call them that can put her back right?"

"I can't. That version of Weavelick's True Form was one of a kind, unique to Tommy. It would take me weeks to figure out something for her."

"Damn it, Gene!" Porter shouted. "You've got to do something before we get crushed and the fire department stumbles on a naked she-troll."

"You mean Bridge Troll—wait, that's it. *Bridge* Troll."

Chairs tumbled past like prairie weeds.

"Huh?"

"The Thinning is a bridge, and technically speaking, your sorority sister now has bridge-based Magickal authority."

"What the hell does any of that—"

"Give me the necklace!"

Porter tossed what remained of the silver necklace to me as if it were a scorpion. "What are you going to do?"

"Something monumentally stupid."

"I'd expect nothing less."

Shelley had already torn her way out of that silky dress, but I was not the sort of person turned on by a middle-aged Bridge Troll—they have all the aesthetic beauty of poorly applied stucco. I laid the end of the torn necklace in her hand and kept hold of the other end myself.

"Ponte Clausi!"

Magick rushed from me and through the torn necklace, before racing out into the Thinning. The walls shook, and the lights flickered on and off.

"Did it work?"

Shelley opened her eyes and gasped, then quickly covered her bare chest. "Holy shit, Porter. What the hell happened?"

I dropped the now-cursed chain into my pocket. "Uh…"

"Remember that party freshman year?" Porter asked, nodding her head knowingly.

Shelley sat up, clutching her hand to her chest. "Crap—I didn't dance on the tables this time, right? Do either of you know where Jeff is?"

The fire department spilled into the room like black ants.

"Last I heard he misses you terribly," I said, helping Shelley to her feet. "Now let's get you two back together.

Porter, would you mind guiding her and the fire department to the men's room?"

"Wait, what are you going to do?"

"I'm going to check on Tommy," I said, finding the prone young man not far from our table.

"And?"

"And if you must know, I'm going to make sure I get a damn pumpkin cake."

FAR AWAY FROM THE BALLROOM, in a section of the hotel that would soon be home to construction crews and jackhammers, a brick shifted in the wall. Dust spilled out from its rough edges, dust driven out by the unpredictable power of Wild Magick surging underneath—awakened from a long and fitful sleep, dark things stirred in the Old Tampa Hotel.

BAHAMA BLUES

The last rays of an orange rind sun cut across the lapping waves. I used a hand to block the worst of it, but the rest of me was otherwise preoccupied with not going overboard. Each bounce of the modest dive boat sent my fingers hunting for a better grip on the metal railing. Beyond the fiberglass hull, the Caribbean's turquoise water stretched to infinity. It shined in the sun's final light, providing a picturesque view I couldn't bring myself to enjoy.

Porter placed a hand on my shoulder. "You okay?"

My wife loved diving. Going all the way back to the early days of our marriage, she'd taken every chance she could to drag me to a potential watery grave.

"Totally," I lied.

While I'd certainly muscled up and soldiered my way through the licensing process—had a little plastic card with my name on it and all—I knew there were things under the water that would love to get a hold of me, things Porter and normal people like her were better off knowing nothing about.

My name is Eugene Law and I'm a Magician.

I don't pull rabbits out of hats, nor do I saw beautiful women in half. I deal in real Magick, the cosmic powers of the universe that are just as dangerous as they sound. It's not a bad gig as jobs go. It basically means I spend most of my time making sure the evil things that bump in the night don't bump into the people I care about, and with the few hours left, I try to keep tabs on the Magickal flotsam and jetsam that washes up in the yard sales and flea markets of Weird Florida. The Sunshine State sits at that geometrically perfect vertex of weird—we get a lot of junk. Now, throw in a teenage daughter and precocious five-year-old, and you'll have a clue just how crazy my life is.

Porter pulled her silky brown hair into a rubber band and checked the zipper on her wetsuit. She'd done that little ritual no less than five times since we pulled out of Grand Bahama.

My wife was excited.

"We're going to be next to a *blue hole*, Gene," she said, putting a hand on my knee. "This is so awesome. I can't believe we got hooked up on such short notice."

Neither can I.

"So, great." You didn't need to be a Magician to feign enthusiasm, but it helped. "Tell me again why we want to do this at night?"

Our dive boat hit a rogue wave and dropped my already loose stomach to my toes.

If Porter noticed, her face didn't show it. She was as keyed up as a kid at Christmas waiting for Santa to drop off that new bike. "One word... bioluminescence."

"That'll win you scrabble."

Porter brushed my comments aside. "Glowing stuff, Gene. The water is going to be full of it. It'll be like swimming in a warm glowing pool of awesome."

"You do know they turn the lights on at the resort pool too, right?"

The twin engines roared and pushed us closer to our destination, a blue hole. Porter had made me watch a nature show on these watery terror factories before we'd booked the trip to the Bahamas, and only just last week I'd returned to having normal nightmares—ones that didn't involve me dying one of a hundred terrible ways at the bottom of a dark and frightening void.

The blue hole was a vertical cave. A rounded drop-off that went down hundreds of meters into the inky abyss before reaching God knows what.

I'd agreed to go on this trip exclusively because I knew we weren't going *in* said hole. We were set to dive the shallows around the entrance and enjoy the sights. There was no impromptu spelunking on tonight's agenda.

The captain joined me in squinting at the setting sun, then pushed the throttle down and sent the boat surging forward into the faded crests. In response, my stomach performed another feat of impressive gastrointestinal acrobatics. I tried to shake it off and distract myself by studying our fellow divers. This was pretty easy since there were only two of them.

Jeremy, the young man with the permanent grin, had been the instigator of this night dive and was almost as excited as my wife. For the past twenty minutes he'd alternated between chatting up the young woman next to him and barely containing a bad case of wandering hands.

The object of his overt affections was a petite young woman. She appeared to be humoring him by doing just enough to feign interest. The entire courtship ritual had been easy enough to pick up, you just needed to be married for a few years and most of these things became a trivial read.

Dad power...

Much like Porter, Jeremy's date wore her hair long, but, unlike my wife who couldn't be troubled to do much more than loop it through a rubber band, this young woman had gone in for the whole massively ornate braid thing. I figured she'd done it for the occasion—a lot of people do crazy things on vacation, and this young woman was clearly on vacation. She didn't have the look of a seasoned dive junkie, and those bright red patches on her neck and shoulders told me her skin wasn't used to the subtropic sun.

Young love.

Still, there was something about her I couldn't quite place, but I didn't have time to figure it out before the jagged rocky coast of our destination popped up on the horizon. The small island of scrubs trees and rocks stuck out of the ocean like a pulled loop of carpet, its leading edge a maze of white caps and barely hidden jagged rocks.

I cranked my hand down on the railing harder. "Shouldn't we slow down…"

The captain didn't share my concern. The old salt bit down on his cigarette and swung the boat back and forth, effortlessly navigating through the potentially capsizing shoals. Thirty heart-stopping seconds later, we were safely on the other side of what had appeared to be certain death. Our captain throttled back, and I checked to make sure my heart was still in my chest.

Yep, just barely.

Thankfully, Jeremy and my dive-crazed wife were too busy hanging over the railing to get a better look at the blue hole to notice all the color had left my face. The lone silver lining came in the form of the young woman across from me who appeared to be just as nervous as I was, if not a little more.

"It'll be alright," I said over the rumbling engines, feigning confidence.

She nodded and slipped her arms into the sleeves of a brand-new wetsuit.

The things we do for love.

Captain Steve cut the engines, and we coasted into the rapidly darkening lagoon. Even in the sun's fading light, I had to admit the blue hole was mesmerizing. Like a perfect void of inky blackness, it absorbed the sun's fading rays and with them what remained of my confidence. I pulled my eyes away from the abyss just long enough to find the young woman looking at me.

"I'm Gene Law," I said, extending a hand.

The petite brunette smiled, a very shaky and not entirely sure version of the one my wife was sporting. "Mira."

"All right everybody. Let's get a move on. We're on the clock," Captain Steve said, grabbing a clipboard.

Like a kid on the first day of summer vacation, Porter practically vibrated in anticipation. She had her gear on in seconds, then set to work helping me suit up.

"This is your bone mic," my wife said, tapping at the small box attached to my mask's strap. "This is how we will all hear your little girly squeals underwater."

"Very funny," I said, running my fingers over the small box. "Remember we do go home together."

Porter pantomimed a swoon. "Be still my heart."

The captain checked us off: Mira and Jeremy, then Porter and her jello-kneed husband.

"All right," he said, rubbing his leathery hand across an unshaven chin. "I figure you've got about five minutes or so before it gets dark enough to see the plankton light up. Unlike the rest of the tourists flailing around at Mosquito Bay, ol' Steve will make sure you'll see the real beauty of the Bahamas."

Something about old Steve told me he wasn't the most trustworthy of sorts, but that was probably just my wallet talking. Our intrepid captain had been big on hefty deposits.

"Where'd you find this nut job again?" I whispered, letting the bone mic pickup my words.

"He can hear you, Gene."

"Oh."

Steve spent a few more minutes going over some last second safety details, but they rolled in and out as my overly excited wife finished strapping up my gear, which included a wicked looking dive knife clamped to my thigh. "Really?"

"Better safe than sorry."

Splash!

Jeremy was in the water first, toppling backwards like a professional, and for all I knew he was. Even with his somewhat punch-drunk vibe, he clearly knew his way around dive gear—it was Mira I wasn't sure of. With Mr. Fun Pants in the water, I gave Mira a thumbs up before she tumbled backwards. Her wide-eyed expression told me exactly what I'd figured—she wasn't much for diving either.

Splash!

Two down and two to go.

I didn't have much time to contemplate the hundreds of potential life-ending possibilities in the water below before Porter's fingers entwined mine and the bone mic rattled her words off my brain stem. "Let's go, Magick man."

Splash!

Bubbles rushed past me, and the familiar falling sensation took over. I'd done enough dives to remember the feeling, and more importantly to focus on what to do next.

Don't hold your breath... Descend slowly...

The bubbles cleared, and I found myself floating not far from Porter and Mira. The young woman was having some issues with her gear and my ever-vigilant mama bear had already taken to making the adjustments for her.

"Is this better?" Porter's voice rumbled against my jawbone.

"Yes. Thank you."

"We sisters have to stick together."

Even through the coming gloom, Mira's surprise was evident on her face. "Huh?"

"I grew up outside of Omaha. You're from the Midwest right?"

"Yeah, how did you—"

"Farmer's tan."

Porter and her new bestie had just finished comparing notes on middle America when the shimmering light of bioluminescent micro-organisms lit up the water. My wife had been right: it was like swimming in a beautiful glowing pool. I swirled my fingers through the iridescent water, giggling like a schoolgirl, but it wasn't long before I noticed Mira wasn't joining in on the merriment. She appeared to be far more keen on keeping track of Jeremy—speaking of which, where was he?

"Jeremy?" I asked, my voice crackling over the mic.

The boat's twin engines roared to life, stirring up a wake of glowing micro-organisms and revealing one young man climbing back onboard.

Huh?

"Gene!" Porter cried. "The boat's leaving!"

Captain Steve's dive boat turned back toward the distant shoals, and I suddenly realized why he was keen on hefty deposits.

Crap.

* * *

"Gene!" Porter cried, watching the boat make for open water. "They're leaving without us!"

With a powerful kick, my wife pushed off for the distant dive boat, then stopped mid-stroke. She backpedaled quickly, her movements awkward. "Lionfish!"

The boat had shaken up the water enough to arouse the interest of bright yellow and brown striped fish. The tropical predators slipped in and out of the glowing plankton around us by the dozens. They weren't much larger than a penny-loafer, but unlike that lazy dress shoe, their fins were covered in venomous spines. For a normal person that venom would hurt like hell, but for my wife it was much worse—Porter was allergic. We'd discovered this on one very bad dive off the coast of Key West. Ever since that harried afternoon, my wife kept an epinephrine shot in her dive bag—the same dive bag still sitting on the deck of Captain Steve's boat.

"Don't move."

Porter froze, her arms and legs drifting gently and doing their best to avoid startling the venomous fish. "I'm trying not to."

A bold predator slid under her arm, its barbs brushing against the wetsuit only to skip off without breaking the soft fabric.

"Just stay calm and everything will be fine."

My bone mic growled with Porter's frustration. "What do you think I'm doing..."

More lionfish slipped in and out of the plankton's glow, surrounding her in a blanket of spines and barbs.

"Go topside," I said, pointing to a narrow opening between the circling fish.

Porter hesitated. "What about you?"

"I'm not allergic to them."

My wife didn't take more convincing. She gently kicked off and pushed her body toward the surface. "Where's Mira?"

A rumble of static shook my bone mic along with a muffled scream.

Porter stopped, the lionfish swimming dangerously close. "Mira?"

"Help," the young woman cried, her voice breaking over the static.

Porter spun around in the water. "I don't see her, Gene!"

"Stop spinning, you're going to get—"

Too late. My wife twisted back just in time to get a barb in the thigh. That short dorsal spike punctured her wet suit and sent a rush of powerful venom into her bloodstream.

"Shit!" Porter clutched at her leg. "Stupid, stupid, stupid!"

"Help!" Mira cried again, the panic in her voice real.

"I see her," my wife said, her words mixed with pain. "She's at the edge."

An arm waved at the cavernous hole's edge and lit up the surrounding plankton. "I can't hold on. The current is too strong."

"Porter?"

"Go, Gene," my wife squeezed her leg with one hand and used the other to push for the surface. "I'll be okay."

"No you won't. If you don't get your Epipen—"

"I've got time. The boat isn't that far away, and I'm a much better swimmer than you are."

Click.

My wife unclipped her gear.

"What are you doing," I cried.

"I'll be faster without all this weight."

"But—"

I didn't get to finish my words before Mira's panicked voice cut over the bone mic. "I'm losing my grip!"

Porter placed a hand on her bone mic, pressing it against the side of her head to make sure I heard her every word. "Go! I'll be fine. She goes over that edge and she's done."

The venom was already having an effect. Porter's voice

had a raspy edge to it, and without that epipen her throat was going to close up tight as a drum in no time.

"Porter!" I locked eyes with my wife.

"Go," she mouthed, dropping her regulator, along with the rest of her gear. The tanks and dive belt slipped past me and into the gloom below.

"Mira, can you hear me?"

The young woman's ragged voice rattled against my jawbone. "Yes. Help!"

I kicked off into the dark water, leaving a stream of glowing blue plankton in my wake. "Turn your dive light on!"

"How?"

"It's on the front of your wet suit."

The distant figure of Mira looked so small and helpless against the inky and infinite darkness of the hole.

"Is this it?"

A bright yellow light popped on, illuminating the young woman and the rocky edge.

"Yes! You got it—"

The petite woman waved, then vanished into the black water of the hole.

"Mira!"

Static.

I pumped my legs and pushed through the plankton-filled water, avoiding rocks and burning through my oxygen at an alarming rate. "Mira!"

Pops and crackles rattled in my head, but the young woman's voice was decidedly absent.

The current picked up the closer I got to the edge. I twisted around and grabbed onto the rocky ledge, extending my feet toward the sucking hole. "Mira!"

The glowing orange of a dive light shined up from the darkness below.

"I'm here," I said, backing closer and kicking my leg. "Take it."

More garbled sounds vibrated against my skull.

"Grab my foot," I cried, desperately clinging to the sharp rocks.

Thin fingers wrapped my ankle, skin on skin, and for an instant it was like standing on a fire ant mound. Outside of those biting insects, there was only one other thing in the world that caused that kind of feeling—Magick.

"I've got you," I cried, digging in and pulling her back from the sucking current.

Mira reappeared above the edge, her regulator out of her mouth and streaming bubbles into the dark water. The current pulled harder and sent the young woman's braid twisting in the dark behind her. The blue hole had enjoyed a taste and wanted more.

"Kick," I cried, wondering if she could even hear me.

Her mask pushed to one side, and half full of water, Mira nodded. She kicked her legs and clawed her way up mine. I dug my hands into the sharp rocks and pulled, dragging the young woman free of the watery vortex.

"Hold here." I reached back and directed her wrist to a jagged gap in the rocks. "I'll get your air."

She clutched at the hold while I tracked down the snaking cord of her free-spinning regulator.

"Breathe," I said, getting the regulator back to her mouth.

Her air restored, Mira took huge gasps.

"No. Slow down. Don't panic. Nice even breaths."

Mira nodded, but the panic in her eyes hadn't dialed back one bit. "We have to go."

"And we will." I checked my oxygen levels along with hers. "But I need you to calm down before we—"

"No. You don't understand. We have to go now! I lost the scrimshaw. I can't close the gate."

"What are you talking about?"

Mira crawled away from the hole's edge, motioning me to follow her. "I've been on Grand Bahama for a few weeks. We aren't their first sacrifice. They've been doing this for a long time. They find unsuspecting people to bring to this hole, summon the beast, and feed it."

"Beast? What beast?"

The young woman shook her head. "I don't know exactly."

"That's crazy. If there'd been a summoning, I'd know it. I'd feel the—"

The current shifted. The blue hole that had been on set on suck switched to blow, and the force of that sudden change threw Mira and me off our rocky perch.

"Take my hand," I cried, catching the young woman's fingers in mine.

Mira turned to face the dark void. "It's coming"

A great ripple of alien Magick washed over the hole's edge—something was coming. Something big.

"We were going to close the gate," she cried, floundering in the surging current. "We worked on that scrimshaw whale tooth for weeks. It was our best hope and I lost it."

"Shit happens, kid." I pulled Mira toward the distant shoals, using the strong current and my legs to propel us forward. "We'll figure something out, but let's not use up the rest of our air debating the finer points of that plan."

"But the scrim—"

I lost the young woman's words in the onrush of bubbles. My mask was yanked to the side, sending saltwater flooding over my face.

Argh!

Sharp claws dug into my leg and yanked me backward. The young woman's fingers slipped out of mine, and the reflection in her mask filled with exactly what I was afraid of —tentacles, lots of tentacles.

Let's go diving, Gene. It'll be fun... Why do I listen to her?

* * *

WHATEVER WAS at the other end of those tentacles, it was strong enough to whisk me away from Mira and against the spewing current. I grabbed at the rocks, but the beast was too powerful. The current shifted again, this time joining the powerful tentacles and pulling me toward the hole, and whatever lay at the far end of those sharp suckers.

My knife!

The dive knife Porter had strapped to my thigh suddenly seemed a lot more important than it had on the boat. But no sooner had I gotten a hand on the hilt than another tentacle caught that arm and pinned it to me, making it impossible to get the blade out of its scabbard.

Son of a bitch.

Sharp suckers dug into my skin, cutting through the wet suit and sending puffs of dark blood into the glowing water. The Magick of the summoning was everywhere, it poured out of the dark abyss beyond the hole's edge and saturated the surrounding water.

This was no Johnny-come-lately conjuring, this was Deep Magick.

I twisted and used my one free hand to catch the hole's edge. I hung on for dear life, the tentacles digging harder into what remained of my wetsuit. Bones ached and tendons stretched as the creature tried to drag me into the impenetrable darkness below.

Another shape moved in front of me, but with my mask twisted, it was hazy and hard to make out in the glowing water. A hand grabbed mine.

Porter!

No, there was Magick in those fingers, a subtle Magick born of complex ritual, incantations, and the combined efforts of tremendous focus.

Mira.

The young woman slipped out my dive knife and cut into the closest tentacle, forcing the creature to loosen its grip enough for me to free my other hand.

Mira slapped the bone mic against my temple, and her panic rattled my skull. "I can't close the gate without the scrimshaw!"

In the distance, the low rumble of the boat's engines tied my stomach in knots—I could only hope Porter had found a way to get to safety. More tentacles rose out of the abyss beneath me. Mira cut at the rubbery appendages frantically, her efforts filling the surrounding water with bubbles and burning through her air at an alarming rate.

Your air!

Mira's gauge drifted past and told me what I didn't want to know—she didn't have much time. I pressed the bone mic to my skull. "Go! You're running out of air. You've got to get out of here."

"What about you?"

"I'll be fine," I said, my own air running thin. "Florida man here, I do this sort of thing all the time."

Mira slashed at another tentacle but refused to swim away. "No, I've got to get the scrimshaw."

The young woman kicked toward the hole's edge, but I caught her arm. "You go down there, you are as good as dead. The pressure will crush you like a soda can."

"But the knife isn't working!"

Mira was right; she might as well have been stabbing at clay for all the headway she was making.

"I'm getting dizzy," she said, her arms slowing.

"It's the air. You are running out."

"I'm not leaving you here."

"You might not have a choice."

Just then, something swam past, something that even my saltwater stung eyes could identify immediately—lionfish.

"Put your hand on mine," I said, holding on for dear life against the creature's pull.

Mira stabbed at another tentacle. "Gene, what are you doing?"

"Magick, and you're going to help me," I said, the bone mic rattling against my skull.

"We're underwater! How the hell are we going to—"

"You want to see what's at the bottom of that hole?"

Mira didn't respond, but her wide eyes told me all I needed to know—she didn't.

"We've got one shot at this. See that lionfish there?"

"Yeah."

"How much Magick do you think it would take to find one a hundred times larger?"

"Gene, you're crazy."

"Nope, I'm from Florida. There's a difference, but it's subtle." I kicked my legs, sending a fresh puff of blood into the glowing water.

Mira switched the knife into her other hand and reached for mine. "But what about the karma backlash? The part where you end up worse off because of Magick."

"Yeah, that's basically my whole life."

The young woman shook her head. "No, you don't understand—"

"Kid, karma can suck it."

Mira kicked at a tentacle reaching for her leg. "You are one weird wizard, Gene."

"Magician. And if you think I'm strange, just wait until you meet my apprentice."

The young girl closed her eyes and unleashed her Magick. I couldn't help but be inspired. This young girl represented the future of Magick, and it was glorious to behold. Mira was a complex and mysterious creature, and her Magick was more of the same. Ritualistic and by the book, it colored between the lines, but I got the sense it also slipped outside those borders whenever she deemed it necessary. There was more to this petite brunette than she let on—a lot more. Physically, she might be young, but Magickally Mira was an old soul, and her cosmic powers had heart, not to mention a crap-load of natural talent.

This is gonna work.

"Maximus!"

In stark contrast to Mira, my Magick was a raucous display of reality-bending prowess. Unlike the far more subtle and complicated young woman, I was an envelope-pushing Magician with the battle scars to prove it. I was going to have my monster-sized lionfish, and reality was just going to have to deal with it.

Mira opened her eyes and pointed toward the distant shoals where something large floated into view like a Thanksgiving Day parade balloon. It was, without question, the single largest lionfish ever to have existed, and technically it probably didn't exist at all, but this time reality had to get in the back seat, because Eugene Law and his Magick were riding shotgun.

The spiny predator lumbered into view, its massive spikes like wide sweeping broomsticks ready to dump a heart-stopping load of venom on the first thing stupid enough to squeeze them.

Just a little closer.

Something bright and red flashed on my wrist—the tank gauge.

OXYGEN LEVELS LOW.

I turned my wrist away, but a second red light appeared, this one on Mira's arm.

OXYGEN LEVELS LOW. Of course they are...

The lionfish floated closer, those wide barbs sweeping back and forth in the glowing water. All I needed was one tentacle, just one and that fish would pump a monster amount of venom in an instant. A slippery appendage slid past me, and I had my wish. It latched on to the Volkswagen-sized lionfish and dragged it toward the hole's edge.

A tasty treat, but, unlike Mira or me, this snack came with a hefty price tag.

One of predator's many barbs pierced the tentacle, and its hollow core sent a flood of neuro-toxin coursing through the monster. The effect was immediate and expected. Mira and I found ourselves instantly free of the monster's grasp and only fighting the pulling current. The bone mic buzzed in the water, but I didn't bother reaching for it. There was nothing up for debate: we had to leave, and we had to do it now.

I pulled the young woman, and together we kicked toward the shoals. More blood leeched out of the tears in my wetsuit, but I kept pushing, knowing that to stay near the hole meant certain death.

We clawed and kicked our way across the jagged rocks. The shoals were too far away, and the flashing displays on our wrists agreed with that assessment.

Think, Gene!

I tugged on the young woman's arm and pointed up. She nodded, and together we scrambled for the surface.

Mira rose fast, too fast, and I had to grab on to her leg to slow her down. Surface too quickly and you're in for a world of problems, plus, to make matters worse, no bubbles escaped her regulator—she was holding her breath.

Stop! Don't hold your breath!

I didn't have the bone mic, so I had no way to telling her

to resist the natural inclinations that down here would get you killed. I squeezed her stomach and an air bubble escaped her lips. Her wide and panic-filled eyes watched me pantomime proper breathing, and her proceeding breaths made me pretty certain I'd gotten through to her.

Like a dark angel against the glowing plankton-filled water, she ascended toward the surface. Her braids undone and her hair streaming out behind the mask, she really did remind me a lot of Porter, and for a moment I wondered if we'd all laugh about this years from now.

It was in that moment, when I thought for sure we would make it out, that a very strong and capable tentacle hooked my mid-section and pulled me into the frigid darkness of the blue hole.

* * *

AN EVER-SHRINKING halo of blue vanished above me. Like the light at the end of the tunnel in reverse, it faded in the bone-chilling cold of the inky water. My tank monitor and its angry red pulse kept time with a frantic heart as we tumbled toward oblivion. At one point, the pressure gauge swung past my face, but I didn't need to see it to know I was rapidly approaching the point of no return. Even if I'd found a way to get free, the ascent would be the end of me.

I sucked at what air was left in my tank, and my ears popped. So this was going to be how it ended? A watery grave somewhere off to the coast of Grand Bahama? I didn't bother fighting the monster's grip; I had almost nothing left to fight with, and the alien creature's cold embrace was almost comforting in the darkness

It might have been the low-oxygen hypoxia kicking in, but it felt like my rapid descent slowed. The flashing red of the gauge confirmed my suspicion, the rock wall no longer streamed past, but now hovered just beyond my fingers. With little sense of direction, I squinted in the darkness where I thought up would be, but there was no distant halo. Instead, I found only myself, a small and helpless reflection floating weightless in the mirror of an enormous eye. The cat-like pupil narrowed, focusing on my embryonic form. High-pitched and distorted, alien sounds like a scratched record tore through my head. They shifted and settled, until the sounds weren't so much words as feelings and thoughts, images that came too fast to comprehend and reverberated against my oxygen-deprived skull.

Cold... Hungry...

A barren landscape, blue-black and watery, appeared in my mind. Dark and all but formless, the unbroken horizon of murky sand stretched out to infinity and filled me with a sense of despair and frustration. Hunger, unceasing hunger, ravaged me—there was nothing left in that barren world to eat but each other.

Death... Pain...

Flashing images of blood and tentacles under a faded and filtered blue light filled my eyes, and I couldn't look away. I felt each tear, and my throat roared each scream.

Magick...

The creature had no words to explain the forces of Magick, but its six-sphere brain understood the power, and more importantly it knew it needed it. The cosmic energy that flowed in our world, and in my blood, was a powerful lure.

More!

Visions of an untold number of the creatures filled my mind. An army—too many to count—waited just beyond. They needed Magick, and they'd found it in me.

Key...

I was the key.

Devouring me would shatter the lock that held them back. I would be the beginning of the end. A great and noble sacrifice. My image would live on in the alien minds of our new conquerors. I sucked at the last gasps of air and let the current swim past my face. The creature's eye faded into the abyss, something else was coming, something sharp and piercing.

Purpose...

A great beak appeared from the gloom, jagged and quivering. There was excitement in the water—Magick was coming—and with it would be salvation.

My eyes fluttered in and out. I didn't have the strength to fight or the will to run. This would be a grand beginning, a great re-awakening, the dawning of a new age.

The beak opened wide, and I rushed toward it, propelled by the beast and its thoughts. Bliss was awaiting me on the other side of those jaws. An unshakable joy that tugged at my heart.

I slowed to push past something white that flashed along the razor's edge.

A scrimshaw tooth.

Somewhere deep down in the animal part of my brain, a fierce and frustrated voice fought for control.

Get the tooth!

The tentacle relaxed and let me float the final few feet, the monster's powerful mind crushing my thoughts and snuffing out the last bits of that survival voice. The sigil-covered tooth teetered in and out of the great beast's mouth like a carnival game. Purely out of reflex I extended my numb fingers for the prize, not entirely sure why, but keen to touch it nevertheless.

A deep sucking sound signaled my end as the creature pulled in the water around it like an open drain. The tooth rushed up on me, and in the waning seconds I brought it to my chest.

Mira's Magick, a complex and powerful force of nature that had been locked up in that tooth with the help of many hands, rushed over me like the warming sun on a summer's day. Alien thoughts burned away in her Deep Magick. In that instant, I remembered something very important—I was Eugene Law, and I wasn't about to be anybody's sacrificial lamb.

The beak chattered and snapped, catching my gear and tearing away my tank. I spun in the dark, my hands clutching to the tooth. Numb fingers ran across the complex swirls of ritual Magick.

If I'm going down, I'm taking you with me.

The creature's thoughts, laced with panic, hit me like a sucker punch to the gut. Images of Porter flooded my mind, her long hair and smiling face. Those still frames vanished only to be replaced by scenes of Cathy and Kris, smiling and playing in the yard. More happy images roared past in gut-churning detail. The beast probed my thoughts for the right words, but failing that, settled on a single nine-inch nail of desire and hammered it into my head.

Deal?

I tumbled end-over-end in the cold dark, my fingers tracing the sigil and unlocking the scrimshaw's Magick.

No deal.

* * *

"GENE?! Can you hear me? He's not moving!"

My wife's words were hazy and broken in the warm dark.

"I'm doing what I can, but he's got to want it," a young woman said, the soft Midwestern accent coloring her voice.

Five more minutes.

I tugged tight to the thick blanket of mind-numbing night.

"Damn it, you bastard. Wake up or so help me God I'll find a way to drag your spirit back to your body so hard it'll leave a mark."

Sigh...

I groaned and pushed the mental blankets aside.

"He's coming around," Mira said, hope in her voice.

I peeled open one tired eye and then the other.

"Gene!" Porter's hug forced the last of the saltwater from my body and across the deck of the dive boat like splatter art.

"Ugh..."

The ladies me propped up against the side of the skiff, but as bad as I felt, the other guys onboard looked worse. I was getting the star treatment compared to Captain Steve and Jeremy—tied up and subdued with more than a handful of cuts, they appeared honestly pleased I'd survived.

I could only imagine what my wife would have done to them if I hadn't.

"Gene, we found you bobbing on the surface. What happened down there?"

"I... I really don't know. I can't remember."

Porter took a few minutes to make sure I wasn't going to topple overboard and then got the engines in gear. We sped off toward Grand Bahama, and an all but certain trip to the hospital. Mira dropped down next to me. "You found the tooth."

"I think I did."

The young woman and I sat in silence for a few moments letting the waves lap against the boat before Mira spoke again. "Your wife is kinda scary."

"Yeah, you should see her when she gets mad."

It was hard to tell in the gloom, but I was pretty sure Mira smiled. "She said I should come visit you guys in Florida sometime, but honestly, after spending an evening with you I'm not quite sure. Are all your days like this?"

My wife's hair whipped in the wind like a Caribbean pirate as she gunned the engine for home.

"Nah," I said, leaning my head against the railing. "You caught us on a good day. Most are way worse."

PLASMA PISTOLS

I cut the Dad Wagon across three lanes of traffic, single-finger salutes erupting from the hands of half a dozen drivers. I didn't have time to focus on any of them—I was on a mission.

How could you have forgotten?

I hit the gas and the old Mazda dug in, surging around a slow-moving minivan.

It's not your fault. The holiday sneaks up on you.

I shook my head and checked the clock on the dash—nine-fifty.

Christmas does not sneak up on you. It comes on December 25th each and every year. There's no magic to it, you mark it on the calendar and you get to work.

The newspaper's holiday insert smiled up at me from the passenger seat. Glossy folds featured happy children playing with a folksy orange space cowboy. Judging by the looks on their cherubic faces, he came with ice cream, puppies, and a new bike. Commander Keen was the 'it' toy for this year, and the only thing my youngest son wanted.

"You got it? Right, Gene?" Porter's words stuck in my

head, alongside that image of her crossed arms and tapping foot.

Crap.

Bold words in thick black marker on a colorful sticky note spelled out my mistake in vivid detail.

Get Commander Keen over lunch. Love, Porter. PS - If they have Spotty the Wonder Pup, get that too.

The dash clocked showed nine fifty-five, and I slammed down the accelerator. Roaring in excitement, the Dad Wagon was not entirely sure why we were racing down I-275, but was happy to burn through my gas just the same.

Lunch back on the day Porter handed me the note had come and gone, as had dinner, and then three more weeks of the same. Yes, I'd forgotten to get Commander Keen and the Wonder Weasel, but it wasn't hard to see why. I'd had two impromptu exorcisms already this month, and a derelict New Dead hanging out near the old bowling alley that proved to be more than a little frustrating.

My name is Eugene Law, and I'm a Magician. I don't do kids parties, or balloon animals, I deal in real Magick and the cosmic forces of the universe hellbent on our shared destruction. It's a full-time job with zero pay and terrible benefits—I love it.

The mall's bright lights consumed the horizon, the metropolitan mecca rising out of the ground like a modern-day castle. Large lamps cast their invigorating glow over its car-filled moat, while the rest of that fortress lay decked out in happy green and red Christmas bulbs. Those flashing lights chased each other in merry patterns across the stark walls, their twinkling colors playing through the garland balls and bells that dangled above the jockeying cars.

"The holiday didn't sneak up on them," I said, counting out the stacked-up vehicles and trying to find a space for the

Dad Wagon. I could almost hear Porter's voice in my head as I pulled off the highway.

It's all he wants for Christmas, Gene.

My son was a tough one to shop for. Unlike his sister, who had a dozen interests, Kris was an old soul. He found something he liked and didn't put it down—ever.

Nine fifty-six...

The Mazda and I fought our way into the lot, cutting off a rumbling truck and racing around a pair of undersized imports. A heavily overburdened minivan popped its tail-lights on, signaling my opportunity, and I pounced.

"Come on, come on!" I wedged the Dad Wagon as close to the backing vehicle as I could get, but it wasn't enough. "Son of a—"

Vroom.

A jet-black sedan shot into the parking lot like he owned the place, cut in front of me, and slipped directly into the newly opened space.

"Hey! That was my spot!"

A teenager popped out of the driver seat and shrugged, apparently uneducated on the basic tenets of parking space etiquette.

Magick swirled in my chest, frustrated and ready to lash out, but I tamped it down. There would be no impromptu cosmic displays today.

The kid grabbed a navy shirt off the seat and pulled it on.

PICKT.

The bright white letters were for a delivery service often used by rich people who didn't want to be bothered by going to the actual store to purchase their fancy-pants items.

Sitting in the car getting honked at by other drivers, I came to the immediate decision that I hated said rich people —every last one of them.

It took three more passes through the lot before a

compact space opened up. I rammed the old Mazda into it as best I could and beat a path for the distant entrance. Supplicants to the gods of commerce streamed in and out of the revolving doors, but these weren't the happy-go-lucky types you might find on a normal day. Those loving souls were home, most likely enjoying holiday beverages and entertaining family. Hungry eyes and frustrated faces filed in and out of those glass doors to the high temple of empty wallets.

I pushed my way past the angry mob, pausing only long enough to check the oversized map that told me where the toy store was. As it turned out, I didn't need it—a monstrously large statue of Commander Keen stood tall outside the nearby toy store's wide-open entrance.

See, you've got plenty of time.

The store's metal gate lowered from that hidden seam in the top.

Run!

"Hang on," I cried, waving my hands frantically to get the attention of a pimply faced teenager rolling down the steel gate on my son's Christmas hopes.

"Sir, we are closing."

"Commander Keen," I stammered, crawling under the half-open gate and trying to catch my breath.

Before the young man could respond I found what I'd come for. According to my young son, Commander Keen was the single greatest Christmas toy of all time. Given the difficulty in locating one, I was inclined to agree with him. The folksy space cowboy with his wide brim hat sat on an otherwise empty shelf, a sly smile on his orange face. A pair of plasma pistols dangled from low hanging holsters, while beneath them the flowing script proclaimed what I already knew.

Space Cowboy and Defender from the Horsehead Nebula.

"We're out," the teenage clerk said, frowning in the process.

"What do you mean you're out?" I said, reaching for the last space cowboy on the barren rack. "I see one right here."

A second set of hands popped out around the display and grabbed Commander Keen before I could get there. Those hands were attached to arms, arms that disappeared into a dark navy 'PICKT' shirt.

You!

"Thanks, Mike," the delivery kid said, tucking my toy under his arm. "I appreciate you holding it for me. You wouldn't believe what this woman is willing to pay for it."

"No problem. Yeah, it's a hot item for sure."

"W…Wait a second," I said, stammering over my words in a fit of frustration. "I was going to buy that. I need it for my son for Christmas."

The delivery boy shook his head. "And I need it for my client." He held up his phone for the teenage clerk.

"Wait! Stop. I'll pay more."

The clerk hesitated. "I don't think I can—"

"Of course you can," I said, pulling out my wallet and thumbing through the receipts in search of some cash. "I've got an extra twenty."

The delivery kid pulled back his phone and pressed a few buttons. "I am authorized to spend this much." He flashed the screen at the young clerk.

"Uh… I don't." The checkout scanner hesitated in the young man's hands.

"Cash is king, son," I said, waving the bill. "Besides, who cares what that rich woman wants, right, guys? I mean, you two could split the extra and maybe go get ice cream or something."

Both young men frowned.

Beep!

A scanner swipe later, and Commander Keen vanished into the PICKT kid's bag.

"What?!"

The ten foot cardboard Commander Keen display stared down at me. He might have been smiling, but I couldn't help but shake the feeling that oversized space cowboy was mocking me in every sense of the word.

"Thanks, Mike." The delivery kid tucked my son's toy under his arm and slipped out under the half-closed gate.

Breathe, Gene. Be calm.

"Please tell me that wasn't your last one."

"Sorry, sir. We're out."

"It's Christmas Eve, you don't have even a single one?"

The teenager nodded, his face completely devoid of empathy. I'd seen fine art statues with more expression. "That's what *out* means."

"But you have a giant display right outside the store?!"

The kid didn't put two and two together into anything meaningful. "And..."

"And that thing is like a giant magnet that says you've got Commander Keens by the case full."

"Yeah, we did—we don't now."

The swinging metal gate kicked back into motion and signaled just how little time I had left.

"Come on, you've got to have one in the back, right?"

"No."

"You aren't even going to look?"

The kid let out a long sigh. "Listen, here's the thing. It's Christmas Eve. I'm cleaned out. I don't have Commander Keen. I don't have the Space Raider's Plasma Rifle, the Moon Pals Phase Base, or the Star Cow Stampede. I don't have—"

"Do you have the Wonder Pup?"

"You mean Spotty?"

"Yes! That's it. Spotty the Wonder Pup."

"Nope." The teenager shook his head. "The Wonder Pup, Killer Kat, and the Dog of Doom are on backorder until New Year."

"Ugh."

"Yeah. It's time to go. I'm tired, man."

My mind scrambled. I couldn't go home empty handed. "What do you have?"

The young kid shook his head. "If I find you something will you promise to leave?"

"Yes!"

The teenager left me to fish something out from behind the counter.

"Here," he said, placing the purple action figure trapped in its clear blister pack prison on the counter top. "This is the best I've got."

I wrinkled up my face trying to read the flowing script. "The Dark Petunia?"

"The Dark Phantasm."

I frowned. "I see, and that's…"

"The Evil Master of Space and Time." The kid continued to read from the package. "The Phantasm has the power of… You know what, I just don't care. It's the best I can do. Do you want it or not?"

The tiny figure frowned at me from inside his plastic coffin. An assortment of oversized muscles and devilish purple eyebrows gave me the distinct impression this wasn't one of Commander Keen's loving sidekicks.

"How much?"

* * *

THE TINY PURPLE man glared at me from inside his clear plastic cage.

"Oh, don't give me that," I said, holding the angry little

alien up to the light. "I didn't ask for this. I try really hard, you know?"

The Dark Phantasm's eyebrows told me he didn't care.

I dropped down on a wide circular bench that surrounded the mall's largest fountain. My daughter lovingly referred to this spot as the 'Geez Bench,' and tonight I felt every one of my middle-aged man years.

"It's true," I said to the doll, propping him up next to me. "I work my butt off. Do you have any idea how hard it is to fight off the forces of supernatural evil *and* get home for dinner on time most nights?"

The Dark Phantasm frowned.

"Exactly. It's damn tough. I mean, who makes sure the bills get paid? Who squishes the bugs and cuts the grass when he remembers?"

My purple pal didn't answer.

"I'll tell you who. This guy." I shoved a thumb against my chest. "You're looking at him."

Gene, you're talking to a doll.

I picked up the Dark Phantasm and flipped the package over.

The Dark Phantasm is the master of space and time. Thanks to the powers of the Temporum Timepiece, the malevolent one can manipulate reality and bend the very forces of nature to his will. Will he be too much for Commander Keen and the Moon Pals? Find out when...

"Master of space and time, eh?" I turned the package back over and frowned at the little purple man. "Yeah, well. I'm a Magician, and I can tell you, it's not always all it's cracked up to be."

A pleasant chime rang out in the wide expanse of the mall. That sound was followed shortly after by an equally cheery yet altogether curt announcement. "The mall will be closing in fifteen minutes. We wish you a Merry Christmas. Please proceed to the nearest exit."

In other words, last call. We don't care where you go, but you can't stay here.

I tucked Captain Frowny-brows under my arm and was busy trying to figure out how I explain this to Porter when I noticed the PICKT kid hanging out next to one of my daughter's favorite clothing stores.

Why are we paying for ripped clothes, Cathy? I mean, shouldn't they come not ripped?

That comment had won me an eye-roll from both my daughter and my wife, and somehow we'd still ended up with torn clothing.

Right now the delivery weasel didn't appear to be there to get some fashionably damaged duds.

Is he flirting with her?

I couldn't tell for sure, but it appeared the kid was doing his best to get the attention of a young girl who couldn't have been more than sixteen. My mental dad-alarm went off. They might have been roughly the same age, but that kid was bad news.

Why? Because he has a job and got the last doll? Gene, listen to yourself.

It was sound advice, so of course I ignored it completely.

The action figure...

PICKT boy set his bag down to get a hand on the young woman's shoulder.

And see, he's handsy too!

I shook that thought out of my head and focused on the bag.

Don't do it, Gene. That would be stealing. Stealing! What sort of example does that set for your kids?

I reached into the wellspring of Magick swirling in my

chest. Cosmic power danced and twirled, bouncing like a puppy.

So let me get this straight. You're going to use Magick to steal a toy for your son on Christmas? Is this the level of depravity you've come to? Gene, look at yourself. Stop for one second and think about what your are doing.

The delivery kid said something and the young girl he'd been talking with immediately frowned. She shrugged off his hand and pushed him back. Undeterred, he took a few steps after her.

Second thought, he's a jerk, and you'd be doing some other dad a favor. It's go time—Magick away.

I dropped the Dark Phantasm back in his bag and tucked him under my arm. My Magick bubbled up like the fountain behind me.

"Veni," I whispered, sending that cosmic power toward the unguarded bag. "Veni…"

The paper bag wriggled slightly, the delivery boy far too concerned with ripped clothing girl to pay any attention to this bag and the Commander Keen inside.

Come on...

"Veni!"

The bag toppled over and skid across the floor like it'd been kicked.

Ah, ha! Nice work, Gene.

I left the old man bench and scooped up the bag, pausing to get a look at Commander Keen's judging grin.

"Don't give me that. Trust me, that kid was bad news."

I tucked the judgmental little action figure and his bag under my arm next to his evil twin and headed toward the door.

"Sir!"

I hadn't made it more than ten feet before a physically imposing member of mall security blocked my path.

"Uh, yes?"

"I'm going to have to ask you to return the bag to that young man."

I hesitated. "I think you've got me confused with someone else."

Barrel-chested and with little in the way of social grace, the security guard's thick hands pointed at my newly acquired bag. "No, I don't. I watched you pick up that kid's bag. I'm going to assume you meant to return it to him. In fact, I'm going to give you an opportunity to do that right now."

The way he said opportunity made me imagine being stuck in mall jail on Christmas Eve.

Yeah, Porter. So, I'm in mall jail. No, I didn't get Commander Keen, funny story...

"Oh, this?" I said, holding up the toy store bag. "I was just going to take it to the lost and found."

"Of course you were, sir."

Something about the way those forearm muscles rippled as he spoke made me think maybe he didn't believe me.

The PICKT delivery boy appeared behind the security guard. "That's my bag!"

"Yes, it is. This gentleman picked it up and is happy to return it to you."

Sigh.

"Yes," I said through gritted teeth. "You must have dropped it while you were bothering—I mean talking—to the young lady from the ripped-up denim store."

"She's my cousin."

Oh.

"Anyway," I shoved the bag in his hand, "here's your bag. I'm so glad I could return it to you. I wish both of you a very Merry Christmas and Happy New Year."

What are you doing, Gene? Stop. Don't do it.

I hadn't gone two feet before the kid opened his bag. "Hey, this is the wrong one. This is the Dark Phantasm. I bought Commander Keen!"

This really isn't one of your finer moments, is it?

I tried to run, but Manly Forearms was surprisingly fast on his feet. He knocked me to the ground and sent Commander Keen spinning out of its bag.

Ugh.

A couple hundred pounds of mall security pinned me down while the delivery boy collected his space cowboy, then flashed his phone at the gorilla-sized guard. "This is mine and I can prove it. Here's the order and the pickup number."

Mall security held me down with very little in the way of effort. He held the toy up and compared it to the phone. "Uh, huh. It looks like this is yours."

"Listen, guys, this was totally a misunderstanding. I meant to give him the other bag. You know, things like this happen all the time. In a few years, we'll all chuckle about this."

The kid shoved Commander Keen under his arm and tucked the phone in his pocket. "Thanks."

The muscular man unhooked his radio. "We've got a situation in front of Dang Girl Denim."

I squirmed under the massive man's bulk. "No, no situation. We're good. I'll just take my bag and head out. Merry Christmas one and all. No mall jail for me. No sir. Just gonna head out to the car."

"Sir, I need you to calm down."

Magick bubbled up in my chest and I had to fight to force it back down. The panic reflex was kicking in.

"I am calm."

I wasn't.

Kris's toy was headed toward the distant door, and it

looked for all the world like I was sure to join the shopping center's chain gang before the day was through. That call to Porter was looking more likely by the second.

You're where?!

I cringed at the sound of her voice in my head.

On Christmas Eve, Gene! Really?!

Magick surged in the worst of ways. "No, not now!"

Too late.

Cosmic power erupted like a dog slipping out an open door. It shot between my arms and over the security guard, expertly finding its way into the taser at his belt.

"Oh, hell."

Whrrr zap!

I'd never been hit by a Magickally induced taser before—turned out it really sucked.

* * *

UNCONTROLLED OR WILD Magick is almost always unpredictable, hence the name. Couple that nascent insanity with the finest in rental tasing equipment and you had a domino chain of disaster just waiting to topple. Lucky for me, I happened to be the bottom tile.

Zap!

I couldn't fault the taser. That tiny gun-looking arc thrower was just doing what it was made to do—reduce bad guys to jelly-kneed morons. It had no idea what Wild Magick was, nor why it should not be juicing up a Magician while he was having a tough time holding on to his Magick. These were obviously things they didn't cover in zapping-people safety classes.

Ugh.

Electricity flooded my body. Neurons fired and synapses closed in rapid succession. Muscles I didn't know I had contracted, sending my legs and arms curling in like a dead spider. The taser didn't stop there, since the security guard and I were only a fancy dinner away from being too close for comfort, it flooded his body too.

My teeth chattered and cheeks twitched. The Wild Magick swirling around me, doing its damndest to pull more power from my chest. It was like a pair of preschoolers egging each other on to new heights of stupidity.

Not gonna happen.

I tried to wrangle that power back under control, but much like my teenage daughter, it ignored me. Magick swept over the polished floor and raced up marbled columns in great streamers of energy. It twirled through holiday decorations, playing like a chorus line of sugar plum fairies. One by one, great garland creations popped, sending a dusting of torn tinsel and broken lights raining down around us.

The Magick wanted a target—something exciting, something it could really sink its cosmic teeth into—something like a fifteen-foot space cowboy statue.

Oh, hell no.

My Magick didn't listen. It poured into the over-sized Commander Keen. He swelled up like a Thanksgiving Day balloon, his already comically large body now easily twice its prior size. That wide-brimmed hat pressed against the second-floor balcony, while his space boots bumped up against the toy store's glass.

The clerk's wide eyes stared back at us.

"Well, howdy there, space partners," the jolly orange giant said, his voice booming. The support tethers that kept him from falling over snapped like overworked rubber bands, freeing Commander Keen to tuck one hand in his belt and the other to tip that goofy-looking hat.

Screams erupted in the mall. Shoppers dropped their

bags, and clerks ran for cover. If nothing, this was going to be a Christmas Eve to remember.

Great.

The delivery kid dropped his bag, his own mouth falling open along with it. "What in the—"

Commander Keen popped a monstrous pistol out of its holster and spun it in the air on his giant finger. "Well hello there, son. Would you like to see my trick shooting?"

"No," I said, trying to untangle myself from the mess of still tingling security personnel. "He would not like to see your trick shooting. You need to go back to where you came from, now. No Wild Magick on Christmas Eve. I have a hard and fast rule about that."

Commander Keen frowned and fired off a few rounds from his plasma sidearm just the same.

"Duck!" I yelled, grabbing the kid and knocking him to the ground before a brilliant laser blast ripped through the air where he'd been standing only moments earlier.

Boom!

The top half of the fountain tumbled into its watery basin, sheared perfectly in two by the space cowboy's hip cannon. Any shoppers not already in a state of full on panic took it upon themselves to break out in hysteria. They surged for the exits in droves, while rolling store gates dropped like medieval portcullis.

It's not a trip to the mall if someone isn't screaming.

The delivery kid scrambled to his feet. "What the hell is that?"

"That's Commander Keen," I said, helping him up. "He won't be around long, and there's very little chance you'll remember any of this, but hey, it's been a fun way to spend Christmas Eve."

"I don't understand."

"Don't hurt yourself, kid." I pushed the delivery boy

behind me. "All right, Commander Keen, really nifty gun show and all, but I'm afraid we're at the end of the road. Time for you to go back to being an inanimate object, and for me to go home to my family."

The orange cowboy frowned.

"Inanimate object?" The monstrous man scratched his head. "That's fancy talk. It sounds to me like someone's been hanging out with the Dark Phantasm and his band of space bandits."

"Purple guy, eyebrows for miles? Yeah, if I recall he was a lot quieter."

Boom!

Commander Keen fired off another blast from that plasma pistol. This shot exploded a nearby trash can, ionizing uneaten fries and sending a fine mist of milk shake spray into the air. This time it was the kid's turn to pull me out of the way. A half-second slower and there'd only have been space dust left to bury.

"Thanks, kid."

The young man nodded. "Sure. We need to get out of—"

The delivery boy didn't get to finish his words before fire alarms kicked on. Ear-piercing wails and bright flashing lights made it next to impossible to hear anything—well, anything except the two-story space cowboy.

"Red alert! Quick, Moon Pals, the Dark Phantasm has breached the perimeter. We need to protect the Horsehead Nebula from his evil plans." Commander Keen swung his pistols from side to side, the six-foot plasma cannons scanning the promenade. "He's got to be drawing dark energy from the black hole to power his time weapons. This is a job for Commander Keen and the Moon Pals."

The kid grabbed my arm and pointed. At least a dozen more mall security guards streamed into the potential blast radius of Keen's cannons.

Isn't Magick great?

"What do we do?" the kid shouted over the alarm.

Boom! Boom!

More plasma blasts tore through the mall. Mall security guards scattered like roaches when you turn the lights on. The delivery kid and I ducked behind a second trash can, lest we lose the important appendages.

A handful of mall cops filed in around us, confused and unsure what to make of the fifteen-foot space cowboy and his plasma pistols. The kid tried to make a break for the exit, but a rogue plasma pistol blast almost cost him the better part of his head.

"Hold on," I said, grabbing the young man's arm. "I've got this."

"Huh?"

I yanked him out of the way and reached for the Magick still swirling inside me. It was time for Commander Keen to go back wherever it was he came from.

"Looks like the Dark Phantasm's space bandits are itchin' for a fight," the space cowboy said, swinging his plasma pistols left and right. "Well, if it's a tussle you want, I'm more than happy to give it to ya."

Oh, no you won't.

I pulled on my Magick like I was trying to land a big fish, drawing deep into that well of power and dragging up enough to unmake the oversized orange pain in my butt.

"Infecit!" I cried, forcing the Magick to bend to my will.

No sooner had I spoke the word and summoned up a can of cosmic beatdown for the space jerk than my eye began to twitch, followed shortly by my cheeks, and my hands. Muscles great and small spasmed like a drug addict on recovery day. I hadn't been tased before, but I now had the distinct impression those effects might be a little longer acting than I'd originally thought.

Well, isn't this just swell?

Seeing its opportunity, my Magick turned on me like a rabid dog. The capricious power juked left, then right, cutting corners and skirting the edges of my shaky will. I closed my twitchy eyes and doubled down. "Infecit!"

Magick shot out of my grasp and into the air, swirling around the space cowboy like sparkler drippings in the smoky air.

"What are you doing?" the delivery kid cried, yanking his arm back.

"I'm trying to save our butts, kid."

Magick condensed into new shapes, almost as large as that big orange idiot.

Oh no...

A ten-foot husky, an equally large yellow puma, and a sheep dog that towered over both of them emerged from the cosmic light show.

The kid grabbed my arm. "What the hell are those?"

"I'm going to guess Spotty the Wonder Pup, Killer Kat, and the Dog of Doom."

The Moon Pals... backordered till New Year my butt.

* * *

Bark! Bark!

Spotty's bark shook the walls and rattled my already tired head.

Great, so he has a sonic bark? No wonder Kris loves this show.

I turned to the delivery boy, then grabbed the closest security guard. "Okay, I need a distraction. You two keep them busy long enough for me to get close to that folksy orange pain in the—"

Boom!

Another plasma blast ionized the air and cut a path

through the ripped jeans store. I mentally chuckled imagining them try to claim that on insurance

But everything's already ripped?

"Hell no," the skinny guard dropped his radio and taser, "I didn't sign up for this. I'm out of here."

"Wait, don't—"

The skinny man didn't make it more than five feet before a white-hot blast from Commander Keen's sidearm reduced him to space dust.

Crap, crap, crap!

I shoved the plastic taser and radio in the delivery kid's hands. "Don't get shot. You hear me?"

PICKT kid's wide eyes didn't waver from the swirling cloud that had been the security guard.

"Look at me." I pulled his head around and locked eyes with the teenager. "I'm not gonna let that happen to you. You hear me? Stay behind the trash can and we'll think of something."

Boom! Boom!

More super-heated plasma zipped past. Store fronts exploded, shattered glass falling like parade tape around us.

"Look out," the kid said, yanking me away from the trash can only seconds before Killer Kat's razor-sharp claws tore a deep gash in the heavy plastic.

Roar!

We scrambled out of the way of two more paw swipes, that giant yellow puma herding us into the firing line.

Boom!

Plasma cut through the gate of a sporting goods store and gave me an idea. "New plan, kid." I pointed to the oversized novelty box just inside the sheared-off gate. "You ever had a cat?"

The delivery boy shook his head.

"Me neither, but my daughter shows me all the damn videos. She's your age, maybe you know her?"

The kid pushed me down. "Duck!"

Killer Kat's claws caught the edge of my shirt and sliced it to ribbons.

I bet they sell one just like it at the ripped jeans store.

"Get the box, kid," I cried, pointing at the novelty gift box still largely intact inside Sporty's Sports. "Leave the lid. Go!"

"What about you?"

I pulled the antenna out on the cheap radio. "I've got an idea."

You do?

The kid took off like a sprinter, while I turned to face the monstrous puma. "Here, kitty…"

I snapped the antenna off and whipped it around like a fishing pole. Like I told the kid, I'd never owned a cat, but I had a decent amount of cat video watching experience to pull from.

Thanks, Cathy. I owe you one.

Killer Kat hissed and swiped at the dangling antenna.

Boom!

Another plasma blast vaporized the trash can. Killer Kat leapt off the ionized plastic and caught the antenna, tossing it aside.

"Box, kid!"

My PICKT pal reemerged from Sporty's Sports pushing a six-foot novelty box. "What do I do?"

"I said no lid!"

"Oh, right."

The teenager pulled the top off and tossed it aside.

"Now, get it between me and the yellow ball of clawed destruction," I cried, backing up from the angry feline.

Thump.

The kid slid the giant box between me and Killer Kat.

Please work.

The ferocious feline put two paws on the lip and sniffed the edge.

Please.

Killer Kat climbed inside and purred, the box shaking around him.

The kid stood dumbfounded. "Holy crap, it worked."

"Of course it—"

Boom!

Another blast of plasma cut a mannequin in half at a nearby sexy woman's clothing store.

Porter wouldn't have worn that anyway.

"Whoa," the kid said, his eyes on the now topless model.

"Hey, eyes over here. We still need a plan for Spotty the Wonder Pup and the Dog of Doom!"

Bark! Bark!

As if on cue, the monstrous husky and his sheep dog brother bounded into view.

"Okay," I scrambled to my feet, "I haven't seen many dog videos. Any ideas, kid?"

No answer.

"Kid?!"

The delivery boy was gone.

Crap.

I put my hands up and backed away from the advancing canines. "Listen, fellas, I bet we can get you guys some nice milk bones. You'd like that, wouldn't you?"

Grrr...

If it were possible, the Dog of Doom's growl was even worse than Spotty the Wonder Pup's sonic bark. The hairs on my arms rocketed to attention.

Damn it, kid. I swear if I die, I'm going to haunt every date you have the rest of your—

"Hey, over here," the delivery boy cried from just outside

Sporty's. The kid held a giant exercise ball in his hands. "Who wants to play?"

Spotty the Wonder Pup tilted his head, and the Dog of Doom ceased his growl.

"It's working!"

The kid dribbled the over-sized ball. "It's a ball. Everybody loves a ball. Ready, set..."

Boom!

Superheated plasma rocketed past only to slam into the mall's candy store. Piping hot sugar oozed onto the promenade. "Now, kid, throw the damn ball!"

The exercise ball bounced past, rolling through the candied muck and toward the distant exit.

"Hold up, Wonder Pup, it's a trap," Commander Keen cried, but that space cowboy was no better than the rest of us when it came to keeping a dog under control when faced with a bouncing sugar-coated ball.

"Nice work, kid." Seizing my opportunity, I made a break for the bright orange space annoyance.

Boom! Boom!

Plasma blasts tore apart the marbled floor, and I bounced like Spotty's new toy trying to stay one step ahead of the evaporation pistols.

Almost there...

Commander Keen kicked at me with an oversized space boot, and I knew what I had to do.

"Geronimo!" I shouted, jumping onto that bright orange instep. "It's time to go home, Commander Keen."

I pulled at the Wild Magick trapped in that monstrous space jerk. It rumbled like an out-of-control stampede of space cows. "Argh!"

The cosmic power fought back, my hands and arms still twitchy, and not nearly in the position to wrangle a force of nature like that.

Crap.

Commander Keen kicked me off his boot like a stray soccer ball. I hit the broken marble hard and tumbled end over end to stop at the delivery kid's feet. "Ugh."

I shook the sense back into my head, and found us at the business end of two still smoking plasma cannons. "Give the Dark Phantasm my regards."

That's it!

I found the broken blister pack for purple-power-brows nearby and pulled it to my chest. "Hit me with the taser kid."

The delivery boy pulled the mall cop's zapper out of his pocket. "Are you sure?"

Whrrr...

The plasma cannons warmed up for an evaporating blast.

"Do it!"

Zap!

For the second time tonight, I took the full charge from an arc-throwing taser. Muscles contracted and tendons pulled in on themselves. The broken blister pack and its purple prisoner crumpled against my chest. Magick erupted like Commander Keen's plasma pistols. Turned out the orange cowpoke wasn't the only one with a little power to swing around.

Okay, eyebrows, it's time for you to be the little plastic Master of Space and Time.

Magick roared, swirling like the unstoppable heart of a black hole. The plastic prison crumbled in my hands.

"You... can... stop...." I chattered over the arcing juice.

"Oh, shit, sorry." The kid switched off the taser, then dropped it an instant later when a bright purple space master sauntered into view.

"Commander Keen," the Dark Phantasm said, mild annoyance in his gravelly voice. "Must we do this all the time?"

The Space Cowboy raised his pistols. "The Dark Phantasm! I'll stop you from—"

"Wait," the purple alien raised a muscular hand. "Hold on. Listen, Keith, it's Christmas Eve. How about we just bury the hatchet for one night? Word on the street is Star Dust Sue's got a party going at the Stellar Saloon."

Commander Keen hesitated, those plasma cannons still humming. "I don't know…"

"I've been doing some future seeing, and I totally think you two end up together."

The Space Cowboy blushed. "Nah… ya think?"

"Totally."

"Well, shoot." Commander Keen holstered his pistols. "We can just take this back up tomorrow, right?"

The Dark Phantasm extended a hand. "I wouldn't have it any other way."

"Merry Christmas, Derek," Commander Keen said, shaking the Dark Phantasm's bright purple hand.

"Right back at you, you orange pain in the butt."

"Hey…" I stumbled to my feet, the rest of me still twitching like fresh roadkill. "This is really nice and all, but would you two manifestations of *my* Magick mind giving me a hand?"

The Dark Phantasm turned his monstrous eyebrows on me, and for a brief moment I understood how those cockroaches in the kitchen felt when you turned the lights on.

"I suppose… I'm not the Master of Space and Time for nothing."

And with that, my world went white.

* * *

"WHEN DID you get in last night?" Porter asked, pushing a cup of morning coffee into my hand.

Sigh.

"Late. Really, really late." I rubbed at the bruises on my chest, my fingers still a little twitchy.

"Well, I got the presents wrapped and under the tree."

"Thanks, sweetheart," I said, enjoying the first sip of holiday blend. "Merry Christmas."

"Merry Christmas, Gene." Porter slipped her arms around me and squeezed.

"Ouch!"

My wife let go. "Where were you last night?"

"It's a long story. I promise I'll fill you in."

"Did you know I—"

My wife didn't get to finish her sentence before Kris's bedroom door burst open. "It's Christmas!"

The kid bounced across our living room like an electrified pinball.

"You can't open anything until your sister is—"

I don't know why I bothered. My son knew the drill. He shot into Cathy's room and flipped on all the lights. "It's Christmas, Cathy!"

My daughter grunted and pulled the blanket over her head.

"She's up, Dad!"

"That's not technically what—"

Porter put a hand on my arm. "It's Christmas, Gene. Let him open his gifts."

Gifts!

Kris didn't wait for me to respond before diving into the brightly wrapped presents like a duck at the pond.

"Porter," I pulled my wife gently back toward the kitchen, "about the gifts. Listen, I had a problem getting the—"

"Commander Keen!" my son shouted, flying past us with the bright orange space jerk in his hands. "Commander Keen! Commander Keen!"

"But... how?"

Porter smiled, clinking her mug against mine. "I used that PICKT app. Cathy showed it to me. Can you believe the delivery kid got hassled by some middle-aged man? The things people will do on Christmas Eve..."

"Yeah," I held my mug up to cover my face. "People, right? Sheez..."

LIGHTS OUT

The tiny house lacked air conditioning. In the Florida summer, that meant it was hot enough to cook a meal on the artfully decorated antique table that dominated this early settler remix. Sawgrass and sea grape swung in a breeze that didn't make it past the period-accurate, blurry windows. My wife wiped the sweat from her face with the edge of her sleeve, patiently listening to the tour guide whose job it was to enthrall us with the histories of old Florida frontier living. I was doing my best not to pass out from either boredom and heat exhaustion, both of which were a distinct possibility.

"Early settlers in South Florida faced many challenges," the perky young woman said, somehow immune to the soul-sapping heat that was the Atlantic coast in early August. "And they figured out inventive ways to cope with those hardships. If you'll follow me I'll show you how they turned sea grapes in an edible jam."

My wife nodded her head like she was taking mental notes for a quiz that would never come. "Fascinating."

"Totally." I peeled up my shirt and flapped it to push some

of that oven hot air over my sweaty mid-section. "Did any of those sea grapes become sea wine?"

The tour guide frowned. "No."

"Had to ask."

The young woman directed our small group's attention to the pot-belly stove in the corner of the room, and I said a silent prayer that she wouldn't light it up.

"Can you at least *try* to care?" Porter whispered, letting the rest of the oversized Midwesterners shuffle past to check out that old-time face-melter.

Sigh.

"One evening." I pointed to a reddish shape outside the streak-smeared windows. "We're on vacation with your parents and we get *one* evening without the kids and you wanted to come to the Jupiter lighthouse?"

The iconic tower's bright red spire rose out of the ground like a giant's discarded crayon, its black top shining in the late day sun.

Porter frowned. "We can go to the beach anytime."

I waved her off. "Beach? We have no kids right now. *No kids.*" I said it a second time hoping the words would have some effective on repeat.

My wife tilted her head. "I'm not following."

"Your parents have Cathy and Kris for a few hours."

"Yes?"

Come on, Porter. Connect the dots here.

"Which means they won't be around us."

"What are you getting at?"

It was my turn to frown and tap at the plastic hotel key in my shirt pocket.

"What, Gene? Just tell me." Porter crossed her arms, her dark hair tied up and tucked beneath a KC baseball cap. The navy blue hat had come from her dad. They always brought things like that for her when they came down to visit. They brought me gifts too—they left on time and occasionally watched the kids.

Almost makes it worth the pain.

I stuck my hands in the pockets of my loose fitting shorts, the only thing you can really wear this close to the equator. "Well, they aren't at the hotel... So I was thinking, maybe, you know—"

The young tour guide's voice cut off my fumbling attempt at sexy time. "For most pioneer women life was very challenging. Childcare was a round-the-clock activity, plus they had to tend the garden, make clothing, and keep the house."

My wife nodded. "Huh? I had no idea I was a pioneer woman. Did you know I was a pioneer woman?"

That comment got a chuckle from the rest of visitors, but not me. I was busy paying attention to something far more concerning. The telltale prickle of the dead settled on my skin like a clammy wet hand. Not that it wasn't welcome in this heat, but it meant something worse than a lack of 'special couple time' might be in my future.

My name is Eugene Law and I'm a Magician. I don't pull rabbits out of hats, or produce turtle doves from my sleeves. I deal in real Magick, the cosmic powers of the universe, and all the amazingly terrible things they attract.

The tour guide pushed open a narrow door and ushered us into a small side room. The entire house couldn't have been larger than our garage back home, with this new little room tucked off the kitchen. "Now, let me show you the bedroom."

Porter joined the tiny crowd and left me in the oven-hot kitchen.

Now why couldn't I have just said that?

I slid in behind my wife and immediately regretted that decision. If there was a ground zero in the pioneer house for unhappy spirits, it was the bedroom.

Ironic? I think not.

I stifled a chuckle and did my best to not sweat on any of the other tourists while I struggled to figure out where the spirit had settled. Ticked off dead tended to pin themselves on something, and sadly the tour company had done a number on filling this room with as many period accurate items as they could, any of which could easily have been an ectoplasmic anchor to the real world.

"This tiny bedroom would have been used sparingly given the demands of the frontier life."

Go figure.

I tried to give Porter a look, but she was an expert at pretending she didn't notice me—the woman was nothing if not talented.

"Here you'll see some period accurate weapons. They should give you a good idea of what the original settlers would have to have used in the event they were attacked by bears, panthers, or pirates."

That last word caught me off guard. "Excuse me, pirates? Like 'Yo, ho, ho and a bottle of rum?' You mean that kind of pirates?"

The young woman nodded and pointed to a cutlass and an old rifle mounted on the wall. "They don't call this the treasure coast because it has great malls."

That elicited a few chuckles from the peanut gallery, but it also got me focused on the far wall. I reached out with my Magick, doing my best to push the power through that stifling heat and probe at the oiled metal.

Bingo.

"Now, if you'll follow me, I'd like to show you the garden and the wash basin."

Tourists turned to file out, and I stepped to the side to let them slip past.

"Are you coming?" Porter asked, seeing me staying back.

"There's a problem in this bedroom."

My wife rolled her eyes. "Gene, enough already. It's like a thousand degrees. I'm just not feeling—"

I raised a hand and cut her off. "That's not what I'm talking about—even if you are ten times more sexy when sweaty. I'm talking about that." I pointed to the gun and cutlass on the wall.

"Uh..." My wife took a second to process the words then frowned all the more. "I'm sure they're safe. Come on, let's check out the garden."

The buzzing of an unhappy specter rattled in my ears.

"I don't like it."

"Since when do you care what happens in tourist traps?"

Part of me wanted to tell her it was because I was trying to turn over a new leaf and be more proactive when it came to my unique set of skills, but the truth of the matter was I thought Porter's interest in me went way up after a bit of Magickal butt-kicking.

The setting sun in those blurry windows told me I'd need to get that butt-kicking in gear if we would get any fun in before the in-laws brought back our kids.

It's Magick time.

"Do you have one of Kris's crayons?"

My wife shook her head. "You will not draw Magick doodles on the historically accurate frontier bedroom floor."

I shook my head. "Of course not. Do you have one?"

"Yes."

"May I have it?"

Porter hesitated, her hand already in the oversized purse she'd started carrying when we had our first child. "Gene..."

"It'll be fine, trust me."

I wasn't sure those last words would push me over the top, but Porter pulled out the crayon so maybe my subconscious was on to something.

"What are you going to do with it?" Her eyes checked the open door as if any minute the old Florida historical accuracy police would barge in and arrest us.

"What I do best." I pulled back the bedspread to draw Benard's Bigly Banishment on the scratchy sheets. "I'm going to clear out this spirit and then we can go see the lighthouse."

Nice move, Gene. You didn't even mention potential sexy time.

I traced the black crayon across the white cotton and Porter practically had a coronary. "They'll see that!"

"I'll put the bedspread back. Besides, they're going to thank me for this. Once I'm done, they won't have any more hauntings, and a much lower incidence of random injury."

My wife bit her lip as I put the finishing touches on the sigil. I knew she didn't do it on purpose, but that little move always got my blood pumping.

"There." I pressed my sweaty hand against Bernard's seal. "Now, let's do a little Magick."

"Gene!" Porter jumped back, her eyes wide.

I hadn't pumped the first drop of cosmic go juice into the symbol before the cold barrel of an old-time rifle pressed nicely against the base of my skull.

Aw, hell.

I HELD up both hands and told Porter not to move. Of course, she promptly ignored me and dug into her purse.

"I have the holy water you gave me in here somewhere..."

Click.

Magick twisted inside the barrel. The gun might not be functional, but it sure puckered up my butt cheeks like it was.

Ghost bullets would still suck.

Porter gave up digging and spilled the contents from her bag onto the dirty wood floor. "I know I kept it."

I took a deep breath and tried to dig through my mental options. Bernard's Bigly Banishment would have worked great, but I wasn't going to try to race the itchy trigger-finger of the floating weapon behind me.

"Damn it." Porter tossed more crayons, a couple packages of half-used tissues, and Cathy's phone charger. "I know it's in here."

"It's fine. I can handle—" The gun pressed harder into the base of my skull and I winced. "Easy there, Pirate Pete."

My wife looked up. "Pirate?"

I frowned. "Yes and no. I'm betting this is an unfocused emanation of non-corporeal aggression."

It was my wife's turn to frown.

"It's like Cathy when she's moody."

Porter's eyes got a tiny bit wider, and she returned to the strewn contents of her upturned purse. Our teenage daughter's emotions were stuff of legend. "But you said pirate."

"I'm getting a distinct nautical vibe about the whole place."

"It's next to the ocean, Gene. You don't think that would have something to do with it?"

"Are you a Magician?" I asked her.

My wife furrowed her brow and went back to the mess on the floor. "No, but I was stupid enough to marry one..."

"What's that?"

"Got it." She retrieved a small plastic bottle from the pile of junk at her feet.

"Great. Now I need you to—"

The half-empty bottle popped out of her fingers and danced in the air like someone had decided to turn off gravity.

"That's a problem," I said, just before the bedspread

jumped up and looped around my head like a scratchy blind-fold. The stinky sheet yanked me to the ground and twisted tight. I got a faded blue-gray view of the room and my wife jumping to grab at the small bottle. It would have been funny had I not been struggling to breathe.

I tugged at the sheet. "Ignore the water and give me your hand."

"Huh?"

"Get this off my head!"

Porter grabbed the twisted knot behind my neck and pulled at it. "This is tight."

"You think?"

"Gene, the gun—"

Thunk!

The heavy rifle butt smacked into Porter's head. My wife's fingers disappeared from the knot. "Porter?"

No response.

Crap.

Something shiny moved in the sheet's hazy blur.

The cutlass.

This had just gone from bad to worse.

The things I do to get a little sexy time.

I pulled at the scratchy spread and kept an eye on the mesmerizing blade. "Come on, you don't want to do this, trust me. Let's just get a nice little banishment going and everything will be better. You can move on to something else. You know, the hotel we've been staying at has all manner of amenities, just think of the fun you could have there."

The curved blade sliced at my face. Sharp steel tore the cheap fabric and just missed my ear by inches.

"Gene!"

I tore the rest of the spread off and scrambled to my feet. Porter had a nice red welt on the side of her head courtesy of the floating firearm. Condensed Magick twisted in its barrel. My best defense was Bernard's Bigly Banishment, but that lay on the bed along with Kris's crayon just out of reach.

"On the count of three I need you to jump."

"Jump?! Where?"

Damn it, woman. I don't know. I'm a big picture sort of guy.

"Over there." I pointed to the corner.

My wife shook her head. "What am I? A word-class long jumper."

The Bigly Banishment was only a few feet away.

"You can do it."

The rifle drifted closer. Magick swirled inside the chamber.

"Gene..."

"Three!" I shouted.

Porter lunged for the corner and I threw myself at the seal. My wife wasn't much of a longer jumper, but neither was I.

Boom!

Magick exploded against the far wall. Cosmic energy tore a decent chunk of out of the historically accurate stacked logs, while I slapped my hand down on the seal and pumped Magick into it.

Click!

That wasn't the sound a banishment made. That was the sound of a rifle hammer resetting for another shot.

"Gene!"

The floating gun had my wife pinned against the wall.

"I'm working on it."

"Could you try working faster?"

I traced the lines of Bernard's sigil with my fingers. It wasn't complicated Magick, but something had to be wrong for it to be failing like this.

"Any second now would be good, Gene."

The rabbit runs around the hole then drops inside, only to come up next to the five lines of—shit!

There was another line. It wasn't just any line. It was the body of a tiny stick figure. Its round head and frowning eyes glared at me from the dingy sheets.

"What in the hell?"

Kris's crayon popped up and spun around the bed sheet like an ice skater. The tiny stick cut side to side and left a mess of broken lines all over my perfect sigil canvas.

"Why you little—"

"Gene!" Porter had her back against the wall. "The sword."

"Huh?"

Shiny steel shot past my head.

"Crap!"

I ducked, but not before the cutlass sliced Kris's crayon in two.

"What do we do?"

I snatched one of the broken crayon halves off the bed. I'd had just about enough of this ghost. It was time to show the spiritual swashbuckler who was in charge.

"Duck!" Porter dropped, and I grabbed the rifle. The antique wood and steel shook in my hand, while Magick flashed beneath the hammer. "Oh no, we're all done with that."

I scratched the worst possible version of Bernard's Bigly Banishment across the gunstock. My five-year-old son could have done a better job.

Magick beamed like a search light from the rifle tip.

Porter put her hands up as the gun swung left and right. "Watch where you point that thing!"

I slapped a hand against the makeshift sigil and pumped as much Magick as I could into the old weapon. "Let's see how you like that."

Cosmic power roared into the ancient firearm, and whatever spirit was driving the wood and steel vanished like smoke in the wind.

Porter eyed the gun warily. "Is it... safe?"

"Yeah."

Thump!

The cutlass hit the ground behind me and startled both of us.

"Holy crap, Gene," Porter said as I helped her up. "Please tell me it's over."

I tucked the gun under my arm like the westerns I'd watched as a kid. "Yes, Ma'am. We got em."

Porter punched my arm. "Why on earth did you do that?"

"Like I said, I was just doing what I do to—"

"Damn near get us killed so you could try to impress me with your manliness?"

"Uh..."

The woman has to be descended from Arthur Conan Doyle.

"I'm sure you'll be surprised to know it *didn't* work." Porter bent down to reload her purse. "We need to clean this place up and get out of here before something worse happens."

"But... I was just trying to—"

"Now, Gene."

I remounted the weapons on the wall while my wife got the sheets back in order. I made sure the gunstock and its new design were facing the wall, then turned to give her a hand with the sheets. Given the look on her face I had the distinct impression that was the closest either of us would be getting to a bed together anytime soon.

I wonder how the hotel couch is?

Porter pulled the ends tight and pointed to the door. "Come on, let's wrap this up and get out of here."

We caught up with the tour group outside the pioneer

house. The sun had almost set beneath a murky watercolor horizon of grays and dark blues.

"So, basically that's the story," the young tour guide said. "Any questions?"

My wife pointed to our car in the distant lot and I nodded.

"Yeah." One of the more portly tourists raised a hand. "So what you are saying is the original people who owned the house was a mother and her son?"

"No, she had two children."

Porter took a few steps, then stopped and shot me a look.

"Ah, two kids." The heavy set man nodded. "Pirates got them all?"

"Yes. The way to story goes, the young mother's turned out the lamp in the lighthouse, but somehow it got turned back on and the pirate's ship sailed safely into the harbor. They ransacked the house and murdered the family."

I met Porter's stare and waved her off. "See, told you. All handled now, how about we—"

The lamp at the top of the lighthouse flickered on and cast its light across the choppy sea.

The wide bodied tourist adjusted his sweaty collar. "Huh, I thought you said the lamp didn't work?"

The young tour guide tilted her head. "Maybe they fixed it..."

Past the newly lit red spire, I caught something bobbing on the distant swells. A dark shape with black flags that snapped in the rising wind.

Porter grabbed my arm. "What is it? What do you see?"

"A problem."

* * *

"ALL RIGHT, if you'll follow me, we can wrap up the rest of our tour at the gift shop." The perky tour guide pointed to a distant building on the water's rocky edge.

The distant bow of that black and moss covered hull cut through the swelling waves with purpose and a destination in mind. Portly visitors shambled past us toward the money removal center with no knowledge of the spectral murders bearing down on them.

"What do we do, Gene?"

Jupiter's painted brick lighthouse loomed high above the nearby trees, its powerful lamp giving the marauders exactly what they needed, safe passage.

"We turn that off." I grabbed Porter's hand and made a run for the lighthouse door. Gravel slipped under foot as we climbed the jagged slope.

"What did you see?"

"Pirates."

My wife slowed. "Huh? You mean like eye-patches and scurvy?"

The ship blast through a white-cap in the coming dark. Hellish shapes moved across its distant deck. Pale and rotted flesh flashed in the lighthouse's high-beam.

"Yes, but with swords and extra murder vibes."

Porter pulled her hand out of mine and picked up the pace. "Did you banish a mother ghost and her kids?"

I didn't want to answer her, but I couldn't shake the feeling that was exactly what I'd done. "Maybe..."

"Can you, like, unbanish them?"

In the world of Magick, very little can be undone without risking far worse outcomes than the original action precipitated. So, while I could try to make up something as crazy as an unbanishment, I was just as likely to launch the lighthouse into space as I was restore the forcibly removed spirits.

"Maybe..."

Smooth, Gene. Really smooth.

Porter cut past me and reached the steps first. She had the advantage of being a few years younger and doing far more to take care of her general health and well-being than I ever had. Sadly, had I known I might one day be required to outrun a ship a ravaging sea-demons, I might have spent a few more minutes on the treadmill.

My wife skipped up the steps and grabbed the door handle with both hands. The lighthouse's heavy metal hatch didn't budge. She yanked a second time for good measure, then put her feet on the frame and pulled. "It's locked!"

I stumbled up behind her and extended a hand toward the folded steel. Magick rumbled in my chest, happy to be used.

"Resere!" The cosmic power slipped from my fingers and into the obstinate metal. Deep inside the ancient door bolts turned and dropped into position.

Clunk!

"How you locked yourself out of the house I'll never understand." Porter pulled on the heavy steel. The dark metal groaned in protest against the weathered stone.

"It's a long story."

The first drops of a stinging rain hit me in the face and Porter grabbed my hand. "Come on, the lamp has to be at the top."

A twisting spiral staircase extended up into the gloom. Steel and stone steps alternated in wildly terrifying states of disrepair against the aging walls.

"Hold on. We need to think this through before—"

My wife did what she was best at and completely ignored me, taking the steps two at a time like she were running stadiums in college. "Come on, Gene."

Sigh.

After the third turn I was wheezing, and by the sixth I had the distinct impression of darkness closing in. Somewhere around the ninth I could no longer see the bottom of Porter's sneakers.

She'd gotten far enough ahead of me that I was alone in the dark of the lighthouse, my only companion the misty rain and the occasional flash of lightning through nearby windows. With no glass to block it, the rain streamed in and soaked the nearest steps. I took that as an opportunity to lean against the wall and catch my breath.

"Gene," Porter called down. "Come on. We're almost there."

I shook my head. My wife might be almost there, but judging by the sound of her voice I had a lot more steps to take.

"Right... behind.... you."

I pushed off the damp stone, but stopped when something caught under the edge of my fingers.

What's this?

A crudely carved heart lay in the weathered stone, and inside that heart were two pairs of initials. It was just like the sort of thing my daughter doodled all over her notebooks. The secondary initials changed, but Cathy's desire to immortalize them in ballpoint ink didn't.

Teenagers.

"Gene!"

"Coming."

The next ten rotations popped my knees in strange and unpleasant ways, but I soldiered on.

"The top door is locked," Porter said as I wheezed my way onto the final landing. "Magick it up."

"Res... Reser..."

My wife placed her hands on her hips. "Eugene Law, you are going to run with me next week."

I frowned and stepped past her to lean against the door,

my fingers tracing the simplest of unlocking sigils on the dusty metal.

Clunk!

Porter pushed past me and into the tiny lamp room. The lamp's blinding light passed over her and she immediately had a hand over her eyes. "Holy crap!"

"Yeah, don't look at it."

My wife stumbled to the side, grasping at the wall. "You could have warned me."

"I just did."

I found the main power switch on the far side of the circular room. The lighthouse must have long ago switched from actual fuel and fire to good old-fashioned electricity. Sadly I hadn't considered that before we raced up the stairs. There might have been a cut off down below.

Really need to start thinking these things through.

I shielded my eyes and cut a path across the circular room. "I got it."

Thump!

It didn't take much effort to throw the lever down and kill the power. The instant I did, the light went out, plunging Porter and I into a relative darkness punctuated only by the occasional flashes of lightning in the early evening sky.

"Did it work?" My wife asked, blinking and rubbing her eyes.

The dark ship bobbed on an angry tide, but it appeared without their guiding light they'd drifted off course. The jagged shoals awaited them.

"Sure did."

"Great." Porter put a hand on my arm. "Nice work, Gene."

There it is. Do not screw this up. There's still time.

"Thanks. Say, isn't there a bar at the hotel?"

My wife hesitated, her eyes still not fully restored. "I think so..."

"Maybe we could get a little celebratory drink, then perhaps—"

I guided Porter toward the door only to have the lamp burst back to life.

Thwump!

"Ah!" My wife took the flash head on again, this time at point-blank range. She stumbled to her knees at exactly the same moment a polished metal cutlass sliced the air where she'd stood on moments ago.

"Gene!"

"Stay down."

The disembodied sword danced between us like an angry butterfly.

"I can't see anything," my wife cried, crawling along the sandy floor.

I ducked a swipe of the sword, then turned my head before I ended up on the wrong end of the world's brightest flashlight.

It's a shame we can't see anything... That's it!

"Et Vidit!"

Magick swelled in my chest like the crashing waves and I sent it into the lamp's light. The next time it swept the room it gave shape to the invisible spirit.

"What the hell?"

A sword-wielding pirate, complete with ruddy cheeks and a patch-work beard, filled the space in front of me. He couldn't have been much older than his teens, with that same scraggly bedhead look that our daughter had gone gaga over as of late.

Please be a phase.

The blade spun in his hand with the casual confidence of youth. The same confidence that got me in plenty of trouble at that age. So I did what any older, self-respecting adult would do. I grabbed the closest railing and filled it with enough Magick to snap off a baseball bat sized chunk.

The pirate boy hesitated.

"Yeah, bet you didn't see that coming."

The young man lunched and sent his blade in a wide arc.

Cling!

The sound of metal on metal rang out in the tiny space.

"What the hell was that?" Porter said, still fumbling on the ground.

"Sword. It's a long story. You're close to the cut-off switch," I said, parrying another cutting slice and really appreciating having watched late-night pirate movies with my son.

"I am?" Porter passed underneath the metal box.

"Yes! Stand up now."

Clunk!

My wife banged her head against the lever. "Damn it!"

"Watch it."

Porter rubbed at her head. "You want to try providing those warnings a little earlier?"

Cling!

Another slash, parried again, but not without drawing a thin line of blood from my wrist. The teenage pirate had me backed up to an open window. Beyond it the dark ship had adjusted its direction and was now cutting a sharp line toward the souvenir shop. I had the distinct impression they weren't stopping in for Jupiter T-shirts or a lighthouse snow globe.

"Kill the lamp, Porter!"

My wife got her hands on the box and found the lever. "Got it!"

"Pull!"

She never got the chance. A pair of ghostly arms in ornate dress sleeves yanked her backward and out of sight.

Crap!

* * *

THE YOUNG PIRATE saw my confusion and pressed his advantage. His sword clanged against my piece of railing. The curved blade kept me on my toes, but that didn't stop me from searching for my wife.

"Porter!"

The woman I married had plenty of her own problems. I was just thankful none of them involved swords. She wrestled with a second teenage spirit in a long dress. Ghostly arms flailed beneath luxurious hair tied up in ornate braids. The young woman would have been more at home in some sort of cotillion ball than slumming it with Pirate Pete.

Porter swung her fists frantically, each wild strike disappearing into the frilly folds of her assailant's dress. "I can't see!"

Given how poorly we were doing at present, that wasn't necessarily a bad thing.

The young woman used Porter's confusion to her advantage. My wife scrambled forward only to have her arms pulled out from under her.

Thump.

The pale girl was on Porter in an instant. A mountain of ruffled dress folds smothered my wife, while ghostly hands wrapped her neck.

"Gene!"

Slender fingers tightened against Porter's sun-bronzed skin and I knew I had to hurry.

"Hang on." I pushed back against the pirate and his blade, my arm-length pipe doing what it could against the spectral steel. There was a reason sword fights used actual blades and not old pipes—balance. A single aggressive swing later and the young ghost had my late-night television offense on the ropes, and me hopelessly over-extended.

His sword flashed in the lamp's swinging light. The bright beam lit me up like the wrong end of a movie premiere's search lights. I covered my eyes and stumbled out of the way of his counter-attack only to find my face turned to the stinging rain from an open window.

"Gah!"

My blurry eyes followed the bright golden rays beyond the lighthouse. They shined down on that black ship and revealed its crew in terrifying detail. Pale and bloodied, the ghostly pirates made my assailant look like something from the amusement park. Curved blades shined in the lamp's glow, while above them angry red eyes remained locked on the fast-approaching shore. The souvenir store sat close to the water's edge, its warm window light reflecting on the choppy waves. They had no defense, and no way to know what was coming.

The ship caught another swell and surged forward. The marauders had made it past the worst of the rocks now, turning out the light wasn't going to stop these guys.

Clang!

A swinging strike from Pirate Pete caught me off guard and cost me my grip on the pipe. It clanked against the floor, then tumbled down the stone steps only to vanish into the dark center of the lighthouse.

That's a problem.

I put my hands up and tried to keep a sufficient distance between us.

"Whoa there, kid," I said, avoiding the sharp edge of a slashing swing at my mid-section. "What's the deal?"

The pimply swashbuckler growled and pressed the attack. His blade moved like the inside of a blender on high and it took all I had to not get caught up in that metallic wave of destruction.

"Gene, I can't breathe!" Porter swung her arms frantically, her fingers passing through the pale party-goer like she wasn't there.

I ducked an angry swing. "I'm working on that."

"Work... faster..."

"What do you think I'm doing?" I asked, sucking in my gut to avoid an impromptu belly-button cleaning.

Porter's response was a garble of words that told me I whatever it was I was doing, I needed to wrap it up, and fast.

"Listen, Pirate Pete. What's the unresolved issue here?"

The young ghost only sneered and pressed harder, his sword arm moving almost too fast to follow.

Most spirits have some sort of communication skills. Sometimes it's limited, but never this bad. I mean, when you don't get to talk to anyone for a few hundred years you tend to gab like Cathy when her girlfriends are over.

Loopers!

Unlike New Dead with their tarry eyes and burning hatred of the living, unfocused emanations like Pirate Pete and the Lady Strangler were lost in a loop. Like a scratched-up CD stuck on repeat, they'd keep doing exactly what they wanted again and again. They couldn't be reasoned with, because they weren't much more than a symptom of a far more complicated problem.

They aren't the dreamer, they're part of someone else's dream.

I tried to think back to the bits and pieces of the young tour guide's story. After a poorly timed dodge of yet another powerful swing, I really wished I'd paid more attention and not spent that time thinking about my wife's butt.

It's a nice butt.

That thought didn't help.

Porter's frantic fingers slowed, and I knew I didn't have much time left.

There was a mother and two kids...

I dodged another sword swing and decided to fill in the blanks on my own. If there were two kids, what if they were like Cathy and Kris? What is the Lady Strangler over there had fallen for a classic bad influence?

Pirate Pete pressed in on me and I ducked another strike.

Classic bad influence.

These two must have been kept apart by someone.

The mother.

Way to go, Gene. You must have banished mom—the lone woman keeping her love-crazed daughter from hooking up with Swashy McBuckle and the rest of the murder posse and raining hell down on her family.

You need an un-banishment.

I shook my head. Magick like that wasn't something I kept in my short-term memory. Any effort that complex would take intelligence and time, neither of which I had in any abundance.

You just need to try.

The young pirate lunged. His sword arm cut a perfect arc and forced me to jump backward to avoid becoming human sushi. My feet slipped on the wet steps and I reached for the metal railing—the same railing I'd removed earlier in a fit of highly questionable inspiration.

Damn.

I tumbled down the stone steps, thankful to not slide off of them entirely, but certain if I lived to see tomorrow I'd have some pretty terrible bruises.

The young swashbuckler loomed above me, his blade high, while nearby Porter's unfocused eyes stared out beyond the sea. Judging by the distant cries against the raging surf, the rest of Team Pillage was zeroing in on their final destination.

I reached into my Magick and my memory. There had to be something, anything, I could try.

A mother and her two children...

I'd banished the mother. She must have been the one with the rifle. Thinking back on the tiny bedroom brought everything into focus. The rifle had been hers, a homesteader's weapon and source of food for her small family. My mind raced through options while the tour guides words rolled on repeat.

Two children.

The smiling face of a little stick figure appeared in my head. There was one more, a younger one, a little kid. Was this his nightmare? Maybe the story had become confused over the years? Perhaps it was a young boy who had tried to stop his sister and failed.

Were we reliving his past?

A gentle hand tugged on my shirt from behind.

"Huh?"

The young boy couldn't have been more than five or six. He brought back memories of my son, with his wide-eyes and innocent face. Tears streaked those cheeks, tears born of helplessness.

"How can I help?" I asked.

Pirate Pete stormed down the stairs toward us. In an instant his cutlass would remove my head from my shoulders.

The young boy held out Kris's crayon in his dirt-streaked fingers.

"I don't have the time to do—"

The kid shook his head and pointed to a Bigly Banishment perfectly drawn on the dusty concrete. He'd added a smiling stick figure next to it, a reminder of a happier time.

"I do this and you're gone too. You understand that right?"

The little man nodded, wise beyond his years. I found myself reflected in his glassy eyes and I didn't like what I saw.

This was my mistake. Had I not tried to get Porter in the mood, this boy's mother would still be here, and most likely taking far better care of her insane daughter than I had.

"I'm sorry."

The kid only nodded and sat down on the step like he were resigned to wait for whatever came next.

Pirate Pete's boots clunked against the stone while the rest of his body was in route to remove my head from its perch on my shoulders.

"I've got an idea. It might not be perfect, but it'll have to do. I'm sorry, kid, I'll make it right." I grabbed the crayon and encased the little stick boy in the sigil, hoping I wasn't as rusty on Bernard's Banishment as I felt. "Promise me you'll let us win at the windmill, okay?"

I didn't wait for the kid to respond. One hand on the sigil and the other on the boy, I let my Magick go. The sound of the pirate ship hitting the dock timed up with the rolling thunder and a flash of cold steel. I lost all of that in the sigil. Cosmic power swelled like the rolling surf and raced through cobbled-together design, twisting and turning into what I hoped was something beyond a simple banishment.

Here goes nothing.

* * *

"Did you see it, Dad?" My son hopped up and down, swinging his tiny golf club like a sword. "Did you? Did you?"

"I saw it and I still can't believe it," I said, my hand on the scorecard for Pirate Pete's Putt-Putt Emporium. "Should I mark that as an assist, Porter?"

My wife shrugged her shoulders. "I don't know. I mean, the ball bounced off the windmill, between the pirate's legs twice, and then off a lizard before landing in the hole."

The scaly green local scampered into the bushes, no doubt highly displeased to be used as a bumper.

"Come on, Kris!" My daughter waved from the next hole, her grandparents behind her and fumbling through their strokes. "This one has a huge flamingo."

"Oh, yeah!" My young son plucked his ball out of the cup and raced past the still turning windmill.

"You coming, Gene?" Porter asked, placing the putter against her shoulder before turning to follow Kris.

"I'll be right there." I marked down my son's improbable shot and stuffed the score sheet in my pocket, then picked up my club. With the handle tucked under my arm, I sauntered past the novelty windmill only to have something catch my eye. It was small, faded, and almost impossible to see, but once I did, I smiled.

A stick boy and his stick mom waved at me from the marked up wood and I waved back.

"Come on, Dad!" My daughter shouted.

"Yeah, yeah. I'm coming." I caught up to them and put an arm around my teenager's shoulder. "So, we need to have a talk about your taste in boys."

"Dad!"

MOURNING PAPER

*D**ing!*

My eyes shot open, taking in the faint pre-dawn light and immediately coming into focus. Much like Pavlov's dog, my grey matter knew what was coming next and already had the appropriate systems in gear.

Coffee time.

I kicked off my sheets and stumbled into the kitchen. That was one of the many benefits of such a tiny apartment —just about everything was close, and it was next to impossible to get lost.

My feet worked their way around a few piles of expertly lumped clothes. There was the dirty pile—somewhat larger than I remembered it—and the clean pile. The latter was basically a loose clumping of mis-matched socks.

That might be a problem.

I waved off my early morning brain's concerns and directed the whole of my frontal lobe toward the percolating coffee machine in the apartment's tiny kitchen. My grey matter's worries melted away on the heady aroma of dark roast. If heaven had a coffee, it was dark roast—let the Demons have their lattes and heart-killing sugary confections—true bliss resided in a black cup of perfection.

I need a cup...

In my apartment, clean cups occupied the same environmentally precarious position that timber wolves and the monarch butterfly enjoyed—endangered. I fished a mug out of the sink and examined its rings. You can tell a lot about a cup by its rings, but first you have to check for lipstick.

No lipstick.

I sighed, the chances of lipstick on a mug in the kitchen at this point were low—very, very low. It wasn't that I had a problem with the ladies, it was more them having a problem with me, or more accurately, my lifestyle.

It's not for everybody.

I nodded to myself. It was nothing if not fun—wildly dangerous—but fun.

Four? Or is that Twelve?

The coffee rings blurred together on the sides of the mug, and I had to squint to count them. I had a hard and fast rule about double digit rings—always rinse—but anything less was just added flavor.

You need glasses.

I squinted harder, holding the cup up at an angle sure to keep me from needing my glasses. My eyes weren't perfect. Heck, they were far from perfect, which was why I should have worn glasses, but the trick with Demon Hunting, and really all manner of supernatural work is *not* to show them a weakness.

Glasses aren't a weakness. Lots of great men and woman wear glasses.

"Do they hunt Demons?" I asked myself, blinking at the blurry rings.

No.

"Damn straight," I said to no one but the mug in my hand. It read 'Ed Lovely, World's Best Demon Hunter,' in flowing script.

I smiled and rinsed it out for good measure.

Thanks, Mom.

My name is Edwin Lovely, but everyone calls me Ed. I'm what you'd call a Demon Hunter. I make sure the dark things that bump in the night get bumped back—hard.

The first cup of black magic poured smooth from the pot, its velvety richness filling my nose with caffeinated joy. I patted the happy little appliance gently. It had taken almost a year to get the coffee maker back to proper function. The last overnight visitor had decided to clean it with vinegar, effectively ending that amorous relationship before it progressed beyond the infatuation stage.

"Eddie, your pot looked like you've never cleaned it," she'd said, no doubt appealing to some sense of cosmic decency I didn't possess.

I chuckled and pulled a stool out at my tiny counter. I could laugh about it now, but in the moment it had taken all I had to keep from handing her the Gordian Shoelace, and tossing the both of them out the window.

I took a slow sip and waited, not so much for the coffee to work its magic, but for the daily news to make its way to me.

Come on, Scotty. You can do it.

I glanced at the clock—it was the papering hour, but no Scotty. It was hard to get mad at the kid; I had to be the last of his clients in this backwater part of the state. Still, I was a paying customer, and we had an arrangement.

He's not late until the clock hits six fifteen.

"Six fourteen and thirty seconds, Scotty. That's cutting it—"

Whack!

I smiled—like I said, we had an arrangement.

Good kid. Now to open the door...

While at face value that sounded like a simple task, in my line of work doors were anything but simple. First, there were the protective locks, then came the layers of enchanted tape, and lastly the peep-hole-covering groundhog skull—it was a process.

With all the steps complete, I twisted the dead bolt and opened the door. You can imagine my shock to find the short redhead and freckled Scotty standing on my welcome mat and holding today's paper hostage. "You never paid," he said, the steely look in his twelve-year-old eyes oddly troubling.

"I certainly did," I said, wondering if that was true as I reached for the plastic-wrapped paper.

"According to the office you didn't. They said I can't give you the paper unless you give me cash."

"What?" I scrunched up my face. "Cash?"

The truculent young bill collector folded his arms. "Yeah, they said your last check bounced like a rubber ball."

"Did they use those words?"

Scotty shook his freckled head. "No, but it's too early for cussing."

I took a deep breath. Scotty was right, it was too early for cussing, and for cash.

"You had any coffee yet?" I asked, letting the aroma of dark roast settle over the hard-edged delivery boy.

"No…"

"Won't stunt your growth, right?" I directed him toward the counter. "Let me get you a mug."

Dropping his shoulders like a practiced teamster, the twelve-year-old pushed past me and climbed onto my chair, and then, without asking, took it upon himself to enjoy my cup. "Thanks, this'll work."

Must resist the urge to throttle him.

"I'll get that checkbook," I said, the words not coming out nearly as smooth as they would have had he not been drinking out of *my* mug.

He's not *the World's Best Demon Hunter.*

"How much do I owe?"

"Two-fifty, and no checks," Scotty said, again channeling his inner enforcer. The kid clearly had a future in collections, illicit or otherwise.

"Two dollars and—"

"Two-hundred and fifty dollars, Ed."

Deep breath.

"Right, two-hundred and fifty dollars, but isn't there a discount for new—"

Scotty shook his head and expertly delivered a deadpan response. "You haven't been a new customer in three years. Two-hundred fifty, or they cut you off permanently."

A crowbar to the knee would have been softer than the young man's delivery of my potential punishment.

"Permanently?"

The kid only nodded.

He must be fun at parties.

"Fine." I pulled my wallet out of the drawer and wondered if it had anything in way of cash in it. "Can you maybe do me a favor though? You know, since we go back three years now?"

"Depends…" My coffee-sipping mobster-in-training raised a ginger eyebrow.

"I can give you," I opened the wallet, "twenty dollars now, and the rest on Friday. That's not too much to ask, is it?"

I'm negotiating with a twelve-year-old…

Scotty stared at me over the cup without a hint of compassion in his eyes. "Wednesday, that's the best I can do."

Why you little…

"That'll work. Thank you," I said, yanking out my last twenty a little more forcefully than I would have under less stressful circumstances and depositing it on the counter. "Now if you don't mind, I'd like to read my paper in peace."

Scotty pushed the plastic-wrapped news across the counter to me, then held up the bill to the light.

I ignored the tiny gangster and shucked the plastic-wrap, careful to wad it up just so before tossing it in the appropriate corner of the kitchen.

Local section...

I tossed the front page aside—it was always bad news, and more often than not the work of the big guns, the monsters and Demons way out of my weight class. It was depressing to read and I didn't need depressing.

Scotty picked up the national section and flipped through it, and for a moment I contemplated charging him a reading fee, but then I remembered that he controlled the flow of information and thought better of it.

I found the local page exactly where I expected it and not far behind it the classifieds. Those were a Demon Hunter's bread and butter, and they never failed to produce work, and work sometimes meant money. I skimmed the first page and made a few mental notes regarding a new speed trap on US301—which would have been important had I possessed a functioning car—before jumping to the obituaries.

The obits were a critical part of my day-to-day job, but what I found in the first listing was enough to twist my empty stomach in knots.

Bernard "Bernie" Holmes, passed away peacefully at...

If it had made the paper, then I didn't have much time.

"Shit, Scotty, I've got to go." I snatched back my cup and downed what little coffee remained. "I trust you can see yourself out."

"Sure. I'll be back on Wednesday for the—"

"Rest of the money, right? Yeah, totally."

Damn you.

I didn't waste any time sorting through the clean pile and just left the dingy shirt and scuffed jeans I'd slept in on, pausing briefly to apply a fresh coat of deodorant before grabbing shoes, keys, and my backpack.

I was halfway out of the bedroom when I stopped and went back for something. I found them under the bed—two white sweatbands. I checked the insides, confirming which was left and which was right, and slid them on before heading for the door.

Scotty followed me out, but didn't bother waiting for me to complete the elaborate ritual of locks and enchantments necessary to keep my humble abode mine—I had coffee cups to protect.

Satisfied the door was secure, I turned to the lot. The apartments were old, so old the roof curled like wet paper in spots, and there was only four of them. At least two of which I was pretty sure weren't occupied, given the fire damage and all.

Which was completely not my fault.

Scotty's low whistle had my hackles up before I stepped off the sidewalk.

"Somebody took your wheels, Ed."

My bike!

Scotty's brilliant assessment of the obvious was breathtaking. My bike was gone, and in its place all that remained was a broken lock and a single wheel.

"Did you just lock the wheel?" the hard-nosed paperboy asked, with more than a hint of derision in his voice. "'Cause that's easy to break."

"Gah!"

Scotty climbed on his own bike, a majestic ten-speed with all the trimmings—clearly a product of his dedication to paper delivery and stubborn unwillingness to bend the rules. "Sucks to be you."

No, Scotty, it sucks to be us.

I grabbed the kid's handlebars. "If you don't get me to The Sunset Funeral home in Starke, Bernie's soul will be forfeit."

* * *

"Huh?"

"I need a ride," I said, pointing at Scotty's wheels.

"What do I look like? A taxi?"

"Have you delivered their paper yet?"

"Papers... and no."

"Whoa, running late?"

Scotty frowned. "I do not run late. Do you have any understanding of the importance of prompt delivery as it relates to holiday gifts and gratuities?"

I shook my head. "No, but it's summer and—"

Scotty pushed away my hands. "And this is when you earn your tips, Ed. Summer is when you put in the work that pays off at Christmas."

"Great, we'll be quick, I promise," I said, hopping up on his handlebars. Already heavily laden with wrapped papers in wide sacks, Scotty and his bike looked positively comical with me perched precariously on the front.

"Get off!"

"I will as soon as we get there."

I couldn't see it, but it wasn't hard to imagine the twelve-year-old's face turning beet-red behind me.

"It's all about the look, damn it. I've got a brand to uphold, and I'm not going to be able to do that with some gangly looking guy sitting on my handlebars."

This kid's a master class in marketing and manipulation. I should be taking notes.

I swung my bag around and produced a second twenty. It represented the last of the emergency money, but technically this was about as close to an actual emergency I was going to have today—my lack of coffee notwithstanding.

Scotty snapped the bill out of my fingers with the same honed skill I'd expect at the Seminole Gaming Casinos. "Fine, only to Sunset Funeral and no further. If anyone asks, you're my out-of-work cousin that was dropped on his head as a kid."

"I can handle that," I said, adjusting my butt. "Now, tally-ho! Chop, chop! Get a move on, little doggie."

I rattled off a few more pithy sayings while the poor kid struggled to overcome inertia. I didn't know if they helped, but they made me laugh, and given our destination, I needed all the comedy I could get.

* * *

ONCE UNDERWAY, my pint-sized navigator proved himself a more than acceptable steed. Scotty appeared to know every shortcut between my derelict apartment and the Sunset Funeral home in Starke, and that was saying something. He did prefer the routes that took us over uneven ground, and was quite adept at making sure to hit every single street reflector in the process, but judging by his puffing chest when we pulled into the lot, he'd earned every cent of that twenty.

"Nice work, Scotty," I said, hopping off the handlebars and rubbing at my sore butt. "Did you have to hit every reflector along the way?"

The perturbed twelve-year-old popped out his kickstand. "I got you here didn't I?"

"Indeed, you did, and for that I am eternally grateful."

The sun had only recently gotten underway, but already the pavement outside Starke's favorite funeral home was hot enough to make me thankful I'd remembered shoes and actually put them on this time. That last barefoot banishing had been difficult to put behind me—I still harbored an unhealthy fear of microscopic glass shards.

That's for the best, really.

Scotty retrieved what I assumed were Sunset Funeral's daily papers. The commercial outfit was a big spender, getting three copies delivered by the local ginger-haired delivery gestapo.

"When do they open?" I asked, rubbing my chin and wondering how I didn't think to ask that before we left.

"Got me." Scotty tucked the plastic-wrapped papers under his arm and fished a set of keys out of his pocket.

"Holy Moses! They gave you a key?"

The newspaper boy shot me a look that, had it been delivered by a Felengus Demon, would have charred me to a crisp where I stood—shoes and all. "This is official newspaper business, Ed. I key in and deposit the papers in the lobby."

"This is perfect!" I said, not even trying to hide the excitement in my voice. "Here I was thinking I was going to have to use Jeffers' Knob Sock."

Scotty stopped halfway up the squat building's steps, most likely wondering if I'd said something crude.

"Dude, the Knob Sock is just a sock you put over the knob to unlock doors. Well, not all doors, but some doors."

The twelve-year-old shook his head, not unlike some of my older and far more wrinkled customers. The ones that know for a fact that 'everything I do is bullshit,' but still can't quite bring themselves to call me a fraud and kick me off the property.

Demon hunting is more of a calling than an actual money-producing business, per se.

Scotty shoved the key in the lock, then turned to deliver a steely glare that would have made Clint Eastwood proud. "Don't even think about it."

"Scotty, it's imperative I get inside before Bernie's soul is forfeit."

"I don't care if the devil himself is inside those doors ready to devour my soul. You don't get to go in with my key."

"You aren't that far off." I pointed at the dark glass on the other side of the newly christened doorman. "It's not 'the devil,' because honestly the underworld isn't nearly that organized. There's a lot of jockeying for position. It's next to impossible to keep up with all of it, so I don't bother. Still, I'm guessing this contract doesn't terminate nearly that far up the food chain."

Scotty yanked the door open and stepped inside, then slammed it shut behind him. The twelve-year-old stood on the other side, his face pressed up against the glass and doing exactly what normal twelve-year-olds did.

A solitary rooster crowed in the distance, the normally invigorating sound setting the hairs on my arm at attention. "I don't have time for this, Scotty."

I have exactly two rooster calls left.

I fished a lighter out of my backpack. It was one of those nice shiny ones. It wasn't Magickal, but it did work really well, which was a sort of Magick all on its own.

Scotty's eyes caught the shine of the lighter, and his mouth froze in its fishlike position against the distant glass.

I ran back to his bike, holding the flicking flame below a helpless pouch of dangling papers. Even wrapped in plastic, they'd be toast if I let the fire catch hold.

"You wouldn't!" he cried from behind the glass.

I let the flames lick at the edge of his canvas saddlebags. "Let me in and the route goes on as normal, or stay inside and see what happens to your brand."

I wasn't exactly proud of myself in that moment, but it was creative, and I did award mental points for creativity.

Scotty hesitated, clearly waffling between his commitment to exceptional newspaper delivery and the sacred rules regarding the bestowment of business keys.

"I don't have all day." The fire left a sooty streak on his canvas sack.

"Fine!" The ginger-haired paperboy pushed the door open. "Five minutes."

"I make no promises," I said, clicking the lighter closed and bounding up the tiny steps. "I have no idea who we're dealing with... yet."

* * *

"Where's the light switch?" I asked, struggling to see using only the light making its way through the tinted door.

"I don't work here."

I couldn't see his face, but his tone made my think Scotty might not be overjoyed at allowing me inside the building.

"No problem, I'll find it." I ran my hands along the wall.

Crash!

I hadn't expected a falling framed painting to make that much noise, then again, it really was the breaking glass that gave it that heart-stopping sound.

"What did you do?" the paperboy cried.

"It's not my fault. Who puts a painting there?"

"You mean on the wall?!"

He's got a point.

"Accidents happen. I won't hold the funeral home liable

for the heart palpitations I'm sure to have now," I said, my shoes crunching on the broken glass.

"You won't hold the—"

"Nope," I said, a smile on my face as my fingers grazed a light switch. "I'm just *that* understanding. You should really try it sometime. The world is a much nicer place if you tried a little compassion. Your word for today is 'forgiveness,' Scotty."

I wasn't sure if you had to be older to have a psychotic break—I figured you did—but to look at Scotty's face I wasn't positive. He appeared to have shot past beet-red and gone straight to plaid.

Well, that's not healthy, then again, you did give a twelve-year-old coffee. You're at least partially responsible.

"I…"

My favorite information dealer stuttered his response, no doubt trying to find the best way to show a little compassion.

"Don't hurt yourself, Scotty. It'll come to you. I believe you're still a good seed at the end of the day."

I turned away from the volcanic paperboy and instead focused my attention on the wide archway that lead into the viewing room. Bernie wasn't the religious type, but I was pretty damn sure there'd be an open casket viewing.

"Ah, ha!" I pointed to the resting old man in the distant casket. "Hey, somebody sprung for the titanium. Nice touch. I mean, it's a little sci-fi for me, but Bernie was a huge Trekkie—totally fits."

Scotty dropped the papers on a small reception table. He appeared to be contemplating removing them from their plastic, but then looked at the broken picture and decided better of it. "I'm so screwed."

"Nah," I unzipped my backpack. "Screwed is what Bernie here's gonna be if we don't hurry. Get me some of that broken glass."

"What?"

Sigh.

"Okay, here's the short version. I need to bring the old pinball wizard here's spirit back to get him untangled from a very much inadvertent sub-infernal binding third-party soul-based resolution."

The twelve-year-old tilted his head to one side. "That's the short version?"

"Yes. Are you a Demon Hunter?"

"I deliver papers."

"Close enough." I shrugged. "Get me a hand-sized piece of glass, and don't cut yourself on it."

"Why?"

"Cause it would hurt, that's why. Geez, does your family have to tell you to come in out of the rain and blow your nose too?"

Scotty grumbled something unintelligible, then trudged off to collect the glass.

"No, something bigger," I said after he picked up his first piece and tossed it aside. "That's too big, keep trying."

Scotty continued to mumble his way through the broken glass while I turned my attention to the casket.

Bernard didn't look good.

He's dead. How did you expect him to look?

I really didn't have much in the way of expectations. I hadn't seen the old arcade owner in years, not since that fateful day back in the eighties.

Dragon's Lair.

It was Mecca for any kid worth their video game salt growing up—the greatest game never won, a nigh impossible cartoon adventure to save princess Daphne from the dragon. I sacrificed too many quarters on the altar of that gaming console, quarters I really could have used today.

"Sorry, Bernie," I said, setting my backpack on the ground

and pulling out a small bottle of aftershave. It wasn't the expensive stuff, as I didn't have those quarters, or the interest they would have made me, but it wasn't the cheap stuff either.

"Here's the—Whoa..." Scotty said, his words trailing off at the sight of the old man's expertly preserved body lying in the open casket. "Are we supposed to be here?"

"You? No. Me? Absolutely. I owe him, and I always pay my debts."

Scotty raised an eyebrow.

"Well, the paper's a different story. I'm fairly certain I paid that with a check."

The ginger-haired delivery boy shook his head.

"Banks," I said, waving him off. "Put the glass there." I pointed to a bare spot in the ornate carpet. The viewing room was vintage old Florida: ornate rugs, cheap folding chairs, and what looked like a cloth-covered card table holding up the casket. A nearby podium was barren, and no picture of a younger or more vibrant Bernie lay against it. Only a lone lamp stood dark above the empty top.

While there was nothing inherently evil about the viewing room, or the old arcade purveyor in the casket, I could still feel the slick chill of malevolence. A darkness that had waited a long time to collect on a quarter spent years ago was ready for its turn.

"What are you going to do?" Scotty asked, setting the jagged piece of glass on the ground.

"First, I'm going to get Bernie back and apologize, then I'm going to stop a Demon."

"Huh?"

I poured three drops of aftershave on the glass and retrieved my keys. The boomerang key-chain clunked against my palm.

"So, the boomerang brings his spirit back?" Scotty asked,

his tone more inquisitive than I'd originally given him credit for.

"Nah, that's a great idea, though," I said, setting the tiny key-chain ornament on the glass. "Bernie was a big Crocodile Dundee fan. You know, 'That's not a knife, this is a knife.'"

The under-sized newspaper boy scrunched up his face in confusion.

And you've lost him... This generation doesn't understand good cinema, just accept that.

"After this is over—should we survive—we can watch it together. I have it on VHS."

"What's that?"

A rooster crowed somewhere outside, its shrill cry just loud enough to reach the viewing room.

That's number two.

"No time, Scotty. I'm one rooster call short of a major mistake. I need you to take the last thing out of my backpack," I said, already feeling the skin tingling sensation of what was coming.

"No way, I'm not sticking my hands in there."

The lights flickered, a gentle brownout that rattled the bulbs in their casings. "Shit, Scotty. You've got to. You're the only one who can do it."

"What do you mean?"

I grabbed the kid's shirt. "Are you a delivery boy or a delivery man?"

"... Man?"

"With conviction, son!"

"Man!"

I nodded my head. "Damn straight. Now, delivery man, please remove the box from my backpack."

Scotty hesitated, looking at my bag as if a pit viper were about to spring out of it and bite his delivery-man-parts. The lights flickered again, and this time they didn't come back on. "Scotty, get the box!"

The ginger-haired delivery man reached into my bag and retrieved The Undeliverable Box. It's Magick flooded the tiny room with potential and anticipation. It was like the feeling the moment before you raced downstairs at Christmas only to find your passed out uncle sleeping off eggnog under the tree. But somehow better, like instead of an old man you might find presents.

Scotty held the box like it was seconds away from exploding and showering him in live scorpions—which was entirely possible when dealing with Magickal items from an age long past—and searched the floor for a place to put it down. "What do I do?"

"Deliver it to me," I cried, holding out my hands. "Deliver to me the soul of Bernard Holmes."

Scotty dropped the tape-covered and stamp-ridden box into my hands, his delivery triggering the latent power in the Undeliverable Box.

The corpse of Bernard Holmes shot up in its casket. "Mrmph!"

"They sewed his mouth shut," I said, handing the box back to a colorless Scotty.

"Uh…"

"Relax, it's just a little thread in the lips, geez."

The twelve-year-old delivery boy clutched the box his chest while his head appeared to be vacuuming up nightmare material for at least the next few months.

I pulled my multi-tool out of my bag and set to work undoing Bernie's threads.

"Eddie Lovely?" the corpse asked, once his lips free of the thread. "What the hell is going on?"

"Save your strength, Bernie. I've got to get you out of here before—"

The rooster crowed a third and final time.

Damn.

* * *

CLUNK!

That was the Undeliverable Box hitting the ground. Scotty had dropped it, along with his jaws, when his eyes zeroed in on what was standing at the pulpit.

"Edwin Lovely, of all the people come to see 'The Bern' off to parts unknown," the Demon said, his bright red face and long curving horns a sharp contrast to the drab viewing room.

"Is that the—"

"Devil?" I said, helping Bernie's corpse out of the casket. "No, it's not. It's a Gillyfinkus Demon, and if I'm not mistaken when we were kids he went by the name...Jeffery."

If it were possible to take the infernal wind out of Demon's sails, I'd done exactly that. His face drooped, and those proud shoulders sunk behind the podium. "How did—"

I got Bernie to his feet and pushed the old arcade owner behind me. 'The Bern,' as we'd called him, had grown out as much as the rest of us had grown up over last fifteen years or so. He still had his mustache—it had been trendy back in the days of Magnum PI—but now it just looked old, tired, and scraggly. The rest of his face had a light sheen of make-up, no doubt to remove the decaying flesh look common among dead bodies.

"How did I figure it out?" I asked, propping up the corpse of my old Frogger-genius on shaky legs. "The voice. You Demons can mask everything but the voice."

"Well," the Jeffery Demon said, stepping out from around the podium to reveal his bulging gut and spindly legs. "Then you know why I'm here."

If I didn't know better, I'd have said he was either ten months pregnant or he'd drank all the beer in a three town radius. But I knew better—that was just how Gillys looked.

"I don't…" Bernie pressed a hand to his head and smeared the lovingly applied foundation. "Would someone please explain to me what's going on?"

"You played the quarter, and lost, therefore your soul is mine." The Gillyfinkus tapped his claw-like fingers in his palm. "It's a simple arrangement. In fact, if I recall correctly it was supposed to be your soul, Ed. Wasn't it?"

It had been a long time since I'd thought about that day, but here in the funeral home, the memory came back like an extra life.

Dragon's Lair.

The massive arcade console loomed above us. Jeffery and I took turns playing as Dirk the Daring and trying desperately to save the lovely and oddly tingle-inducing Princess Daphne. The game was a quarter-eating monster, capable of cleaning me out in no time, but Jeffery always had extras, which was why I tolerated him.

"I'll bet you your soul you can't win it," he'd said, braces-bound teeth adding a slight lisp to his words.

"Whatever." I banged the top of the cabinet. "Put up or shut up."

The Demon-child laid a single dingy quarter next to the joystick. "Here you go. If you play this quarter and lose the game, your soul is mine."

"Sure, you want fries with that?" I'd asked, reaching for the quarter, but a much larger and faster hand snaked it out from under my fingers.

"Sorry, kiddos. It's time for you guys to feel 'The Bern.' I'll show you how the game is meant to be played." A much younger and more hip Bernie bumped me aside and droped in the soul-bargain quarter.

"I didn't win." The old arcade salt's corpse braced himself against the casket.

"No, you didn't," both the Demon and I said.

Bernie's stuffed body shook its head. "Well, I wasn't part of that bet, I shouldn't—"

The Gillyfinkus Demon stretched out his claws and scratched at his nether regions, which were blissfully covered in enough hair to keep the entire visual hovering just inside a PG-13 rating. Sadly, Scotty wasn't going to be forgetting any of this anytime soon, and none of us would if my plan failed.

"Doesn't matter, that's how eternal soul-based transactions work when delivered in a gaming establishment on non-consecutive holidays, isn't it, Eddie?" the Demon said, flicking sulfur off his nail. "All of this is completely above board, I assure you. Now, if you'll come with me, I've got a whole new 'Bern' for you to feel."

"Wait," the corpse cried, grabbing my arm. "You've got to do something. I let you play for free that time. Remember? After your Aunt died, I let you play for free. That's got to be worth something."

It wasn't much, but he had done something.

"Jeffery, how about we up the ante? I know you didn't really want Bernie's soul, and nearest I can tell, mine's not promised to anybody."

The Gillyfinkus hesitated. "Tempting, but I've got to taste the goods."

Sigh. Demons...

"Fine, make it quick."

The monster was on me in an instant, his claws tracing the edge of my neck and running down my sternum. "Eddie, your soul's been stitched. You know that?"

"Yeah, it's a long story."

"Listen, I hate to break it to you, but I don't really go in for stitched souls. It's just, you know, everybody has their thing. There are Demons out there that totally dig on stitched souls. I mean, it's their cadaver caviar, but it's just not mine." The Demon cupped a clawed hand under Bernie's arm. "Let's get a move on, we'll miss the sinner brunch."

A twinkle of hope appeared in Bernie's eyes. "There's a brunch?"

"Of course, and who do you think is on the menu?" The Gillyfinkus tapped a single finger on the old corpse's chest.

"Eddie!"

"Wait, how about this," I said, not ready to let go of Bernie just yet. "You get my stitched soul, and I'll throw in the soul of this delivery man."

"What?!" Scotty cried, his twelve-year-old voice breaking at just the wrong moment. "I'm just a boy. I'm not a delivery man, I swear!"

"Hmm," the Demon placed a claw on his chin, "and is that 'The Undeliverable Box?'"

"It is. Here's my super special, one time only, bestest deal. You ready?"

"Shoot."

Scotty appeared ready to fall over, as if his entire delivery life flashing before his eyes.

Here we go.

I scooped up the broken glass and held it in my hands. "One more game of Dragon's Lair. I win and you lose everything—no Bernie, no me, no delivery man, and you go scratch for nine-hundred years. But—"

"If you lose, then I get it all, plus the Undeliverable Box."

"What are you doing?" Scotty cried, his eyes a mixture of fear and abject hatred.

"Chill, Scotty. I've got this," I said, trying to muster enough bravado in my voice to console the kid. "I think."

"I accept." The Jeffery Demon wrapped his spindly

claws around my hand and pressed the sharp glass against my skin. A single line of blood dripped from my palm. "Just for good measure, Eddie. I'm sure you understand."

"Totally."

The Demon took the glass from my hands and held it up. It stretched like pulled taffy, expanding and twisting to form the shape of my single favorite video game of all time.

"Dragon's Lair," Bernie and I breathed as the brilliant glow of the cartoon screen washed over us.

"Quarter me, Jeffery."

The Gillyfinkus held up a single dingy quarter. "Wait a second, how do I know you aren't using some sort of Magick?"

"I'm not a Magician. You know that."

The Demon shook his head. "Since when has that ever stopped you? Empty your pockets."

"Jeffery, we go way back—"

"Empty them!" the Demon's voice rattled the casket and shook Bernie enough to elicit a sawdust toot in the process. I turned my pockets inside out, dropping a few items to the floor.

"Ah ha! Is that the Roger's Rabbit Foot?"

"No, it's—"

Jeffery held the tiny white paw to his crooked nose. "It is! You were going to cheat."

"No, I just forgot it was in there," I said, wiping the sweat that had begun beading on my brow with one of the bands on my wrist.

"Sweat bands." The Demon held out his hands.

"No, I need them to keep my palms from getting slippery."

The Demon squinted his eyes at me. I pulled off one of the bands and tossed it to him. "Here, smell it."

He pressed it against his nose and frowned. "It smells like you."

"Damn straight it does. Now, give it back."

The monster returned my wrist band and handed me the quarter, the coin cold in his warm hands. "You never could get past the whirlpools."

"We'll see."

* * *

"THE WHIRLPOOLS." Bernie leaned his overstuffed corpse on the arcade cabinet, completely absorbed by the cartoon-like scene playing out across the screen. "He's going to do it."

Jeffrey the Demon stood next to me, his long arms folded and very much displeased. "Impressive, but there are a lot of scenes on the other side. One wrong move, Eddie. Just one wrong move and your souls are mine."

"Wrong, I've still got two lives left." I said, timing the left push just in time to send Dirk the Daring paddling down the proper tunnel. "Scotty, hydration. Get me a Diet Coke."

"Huh?" the delivery man said, his head popping up in the reflection on the screen. "Are you serious?"

I wiped more sweat from my face, then narrowly timed the attack button quick enough to block the floating sword from removing Dirk the Daring's head. "Deadly serious, check the other rooms. This is a funeral home, they're going to have sodas. Diet Coke only, you got it?"

"I..."

I timed the next right pull on the joystick just so, and sent Dirk dodging the swing of a floating mace. "Scotty, I'm fading over here."

The delivery man's fiery gaze disappeared from the glass, only to be replaced by the Gillyfinkus Demon's reflection. "Recruiting young, eh?"

"Kid's got spunk. Reminds me a lot of me at that age."

The Demon bobbed his head from side to side as if processing my statement. "You were more positive—it was irritating as hell."

"Amen." I timed up the next two pulls perfectly and kept the less-than-intelligent Dirk from consuming the bottle marked 'Drink Me.'

Clunk.

A can of soda landed on the arcade cabinet and I grabbed it, tossing back the sugary goodness.

"Gah!" I spit out the vile drink and missed the next turn. Dirk the Daring became Dirk the Decapitated in an instant. "Scotty, what is… RC Cola!"

"All they had."

"You gave me RC Cola? Our immortal souls on the line and you give me RC Cola? What were you thinking?"

Jeffrey the Demon sharp teeth and curling horns shined in the black screen's reflection. "One more life, Eddie. One more and your souls are mine."

Scotty removed the offending can from my view. "Sorry, I just… It was all they had."

I took a deep breath while the laserdisc inside that infernal arcade game spun up. "It's okay. Just never do it again—ever."

Bernie patted my shoulder, his corpse-hands heavy with preservatives. "You've got this, Eddie. You know you don't have much further. You can do it."

"Actually," the Gillyfinkus said, leaning against the arcade cabinet. "He's got a long way to go, and a single life left to do it. It only gets harder from there."

"How would you know?"

"The game was popular in the lower hells for a while." He shrugged. "I got to see almost all of it."

"Wait," I said as the video screen queued up. "You've never seen anyone beat this damn thing either?"

The Jeffrey Demon's smile was positively feral. "Nope."

Damn.

The screen lit back up and I wiped my brow, then planted a kiss on my joystick hand's sweatband. "Let's do this."

* * *

"HE'S GOING TO DO IT..." Bernie breathed, his face taking up half the display's reflection. Next to it, an equally large Demonic scowl deepened with each scene.

"Impossible."

It should have been, but there I was, deeper into the game than any mortal man had ever been. It was no longer a simple video game; it was life and death, and with each joystick pull and button press, I made it one step closer to freedom.

Bernie clutched the cabinet. "Eddie, the—"

"I've got it," I said, popping the joystick with near flawless timing.

"He's going to do it!" Bernie's makeup-laden face lit up with cherubic joy.

Scotty's steely gaze appeared in the bottom of the reflection. "This looks like a cartoon."

"Yeah." I hit the attack button in perfect time with the next scene. "That's how it was designed, and that's why it's one of the greatest video games ever created."

"I always liked Double Dragon 3," the ginger-haired kid said.

The three of us froze. Bernie, the Demon, and I simply stared at him in the dark reflection as the next scene loaded.

"What?"

"How about I take his soul anyway?" the Demon said,

pursing his infernal lips. "I mean, just to do the world a favor."

"Whatever, it was better than this old man game." Scotty frowned and his face disappeared from the glass.

"It's back, Eddie," Bernie said, pulling my attention to the screen.

The beautiful Princess Daphne appeared on the screen. Her long blonde hair and plunging neckline reminded me of exactly why I'd loved this game so much as a kid.

"To slay the dragon, you need the magic sword," she said, her eyelashes batting beautifully.

Scotty's face reappeared in the glass. "Is that the princess?"

"Yeah," the three of us said in unison.

"She's hot."

"Damn straight," I said, sending Dirk after the sword.

Scotty's reflected eyes lit up each time Daphne made an appearance. "This game's kinda cool."

Dragon fire filled the screen and I knew I had scant seconds to make my moves.

"No one beats the dragon," the Gillyfinkus said. "There's no one alive with that level of hand-eye coordination. This is where you lose, Edwin Lovely."

The Demon was right, there was no one alive that could make those maneuvers, but I could think of at least one person long gone that might have been that talented.

I just hope it extends to video games.

I twisted the sweatband on my joystick wrist. "Here goes nothing."

I parried and spun in a flurry of movement, sending Dirk the Daring on an unstoppable rampage through the Dragon's golden lair. The cartoon knight ducked claws and slipped away from falling treasure, then swung his sword and caught the dragon's fire.

"He's doing it!" Bernie cried, his decaying hands clutching the cabinet. "He's going to win!"

Doubt crept into the Demon's confident smile. "Impossible."

I slammed the attack button down and sent the magic sword into the dragon. With a single button press, I beat the greatest game ever made on a single quarter. "Take that!"

Unable to tear ourselves away, we all stood in transfixed wonder as the beautiful Princess Daphne leapt into Dirk's arms and the screen faded to a heart-shaped cutaway.

"You cheated!" The Demon smashed the arcade cabinet with his claws. "I don't know how, but you cheated. No living human is that coordinated. It's just not—"

"Ah, but I am." I used a sweatband to wipe the RC Cola taste from my lips. "And I believe you have lost."

"Argh!" the Demon stomped around the tiny viewing room, his spindly arms flailing. "I couldn't lose. It was impossible! I'll find out how you cheated. No mortal man beats Dragon's Lair. No one!"

I pulled off the sweatbands. "Time to go scratch, Jeffrey. You'll be someone else's problem the next time around."

The Demon shriveled like an old grape, his skin pulling in on itself while his body folded like a collapsing star. "Damn you, Edwin Lovely!"

Pop!

The Gillyfinkus vanished in a pop of sulfurous smoke, taking with him the arcade cabinet and Daphne's smiling face.

"Hooray," Bernie's corpse slapped a hand on my back. "You've saved my life."

"Nope."

"Huh?"

I pointed at the casket. "You've got a ride to catch. Without the Gilly here, you should get it any minute. They aren't quite as timely as they used to be, but they don't take corpses—it's part of the rules. Now, hop to it."

"What?" the arcade owner said, his makeup laden face falling. "You mean I'm still—"

"Dead? Uh huh, you sure are. Sorry, pal, but them's the breaks of the game. Still, I'm guessing there're a lot of great video games where you're headed."

"Like Double Dragon 3!" Scotty shouted behind me.

Bernie frowned.

"I'll work on the kid, don't worry." I helped the old corpse back into his space-age casket. "Now, let's get you off to paradise."

Bernie sighed and gingerly climbing back into the coffin. "You think I'll be okay?"

"Handsome guy like you? Sure. Now, stay put and don't go anywhere," I said, pushing him back against the cushions. "Your ride will be here shortly."

Bernie's eyes closed and his corpse returned to its normal decaying self.

"How'd you do it?" Scotty asked, standing beside the steel tube. "I've never seen hands move that fast."

I pulled off the opposite sweatband, the one I hadn't handed to the Demon. "Arthur Ashe's sweatband."

"Who?"

I shook my head. "Only one of the greatest tennis players who ever lived."

"My dad says that's John McEnroe."

I patted the newly re-christened delivery boy on the head. "Scotty, your Dad's an idiot. How about I get some breakfast?"

"I thought you were broke," the kid said, helping me load my bag but unwilling to touch the Undeliverable Box.

"I am, but I know you've got a couple twenties, and I did save your soul."

"You risked my soul—"

"And I saved it," I said as I wrapped my arm on the delivery boy's shoulder and guided him toward the door. "I believe protocol dictates the presentation of one Egg McMuffin—with sausage."

"But…"

"Sausage, Scotty. Don't cheap out on me."

IGNORANCE AND UNLEADED

*S*team mixed with white smoke billowed from the seams of the Dad Wagon's hood. The toxic cloud covered my windshield and made the panicked turn off the highway an altogether harrowing experience—one I was lucky to survive in one piece.

The Mazda and I found a derelict gas station not far from the offramp, and together we coaxed enough yards out of the rattling engine to get her to the pumps, but only just barely. We rolled to a stop between premium and diesel, and while I had enough cash for both neither would be delivering fuel anytime soon.

The pumps, along with the rest of the gas station, were non-functional, their old glass displays long since cracked and their nozzles wrapped in grocery bags.

I turned off the engine and popped the hood, sending another plume of white smoke into the air.

That can't be good.

Being on the road month after month meant the Dad Wagon and I had been away from *The Qwik Fix* for too long, and my four-wheeled friend was more than happy to use smoke signals to remind me.

Rob and his mechanics had been my one stop shop for all things automotive over the last few years, but out here on the highway somewhere between Orlando and Daytona, the ginger-haired and his master-level grease monkeys were nowhere to be found.

I pulled the trunk latch, then stepped out into the late-day sun. The Dad Wagon's dash had read five o'clock, and while it sure felt like we were getting close to dinner time, the clock had stopped working a few weeks prior.

Even a stopped clock tells the right time twice a day.

I slammed the door behind me and hadn't gone three feet before my stomach started churning. It'd been building up an industrial helping of acid ever since I'd left Ocala the previous night. My guts weren't used to Korean food, and they were doing all they could to let me know that.

Black noodles be damned.

I fished some antacids out of my pocket and choked down a few chalky white capsules.

You're going through these like candy, Gene.

My stomach rumbled in protest as the mint slurry did its magic. I did my best to ignore it and instead pried open the Dad Wagon's trunk. Ever since I'd started working for the house the back half of my car had become a junk magnet. There were empty boxes, jumper cables, a crowbar, and even a few non-Magickal items. It was just one of those things I needed.

Oil. Where did I put the oil?

That pimply faced kid at Pep Boys would have been proud I'd actually learned a few things that rainy afternoon regarding the value of lubrication for the modern automotive engine. I'd bought a quart of oil for his trouble, but, I hadn't been there for the auto shop lesson.

Another day, another exorcism.

I gave the rubbery oil can a shake, and what sloshed around inside told me I'd done this trick a few too many times—less than half full.

You've got a leak. Eventually you'll have to find a real mechanic to patch that up for you—can't keep feeding it oil forever.

I returned to the front of the car and opened the hood, letting the pent-up steam and burning oil escape into the late afternoon air while I got a look at the problem.

How hard can it be?

I tugged at a few wires, then burned my fingers on the hot metal, still with no real idea what I was looking for. I did, however, find the spot to refill the oil, and used up what was left in the jug. Having reached the full extent of my mechanical knowledge, I let the engine cool while I checked out the gas station itself.

Gulf? Haven't seen one of them in years.

What remained of the bright orange-and-blue sign swung gently in the afternoon breeze above the door, its missing plastic pieces long since lost among the weeds and encroaching scrub brush. The front of the building itself hadn't fared much better—the boarded windows and blacked-out door were ample evidence of that.

I found a few yellowed newspapers wadded up against that door and kicked them aside to make a spot to sit down. With my back against the darkened glass, I pulled out my phone.

No signal. Damn it.

I shoved the phone back in my pocket and tried to distract myself with the setting sun. It was one of those Florida evenings where the sky glowed in bright bands of red, pink, and azure that swirled above the tree tops. My stomach had settled down just enough for me to get comfortable with the beauty of the coming night, when a minivan tore down the off-ramp and yanked me out of my meditative state.

The dull blue van kicked up dust coming off the highway like a contrail then turned hard into the gas station, following practically the same harried route I had. They bounced over the broken pavement, then hit the brakes and came to a stop one row over from the Dad Wagon.

They'd idled for barely a second before the sliding door shot open and a young woman carrying a baby like heavy ordnance leapt onto the pebbly asphalt.

"Oh my God, it's everywhere!" a man yelled from inside the van.

The woman didn't turn back. Instead, she stripped down the vomit-smothered child like she was handling a hot-zone patient, unzipping the onesie while at the same time avoiding direct contact with the hazardous material it was coated in. "Deal with it, Tommy. I've got my own problems!"

The woman was right, she did: her son was a puke-coated mess. God knows I'd seen the same thing when Cathy was little. That girl had been a vomit factory in the early years, and both Porter and I had shared similar experiences count-less times.

"What do I do with the car seat?!"

"You need to clean it, Tommy," the woman said, wadding up her son's onesie.

The van tilted side to side a few more times before a skinny, bearded hipster climbed out carrying a slimy white car seat. "It smells like death in there."

"Then next time don't let your dad feed him before we get on the road."

The young man set the car seat down; neither of them had slowed down enough to notice me sitting against the old gas station door.

"There are some water bottles in the cooler," the mother

said, sliding her baby under one arm and using the other to wipe vomit off with the wadded-up onesie.

"Where did you pu—"

"In the trunk."

Dad opened the trunk and removed water bottles.

"When's he going to need his meds again?" Mom wiped her forehead with the back of her arm.

"What time is it?"

The young woman looked at her watch. "Five."

Ha!

Her husband's face darkened. "Very soon."

"Okay, you can give them to him as soon as you take care of this." The young mother shoved a vomit-covered onesie into her husband's hands. "See if there's a trash can around back."

"Ugh, Joyce, it smells terrible."

"Sure does. Now go get rid of it."

Tommy held the biohazard at arm's length and jogged around the back of the old gas station while his wife continued to attend to her son.

"Who's a good baby? You're a good baby. Yes, you are. Yes, you—" The young mother paused, finally noticing my car for the first time. "Tommy?!"

"Hang on, I can't get the lid open all the way."

"There's somebody here…"

"Huh?"

"There's a car with the trunk open," Joyce said, taking a moment to look at my collection of road trash. "We aren't alone."

"Yeah, just me waiting for the engine to cool," I said, waving from my seat in front of the door.

"Hello…" Joyce said, switching arms and bringing her young son tight to her chest. "Tommy!"

Clang!

"I almost got it open," her husband called from behind the building.

"You can just put it on top, I don't think they'll mind. Let's get back on the road."

The young mother's eyes stayed locked to me like a tractor beam.

"Just about there."

Boom!

"Got it!"

I stood and brushed the dirt from my pants, all the while keeping a wide berth. I had no interest in spooking the young mother further.

"That's great, honey," Joyce said before turning her attention to me. "Don't you think that's great, Gene?"

It was subtle, and if I hadn't been getting good at catching it, I would have missed the shift in her tone.

69 Mallory Lane.

"What are you—"

"Doing?" the house said, shifting her baby from one arm to another. "I'm appealing to your fatherly instincts."

The young child squirmed in his mother's arms.

"Don't hurt the kid."

The Joyce-shaped house squeezed the baby to her chest. "Why, Gene, I would never dream of such a thing."

"What do you want?"

"I want you to save this baby."

"Huh?! Save him from what?"

The house smiled and waved to the young woman's husband as he rounded the old building. "From him."

* * *

161

Either the house was gone, or it had disguised its voice perfectly to mimic the young mother's tone. "Tommy, you'll never believe who I ran into."

The young man rounded the corner, slightly out of breath. "Huh?"

"I was so busy with Jason that I didn't even notice the other car. Did you?"

"No." The young father's guard went up as soon as he laid eyes on me. The guy had a reason to be worried—I looked more than a little rough around the edges. Months of highway cuisine and cheap hotels can take the shine off even the best of us.

Tommy gave me a wide berth, jogging past as casually as he could to stand next to his wife and son.

The Joyce-shaped house switched the baby to her opposite arm. "Yeah, what are the chances I'd run into the father of my old babysitter at an old beat-up gas station outside of Deltona?"

Come on, how old do you think I am?

"Not very high, I'd guess," her husband said, keeping his eyes on me.

"Tommy, this is Eugene Law."

"Hey," I said, keeping my distance and giving the young man a friendly nod.

Joyce handed her baby to Tommy, and I exhaled. The thought of the house with a small child was too much to take.

"I'll be right back. I'm going to get him some new clothes."

Tommy didn't take his eyes off me. "Sure."

Joyce smiled and disappeared into the bowels of the minivan.

"So what are you going to do, Gene?" That might have been Tommy's mouth moving, but it was the house's voice. "This is my favorite part, you know? The part where I get to watch your monkey brain break down a problem all while you try to stay within the guardrails of self-prescribed morality. So, while we're waiting for her to come back, tell me, what are you going to do? The suspense is palpable and I love it."

"Nothing," I said, pointing to the Dad Wagon. "I'm going to drive out of here and leave this family out of it."

"Gene," the house tickled his child, "you won't do that."

"And why not?"

"Because you couldn't live with yourself if you did nothing."

"You'd be surprised at what I can live with," I said, walking toward my car.

"Murder? What happened to the Eugene Law of last night —the staunch defender of the sanctity of life? Where did he go?"

I held my hand above the Mazda's engine compartment.

Cool enough for me.

Then I slammed the hood shut. "His stomach is still screwed up from black noodles."

The house switched hands and the baby giggled. "I'm disappointed in you. I thought you were better than this."

"Why? Isn't this what you've wanted all along? You've systematically removed my contact with the outside world to leave me isolated and angry, and *now* you want me to care?"

"I want you to save this child."

I shook my head. "No you don't. You want me to kill that man. That's all you've ever wanted, and I'm not going to do it."

"Even if it means this little boy dies?"

The baby giggled again and tugged on his father's ear.

I can't let that happen... can I?

"You're making this up. I'm not going to worry about them, because you won't do anything, and even if you did I couldn't stop you, so why bother?" I was lying, and the house knew it; everything 69 Mallory Lane did was on me.

Joyce reappeared with fresh clothes for her son. "Tommy, is it time for his medicine?"

The young man blinked his eyes as if waking up from a short nap. "What? The medicine, right…"

The young man returned his son to the boy's mother.

Joyce smiled and waited for her husband to get behind the van before she spoke again. "Gene, we don't have a lot of time here. You need to stop him before it's too late."

"I don't get it. Why do you care? It's not like this small family is remotely important to you."

Joyce tucked her son's legs into the tiny onesie. "If I pulled a single word out of the book of your life would it make sense? Without context you couldn't possibly understand the significance of what you were looking at."

"Well, then give me some context?"

Joyce shook her head and coaxed her son's arms though the sleeve holes. "Nice try, Gene, but it's too much for your primate brain. There are layers within layers here."

"Whatever," I said, pulling open the Dad Wagon's door. "I'm not biting."

"The medicine," Joyce said, pulling the zipper up. "He's killing his son with that medicine."

"What are you talkin—"

"I got it, honey," the young husband said, returning with a small plastic syringe. It was just like the kind we'd used on Cathy and Kris when they needed an antibiotic. No needles, just a simple way to deliver medications to an infant not accustomed to drinking from a cup. "Only a few doses left."

"Oh, that's a relief," the Joyce-shaped house said, keeping a furtive eye on me. "I just wish he would start getting better."

"He will. I promise you he will. Just a few more doses."

"What's wrong with the little guy?" I asked, unable to do what I'd boasted about only moments earlier. The house had a hook in me and knew how to exploit it.

Damn you...

"What did his doctor say again, Tommy? You were the one that took him there..." the house said, letting the young woman's words hang in the air expectantly.

"We went over this before, sweetheart. It's a rare disorder that runs in my family. However, if we catch it early, he'll be fine... just fine."

The house knelt down and sat the baby against her knee. "That's right. I'm sorry."

Tommy knelt next to her, checking the level of the pink goo in the tiny plastic syringe. "I just wish you would trust me. I know what's best for my son."

"I'm sorry, honey. Sometimes I just can't *see* where it's all going."

You sneaky bastard.

I reached out for my Magick, letting my mind brush across the house's corrupted wellspring boiling inside me. The power was there, I had only to reach for it—but each time I did it brought me one step closer to 69 Mallory Lane. At some point I would use enough of that Magick and forget where the house ended and I began.

"Now hold him still—you know how he likes to squirm."

That's it. I can't take any more.

I accepted the twisted power of the house and let the Magick bubble up inside me.

What is it the house want me to see?

Magick!

It flooded the young boy. What I was seeing shouldn't have been possible, yet there it was, plain as day in the setting sun. The infant practically exuded Magick from his pores, but there was something else, something dark slithering just below the surface of his skin.

The kid has Magick in his blood. How the hell is that even possible?

Typically, Magicians didn't come into anything that resembled Magick until they hit puberty, but this kid had turned that rule on its head.

Where did you come from?

The baby may have had his mother's eyes, but the similarities didn't extend to the supernatural. There was nothing remotely Magickal about Joyce. In fact, she reminded me a little of my own wife, a bastion of normalcy next to her miracle baby.

The father...

The syringe, and whatever swirled inside it, pulsed in Tommy's hand. With the illusions removed it was easy to see it for what it was. That wasn't medicine, at least no medicine a sane person would take. That was a living thing, vile and black, and squirming within the cheap plastic.

Night Seepers?!

I'd only ever read about them—they were stuff of nightmares for Magicians. Tiny leeches that fed off Magick, drinking it like it was their mother's milk, and more often than not killing their host in the process.

In a far less enlightened era, Night Seepers had been an effective tool to subdue Magicians deemed too dangerous for humanity. Their use, as well the use of other tools that separated a Magician from their Magick, had been outlawed decades ago. As a loose community of oddballs we Magicians had tried our best to eradicate them; however, we must not have done enough, because there I was, not ten feet away from what had to be dozens.

"Stop!"

The husband hesitated and turned his eyes to me. Black

worms swam circles around his pupils, twisting and turning like hungry weevils. Tommy had Night Seepers in his blood too—lots of them.

"Joyce, get in the car," I said, taking a step toward the young family.

* * *

JOYCE HELD HER GROUND.

"Put him in the car, honey," the young father said, turning his attention to me. "I'll take care of this."

His wife nodded and climbed into the van, not a hint of the house in her actions. Once Joyce and her Magickal son were safely in the van, the young father turned his focus and the devilish Seepers on me.

"This isn't your concern, Magician. You need to leave."

He's right, this isn't your concern. Just get back in that car and drive off. It's his son...

"Like hell it isn't," I said, obviously not interested in listening to my own advice. "Those things are killing him and you know it."

"Killing him? Hardly. Does he look like he's dying?"

"No, but—"

"Exactly. I don't blame you, Magician. Don't act surprised. I may be more enlightened than you, but it doesn't mean I can't smell the evil Magick on you."

"More enlightened? You were about to give Night Seepers to your son."

Tommy nodded. "Correct. However, we don't use that name. They're a helpful symbiote that keeps Magick from destroying our lives. Haven't you read the doctrine?"

The doctrine?

The young man didn't give me time to respond.

"I get it, you're older, and you come from a different time, but you should know that the younger generation has smartened up. We *know* Magick is there to control us, to keep us hungry for our next fix, and to make us targets for the monsters just beyond the visible world."

"No! Magick is a gift."

The young father sighed as if he were trying to explain computers to a caveman.

"That's what you've been led to believe, but it's a lie. It's all a lie. The doctrine proves it. Let me ask you, do you have children, Mr. Law?"

"Yes, and—"

"And where are they?" the young man asked, cutting me off before I could finish.

"They're—"

"Safe," the young father interrupted again. "You've kept them as far away from this as you could, haven't you?"

"No, I—"

"No? You let them find their Magick, and what has that brought you?"

The Hellgate appeared in my mind—and clinging to it, the fading form of my daughter. Fires raged beyond that portal, along with the slithering arms of The Defiler.

Did I make the right choice? What awaits Cathy around the next corner? Or Kris?

"You can't make the decision for him. If your son grows up and chooses to take the Night Seepers, that's his choice, but you can't take Magick from him. You have no right—"

"I'm his father. I have *every* right."

"What about Joyce? What does she think?"

Tommy shook his head. "She doesn't matter. She's not a Magician and never will be. She doesn't know what we know, and it's going to stay that way. She believes this will save her son, and she's right."

I took a small step closer, keeping my eyes on the twisting

Seepers in the tiny syringe. "You think you're the first Magician to deal with kids?"

"Of course not, but unlike you I'm willing to make the sacrifice for my son. Thanks to me he'll grow up in a world without Magick."

Where is the house? Why isn't it getting Joyce and Jason out of the van?

I inched closer. "Please, just think about what you are doing. The Seepers won't stop with his Magick, they'll colonize his frontal lobe. Those tiny devils will burrow their way into his mind like weevils. He'll never be right after that —never."

Tommy gripped the syringe tighter. "You don't know that. The doctrine states tha—"

"The doctrine is a load of crap. You've been fooled."

"The doctrine talked about Magicians like you: unenlightened, power hungry, weak. It warned us of your evil. You've sent your waves against us, but Joyce and I prevailed."

"What the hell are you talking about?"

"Please, show me a little respect. You expect me to believe you just happened to break down here? You're the fourth I think; its hard to keep track of how many Magicians have come after my family."

"I'm not after your family," I said, keeping a close eye on the Seepers in the young man's hand.

"You should have told that to Jason's last babysitter. She didn't last as long as you. She crumpled like wet tissue paper. Now, you haven't touched my son, so I'm going to give you something I didn't give her: a chance to walk away."

Do it, Gene. Walk away, now.

"I'm not going to let you murder your son."

Or don't. Just stay here and risk exposure to Night Seepers...

"Don't pretend to care about my son and his Magick. You'll do whatever *they* tell you to do. Don't you see? That's what Magick has brought you, slavery. You're a slave to their whims."

Whose whims? The Seepers must be deep in his brain, sowing seeds of doubt and paranoia.

"I'm a slave to no one," I said, letting my Magick boil up a good bit faster than I'd expected.

The Night Seepers squirmed below the young man's skin. Tiny black worms wriggled through the whites of his eyes, their voracious maws churning. They sensed my Magick and were hungry.

"You think you are protected, Magician? You think your evil, your age, or the fact that you have a family means anything to the Seepers? They will devour you, and in the end you'll become just like me."

"What's that? Crazy?"

"Normal."

"Hardly." I shook my head, trying to tamp down the Magick welling up inside me. "You're a walking worm farm. There's not a damn thing normal about you."

"The Seepers have made sure I'll never end up like you."

"Ruggedly handsome?"

Tommy ignored me. "I'm going to get in the van now, and you're going to let us leave."

"And if I don't?"

Tommy glared at me, the Seepers squirming across his face. "I will introduce you to the doctrine."

My Magick rumbled, and the power of 69 Mallory Lane coursed through my veins, chumming the air with feed for the hungry Seepers.

"Let the boy go with his mother."

"That's not going to happen. Joyce knows nothing about Magick. She's normal, and wouldn't stand a chance as he got older. You know that."

As much as I hated to admit it, Tommy was right. A

mundane person like Joyce wouldn't know what to do when her son's Magick began to assert itself; without a willing teacher and a lot of patience the young boy's mother wouldn't survive to see him reach puberty. Still, a young child with Magick was too important to pass up, too special.

Is that you thinking, or the house?

Tommy backed toward the car, slipping the syringe in his shirt pocket before opening the driver's side door. "Don't try to follow us…"

His young son's wailing cries washed over me from somewhere within the recesses of the van.

"Damn it, Joyce, can't you shut him up?"

I'd only lost control of my Magick a few times in my life. Most of the time they'd been minor lapses, however I'd never had the full power of 69 Mallory Lane backing me up before. The house's will surged in my blood and I unleashed that unfocused anger-fueled rage at the young man and his Seepers.

"Frangit!" I shouted, my mouth barely forming cohesive syllables. It didn't matter—the Magick still listened, it always listened. Righteous power roared from my hands, tearing the driver's door from its frame and tossing it aside like a discarded candy bar wrapper.

Tommy didn't move. "Don't do it."

"Ledo!"

My rage had taken over. There was no stopping the Magick now. I raged at a young man willing to sacrifice his son out of ignorance. I raged at a world full of monsters that made him feel the way he did. Most of all I raged at my own fear: of the unknown, of being a father, and of the future.

The house's power slammed into the young man, hitting him with the force of a wrecking ball. Or so I would have thought.

With barely a whisper, the destructive force dissipated harmlessly into the humid twilight.

Oh, shit.

"I told you not to do that," Tommy said calmly, stepping out van, his son's cries mixed with the screams of his mother.

"What the—"

"Now you've made them hungry."

The Seepers?! They'd consumed my Magick like a Little Debbie Snack Cake.

The young man leapt at me, throwing his weight against my chest and knocking me back against the Dad Wagon's open trunk. He pinned me down against the boxes, his eyes wild and unfocused. Night Seepers clamored beneath the young father's skin, those tiny black eels twisting around each other in ravenous delight.

Think, Gene! Think!

Tommy brought his face above mine, then opened his mouth, letting an untold number of hungry devils extend out into the evening air. Like addicts searching for their next hit, the Seepers whipped back and forth, licking the air and clawing for my Magick.

* * *

A SWIFT KNEE to the crotch crumpled Tommy, but not before one of his Night Seepers landed on my wrinkled shirt.

Shit! Shit! Shit! Don't touch it, Gene.

The black eel squirmed between the buttons, searching for bare skin. I snapped the edges of my oxford and launched the vile creature into the night air.

The young father didn't stay down long. He got to his feet and coughed a writhing mass of Seepers into his hand, then flung that black wad at me like a revolting snowball.

I grabbed an old pizza box from the Dad Wagon's assorted supply of discarded cardboard and used it like a shield, letting that smiling grandmother's face catch the brunt of the Night Seepers before I batted them toward the unused gas pumps.

Splat!

Writhing Seepers oozed down the broken glass display, clawing at the air for my Magick.

"You can't win," Tommy said, the Night Seepers squirming beneath his skin giving him a distinct cottage cheese look. "You aren't a child. At your age it will just take one. Just a single Night Seeper and you can kiss your Magick goodbye."

I tossed the pizza box aside and grabbed the first thing my hand fell across from the trunk.

Jumper cables?!

Night Seepers oozed from the young man's eyes, streaking his face with living black tears.

What the hell am I supposed to do with—

I didn't get time to finish my thought before the he lunged at me again. This time I got out of the way, letting Tommy ram against the lip of my trunk. I slung the jumper cables around his neck and pulled them tight from behind. I didn't want to kill him, but if he passed out from lack of oxygen that would be just fine by me.

The young man flailed, clawing at the thick black wires that held his neck. It was like trying to hold a wild horse, and while I'd never been remotely fit enough for that, this time I had a few extra pounds of frozen pizza hanging on my frame to help. I cranked down hard on the cables, putting my meager back muscles into it while hoping it would be enough. Night Seepers smeared Tommy's neck like artistic tribal tattoos, but still he kept fighting. "I won't let you curse my son!"

"Damn it, man. I'm not trying to curse him. I'm trying to save him!"

Tommy fell to his knees, his face pressed up against the Dad Wagon's bumper.

Come on... Why won't you just go down?

Tommy's frantic hands slowed—had I finally run him down to zero?

Something black wriggled across my shoes in the last lights of the setting sun.

Shit!

Seepers by the hundreds flooded the broken pavement, squirming over the dusty ground and searching the air for me.

"Gah!"

I skipped back, letting the cables fall away as I kicked at the hungry eels. Tiny Seepers bit at my shoes, slithering across the laces and searching for any hint of bare skin. Tommy tore the cables free and pulled something out of my trunk.

The crowbar? Aw Hell, now why hadn't I thought of that? Because you didn't want to kill him, that's why.

The young father leaned against the Dad Wagon's rear bumper and fought to catch his breath. My jumper cables dangled from his neck like a Pep Boy's boa constrictor, but he ignored them, and instead twisted the wicked-looking crowbar in his fists. Night Seepers covered his face—only angry eyes shone through the living mask of writhing hunger.

"Now, Tommy, let's not get crazy," I said, keeping my hands up while backing away from the Seepers and the young man spewing them like a fire ant mound. "No need to be swinging crowbars."

"Why won't you just let them in?" the young man said, taking a step toward me, Seepers smearing his face like running mascara. "What has Magick done for you? Magick has ruined your life. Why won't you let it go?"

Just keep him talking. There's got to be something you can use.

Night Seepers streamed over the chunks of shattered asphalt, ensuring I wouldn't be throwing any rocks at Tommy. The discarded pizza box vanished beneath the writhing mass of black ooze, and I decided then and there I would not be checking the box for old crusts—the Seepers could have them.

"The Seepers do more than eat your Magick. They burrow into your brain and make you bat-shit crazy. Can't you see that? I mean, think about it. What sort of father gives his son brain worms?"

Tommy swung the crowbar a few times with Seeper-covered arms. "A father that loves his son. Look at you! I can smell the evil on you from here. Magick has brought you nothing but pain and darkness—you would wish that on your own flesh and blood?"

Seepers flicked off Tommy's crowbar, splattering on my jacket and against the cracked glass of the gas pump.

The pump!

Night Seepers bit at the seams, hungry for the Magick beneath. I tore the jacket off and flung it at Tommy. He swatted it away, but not before giving me enough time to grab the nozzle and whisper a quiet prayer.

Please be something left in the tank...

I tore the plastic bag free from the handle and willed my Magick into the hose. It traveled down the line and into the reservoir beneath my feet.

"Autem!"

Nothing happened.

Come on, damn it!

"The Seepers thank you for your Magick!" Tommy said,

his fingers flexing against the oily crowbar. "They will enjoy consuming you."

The Night Seepers surged like a cresting wave, their black shiny bodies consuming everything in their path.

"Autem!"

The nozzle sputtered, puffing a loose mixture of old gas and fume-laden air.

"Just give in," the young man said, his body a living fountain of black death. "Your Magick isn't worth it."

Gasoline stirred in the tank beneath me, banging against the walls and filling the rubber hose.

"No! My Magick is all I have left. Autem!"

The old fuel exploded from the nozzle like a firefighter's hose, spraying Tommy and pushing back against the rising tide of Seepers. The black eels squirmed in the stinging fuel, halting their advance across the jagged ground.

"Argh!" Tommy swung the crowbar wildly.

"Stop!" I yelled, turning the nozzle on the pavement and pushing away Seepers by the thousands. "Just stop! I don't want to have to—"

"Kill him," Tommy said, dropping the crowbar, but it wasn't his voice that spoke to me, it was the house. "He won't stop. Can't you see that now?"

"I'm not going to kill an innocent—"

"Gene," the house wiped fuel and Seepers from its eyes. "He's not innocent, and you know it. He's a murderer. Remember the baby-sitter? If you let him live, he'll do it again. This one's a rabid dog and must be put down."

The spray of gasoline sputtered in my hand. "I'm not that person—"

"Gene, you *are* that person, and so much more. You're the first one in a couple thousand years that actually stands a chance of going the distance. Can't you see that? Finish it!"

The nozzle in my hand shuddered and the flood of fuel

reduced to a trickle, leaving me with a dripping nozzle and a host of angry Seepers.

"No, I won't," I said, throwing the nozzle to the ground and taking a step back from the pooling gasoline.

"Oh my God!" Tommy cried, getting to his feet. "Don't do it. Please, don't do it. I was just trying to keep him safe. What father wouldn't want their child to be safe!"

The house was gone.

"I won't. Just get those Seepers under control and we'll—"

My word were lost in the sound of his son's cries and the metallic slide of the van's side door.

"So close, Gene. So close. But, I'll take this as progress. I mean you did cover him in gasoline—you made this downright easy for me."

"Joyce?" the young father said, confusion in his voice.

"No, honey."

Tommy stepped back from his wife and the silver lighter that flickered in her hand. "Joyce, don't—"

"Goodbye, Thomas."

Whoosh!

Flames roared across the poured gasoline, forcing me to turn away as the fire consumed the young man. Seepers screamed in the smoky air, their shrill cries mixing with the terrible wailing of a lost Magician.

* * *

"WAKE UP, GENE," the Joyce-shaped house said, leaning in through my driver-side window.

"Huh?"

She pointed to the Dad Wagon's fuel gauge. "You've got a full tank, and I took care of that oil leak for now. That should be enough to get you to Cedar Key."

I blinked my eyes at the acrid air. "Tommy."

"He's in the wind," the house said, chuckling at its own joke.

"You—"

"No, Gene, *you* saved a prodigy today. There's a little boy that's going to grow up a healthy and reasonably well-adjusted Magician thanks to you."

"But the Seepers…"

The house smiled. "Nasty little buggers. All taken care of."

"What?! You could have done that at any time and you didn't?"

The house ran a maternal hand down my cheek, the smell of gasoline lingering on its fingers. "Mother knows best, Gene. Now get out of here."

The Dad Wagon lurched forward, and I had to swing the wheel hard to keep from ending up in a ditch. I pulled onto the highway and checked my rear-view mirror. The fire had died down, but I could still see the silhouette of Joyce and her son against the flickering orange.

What have I done?

BLACK VALENTINE

I stabbed my chopsticks into a steaming bowl of black-tinged noodles and sauce-covered vegetables. "What do you call this again?"

"Ramen." The young waitress's voice held more than a hint of frustration.

"I know it's ramen. I mean this," I said, pointing down at the mysterious bowl of dark noodles.

"Jajangmyeon."

I nodded, wiping sauce off my chin. "Yeah, well, whatever it is, it's damn good."

The young girl sighed then slipped into the kitchen, leaving me alone with my noodles. I was pretty sure she had a lot more interesting things to do on a Friday evening than entertain the only guy in the restaurant, but she was stuck with me regardless. Ever since I'd signed on with Team Mallory Lane actual human contact wasn't exactly something I got a lot of, so whenever it came up I took advantage of it—at least as long as it lasted.

The young girl returned with a steaming cup of sake.

"Thanks, sweetheart, but I didn't order any—"

"You're going to need it, Gene. Trust me."

It may have been the young waitress's body, but it wasn't her voice. Instead, it was the twisted tone of a benefactor I'd come to detest over the last few months—the House.

"Can't a guy just get some noodles in peace?"

The House adjusted the girl's top and held up a frying pan to check out her reflection. "I'm telling you, you've got a thing for wait staff. I don't get it, but you totally have a type."

"I'm married."

The house flipped her hair back and giggled. "That old story? Gene, you're eating Black Day noodles by yourself in a Korean bar in Ocala."

"So?"

"So," she placed a soft hand on my arm, "Black Day noodles are for single people. They sit around and eat their noodles and cry about the injustices of life without a partner."

I tossed the chopsticks back in the bowl, suddenly no longer hungry. "Whatever. Do you have a job for me, or are you just bored?"

She smiled with those bubblegum-pink lips. "A little of both."

"Well, out with it. I don't have all day."

The tiny bell above the door jingled.

"Out with what?" the waitress asked, cocking her head to one side—the House was gone.

"Sorry. I'll take the check whenever you're ready."

She didn't hear me, instead my waitress was already halfway down the bar chatting up the latest addition to the lonely heart's noodle club. The new visitor couldn't have been much younger than me. She slipped off her jacket and set it on an open stool, then hooked her purse under the bar before rattling off a response in what I assumed was Korean.

Language Magick wasn't my thing, but then again, neither were noodles.

My name is Eugene Law and I'm a Magician. I don't pull rabbits out of hats, nor do I saw women in half. I leave all those things to the professionals. Instead, I spend my time doing something about the things that go bump in the night. Most of time that meant banishment or protective spells, but ever since I'd taken the deal with 69 Mallory Lane, I'd been doing a lot of bumping back. As bosses went, the House was the worst, but it certainly had a thing for removing as many of the dark and evil creatures hiding in the unseen corners of the Sunshine State as possible—it just used me to do it.

I tossed back the tiny cup of now lukewarm sake and let the rice wine burn my tongue while I fished some dollars out of my pocket. Being what it was, the House wasn't much for money. It made sure I had some, but always in the strangest of ways, and not all of which were—strictly speaking—legal.

My tiny waitress swung back by and scooped up the bills, counting them off in her hands before opening the register.

"Here you go," she said, pulling out what had to have been the restaurant's entire take for the evening and placing it in my hand.

The House.

"You can't do—"

The waitress placed a finger to her lips. "I can do whatever I want, silly. In fact, I could shout right now that you grabbed me and Captain Muscles chopping vegetables in the back would be out here in seconds."

"I didn't—"

"Oh I know that, Gene." She closed the drawer and flashed her perfectly white teeth at me. "However, somewhere down in that lizard brain of yours you thought about it. You think you ended up in this noodle joint powering down Jajangmyeon on accident? Black noodles for my little lonely heart."

That last part came with a squeeze of my cheek.

I slapped away her hand, drawing the attention of the woman at the end of the bar.

"What is it you want?" I whispered through clenched teeth.

"Humans, always in a hurry. Can't you learn to savor it a little? You know something? Your wife might have really appreciated it if you'd taken your time once in a while..."

"That's it!" I pushed back the partially eaten noodles. "I've had it with your bullshit. When you are ready to tell me what the hell it is you want, then come find me. I know you can do that."

The young waitress grabbed my sleeve and let a lone tear glisten in her eye. "I don't love you anymore, and maybe I never did."

Her theatrics once again brought with them the attention of the smartly dressed woman at the end of the bar, however this time the house took notice and laid it on thick.

"You're a fat, ugly piece of shit, and I never want to see you again," she said. Then grabbed my shirt and pulled me in before whispering. "Nice job! That's how we chum the water. Now get out there, little bait fish. You've got work to do."

"What the—"

She cut me off. "Gae!"

"Wait just a minute. What is it you want me to—"

The linebacker-sized vegetable chopper's face appeared in the order window behind the bar. The House was right: I wanted nothing to do with him or his muscles tonight.

"Better go, Gene," she whispered, pointing at the cash stuffed in my pocket. "Otherwise I might have to tell him whose pocket that money ended up in."

I snapped my jacket off the stool and found the woman at

the end of the bar's walnut eyes following me. I reached out with my Magick, but the House was there, and its presence alone was more than enough to overload my senses.

The waitress shouted a few more things at me in Korean, then winked when she knew no one was looking.

It was all a performance; an award-winning act for an audience of one at the end of the bar, and it appeared to have worked. Warm brown eyes steeped in intrigue followed me toward the door, then drank me in like a martini before stopping to lick the olive.

I was bait, but for what?

Jingle.

A light rain covered the sidewalk outside. An evening shower had sprung up while I'd sat in that little noodle bar, and the wind-blown drops blew in my eyes.

I didn't have much time. Knowing the House, the waitress would figure out her cash was missing, and not long after that her resident vegetable chopper would be keen to turn his attentions on me. While I wasn't afraid of him, I *was* afraid of what I could do to him, thanks to the power of 69 Mallory Lane—no human being deserved that.

What happens when it asks for that, though? What happens when the House demands something you won't do?

I shook those thoughts away with the rain. I may have compromised more than a few things to get to where I was, but I wasn't a murder.

Are you sure?

I wasn't.

Downtown Ocala was largely empty that time of night. The horse farms and pastures of the wealthy were a good distance from the city's compact center. With the rain, its four streets and well-manicured park did little to draw the people out that evening.

But it had drawn the attention of the House—never a good thing...

I slipped between the noodle bar and a derelict storefront, then huddled in the darkened alley pressed up against damp concrete.

Jingle.

Someone was coming, and my money was on walnut eyes.

Clack. Clack. Clack.

Heels on the hard ground sharpened my attention, and I reached for my Magick, pushing through the sheen of oily corruption the House left on everything it touched and down into the wellspring of my power.

A flash of dark hair and the smell of perfume—sickly sweet lavender and lilacs—almost shot past me on the open sidewalk.

Magick tingled in my fingers; this wasn't my first Demon, and it wouldn't be my last.

I yanked her into the darkness, pulling that body against mine. It came with the bouquet of her perfume, and something else: fear, uncertainty, and doubt.

It was humanity in its purest form.

* * *

"GET YOUR HANDS OFF ME!" the woman shouted, pushing me away.

I released my Magick and let it vanish into the wet air like the smoke from a spent match. "I'm sorry, I thought you were someone else."

She shook the rain from her jacket and ran a hand through soft, midnight-black hair. "Do you grab all the women you think you know?"

"Yeah, no. Just having some fun. Like I said, sorry." I

checked the quiet street for police, but found none.

Good, I don't need more problems tonight.

"How do you know my sister?"

"Excuse me?"

"She called you a dog."

"Yeah, it happens."

"You don't look like her type."

"Uh, yeah."

Things like this happened all the time when the House got involved—so much so that sometimes it was best to just roll with it. "Maybe she changed her type."

"No offense, but that K-Pop princess doesn't go for old."

Ouch.

"Yeah, well, you and I aren't exactly from different generations."

The wind picked up and barreled down that narrow alley, forcing both of us to shield our eyes from the rain. I tried to use the opportunity to slip past the raven-haired woman, but instead she blocked my only exit.

"You haven't answered my question," the woman said, cocking her hip to the side.

"Right, and I'm not going to. Listen, you don't want anything to do with me. I'm a magnet for problems."

"Are you threatening me?"

Lightning cut across the sky and filled the narrow alley like a flash-bulb, but the woman's eyes didn't waver; she wanted an answer, and I wasn't going to give it to her.

Unstoppable force, meet immovable object...

"I don't have time for this."

I started to push past her, then stopped—something moved in the dark of the wall above us, something that tickled my Magickal senses.

Shit.

"I swear if you don't tell me what you are doing with my sister right now, I'll scream for the cops."

More movement in the hazy dark above the older sister demanded my attention. This wasn't one thing, it was many, and their ravenous whispers set my heart racing. These were hungry shadows and like velvety patches of alien night they slithered down the concrete, their tiny mouths opening and closing in the soft rain.

Shades...

This wasn't my first time dealing with the half-living, but it was my first time doing so while trying to extricate myself from a persistent woman who clearly didn't understand the gravity of the situation.

"We need to go," I said, trying to direct her toward the street.

The older sister remained undeterred and unmoving. "I'm not going anywhere with you until you tell me what your business was with Sun."

"Who?"

"My baby sister!"

The half-living shadows crept closer, hovering just above the raven-haired beauty and her crossed arms. This wasn't a lone Shade out for an evening snack. This was more, a lot more—shadows slithered over shadows, quickly becoming too many to count. What had once been one was now legion, and all with a singular purpose: feeding. Their mouths chittered softly in the light rain, hungry and desperate.

"Well?" she said, tapping a heel against the broken pavement. "I'm waiting."

"Not here you aren't," I said, grabbing her arm and pulling her deeper into the alley.

"Hey, I'm talking to—"

"No time, come on."

The first shadow sprung from the wall above, narrowly

missing the indignant woman before vanishing in the hazy light of the alley's lone bulb. We needed light to keep the Shades at bay, but in this alley light was in short supply. To make matters worse, high above us the rain-laden clouds shifted and blocked what little moonlight we'd had only moments before.

Another flash of lightning found the Shades closer, guided by red eyes and voracious mouths that would never be full.

The woman's tiny fist hammered on my already sore shoulder. "Let me go!"

I could have, but had she known what lay just behind us she would have had second thoughts. Unlike the half-living that had tried to consume my daughter, these Shades were weaker, but their numbers made them just as deadly.

The lone lamp above the distant door shone like a lighthouse in the deepening gloom.

Focus, Gene. Get to the light.

More shadows filled the narrow opening behind us, twisting and blending like dirty water colors.

None of this made any sense. Shades were a nasty evil, sure, but they weren't enough of a challenge for the House to waste my time. Even more strange was their pack-like configuration. I'd only ever seen Shades work in a group once before; they were typically lone wolf predators, like the one that had set up like a catcher's mitt to consume my daughter at her birth.

These weren't the sort of Shades I was used to. These were persistent, motivated, and brought with them memories of my college years I'd just as soon stayed forgotten.

The woman pounded her balled-up fist against my already sore shoulder. "Let go of me!"

Shades streamed down the alley walls and across the alley pavement like an unholy wave.

"Believe me, I'd love to."

But there was no going back now—that path was currently blocked by more nightmare material than I'd want to take on my myself, even with the House's help.

I dragged the raven-haired woman a little deeper into the alley, her eyes wide and her fists quickly becoming more than a little annoying.

"Help! Help! He's trying to molest me!"

Great, this is what you get for trying to save someone's life, Gene. Remember that.

I pulled her kicking and swinging into the dim halo of salvation beneath the only light in the narrow alley. The lone bulb hung above a rust-stained orange door and surrounded us in its protective halo. It wasn't a door to the noodle bar, but if memory served, the store on the other side was empty —or, if not, closed for the evening. Either way it was cold steel and enough to slow the half-living long enough for us to get away.

Beyond the light's dim edge, a rolling wave of Shades clamored over each other like over-anxious children in line for dinner, and I didn't particularly care to be on the menu.

I pressed a hand against the wet metal and called up my Magick; again, I had to reach through the thick sheen of oily corruption Mallory Lane left on everything it touched. It was a little like dipping a hand into fetid water, but that was better than becoming Shade-feed.

"Reserare!"

The deadbolt turned beneath my hands, ending with a satisfying thump as the folded steel dropped into the door.

"Come on," I said, throwing my shoulder against the damp metal.

"I'm not going anywhere with you," my ignorant fugitive said, stomping her heel on the pavement and stepping back outside the bulb's protective halo. "I'm staying right here until you tell me what's going on."

Shades slithered over the walls like black tar and danced between the bricks. The legion was undeterred and hungry.

"I so don't have time for this. Videre!"

The Magick unlocked her eyes and pulled back the veil the rest of the world willingly wears. For the first time in her life, this woman would see what I got to look at every damn day.

Heaven help you.

"Ah! My eyes!"

I yanked her into the light, but she resisted, pulling back and winding up for a wild swing with her purse. That purse never made contact—instead, the Shades tore it apart like tissue paper.

"What the hell are those?!"

"Exactly," I said, holding the door open and pulling her toward the darkness beyond.

Long and twisted fingers, like taffy stretched to the point of absurdity, twisted their way around her arm.

With eyes suddenly awakened, the woman panicked and struggled to break free of the Shade's grasp. "Get it off of me!"

I tilted the lamp shade forward, bathing her and the monsters in the old bulb's dull yellow glow. "Come on!"

A chorus of angry chittering surrounded us. They swirled like a black soap bubble on the weak halo of light.

"My bag!"

"Let it go," I said, holding the door open with my foot.

"But my—"

Lightning lit up the sky, cracking from cloud to cloud before arcing down to earth. The loud rumble of thunder followed immediately; then on its heels came something else.

It sounded like thunder, but having lived in Florida my whole life I knew wasn't.

Boom.

"What's that?"

The dim bulb flickered.

"Transformer," I said, biting my lip.

"Huh?"

"It's about to get really uncomfortable out here."

Shadows pressed in against the flickering light, their clicking mouths insatiable.

Come on, Gene. You don't know that. It might be another part of the grid, it's not necessarily right here—

I didn't get time to finish my mental pep-talk before the small lamp above our heads gave up its ghost, and in that instant dropped the two of us into a near perfect darkness.

A near perfect darkness surrounded by hungry Shades.

Damn, all this for a lousy bowl of black noodles.

* * *

THE LAST FEW seconds had been a blur of activity. Somehow I'd pulled the young woman inside and slammed the door behind us.

"Find a light switch!" I yelled, throwing my shoulder against the swinging metal.

Heels clicked on the hard floor. "I'm trying! Can they get inside?"

Outside Shade claws scraped at the rusty metal. "The door is steel, but it's not going to stop them for long. It would really help if you found some light."

Clang!

"What the hell was that?" I asked pressing a hand against the lock and desperately trying to call up some Magick.

"I think I found something."

Click.

A construction flood lamp blinded me with brilliant white light. Shades clamoring along the door seam screamed and pulled back into the darkness.

"Clauditis."

Thump.

The deadbolt was thrown, but that door wouldn't keep them out for long, we needed a more permanent solution.

"Give me your lipstick."

"What!?"

I pointed to the floor-to-ceiling glass of the storefront. "You want those Shades coming through that glass?"

"No!"

"Then I need your lipstick."

"Sure, it's in my purse. Let me get that for you—oh, right, I can't, because it's out in the alley with enough nightmare material for three lifetimes!"

"Shit."

Even though I couldn't see her behind the flood lamp, I'd been around enough women to know when they were nodding condescendingly—call it a sixth sense.

"How much is left on that battery?" I asked, shielding my eyes and leaving the door.

"I don't know. Do I look like an electricity person?"

Sigh. Deep breaths, Gene.

"You don't have to be an electrician to read the display. Show it to me."

She turned the tiny green screen to face me.

19%

"Great. Listen, sweetheart, we are stuck in here until the Shades either get what they came for, or move on to something even juicier. Now, until the power comes on we need to reduce the number of shadows and figure out some way to get a sigil up on that glass."

For the first time that night, the woman didn't have a snappy response.

"Ji," she said, after a few moments had gone by.

"Come again?"

"My name is Ji."

"Great, thanks," I said, taking a visual inventory of our surroundings.

"Now's when you tell me your name."

The store was clearly post-demo and pre-renovation. The floodlight sat on a pile of unmixed mortar bags and boxes of ornate tile. Bright blue grease pencil markings on the bare concrete let the crews know where and how to lay the tile, and it also gave me an idea.

"Grease pencil."

"Nice to meet you, Grease Pencil."

"Huh?"

"I asked you for your name."

I pushed aside a few boxes of tile before stopping to trace the perimeter of the room. "It's Gene. Can you walk and talk at the same time?"

"Yes."

"Good, then let's get both your jaws and your feet working. They may have left a grease pencil here. If you can find it, I can use it to get a sigil going on that wall of glass, because as it stands right now that glass is not going to stop a single Shade, let alone the horde outside that door."

At the sound of my words, the clawing Shades stopped.

"Okay, now we have to hurry."

"Why?" Ji asked, positioning herself behind the flood-lamp.

14%

"Because they just got quiet."

There has to be something here I can write with. I've never seen a job site where the crews didn't leave at least something *behind.*

A lump of leather and shiny metal caught my eye.

Tool belt—Yahtzee!

"Gene!" Ji's voice had the sharp edge of panic in it. "Look!"

Black and viscous Shades slid along the mist-covered glass, and I suddenly had the distinct feeling of being caught on the wrong side of an aquarium.

I scooped up the tool belt and picked through it: scraper, tape measure, triangle, rubber tile-spacers, but no grease pencil.

"Come on!"

"Gene!"

More inky darkness slithered over the glass, and drifting in that liquid midnight were many sets chattering teeth.

"Turn the light!" I shouted, tossing the tool belt.

Ji twisted the flood-lamp toward the glass, bathing the dark storefront in a burst of brilliant light.

13%

Shade screams clawed at my ears. "Good work, now we just need to hold out until they get the power turned back on, and then—"

Brain-freezing cold wrapped my leg and yanked me to the floor. Taking the light off the steel door had given the Shades a way inside; through the floor seam.

"Gene!" Ji shouted. "What do I do?"

I reached for my Magick, ready to impose my will upon reality, when the queasy taint of the House reared its ugly head. Each trip to the well was one step closer to becoming what the House wanted, to becoming the person I had swore I would never be.

Just use it, you'll be fine. Just this once. Go for something big. Show these Shades who's boss.

It was right there, near-limitless power, but directly

above it, squatting on the surface of my Magick, was the House and all it brought with it.

More twisted claws dug into my leg and pulled me toward the door and the massive Shade perched in front of it. The half-living creature's jaws quivered in anticipation, its mouth stretched wide to consume me whole.

The House or not, I needed my Magick, and I needed it now. I reached for the tainted well of power, but before I could dip my mind into it the flood-lamp swung again, obliterating the Shade and its soul-chilling grasp on my leg.

"Grease Pencil!"

"My name's—"

The thick blue pencil lay not far from the door's crack, practically smiling at me in the flood lamp's brilliant light.

"Shit, nice work!"

I scrambled for the pencil while behind me the glass wall rattled with the force of a hundred Shades.

"I've got it!"

Beep! Beep! Beep!

"What did I do?" Ji cried. "It says ten percent!"

"Just keep swinging it around."

Ji turned the flood-lamp like a booze-crazed party girl, kicking off her heels and twirling fast enough to make me wonder just how long she could keep that up before toppling over from dizziness, exhaustion, or both.

"Gene?!"

"Just keep turning," I said, throwing my body at the glass.

Shade mouths pried at the narrow seams in the storefront, digging into those cracks, hungry for the warm meat that lay just beyond.

I dragged the pencil across the glass, my fingers tracing circles within circles and lines piercing lines. I didn't do the Felberg's Shadowbox very often, and it took me more than a few seconds to remember it—seconds we didn't have.

Think, Gene. The lines intersect here? No, that's different. This one uses a square end, right?

The piercing wail of the flood-lamp ran roughshod of my memory.

"Five percent!"

Chattering faces pressed against the glass, their misshapen mouths reaching for me, clawing at the thick glass.

"I think I've got it."

"You think?" an exasperated Ji cried, her voice tired to the point of exhaustion.

"Yeah, turn the light on the rear door."

Shades slammed against the glass, their wailing quickly reaching a crescendo.

Ji stopped spinning and turned the light on the steel door... and that was right when my memory came roaring back to me.

You missed a line.

The Shades should have been stopped cold in their tracks, but instead without the light or the Shadowbox to keep them back they tore through the seams in the glass.

"Gene!"

"On it!"

Cold shadowy fingers were everywhere, so many my breath seized in my chest, but still I fought for the glass.

Just finish the line.

Shades slipped through like an unholy wave of terrible cold.

Somewhere behind me Ji screamed, and the battery-powered light flickered.

The pencil quivered in my fingers. The glass was so close now, just another few inches.

"Three percent!"

So close...

I stretched out, the blue tip gliding across the glass and finishing the missing line.

"Gene!"

I lost Ji's scream in the explosion of Magick that followed.

"Gene, wake up! Wake up!"

Delicate fingers slapped my stubble-ridden face. "Huh?"

I blinked my eyes in the dark.

The dark!

"Shit, Ji, give me the light, we need to—"

"Gene, it's okay. They're gone."

"What?"

The dim light of the moon filtered through the clouds and cut through the sigil-streaked glass. Ji was right, there were no hungry Shades clawing their way in to devour us.

"She's here."

I sat up and rubbed my eyes. "Who's here?"

Ji didn't respond; instead, she turned her eyes to the glass. She wasn't caught up in the majesty of my grease pencil blue masterwork. Ji was focused on what stood on the other side of it—her sister.

* * *

"Great," I said, pushing myself up to a seated position. "Tell her we'll be right there, just give me a few minutes for the room to stop spinning."

"I understand now."

I rubbed my head. "What do you understand? Listen, all of that was crazy. In a few days you'll forget most of it—that's just what happens. Don't take it the wrong way, but your brain just isn't wired to handle that sort of crazy, and the sooner it figures that out the better you'll be."

"She's been doing this to all of them."

"Huh?"

Bubblegum pink lips blew me a kiss from beyond the glass.

Ji dropped the construction light. "It all makes sense now."

"Come again? I've still got ringing in my ears."

Ji kept talking, but she wasn't looking at me—instead she directed her words at the younger sister standing just beyond the glass.

"It wasn't enough to have Dad's love, you had to take everything from me too?"

Ji's sister didn't move, but something behind her did.

Shades!

"Get the light, Ji! They're outside, your sister is a sitting duck!"

"No, she isn't."

Shades slithered over the younger girl's shoulder, twisting their inky bodies like a pet boa between her arms.

It was my turn to be confused. "What the hell?"

"Each date, anyone I even remotely cared for. They didn't just drop out of my life did, they? This was your doing."

The younger sister nodded, unleashing a perfectly white smile in the process, before stepping through the glass.

Magician! Shit, how did I miss that earlier?

"So you can see them now, huh? That's odd. It doesn't matter, you won't remember. You think this is the first time you've questioned your luck, big sister?"

Shades poured out of the young girl like a flag flapping in the wind. Hungry and chattering, the nightmares hovered mere feet away, held back purely by the force of the young girl's will.

The older sister shook her head. "But why?"

"You and your perfect life." The younger woman pantomimed her older sister. "Hi, I'm Ji, and everything is perfect for me." She swung her tiny hands up into fists then gave herself a gruff, paternal tone. "Why can't you be more like Ji? Her boyfriend is a doctor. *She* passed the bar. She is very smart. Why can't you be more like Ji?"

"I worked hard for—"

The younger sister dropped the act and practically growled her response. "Yeah? You did, huh? All those late nights and weekends? You think I don't look at your Insta? You burned through that money on booze and Adderall, and you thought I wouldn't figure it out?"

"I don't know what you're talking about. You can't prove anything."

"Always the lawyer, eh, Sis? You know something? You're right. I couldn't prove anything, not to Dad, and not to Mom when she was alive. They loved their Ji too much to believe me. But it doesn't sting as much anymore."

"Why's that?"

"Because now I get to watch you eat your Jajangmyeon and I laugh. You drone on and on about the injustices of men and your terrible love-life and I practically giggle inside."

"Dad set you up with a job at the family business."

"Slinging noodles for guys like him?" the younger sister feigned a swoon. "You're right, oh how did I not see it? I get to be queen of the broth bowl. All hail, Madam Noodle!"

"At least you have Dad…"

"Do I? What's the point of living with him when he hates me? Every move I make is held up to the majesty that is Ji. How many kind words do you think that brings me? How many times do you think Dad says he's proud of me?"

Shades clamored in the tight confines of the room. Ji's sister might not have been a full Magician, but she'd mastered the art of controlling the half-living, and that took skill, along with insights from a book I'd once owned. "I'm sure your Dad loves you both, I've got a daughter myself and—"

"Shut up!" both women said in unison.

Shades inched closer, their clicking teeth grating on my nerves like fingers on a chalk board.

Ji pushed me back. "You think I wanted any of this? You think I wanted to go to law school? You think I like living up to his expectations? Every day it's an uphill climb. All those words of praise you think you aren't getting—well, don't believe for one minute they're headed my way, cause they aren't."

Pop!

In the distant dark, a street light flickered on.

Come on, Tampa Electric...

The older sister turned to me, her voice changed. "What are you waiting for, Gene? A signed invitation?"

The House!

"What are you talking about?" the younger sister said, the Shades churning around her.

"Ignore her," Ji said, drawing me in with her eyes. "You have a job to do, remember?"

"But she's just a kid!"

"Hardly. Don't let the pink lipstick fool you. Her soul's as black as the Shades she consorts with."

Magick tingled in my fingers.

No!

"Yes." The House's walnut-brown eyes were mesmerizing in the moonlight. "You don't get to pick and choose, Gene, that's not how this works. You get exactly what I tell you."

My Magick surged, the well of power boiling over with the House's will, and Ji's little sister took notice. "Ji, he's like me. Get back!"

The older sister spun around, her eyes flashing in the distant light of the popping street lamps. "Wrong, Sun, he's nothing like you. He doesn't play with fire, he *is* fire."

The Shades hesitated, their chittering uncertain in the halo of the House's power.

"Get away from him," the younger sister pleaded. "I don't want to hurt you."

The House was in command now and pushing back. "That's all you've ever wanted to do, and I've got to tell you, kid, I admire that. You've done some pretty impressive stuff. I've never been big on the half-living, but you've managed to get them coordinated and semi-functional—not half bad, but you don't hold a candle to him."

The younger sister's tears appeared in the flash of another street lamp "Ji…"

"Oh, come on. You know who I am. I'm sure he told you." The House practically beamed.

"I…"

Ji swung her hair back. "You think you could cuddle up with Shades and somehow *not* get my attention? You've got a knack for insidious revenge, cutie, and my earlier days I would have totally gone in for that sort of thing. However, day late and a dollar short, you know?"

Little sister struggled for words. "Ji—"

"Finish her, Gene."

Magick bubbled up like stomach acid, and I fought the surge of power that crackled in my hands. It was a dark power, a force of destruction and entropy that yearned for a target.

"No!"

Ji turned her attention back to me. "I'm sorry? Did you forget the deal? Are we going to play the game of what happens to Porter, Cathy, and little Kris if you don't listen?"

"I'm not a murderer!"

More street lights burst to life, but not enough to disperse the chattering horde of Shades.

Ji placed a soft hand on my chest. Her warm fingers

splayed out like daggers against my heart. "Gene, let me make this really clear for you. You are whatever I say you are. If I say you are a murderer, then you get your big boy murdering pants on and you murder someone."

"Ji, get back! I can stop him!"

The Magick rumbled. I couldn't hold it back much longer, and there was zero chance little sister would fare any better.

Ji smiled at her younger sibling. "Honey, there is no world where you can untie his sandals. I should know, I've seen them all."

Lights flooded the sidewalk from the small shops across the street, and the Magick inside swelled.

Hold it back, Gene. You can do it. Just a few more seconds...

The House's warm eyes glittered. "Do it, Gene—now!"

Shades surged, unleashed by a kid who knew just enough to be dangerous, but not enough to know better.

Knowledge is power.

Clicking jaws and soul-stealing cold met the brilliant explosion of light and Magick. The power of 69 Mallory Lane erupted, but I wasn't completely lost—deep down there was still a little Eugene Law, and he was still a real sono-fabitch.

"Obliviscatur!"

The blinding Magick peeled the poor girl's mind like a ripe fruit, cutting out memories with the delicacy of a hack saw.

The book—my book—and a young man's face streamed past. I knew that face: it appeared in my dreams. It had lit the fires of my new life, and I would snuff it out.

Tristan.

* * *

"She won't remember anything?" Ji asked, taking a seat next to me on the park bench.

"No."

The older sister blinked back tears. "And I won't either?"

"Not really. This will all seem like a bad dream, and eventually you'll forget it altogether."

Her hands were shaking, but still brought warmth to mine. "You saved my life."

"Nah, your sister wouldn't have hurt you—but I'm pretty sure she would have tried to kill me."

"I found these in her pocket," Ji said, shoving some pages from the stolen grimoire into my hands. "Are they yours?"

"Yeah, I kept an eye on them in another life—a life I want to get back."

Ji's little sister groaned quietly on the soft grass.

"She'll wake up soon. She's going to need a good sister to help her back get on her feet."

Ji nodded. "I will."

"I know." I gave the raven-haired woman one last hug, savoring the human contact for a few more seconds before letting go.

Ji wiped her eyes. "Brooksville."

"What?"

"When they broke-up she said he left for Brooksville."

Tristan.

SOULLESS

"Gene, no!"

Ariadne's Thread stretched out before me, an ethereal lifeline to a world now just beyond my reach. A fiery wind danced the silver cord like a kit string. It was the only thing holding me back from oblivion.

"I love you," I cried, clinging to that strand even as the library's fire roared around me.

"You don't know what love is," he said, just as he'd said hundred times before. It didn't matter how hard I screamed, or how I replayed the vision in my head, it always ended the same.

He cut it.

That moment, that singular soul-crushing instant where I knew I'd failed, where I knew there was no going back, caught like a skipping CD in my mind.

You failed.

It wasn't enough to see it break, my mind made sure I felt it too, again and again in soul-searing detail, and each time it did, it brought the pain.

Fire consumed my body like a matchstick, and I swung

my hands desperate to slow my fall into the library's unknown depths.

"No!"

Splash.

I hit the water hard and struggled to orient myself. The sudden shock of cold sent me clawing for what I hoped was the surface. Everything fought me: my boots, my jacket, all of my clothes wanted to drag me down into that inky dark, but I had to keep pushing.

My lungs screamed out for air.

Please!

I broke through to the air and sucked it down in wild gasps, then pushed through the deep water toward a nearby bank. Heavy in the Sojourner's Jacket, my arms fought me with each push, the muddy water soaking the already thick sleeves. Reluctantly, I let it go, slipping my pale arms out and letting the coat fall into the abyss. Next went my boots. They vanished the instant I kicked them off and sunk to a murky bottom I hoped to never see.

Exhausted and soaked through, I dragged myself onto the sandy beach. Trying to catch my breath, I lay in the soft muck and stared up at the dim half-light of a charcoal sky. Angry and boiling clouds glared at me through a canopy of tall cypress, whose wide roots soaked in the black and muddy water. The rolling sky twisted and turned, and with it came the visions: Gene's face, the breaking Thread, the library's doors.

The library...

A faint wind rustled the cypress, cutting through my wet clothes and making me wish I'd kept the jacket.

I'm on the inside.

I'd been inside the library before. An ill-fated attempt at a jailbreak that—thanks to Gene—had ended badly.

And now you're in here with them...

"Focus, Morgan," I said to no one but myself, and secretly hoped if there was someone listening they wouldn't notice the fear in my words.

I crawled out of the cold muck toward a relatively dry looking patch of rich dirt, and pushed aside the decaying leaves and broken branches until I had a blank canvas to work with, then set to work drawing the sigil.

Remember who you are.

My name is Morgan Crowley, and I am a failure.

I pressed my fingers into the soft earth and traced the circles, lines, and their intersections from memory.

Jelker's Warmth. It warms the hands and the heart.

I was almost finished when my shivering fingers broke the smooth line into jagged dashes.

Do it again, you stupid bitch.

I flinched. I wasn't sure why, it was weak and I knew it, but Dad's voice did that to me, even when it was only between my ears.

I clenched my jaws and swept away the sigil in a fit of frustration.

How can you be so careless?

I took a deep breath and forced the old man's words into that deep, dark, hole I made for him years ago. It took a few calming breaths before he faded and I could start again.

The asshole might have been gone, but he was never far away.

Jelker's Warmth.

This one Mom had taught me—the old man never liked it when I used mom's Magick.

"Morgan, it's simple. You can do it, I know you can. The line curves like this," she'd said, guiding my finger through the ash. "Think of the flame—how it dances on the cold night. Yes, perfect."

I smiled, my teeth chattering as my fingers once again carved a path through the black earth.

Try not to fuck it up this time.

My smile vanished, as I bit my lip and closed the sigil, lining up the Magick like the wheels of a great clock.

"That's it, honey. Magick isn't lawless, it follows rules—like everything in this world. Keys fit their locks, and wheels roll in their grooves. Let the Magick follow the path you've made for it. Guide it like the banks of a mighty river."

Thanks, Mom.

"Ignis," I whispered, letting the Magick flow into the perfectly drawn sigil. It twisted and turned across those lines, bringing with it a bright and roaring fire that sprung to life from the wet earth, its warm glow quickly taking the cold from my fingers.

Take that, Dad.

No sooner had I thought those words than the Magickal fire flickered. I held my breath and for a moment questioned everything: the design, the sigil, myself. Thankfully, that hesitation didn't last, and after a few tense moments Jelker's Warmth was doing exactly what it was supposed to do. I just wished I could say the same for my mind. Now that the old man had made an appearance he wasn't going away without a fight.

So, here you are, muddy like gutter trash and warming your shitty little fingers over one of your mother's parlor tricks. Is that what I taught you? Look at yourself.

I crawled back to the edge of the black water, only to find a reflection I hardly knew staring back up at me.

Mud streaked my hair, the bright green I'd dyed it already fading in the dark of the swamp.

I straightened the tangles and picked at the dead leaves that had taken up residence behind my ears.

How did this happen? I was so careful.

I tried to trace the events that lead me here, but Dad's voice kept throwing me off track.

You let him get to you. You let him inside—you are weak. Did you learn anything I taught you? Magick is precision, dedication, focus—all of which you lack. If you could only focus on something, even for a few minutes, you might have actually prevented all of this.

I slammed my fist into the black water, shattering the shameful reflection. "I was focused. I had everything prepared."

Everything? Sounds to me like someone is making excuses. That's loser talk. Are you a loser, Morgan? Only failures raise failures. Are you calling me a failure?

"No, Dad," I said, startled to hear my broken voice in the cold swamp air.

Good, now go dry off. You look like hell.

I nodded and crawled back to the fire, huddling in front of the flames as my mind ran itself in circles trying to figure out how I'd failed.

He's more powerful than you guessed.

That thought caused me to chuckle. Gene was powerful, sure, but he was also ignorant. He didn't understand the true complexities of Magick. He was wild and erratic—sure they hit hard, but wild haymakers only land so many times. The boy couldn't see beyond what was right in front of him.

He saw beyond you.

I shook my head and tossed a broken branch into the fire. That was luck, pure and simple. Gene wasn't some master Magician, he was a kid, a kid that got lucky.

Luck maybe, but he had help.

Ed Lovely.

The very thought of Gene's roommate sent me searching for more branches to break.

Without Ed, Gene would have failed countless times.

That was my first mistake, not finishing the roommate problem. I'd counted on a Death Shroud, something I should never have done.

A strong woman would have done it herself. If only you were a strong woman, like Porter.

I grabbed another branch and snapped it against my knee. *Porter.*

Ed might have been a problem, but he was nothing compared to Porter. She'd found a way to get to Gene, to take him from me. But how?

Love.

"Ha!" I blurted out, again surprised at the jagged edge to my voice. "Can you love a tree, Gene? Maybe you two will have nice acorns together."

He'll save her.

I shook that thought away.

No, he won't. He's not focused, and he doesn't understand Magick. He wields it like a child with a new toy truck, he won't... he can't.

He will.

I threw more branches into the fire, letting Jelker's Magickal flames consume the wet wood and send a small plume of smoke into the misty air.

You underestimated him.

"Thanks, Dad. I hadn't figured that out yet. Tell me something, did you underestimate me? How'd that work out for you?"

My father's voice faded, no doubt crawling back into that hole in my mind where he laid in wait for my next misstep. And when that time came he would spring out again like a trapdoor spider and inject his venomous thoughts.

Crack!

The breaking branch didn't come from my fire. It came from just beyond the thick cypress trees.

Your smoke has attracted visitors.

I spun, putting my back to the flames and tracing the edges of the dense cypress. Dad was right, the smoke drifting in the sky behind me must have been visible for miles, and my vocal outbursts weren't helping anything.

What do I do?

Crack!

Something moved in the thick brush, and once again I felt the panic rising in my chest, except this time I had no Magick prepared, no sigils, no seals—nothing between me and whatever shifted beyond the tree line but the thin fabric of my damp clothes.

It was in that moment, when I was neck deep and racing through Magickal options like a mad fool, that my visitor stepped out from behind a wide trunk.

You aren't alone.

I grabbed the first stick I could find and held it in front of me.

Thanks, Dad. I never would have guessed.

* * *

Run!

I shook off that base instinct and tightened my grip on the branch.

Crowleys don't run.

I squeezed my fingers around the damp wood and took a few practice swings while the old spider in my head twisted in his web.

Crowleys are precise, focused, and most of all prepared. Sadly, you are none of these things.

I kicked aside the broken twigs and leaves around my feet, immediately reminded of the idiocy of removing my boots.

The man wasn't tall, but he wasn't exactly small either. He was taller than Gene, but not by much. Inwardly I snarled at the fact that the first man I compared him to was Eugene Law.

Get him out of your head.

The man wore a mismatched set of clothing that appeared to have been picked up one item at a time from thrift stores and costume outlets. His pirate-like puffy sleeves clashed terribly with what looked like dirty sweatpants. He did have a one up on me though; he had shoes— caked with mud and practically growing their own moss, but they still beat the hell out of standing on sharp sticks barefoot. His short hair looked like it had been cut without the benefit of a mirror. Uneven and sandy, it shot out at odd angles and curled hopelessly behind his ears.

Prepare yourself, Morgan.

I wound the mental clock in my head, its gears tightening and swinging into place.

Gene is stronger.

I closed my eyes and fought my father's voice back into its hole. It wasn't easy. Once out and about, the spider loved to prowl the dark recesses of my subconscious ready to inject doubt. Gene was stronger, but he lacked precision, focus, and knowledge.

Lovinger's Mourning? No, not enough time. The Seven Confusions? Not enough feathers.

A dozen different Magickal options rolled through the flash cards in my mind, but not one of them was a fit for the situation at hand. I just didn't have anything for barefoot and chilled to the bone.

For you, failure is always an option.

The man stopped to admire the waning flames of Jelker's Warmth, passing his dirty hands above what remained of my sigil fire. Those weren't the hands of someone that needed warmth, they were the hands of someone playing with the gentle tips of flame like an old friend.

Or a lover.

"Beautiful."

His voice was odd; I couldn't place the accent. Dad and I had travelled extensively, and not always places I would have wanted to go. Still, the oddly melodic twist to the strangers words didn't fit anything we'd run into.

No remarks, eh, Dad?

My father's biting tongue was nowhere to be found—no doubt lying in wait for the next mistake.

The stranger gently traced his finger along the outer edge of my sigil, careful to not disrupt the fading Magick. "Is good work."

I took a deep breath and evaluated my options. Damsel in distress? No, can't appear weak until I know what I can gain. Tatiana Tough Tits? No, I have no shoes and a soaking wet top, that's not going to play. Sally Seductress? I had more in common with Sally Swampwater than anything remotely seductive.

You work with what you have.

"Thanks," I said, feeling out the tone in his voice. It wasn't hard—I'd been doing it since as far back as I could remember. It was an important skill to master—separating fact from fiction and drawing out intent like a snake's venom.

Caution, daughter.

I shook Dad's voice out of my head and let the branch in my hand drop.

I got this, Dad. Just watch.

I folded my arms beneath my breasts, just enough to look both cold and alluring all in the same instant. "It's so cold, isn't it?" I asked, letting my voice soften. Not too much, but enough to take the edge off and see just how receptive the stranger was.

"It's one of my favorite designs," he said, stepping back to give me room. Up close he was perhaps a little taller than I gave him credit for, but still, nothing to worry about. It was that accent I couldn't place, a melody that at once sounded both old and oddly new.

"Jelker's Warmth?" I said, keeping a sharp eye on his reactions. "It's an old one, but it works in a pinch"

The stranger tilted his head at me, as if confused by the words coming out of my mouth. "Jelker's Warmth? That's not what I named it. This is the Stubborn Fire."

I had to bite my tongue. If I'd had a nickel for every time some male Magician wanted to explain Magick to me, I'd have long since bought a private island and filled it with their screams. That was Jelker's Warmth, and I knew it. Still, I had to keep up the act, at least until I knew what this odd duck was about.

"Are you sure?" I asked, leaning in enough to show off just a tiny bit more hardly innocent cleavage. "I've always known this as Jelker's Warmth—a fire to warm the hands… and the heart."

You're laying it on too thick, daughter.

I gently shook my head, letting it look as if I was getting the hair out of my eyes.

Shut the hell up, old man.

"Young lady, I am Alexander Jelker, and this is my sigil. It is the Stubborn Fire."

Young lady! Shrug it off. Don't take the bait. He's playing you like a worm on a hook. Focus, Morgan.

"Nice try, but Alexander Jelker would be over five hundred years old," I said, letting out an innocent laugh. "And you don't look a day over thirty."

"Five hundred years?" His face fell. "Has it been that long? What year is it?"

"Last I checked it was nineteen ninety-five."

The odd man clutched at his gut like he'd taken a sucker punch I hadn't seen. "Nineteen hundred?"

"Yeah."

Is this guy really Jelker? I mean, the Jelker?

No, he's got to be lying.

But his body language is saying otherwise.

Before the well-preserved five-hundred-year-old could respond a shrill howl rung out across the dense swamp. Alien and soul-shuddering, the sound set the hairs on my already cold arms on edge. "What was that?"

Jelker's eyes searched the horizon, almost frantically. "Blackhearts."

"What?!"

Blackhearts, Morgan. You remember, don't you?

The old spider spun my memories into a dark tapestry of our first trip together.

"Don't touch it, Morgan." My father pointed at the taxidermy beast rearing up, its claws and fangs shining in the dusty light.

"I won't."

"Do you know what this is?"

"A wolf?"

Somewhere behind me an older man chuckled, his voice thick with smoke. "That's a Blackheart. Magick eaters of the Stalgorian Wastes."

"The eyes, Morgan, look at the eyes."

Twisted and soulless, the eyes of the Blackheart shimmered in a rich purple haze.

"Can you see them?"

"Yes—"

I didn't get to finish my thought before his hand hit my face. The stinging palm striking hard enough to leave a mark and bring tears to my eyes. "Good, now, never look at them again. A Blackheart's eyes will shatter even a great Magician's focus, to say nothing of your weak mind. Never forget that if you value your life."

"Yes, Father."

The vision faded, but the howling didn't.

"You know what Blackhearts are?" Jelker asked, reaching for my arm. "We have to go."

"Go? Go where?" I picked up the stick I'd dropped moments ago. "What we need is defensive Magick. Can you keep them busy while I erect Eldero's Ninth Seal?"

Jelker hesitated, his eyes torn between me and the tree line. "No, not here. There's a house. It's not far. If we run, we can make it."

My bare feet dug into the cold earth. "Not without shoes I can't. The seal is our best option. If you really are Alexander Jelker, then you know that. Take that Stubborn Fire and make us an inferno."

The Magician crouched and reached for my sigil, while I set to work tracing the first lines of Eldero's Ninth Seal. I hadn't completed the initial whorl before Jelker's shout broke my concentration.

"Blackhearts!"

The shadowy wolves broke the tree line in jagged groups, their wide paws digging at the soft earth. Thick fur covered their backs and did very little to conceal the dense muscles underneath. Sharp teeth glistened in the fading light, while their guttural growls rattled my ribs.

"Jelker, the fire!"

The Magician backed away from my modest campfire, its flames dying slowly.

"We can make it if we run," he cried, reaching for my hand.

Finish the Seal, daughter.

"No, we can't—"

"The swamp gets deeper just beyond here, we can outrun them," Alexander Jelker's hand reached for mine, "I promise."

Howl!

I tossed the branch aside and left the half-finished seal in time to grab his cold hand, expecting the shock of a lifetime when I touched his fingers.

Nothing.

Alexander Jelker, one of the greatest Magicians in the last millennia, had no Magick—not a single drop.

* * *

No Magick!

My mind ran in circles at the thought, leaving a deep groove of confusion. If this really was Alexander Jelker, then what had happened to his Magick?

And will the same thing happen to me?

Blackheart howls echoed between the narrow cypress and sent those worries packing—we had much more pressing concerns. It was impossible to tell if they were gaining, but judging by Jelker's sense of urgency there was a very good chance they were.

"Come on." He yanked my hand and pulled me over a fallen trunk. My feet screamed out in protest, but I bit back the pain. I'd endured worse—the old man had seen fit to that.

"Again!" Dad shouted, cracking the wrapped bamboo across my shoulder blades. "That sigil is sloppy, therefore the Magick in it will be sloppy. Is sloppy Magick what we do here?"

"No," I bit my tongue at the sharp pain.

"No, what?"

"No, sir."

Dad dragged his foot through the soft sand and shattered

my near perfect design. "Good. Now, do it again, this time with focus."

Focus.

Dad had been right about one thing: never underestimate the power of laser-like focus.

I used that skill now to push the pain in my feet aside and keep pace with the much faster Magician ahead of me.

We broke the tree line and hit a wide clearing. Tall grass swayed gently in the soft breeze and surrounded a small cottage. If the three little pigs lived here, I wouldn't have been surprised. This was their kind of dwelling—thick-packed mud holding together loose logs under a thatch roof. A thin line of smoke drifted above its bent chimney.

"Hurry!" Jelker shouted, the concern in his voice pushing me faster and driving me toward the cypress plank door. "They're almost upon us."

Blackheart howls sent shivers down my damp back, but Dad's warning kept me from looking back.

I shook my head, forcing the memories away and focusing all my attention on the cottage's small door. Hot breath nipped at my heels. Was it a Blackheart or my imagination? I didn't dare stop to find out.

Jelker hit the door first, his boots far more effective than my bruised and bloodied feet. He pulled the rope handle and swung the cypress planks wide. "Inside!"

I didn't need to be told twice. I pumped my legs and willed myself over the narrow stoop, then threw my body into the warm glow of the cottage.

Bang!

Jelker pulled the door shut behind us, the flimsy boards rattling against the ramshackle frame. "Get me something to brace it." He pointed to a thick log laying against the wall.

Blackheart howls set me in motion, and I didn't have my

hands around the thick trunk before the door began to open against Jelker's thin arms.

He pushed with his legs, but not before the snapping jaws of a Blackheart slipped inside. "Argh!"

The eyes, do not look at the eyes.

I dragged the log and looked away. Anything to keep from seeing their eyes.

"Come on," he cried, pushing back against the burgeoning door. "They're going to get inside!"

The Blackheart's jaws snapped at the air, its teeth long and crooked in the cottage's warm light.

The eyes.

I dragged the log across the floor and used the last of my strength to push it up against the door. Jelker spun around and kicked at the ferocious snout until it vanished.

Together the Magician and I wedged the long trunk in place, pinning the door and sealing us in. We scrambled backward, only to collapse in a heap on an animal skin rug in the center of the one-room shack.

The snarls and banging continued, the beasts clearly displeased to be on the opposite side of those mud and log walls.

Focus, Morgan.

I pushed Dad's voice back and let the smoky air fill my burning lungs. I hadn't run like that in a long time, and it showed. Jelker, for his part, appeared to be in far better shape. He rolled to his knees and checked the log-brace keeping us from becoming Blackheart feed. I, on the other hand, checked my feet, and as soon as I did I was wishing I hadn't. They were black and blue, and streaked with blood. I was sure to lose a toe nail in the not too distant future. The pain that I had most expertly blotted out only minutes ago came back like an unwanted guest.

"Your feet." Jelker let go of the brace and retrieving a

wooden bucket from above his fire. The small cooking fire in the center of the room was low, its only fuel a thick black moss that curled slowly beneath the weak flames.

So much for Jelker's Warmth—or should I say the Stubborn Fire.

"Let me help you." He brought the steaming bucket near my bloody feet. "We need to keep them clean." Jelker set it down and retrieved a small stool. "Here, sit. Soak your feet."

"What's in that?"

"Jellyweed, it grows wild here. It will help with the pain."

I frowned at the soupy concoction. "It'll also make my feet numb. I don't need Jellyweed. I'll heal."

Jelker shook his head. "Not here you won't. Look at your feet."

The odd Magician was right, my feet weren't healing, not in the way I was accustomed to. "Just give it a minute."

"Young lady, you could give it a hundred minutes and it'll still bleed. Worse, by then it will be infected, and you will not survive infection. I don't care how much Magick you have left. Soak your feet in the Jellyweed."

"Left?" I asked, listening to the Blackheart paws scrape the tiny cottage's log frame. "What do you mean 'left?'"

Jelker ignored me, and instead pointed at the bucket at my feet. "You think they won't find a way in? We need you at your strongest if we want to survive."

The pain in my feet was immense, so much so I started to wonder if he wasn't kidding. I should have healed more by now, but instead the throbbing of my toes and ankles only increased.

Jelker pointed to the bucket. "Please, I need you if we're going to survive."

I dropped onto the stool and frowned as it creaked in protest. "We don't have time for this. Those Blackhearts are going to break through that door any minute and we are sitting ducks in here. I've got to get my Magick going."

"And you will," Jelker said, pointing toward the bucket. "But the infection will set in long before you finish. You ran barefoot through Daffel, look at your toes."

He was right, as much as I hated to admit it. It wasn't just scrapes and cuts, it was worse. Broken stems and crushed Daffel flowers, faintly yellow in the fire's light shined up at me.

Daffel flowers, poison in the blood stream. You have no choice, daughter, once again your lack of foresight has all but doomed you.

I plunged my feet into the nigh boiling Jellyweed, sending a fresh wave of pain rocketing up my battered legs. But I didn't cry out. I kept my mouth clamped shut.

Never let them see you suffer.

Had he been here, I would have punched my old man right in his squared-off jaws. But he wasn't, my only companion were the soft and almost baby-like cheeks of Alexander Jelker.

"There," he said, crawling closer to get a better look. "Was that so bad?"

"Yes," I said, my teeth still clamped together. The Jelly-weed was already fast at work pulling the Daffel poison from my flesh, but it was also busy doing what Jellyweed did best —removing all feeling from my legs.

"So, do you always keep a boiling bucket of Jellyweed on the fire, or is it just for the special girls?"

Jelker let out a long sigh and stood up, slowly rolling up his sleeves. "Only for the special ones."

There was something to his words, a subtle sadness I hadn't noticed before. But now, as the Jellyweed worked its way up my past my knees I noticed it, and it sent shivers down my spine.

"What are you doing?" I asked, my tongue thick and

unruly, like an oversized caterpillar languishing in my mouth.

"Shh, it's best if you don't struggle," he said, slowly pulling the bracing log from the door. "Once I have what I need, I promise to end it quickly."

Run, fight, do something damn it.

My mind cried out for action, but the Jellyweed muted its pleas. The noxious plant was stronger than I'd thought. It had already numbed my legs completely and was now working its way up far enough to make my arms all but useless.

"Blackhearts," I said, my tongue tripping over the word.

"Yes, vile creatures, but necessary for survival." Alexander tossed the log aside and gently pushed open the door. A gentle breeze drifted in on the cold night air, chilling my bones and making my bare shoulders shiver.

The eyes!

I did my best to look away, but the Jellyweed was too deep now, and it sapped what little strength I had left. All I could do was watch as the deep and shimmering purple eyes caught the light of the fading fire and stared through me.

* * *

MY VISION DRIFTED in and out, clear in one instant and watery the next.

Jelker retrieved a rag from somewhere in his sweatpants and in the next moment it was covering his eyes. "I'd almost given up, you know that?"

My head lolled to one side. Looking into the Blackheart's shimmering eyes was like staring into the sun.

"It's true," Jelker said, his melodic voice equal parts mesmerizing and soul-crushing. "I've been out here so long I didn't think I'd find another, but then you came along and landed right in my backyard."

Heavy paws padded into the tiny cottage, the Blackhearts' thick hides bunching together as they pushed their way through the narrow entrance. "I might not have found you before the others had you not used my Sigil. What were the chances? A thousand to one? A million? But here we are —kismet."

"Others?" I asked, my brain moving slower by the second, my thoughts congealing like cold oatmeal.

"Yes, the others. Velcurses, Gorbel, and rumor has it even Ten Spins himself is trapped here. I haven't seen him, but I have seen others. It's not safe around them, they have accumulated more Magick than I have, but thanks to you I will be able to heal, and to prepare my defenses. I felt more than enough power in your body to get me through the next winter, and maybe the one after that."

I wanted to close my eyes, but the Blackhearts' stares were too strong. They drew me in like a fly to honey and held me fast.

"Don't fight it," Jelker said, feeling around for a large stick leaning against the wall. "Let the alpha have his prize, and afterwards I promise I'll give you a swift death."

The largest of the Blackhearts pushed its massive snout against my chin, propping up my face and licking my cheek. This wasn't a playful kiss—I was being tasted.

Again the recesses of my mind called out for movement, but the creature's eyes were too strong, and the Jellyweed had made me too pliable, too soft.

Wake up, Morgan! You must fight it. I raised a stronger woman than this. Dig deep and find the will!

I shook my head, or at least I thought I did, nothing appeared to move.

There's nothing I can do.

I was defeated, broken, and a failure. I didn't have the strength to fight the Jellyweed, and nothing could stop the

Blackheart's eyes. I let my shoulders go and my head drift, watching as the beast opened its wide maw, those jagged teeth aiming for my soft neck. Just beyond the monster's thick hide, Jelker raised the heavy stick to his shoulder, his knuckles whitening along the shaft. "I'm sorry to have to do this to you, especially once I saw the sigil. It is so humbling to be remembered."

Remember, Morgan. You need to remember...

The spider in my mind tugged at the gossamer threads of memory, spinning them into yet another tapestry of the past.

"Your old man is not exactly right," the smoking man said, once my father had moved out of earshot. "The Blackheart's eyes aren't unbeatable."

"They aren't?"

The wide man blew a perfectly round smoke ring and let it drift over the stuffed beast like a well placed collar. "Well, they could be, unless you're more cunning."

"Cunning?"

The man placed a heavy hand on my shoulder, his fingers uncomfortable against my chest. "It's like wrestling, little bird. Do you know wrestling?"

"Some."

His fingers squeezed harder, and I bit my lip.

"Good, you must show me sometime—when you're older of course."

His hand lifted and with it the memory began to fade. "Just remember what the deadliest animal is and you'll be fine."

"What is it?"

The smoke ring faded. "Easy, child. The one that wants it more."

The Blackheart's eyes filled my vision, the vibrant purple blotting out the cottage, Jelker, and everything else. It was only the eyes.

Who wants it more?

Somewhere in the depths of those midnight circles something moved, something deep within me. The spider in my mind shuddered, scurrying away at the sight of it.

Is this the end, Morgan Crowley? Or is this the beginning?

The Blackheart's teeth pressed against my neck, and somewhere I knew Jelker readied the winnowing blow.

Who is more cunning?

The wound clock of my Magick stirred, its gears pressed tight together, too tight lest they rupture.

I am.

There were no words, no sigils, and no seals, there was only the Magick. Jelker was right—what had once been an inexhaustible bounty had been reduced to a pauper's pence, but it was Magick, and the Blackheart was hungry for it.

I released the clock springs and let my Magick flow, not at the Blackheart, but at Alexander Jelker himself. I knew his seals, his sigils, and I knew him. Each beating, each painful lesson at the hands of my old man was, at its heart, a lesson in how the mind worked.

Understand the Magician, and you will understand his Magick.

I understood Alexander Jelker, and I knew how to send him my power.

He wasn't ready for it.

The river overflowed its banks, my Magick crashing like a whitecap and knocking him to the ground. Instantly the jaws vanished, as all three Blackhearts pounced on the unprepared Magician.

His screams melted away, lost in the soft gurgling of tearing flesh and cracking bone.

I tumbled forward, still weak from the Jellyweed, but knowing I only had so much time before it was gone. I looped a hand around the largest Blackheart's neck, pulling it away from the Magickal blood feast and bringing its eyes level with my own. The shimmering purple no longer brought fear, but hope.

I siphoned what Magick I could before letting the beasts return to their meal, our minds now one and focused on the task at hand.

Jelker's Magick, my Magick, returned to me, tightening the clock and winding its gears. Glorious precision shut up the spider in my head and sent him crawling back into this hole. I knew he'd be back, that was a given, but I'd grown accustomed to him, and my head wouldn't feel right without his acerbic thoughts and constant honing.

The Blackhearts continued their feast and filled the air with fragments of memory. These weren't like the finely woven tapestry of my past, but they brought with them enough to fill in the gaps. Jelker wasn't the only Magician trapped in here, not by a long shot. There were others, and they were powerful.

But are they cunning?

I left the Blackhearts to their meal, content to curl up against the faint fire and wait for the Jellyweed to subside, my mind drifting in the heady mixture of Magick and memories.

Jelker was the first, and arguably the easiest, but there would be more. This prison was full of Magician's clinging to life and struggling to survive in a dark and Magickless existence.

One down, and many, many more to go...

TEN TURNS

*B*ad music crackled from a tiny set of speakers in the backwater bar. It echoed against the cheap panel walls and bounced over gouged and stained tables. The tinny and static-filled melody drifted through the smoky air, catching on the eddies of cigarette ash before ending up in my ears.

I tried to enjoy it, but the backseat driver in my head had other ideas.

"Sit down."

This is a bar, I'm not twenty-one. They're going to—

"Sit down."

He was stronger now. How many years had it been? It was hard to remember a time before the voice. In the beginning, I'd found ways to skirt the edges of his requests, now I had very little choice. I took a seat at the bar, pulling out a wooden stool sure to be painful.

It was the little things.

Is this better?

My name is Tristan Shelldeck. At least I think that's my

name. There are days I can't remember anymore, and truth be told, I'm not sure I want to.

Sal's Bar wasn't a place you'd find in the guide books, and it certainly wasn't a place I should have been in at night, but that didn't stop him from sending me here.

The old voice grumbled at the cushion-less seat. He wasn't much for irritation.

"I need to work—try to stay quiet. He's been here and I need to know what he knows."

I signaled the matronly woman behind the bar and received a scowl for my efforts. A few dollars later I got a soda. It wasn't much, nor was it cold, but it would do.

Eugene Law.

Everywhere we went, it was always about Cathy's dad. I'd criss-crossed the state, that infernal book in my pack, a cresting wave of forced enlightenment in my wake, and all of it to keep tabs on one Magician.

The voice grew irritated. "Turn around. I need to see the room. Do it slowly."

Magick.

The first time I'd felt it, it had sucked the wind from my chest and left me dumbfounded. I'd never experienced anything like it. The depth and breadth of reality at my command, the connectedness of all things splayed out like an open book in front of me.

Mr. Law.

Cathy's dad walked past as a hazy specter of memory. He was rough around the edges, the fine details missing like low-grade film. I could tell it was him, but he looked bad, really bad. Somewhere along the way he'd grown a patchy beard, most likely from lack of caring more than any conscious effort. His black jacket was wet with rain, something we'd had a lot of recently.

"This is recent," the voice said, more to himself than me.

Something red and unpleasant looking flashed in and out of view and scrambled to extract itself from Gene's grip.

Is that...

"That's an Imp, and a powerful one if memory serves."

Cathy's dad tucked the diminutive Demon beneath the folds of his jacket. He made his way toward the back of the bar, pushing past grainy musicians playing on a now empty stage and a trio of large men taking a more than casual interest in the Magician and his unruly cargo.

"Washroom, now."

I just got this soda and—

My calf cramped up and sent me sliding off the stool, then limping across the dirty floor.

"Much better. Now, washroom."

I stumbled past the mostly empty tables, drawing the predatory attention of my own group of tattooed gentlemen before reaching the men's room.

"Go inside."

Sigh.

I yanked open the door only to be greeted by the aroma of stale cigarettes and urine.

Why are we here?

"Do not interrupt me."

Gene's not here.

The voice's obsession with Eugene Law was relentless. It, along with its growing control over my body, had pushed me up one side of the state and down the other, always one step out of sync of the ever-present specter of Eugene Law.

That memory ghost was here now, again a grainy half-image of the man that haunted my dreams. He stood at the mirror, talking to what I guessed was his reflection.

"Look, it doesn't matter. You did what I told you to do. Cathy's spirit is back in her body—that was part of my deal with the House."

The house? What does that mean?

The voice sent my tongue to the roof of my mouth. "Quiet."

"Six months, three weeks, four days, and…" Gene looked at a static-filled version of his phone. "Two hours ago."

His reflection, or whatever it was he was talking to, said something, but it was lost to a crackle of distortion.

Cathy's dad shook his head and dragged something toward a narrow window on the far side of the bathroom.

Is that the Imp?

"It is an Imp, but not the one I expected." There was a hint of surprise in the voice's tone.

Is it dead?

"Impossible."

It looks dead to me.

Gene stopped and wiped something that sure looked like gore from his face before arguing with the mirror. "What doesn't make sense?"

This time the garbled response from the mirror came in clear enough to pick out most of the words. "I lost her just now."

Her? Who is he—

Gene dropped the dead Imp. "What do you mean 'just now'?"

Again static rattled from the dingy glass and I couldn't make it out.

"What do you mean *just now*?!" Cathy's dad said, returning to the sink visibly shaken.

The voice directed my attention to the mirror. "Get closer…"

I crossed the small bathroom slowly, somewhat ashamed to be eavesdropping, but strangely drawn to the voyeuristic scene playing out in front of me.

Swirls of color and light rolled across the streaked mirror

like a bad TV signal. The picture wasn't coming through, but we had audio. "I've got to go! I'll find her—I made you a promise."

What's wrong with Cathy? You said she would be fine. You said the only way to help her was to break the thread.

"Place your hands on the mirror." The voice ignored my questions and pulled me toward the dirt-streaked glass.

"No." I pushed back and grabbed at the edge of the sink. "Not until you tell me what happened to Cathy."

"Place your hands on the mirror, Tristan."

I shook my head and fought against the pull. "No. You said she would be fine. You said it was the only way."

Cathy's face, her soft hair, and heart-shaped cheeks came back to me like they had a thousand times before. She sat in the Seal of Ariadne, sweat dripping down her skin, while behind her that translucent Thread stretched out to infinity.

You cut it.

"I did nothing of the sort. You broke the thread, and now you are going to put your hands on that mirror," the voice said. "I'm growing tired of your silly games, Tristan. You can lie to yourself all you want, but I know deep down exactly why you broke that Thread."

No! That's not why.

My hands shook against the dirty porcelain.

"Yes it is. It's nothing to be ashamed of. You wanted power. You wanted a way out. Who was there for you?"

You...

"I can't hear you. Who was there for you when you stared into the abyss? Who was there when your body lay shattered on the hospital floor?"

You were.

"Yes, I was. I brought you back, didn't I? Do your limbs work? Are you standing? The fight in your fingers comes from me because I allow it, but now you need to do as I say.

Unless, you want to go back to the way things were before?"

My knees quivered, the muscles holding them upright slowly giving away like bent blades of grass. "Stop!"

"What's wrong? Can't bear to go back to that place? Remember, I gave you this, and I can take it away."

The vitality in my legs returned and I placed my hands on the glass, bracing for the Magick I knew was coming.

Do it.

"Open your eyes, Tristan."

Creak...

The sound of boots on sandy tile pulled me away from the mirror.

"Who you talking to, boy?"

You don't want to know.

"No one," I said, taking my hands off the mirror only to find three large gentlemen blocking the exit.

"You think I'm stupid?"

Are you going to do something?

The voice was infuriatingly silent.

"I don't want any trouble," I said, trying to calculate a path past them to the door.

"He says he doesn't want trouble—you guys hear that? That's special. I don't want trouble either, little man." The man tucked his fingers under an oversized belt buckle. "Now, we can do this the easy way or the hard way."

Please don't... I don't want to hurt anyone else.

They crowded the door, making any escape route impossible. There was a narrow window high up along the far wall, but there was no chance I could reach it.

I was trapped.

Thunk.

One of them locked the door, the dead bolt falling into place with a bone-chilling thump.

"On your knees."

* * *

Whump!

His fist came faster than I could follow, slamming into my stomach and sending what air I'd had rocketing out in a single blast.

Do something!

I clutched at my gut and fell forward, landing on my knees in front of the big man. Stars twinkled at the edges of my vision making it hard to see beyond the imposing buckle.

Stop them.

The voice's words were smooth, almost relaxed, in my head. "Are you sure? After all you've told me I assumed you were tired of fighting back. I thought you wanted to go back to the Tristan of yesteryear. You remember him don't you?"

The strength in my muscles faded.

Please no.

"Are you sure? Because just a few minutes ago you were ready to fight me over the simplest request, but now that you need me, all is supposed to be forgiven?"

Please forgive me.

"I don't know." The voice twisted through my mind like a languid serpent, its thick muscles squeezing my brain in its coils. "Perhaps it would be better for you to remember why you need me in the first place? It seems to me that lately you have forgotten who I am, and who you are without me."

No, I remember now. I need you. I realize that. Please, help me.

"Hold him." The tall man undid his comically large buckle and reached into sweat-stained underpants. His friends grabbed my arms and pulled them back, pinning my hands and forcing my head forward.

"Now, little man. You try anything funny and I'll have

them smash your pretty little face into that sink over there. You get me?"

Please, I swear I was wrong. I need you.

A strong hand grabbed my hair and pulled my head back. "I don't know… I don't think he gets you. Maybe he needs a reminder of who's in charge."

Please, I promise I won't fight any—

Bang!

A knee made contact with the middle of my back and sent a rolling wave of nauseating pain up my spine. "Ugh!"

"That's not a yes. I need to hear a yes, boy."

"What a coincidence," the voice said, its tone calm like the ocean after a storm. "That's almost the same thing I need to hear."

"Yes." The word tumbled out of my mouth like the whimper of a whipped dog.

"Open your mouth, boy."

The voice swelled like a summer thunderstorm in my head. "Yes, what?"

"Yes. Your will be done."

Belt buckle paused. "Hey guys, get a listen to this kid. It's like he wants it. You want it, you little—"

"Do it." I closed my eyes and braced for what was coming.

"Are you certain, Mr. Shelldeck? You are running out of turns at the wheel."

A belt-buckle jingled. "You're damn straight I'm gonna do it."

I accept.

The voice boomed in my head, hungry for the words that would set it free and bring me one step closer to the end. "Say it all."

I, Tristan Shelldeck, give away my eighth turn at the wheel.

Pain exploded in my shoulders: ligaments tore, muscles snapped and bones popped. The voice was rebuilding me, cell by cell, and molecule by molecule, but into what? Ligaments twisted like serpents across my back, while muscles folded over and joints ground back into position.

My arms, now free to move in ways I didn't understand, slipped out of the strong hands holding them back.

"What the—"

My newly recharged hand shot out like the snapping jaws of a pit viper and clamped down on a dangling pair of hairy fruit.

"You like this?" the voice said, its deep timbre speaking through me while steel-like fingers clamped down on those exposed man parts.

"Uh—"

Pop.

"Argh!" Organs popped like fresh grapes beneath my fingers, but I didn't have time to celebrate the victory.

Boom!

Four knuckles to the back of my head sent me crashing into the newly neutered man. No doubt they thought I'd be easy pickings on the ground, but the voice had other plans.

It always had other plans.

He adjusted our trajectory mid-flight and put my shoulder inline with the falling man's knee.

Crack!

Tendons snapped beneath stained denim and tender flesh. Together we landed on the tile, my assailant clutching at what remained of his virility, while I rolled forward.

Do something!

"With pleasure." The voice rolled us back to a fighting position—something I'd never have been able to do on my own.

Holy—

I didn't have time to remark at the impressive maneuver

before the second guy had a knife out and swinging at my face.

Do you—

"I see it." The voice yanked my head back a split second before the sharp metal carved us a second mouth. My hand snapped out again, and if it were possible, this strike was faster than the last. Open palm fingers, straight as their own knife edge, stabbed into the soft spot in the blade wielder's neck.

The smaller man clutched at his throat, but he still had enough to swing the large and crooked steel across my chest. The voice pivoted me just in time, and instead of taking the metal to my sternum, I caught it with my forearm and sent a splatter of blood across the floor.

I'm bleeding.

"We'll live." The voice had my hand twisted into a hook and aimed at the man's wrist. I caught his arm and yanked forward, my knee making contact with his gut.

Whump!

The satisfying sound of expelling air was cut off by my sudden loss of balance. My feet slipped out from under me as the floor rushed up to meet the base of my head.

Boom!

The star-fields returned, this time filling all but a pin hole of my vision.

"Get up! He's got a knife." The voice grumbled and I felt the cold press of steel against my throat. "He's going to—"

Too late.

The blade slashed across my throat and a warm splash of life-giving blood washed over my chest.

Argh!

My lungs struggled for air as they drowned in a sea of red.

"I got him!" A gruff voice shouted, his words suddenly distant and hollow.

"This body is too weak," the voice said, resentment in his words. "I must find another."

My hands, hands that had been trying to hopelessly stem the flow of blood, clawed for another body.

"Maybe one of these..."

"Look at that. The kid's all twitchy and shit. You ever seen that?"

"No..."

No.

The word stuck in my head, echoing with the pounding of my slowing heart.

No.

This wasn't my time, just like it hadn't been my time in the hospital. I was a survivor and I knew it. I hadn't died then and I wasn't going to die now.

You promised me ten turns on the wheel. I have not taken my ninth turn.

The voice sent my hands grasping wildly in the open air. "You are weak. You have alway been weak. I should never have chosen you in the first place."

Bone-chilling cold crept into my legs. My feet and toes faded away in the numbness that followed. My hands continued to feel the air for a warm body, even as my vision faded to black.

No. I have what you need and you know it. I can feel it in your voice. If you let me die you won't make it. They can't sustain you, no one can. Not like me.

"You sure this is what he said to do?" a distant voice asked, his words fading.

"Yeah, I think so. If you ask me he's crazy..."

Death's icy cold crawled into my hips and from there my

chest. My body twitched in the final moments of a life half-lived.

"Say it then." The voice's words boomed between my ears and pressed on my mind like a vise—there was no compassion in those words, no warmth, and no soul. There was only power, resolute and unyielding power.

I, Tristan Shelldeck, give away my ninth turn at the wheel.

"Shit, are you seeing this? The kid's getting up."

"How in the hel—"

* * *

"WE AREN'T IN HELL," I said, my voice no longer my own. My consciousness drifted on a rising tide. My fingers tingled and my heart beat faster, pounding in my chest like a snare drum.

I was no longer in control.

What are you doing?

"Taking my ninth turn at the wheel." The voice was matter-of-fact and direct. Breath had returned to my body and with it came power.

"Shoot him!"

The third man, a jean vest wearing cretin, struggled to remove a pistol from his waistband.

I sprung forward, the voice's power pushing me off the dirty tile and sending me crashing into the knife-wielder.

Wait! The other one has a gun.

I took him down like a jungle cat. His body slammed against the same hard tile I'd been on only moments ago, except this time it was his head bouncing off the ground. My assailant didn't speak, he only swung his blade in hopeless fury, trying desperately to dislodge the thing I'd become.

The knife slashed at my face, but hands I could no longer feel caught his elbow and turned the blade's edge back on its owner.

The metal found its new home in the man's neck. A fresh spray of blood joined mine on the tile.

What are you doing?

"Whatever it takes."

Boom!

A bullet shattered ground next to me and sent hot shards of porcelain into my side.

The voice didn't waste a moment. It rammed the knife deep, then leapt off the bleeding sack of dying flesh and scrambled into one of the bathroom stalls.

They're shooting at me!

The smugness in the voice's response was palpable. "Yes, it is unfortunate for them."

Boom!

Another shot blasted a hole in the cheap pressboard door. A sharp stab of pain raced up my side. I placed a hand against it and it came back red with blood.

I'm bleeding.

"It's a flesh wound. You will survive, that's more than I can say for your attacker."

He's got a gun.

"Yes, and that will be his downfall."

I wasn't sure I believed the voice, but I didn't have a choice. I was on my ninth turn at the wheel—the next would be my last.

I watched with morbid fascination as my hands grabbed the tiny barrel-bolt lock.

What are you doing? Don't open that.

The voice's hands, my hands, threw the lock open with a resounding clunk.

He's going to come in.

"Exactly."

The flurry of motion was almost too fast to follow. Our attacker pulled the door open, his gun ready, but my hands were faster. Fingers snapped out like a whip-crack, catching his wrist and elbow and yanking them forward. The hot gun barked again, the bullet sending a stabbing wave of pain through my already injured side, but the voice didn't let go. Using the man's hand like a counter-balance, it sent a leg into our attacker's mid-section, folding him like a cheap chair.

Hot metal landed in my hand.

The gun.

With a muscle memory I didn't know I had, my hands turned the weapon back on its prior owner.

Stop! Don't shoot him.

I pleaded with the voice, but my words faded on mental tidewaters.

"Don't shoot," he pleaded, one hand on his gut and the other raised. "We just did what you told us to do."

What's he talking about?

The voice took aim with my hands.

"Please, don't shoot," he pulled a wad of crumpled cash from his vest, "here, you can have it, just don't shoot."

Boom!

I couldn't look away, the voice made sure of it. His face exploded, the bullet doing its deadly best. Bile bubbled up in my throat and I fought the urge to vomit.

Oh my God, you killed him!

The voice tucked the gun into my pocket, then picked a path toward the mirror. My hands touched the glass, blood mixing with the grime, cold beneath my fingers.

Here inside my head, I felt the rising tide of Magick. It was a swelling wave that threatened to pull me into the sweet embrace of non-existence.

I can stop it.

The Magick was still part of me. I had control over it, however fleeting that control might be. I could stop it, in here I could reign it in.

"What are you doing," the voice said, angry at the shifting current.

Something I should have done a long time ago—stopping you.

A mental wave rose and fell. The salty brine pushed my head under the pounding surf.

"You can't stop me anymore than you can stop the setting of the sun. This is pointless. Release my Magick before I do worse to you."

My knees shook and my arms twitched. I knew what he was doing, but did he?

Do it then, bring back the disease in all its terror, but you are in the driver's seat now. How will it feel to be a broken little boy?

"Argh!" My hands pounded the glass in frustration, while in the distance a faint siren signaled what was coming.

Let me back in. This is my world, not yours. I'll figure a way out.

My hands left the mirror, the voice giving me control and letting the raging tidewater of Magick subside. I grabbed the edges of the sink and used it to hold myself up.

Breathe. Just breathe.

The destruction was immense. Three men, two of them dead, and one of them mercifully unconscious.

"What will he say when he wakes?" The voice asked, once again communicating at a manageable level.

We won't be around to find out.

I turned to the far window, but movement in the mirror caught my eye. Swirling smoke filled the streaked glass as the tiniest hints of Magick tingled my fingers.

"She's coming." The voice directed my attention to the dirty glass.

Who?

The siren echoed in the tight confines of the bathroom, no longer distant. Bright red and blue light flashed across the ceiling.

We've got to go.

I tried to pull myself away from the cloudy mirror, but the voice held firm, raising my hand to touch the glass.

What are you doing? The cops are going to come through that door any minute.

"All the more reason to place your hand on the glass. Do it, Tristan. You know you want to. Cathy's fate depends on it."

Cathy?

"Place your hands on the glass. If you have ever cared for her, put your hands on the glass."

Behind the streaks of grime, the swirling smoke started to coalesce and form something.

"Put your hands on the glass."

I hesitated, my fingers shaking.

What happened to Cathy?

"Nothing... yet. Her fate is in your hands. Touch the glass and let us see."

Thunk.

Behind us the deadbolt retreated into the door, someone was coming.

"Do it now! Do it before it's too late." The voice's power echoing in my head.

I...

The image bleed and shifted like a motel TV.

Cathy?

"Turn around with your hands up." The cop's voice bounced off the tile, rattling around in a head already full of voices.

"Don't do it." The voice pushed my fingers toward the mirror. "We don't have much time. Touch the glass."

"Did you hear me, kid? I said, turn around and put your damn hands up."

The distorted image started to solidify. Blobs of color took shape—sandy blond and blue.

Cathy?

Radio static crackled behind me, but I couldn't turn away from the shifting scene.

"I'm not going to ask again. Turn around and put your hands up!"

Is that her?

"Place your hands on the glass and we'll find out." The voice pulled at the Magick welling up in my body. "Put your hands on the glass."

"Put your hands up."

The words were blending, but I couldn't take my eyes away from the image. It was Cathy, it had to be, but how? She was safe. He'd promised me she would be, had he lied?

"Put your hands on the glass—"

"Put your hands in the air—"

I extended my arms, the gun becoming visible in the process.

"Gun!"

Wait, no!

Cathy's image popped, vanishing from the glass like a spent bulb.

"No!" I cried, spinning around in frustration.

Boom!

The bullet tore a hole in my gut, shredding flesh and shattering bone.

Cathy... I'm sorry.

"You can still save her," the voice whispered gently, its words tickling at the edges of my conscious mind. "You have one turn remaining..."

* * *

No, that's my last.

Shooting pain surged through what remained of my body followed by the return of cold, numbing cold.

"The shooter is down. Geez, he's just a kid."

The voice was calm, almost serene in my head. "You are dying, Tristan."

No...

"Yes. It is regrettable, but you have reached your end. I've kept you alive too many times as it is. You are right to deny me the tenth turn. Go and enjoy the fruits of your afterlife."

But I don't want to die.

The flashing lights splashed the ceiling and cut across the officer's face. "Stay with me, kid," he said, pressing on the gaping wound with me. "Shit, just hang on."

The voice shifted beneath my skin like a hungry worm. "Who do we have here?"

"Don't leave me."

The cop moped a sleeve across his sweaty brow. "I'm not going to leave you. You need to hold on. The paramedics will be here any second."

"He's tempting." The voice unfurled in my mind like a serpent. "There's a spark of Magick deep inside, perhaps it will be enough?"

"No," I cried, letting go of my wound to try and push the officer's hands away. "Don't touch me."

He ignored my feeble attempts.

The voice probed at the edges of the Good Samaritan's mind. "Family? Well, that's disappointing. Still, they can always be dealt with."

"Please." My voice faded to a whisper. "Don't let him in. Don't make the same mistake I did. He won't help you. He will destroy everything you've ever loved."

The voice pulled away from me like a butterfly shedding its cocoon for finer pastures. "I did exactly what you wanted.

I have never lied to you, Tristan. When you lay on the hospital floor broken and unloved, was I not there?"

"I died that day."

The voice chuckled, a cruel and hollow sound. "Of course you did. Are you just now figuring that out? You were mine, Tristan Shelldeck, but now I am finished with you. You have served your usefulness. I will find another."

My vision faded and I found myself on the cold tile, staring up at the bright lights of my hospital room. The muscles in my body twitched in what would be their final gasp. Soon I wouldn't have enough strength to breath, and in that moment I would suffocate, dying at the hands of this damnable disease. Had I the strength, I would have pounded my hands or screamed at a world that had offered me so much only to take it away, but this was the end, and I knew it.

"It doesn't have to be..." The voice was calm and commanding, settling in my head like a warm blanket after the cold rain.

I'm dying. Let me be.

"Yes, you are, and it is a terrible way to die. Your body giving up on you like a spent shell while your mind continues to toil away."

My breath came in thin and labored gasps. It wasn't long now.

Nothing can be done.

"That's where you are wrong. There are always things that can be done, if you have the stomach for them."

I wanted to laugh, but my body had long since lost the strength to.

They've tried it all: Gene therapy, transfusions, experimental drugs. All of it for nothing. Let me die in peace.

The voice tickled at my mind, twisting and turning

around the edges of my consciousness like a python. "Everything, eh? What about *this*..."

Something stirred in the recesses of my broken flesh, something I'd never felt before—a rush of power more than sufficient to lift my tired muscles. I opened my eyes and watched in amazement as my own fingers moved for the first time in months.

What...

"Only a taste," the voice said, the power fading as quickly as it had come. "There is more out there, an almost inexhaustible amount. The greatest secrets remain trapped in my book. Hidden between the pages such that only I can free them. You will help me get it back, and in return I will see that you walk again."

But how?

"Shall we debate the semantics of how I cheat death while your soul drifts away? Or are you ready to live again, Tristan Shelldeck?"

The door opened and the University's medical staff filed into the room—strange hands pulling my body toward the bed.

What must I do?

"Submit."

I don't understand?

"We're losing him!"

The voice dropped to a whisper, its snake-like coils tightening against my soul. "Repeat after me. I give away my first turn at the wheel..."

I give away my first turn at the wheel.

A shock of pain jolted me back to the present moment. The officer had pulled his hands away from my wound, his eyes cloudy and unfocused.

"Fight it," I pleaded, each word a painful reminder of my

ebbing life. "He lies. Everything he says is a lie. There is no truth but his desires. He will destroy you."

Hands left my body and found the gun on the distant tile. "I understand…"

Fire licked at the edges of my vision. The bathroom was burning.

What's happening?

The voice was strained, stretched to its limit between us. "You think you could do all you've done without repercussion? Did you think cheating death would come without a fee? Don't feel bad. You will fit right in with the damned."

Ashen white faces and clawing hands smothered in spent embers pushed through the flames. Their coal black and hungry eyes filled the void behind the cop.

"Goodbye, child."

Something moved beyond the ashen faces of the damned —dirty blond hair and sparkling blue eyes.

Cathy?

She hovered just past the monsters, her face soft and caring. "Find me. Make it right. There's still time."

There's no time.

"That's right," the voice said, clawing its way from my broken and bleeding form. "There's no time."

Cathy smiled, her lips pink and lush against the burning horde. "There is always time for forgiveness."

I…

Her hand reached for me through the hellish wall of death and pain. "Let go. I won't let you drown."

I can't. It would be my tenth turn.

"The tide will drag you out, but I won't let you sink beneath the waves. There is good in you, Tristan. I won't let that be snuffed out."

I reached for her hand. I let go of the pain, the sadness,

and the disappointment. I reached for her like I'd clawed for life on the hospital floor all those years ago.

Our fingers touched and in that instant I knew what I had to do.

"What are you doing?" The voice was concerned.

"I, Tristan Shelldeck," I coughed, fighting for the strength to push the words out, "I give away my tenth turn at the wheel."

The voice fought me, scrambling for greener and less broken pastures, but I clamped down, dragging the serpent back by its tail.

"The tenth spin on the wheel." The voice twisted around to bare its mental fangs. "You know what this means? You are mine now."

The tide swelled in my mind as dark water pressed against my legs. "I give up my tenth turn—"

"And what if I don't want it!" the voice shouted, banging against the sides of my skull.

The current knocked me over and I clawed for the surface, each wave batting me back down into the black of unconsciousness. "I give up my tenth—"

"Argh!" The voice slammed at the cage like a trapped animal, stuck in the hell of its own creation.

Cathy... I will find you.

I broke the surface, but the waves continued to drag me farther from shore. "My tenth turn..."

"I accept." The voice's words rattled through my mind like a thunderclap. "Say my name, boy. Say it and know the progenitor of your destruction."

The tide pulled me farther away, my voice fading on the roaring sea. "Ten..."

"Say it."

"Ten..."

"Say it!"

"Ten Spins!" I shouted, no longer afraid, no longer the scared boy clinging to a broken life. Cathy was out there and she believed in me.

That was enough.

It had to be.

* * *

I placed my hands on the mirror's glass, in its reflection the bodies of the cop and a handful of paramedics joined the idiot thugs I'd bribed to rough up the kid. It had all gone according to plan.

Light and color swirled inside the mirror, listening to my call and heeding the power of my Magick.

Now, where are you Morgan Crowley?

IRRIGATED

*P*orter crossed her arms and folded them over her chest. It was a look my wife had down pat. She frowned and pointed at the back yard from the window of our living room. "It's dying."

"What is, honey?" I asked, not looking up from the paper. This was the first time in a week I'd actually been able to read the damn thing and I wasn't about to take the bait.

"All of it."

"That sounds terrible, but I don't see anything about the world ending in here. There is a sale on furniture, though, so... close?"

Porter sighed.

That simple exhale represented weapon's grade guilt, and my wife had an expert-level skill at wielding it. "Gene, the whole backyard is dying. Did you check the sprinklers?"

The sprinklers... Damn it.

I knew there had been something else on my todo list.

"I was going to work on them today," I said, even as the thought of spending my day digging up pipes in the mosquito-infested yard ruined the taste of my coffee.

"Today, as in this day? Or some other today. I mean, there are a lot of todays in Eugene Law's world. There's the tomorrow today, that's the one we use for taking out the trash. I'm a huge fan of the next week today, that one really lets the bills marinade nicely. Then there's the—"

I slapped the paper down on the table and downed the last of my coffee. "I'm going."

"Really? You don't have to do it now."

I scooped up my yard shoes from beside the door, shaking my head. I wasn't going to take the bait twice.

Bang!

I closed the garage door behind me and flipped on the light, doing my best to locate the sprinkler control box in the dingy bulb's weak glow. "There you are."

I popped the box open and checked the wires. I didn't have a clue what I was looking for, but they did appear very wiry and connected. These were all things I assumed wires needed.

I hit the garage door button and waited as the large metal accordion rolled up, blinking my eyes at the bright morning sun.

Sprinklers... New Dead would have been easier.

I chuckled at the thought, but brushed away the absurdity of it. Having the spirits of the damned in my garage would not have made it better—not by a long shot.

My name is Eugene Law and I'm a Magician. I don't pull rabbits out of hats, and my card tricks leave a lot to be desired. I deal in real Magick, the cosmic powers of the universe, and all the evil it brings to my front door.

Evil that never offers to fix my sprinklers.

I yanked a big blue box of plumbing parts off the top shelf, and wrinkled my nose at the smell of pipe glue coming off it. I popped the top and found the inside was arguably worse. The bin was a mismatch of odds and ends that couldn't possibly have been useful, but they were better than nothing.

I pulled my tool box out from under the workbench and blew the dust off it. Yeah, I was that kind of handy.

Porter waved from the window by the time I hit the backyard and I nodded, doing my best to look manly in the process. There was something about tools and fixing stuff that got my wife's motor running. At least that was the lie I told myself. She didn't seem to derive the same level of satisfaction from my Magickal pursuits. I guess there's only so many ways you can talk about fending off rogue fairies or thwarting the powers of darkness before it gets boring.

Ah, but get the tools out and you get a wave from the window.

I turned back to check that window again but found her gone.

Want more attention? Fix the sprinklers.

Crunch!

Porter was right: Our once verdant backyard had really gone to hell. Grass blades cracked under my yard shoes, their green luster replaced with a ruddy brown complexion that was not about to impress any garden club—not that we'd have ever been invited to one, but still, one had to keep up appearances.

The dead grass wasn't the worst of it. No, that was the bushes. We'd had a really nice hedge along the fence line, a hedge that had been great at keeping me from seeing the neighbors. It wasn't that I didn't like the people that lived next door, it was that they weren't likable to begin with.

This was an entirely different source of argument between Porter and I, which was why the hedge was so important. If we didn't see them, then we didn't argue about whether they could see us.

It was a process, and one that required a lush green hedge. A lush green hedge we no longer possessed.

Our newly dead line of bushes made Charlie Brown's Christmas Tree look resplendent. Leaves hung like brown caterpillar cocoons. Twisted up cigars of wrinkled death, they'd already begun to pile up on the ground.

Crap.

As if I'd summoned him with some annoyance Magick, my neighbor stepped out into his backyard. Shirtless and hairy, the big man paused to make some genital adjustments that thankfully remained hidden behind his boxers.

"Morning, Gene. Fixing the sprinklers?"

"Uh huh."

The big man waddled down his steps and across a lush green lawn. A lawn my wife must have seen from the window. With Porter, grass envy was a thing.

"Yeah, I got a service for that," Ted said without prompting.

I dropped the tools next to a rusty pump not far from the dead bushes. That old machine was the source of all our irrigation water. It was older than me and twice as cranky, but it didn't look broken.

"You should think about getting a service, Gene."

"Uh huh."

"You know, I've got a cousin in landscaping. I could get him to give you a quote for putting in all new stuff. Since you know me I'm sure he'd give you a deal."

Ted was one of those guys that offered suggestions whether you wanted them or not. He also had a cousin who worked in practically every profession and was more than happy to recommend their services regardless of whether you asked for them.

"Yard's not dead yet," I said, pulling out a few dusty tools.

"Right, right. Sure." Ted produced a coffee cup and

crouched down behind the basically ruined hedge to check out the pump with me. "Looks good to me."

Sigh.

"Yeah. I—"

My back porch door opened and Porter appeared on the step. "You mind giving him a hand, Ted?"

"You got it, P."

Thanks, Sweetheart.

"No. It's fine, Ted. I've got it. I'm sure it's something simple. I don't want to take you away from your coffee."

My heavy-set neighbor shuffled through the dying bushes and sent a pile of curled-up leaves raining down. "It's no problem, neighbor," he said, arriving in my backyard to take a seat next to the pump.

"Thanks!" My wife let the porch door slam and went back inside.

Yeah. Thanks.

Ted slurped his coffee and leaned over the ancient pump. "Damn, Gene. Your wife is a looker. I mean, wow. No offense or nothing, but damn. I'd be out here fixing shit for her all day long if you catch my drift."

I caught his drift, and I didn't like it. "Yeah. You don't need to help, Ted. I've got it."

"Don't worry, Gene. I'll tell her you did all the hard work."

Ted picked up one of my wrenches and spun it in his hands. "Yeah, all the hard—"

Thump!

He lost his grip on the heavy iron pipe wrench and it clunked against the pump, knocking off a decent chunk of rust as well as the metal plate that covered the motor itself.

"Shit! Sorry, Gene."

I ignored him, too focused on the tiny creature that scrambled back up inside the ancient machine's metal housing. I hadn't seen one in years, but it would appear I had one living in my irrigation pump.

Grellic.

Ted leaned over and poked his head right up to the wiring. I half-hoped the tiny creature would chew his face off then and there, but I rarely got that lucky.

"Ah, I think I see your problem." Ted shoved his hand in the open pump.

"Wait, don't!"

"Ouch!"

My neighbor pulled back his finger and immediately stuck it in his mouth. "Must be a loose wire. Damn that smarts."

No, Ted. Smarts are about to be the exact opposite of your problems, and mine.

A nearby sprinkler head popped up, the tiny body of a feral sprite with oversized teeth poking out of it.

Great.

Where there was one Grellic, there was bound to be two, and where there was two...

Three more sprinkler heads popped up around the yard. Tiny eyes perched above oversized jaws and stared back at me.

Ted sucked his finger and bent down to stare into the pump again. "I bet if we..."

I don't know what else my neighbor said, because honestly I wasn't paying attention. All of my focus was on the rest of the slowly rising sprinkler heads each one housing a toothy Grellic.

"Well there's your problem," Ted said, his head practically inside the pump.

Uh huh. Sure is.

* * *

GRELLICS.

Related to Pixie, the ravenous little creatures had more in common with Bone Fairies than their Tooth stealing cousins.

Frustration Fairies.

Ever been working on a task and get increasingly frustrated, to the point of making really questionable decisions to try and solve your problem? You know what I'm talking about. That moment when you decide to jam your screwdriver into the electrical outlet to see if it's hot versus just walking out to the circuit breaker?

Grellic.

A large number of monstrously stupid decisions could be traced back to those irritating Fairies who make their home in the Sunshine State.

Ted dug his hand back into my pump, suddenly oblivious to the blood on his fingers. That was the problem with Grellics: Their natural chemistry disrupted the reason and logic centers in your brain. Now, my neighbor didn't have much in the way of rational logic to begin with, but having been bitten by a Grellic, what he did have was going to go downhill, and fast.

"Ted, why don't you go inside and get that looked at? Don't want it to get infected."

My neighbor brushed me away with his other hand, the rest of his sweaty body pressed up against my irrigation pump.

"Nah. I think I found it. You've got something gumming up the works—ouch!" Ted yanked his arm out and swung it like he's touched the stovetop. "Gotta be a short."

"Ted, don't—"

But it was too late, my neighbor had already re-inserted his twice bitten hand in the rusty pump.

Crap.

As if that wasn't bad enough, the rest of my new found

family of Frustration Fairies had chosen this time to investigate the oversized tasty morsel of neighborly stupid currently wedged in my pump.

"Go! Shoo!"

Like bobblehead dolls with grapefruit-sized heads chock full of razor sharp teeth, Grellics were not something you played around with, especially not in numbers.

A handful of those Frustration Fairies sniffed at the air.

Grellics, much like most of Florida's indigenous supernatural fauna, had plenty of weaknesses, the chief among them being their sense of smell. Frustration had an odor, and it brought them like the ice cream truck lures my kids to the street corner. Still, like my kids, they had smells that sent them packing.

There were few different options, but chief among those was rosemary. Not only tasty on chicken and the occasional beef my wife let us have, the wild herbs I had Cathy tending on the side yard were exactly what the doctor ordered to get these hungry little bastards off my dead lawn. With them gone, I could turn my attention to Ted and make sure he didn't get any more brilliant ideas.

"Hold on, big guy. I'll be right back."

My neighbor only grunted and wedged his hand deeper in the pump cavity.

Grellics congregated on the edges of what remained of my lawn, raising their flat noses to take in that glorious frustration.

"Ted—" I was going to tell him not to do anything crazy, but I stopped the second he started pounding the side of the pump with his hand.

I needed rosemary and I needed it now.

One of Cathy's chores was tending to the great herb bushes I'd planted on the side yard when we'd first moved into this house. They weren't elaborate, but a few bags of high-end fertilizer and a little Magick had given us a pretty solid herb garden.

"Just get a few stems and we should be fine..." I said to myself as I rounded the corner to find an herb garden in the final stages of death and decay.

Cathy!

My daughter had obviously forgotten the tending part of 'tending the garden.' Brown and withered beyond recognition, my rosemary bushes weren't going to be helping anyone anytime soon.

Crap!

"Ouch! You little bastard. I've got just the thing for you." Ted's exclamation raised the short hairs on my neck. "Oh yeah, just the thing."

"Wait, Ted, don't do anything stupid." I returned to the back yard, realizing the idiocy of my own statement, only to find it empty.

There were no Grellics, but there was no Ted.

Bang!

My neighbor emerged from his house covered in pint-sized frustration magnets, their melon-shaped heads dangling on his exposed flesh like possum babies clinging to their mother.

All of that wasn't nearly as concerning as the chainsaw in his hand.

"Ted!"

"Stand back, Gene." My neighbor yanked the pull cord and the angry blade rumbled to life. "I'm gonna slice the back end off so I can get to those wires."

"You can't cut the pump with a *chainsaw*!"

My neighbor hesitated, confusion in his eyes.

"Put the chainsaw away and we'll figure this out."

Ted lowered the blade and reached for the off button.

"There you go," I said, keeping an eye on the sharp edge of his impromptu pump fixer. "I'll take care of it."

"You sure?"

"Completely. Just turn off the—"

A chunky Grellic scrambled up his leg, frowned at me, then took a nice bite out of my neighbor's thigh.

Whrr!

"I got this, Gene. Stand back!" His frustration back in gear, my neighbor spun the chainsaw up to full speed.

Gah!

"Gene," Porter chose that moment to poke her head out the porch door. "Can I get you guys any—Holy shit?!"

"Grellics," I said, backing away from the 80s horror movie villain advancing on my irrigation pump. "We've got a whole damn warren of them back here."

"What about the rosemary?"

I shook my head. "Cathy let it go to pot."

Whrr!

Ted hovered over my irrigation pump, the chainsaw roaring in his hands. "Yeah, Gene. This is gonna get that back off no problem. Then we can tackle the wiring."

The wiring! Crap.

The irrigation pump was still wired to house power. It might not be enough to kill him, but it certainly would do wonders at increasing his already epic frustration.

"Porter, throw the breaker for outside."

No response.

"Honey, I need you to throw the circuit for—"

Porter wasn't going to be doing any circuit breaking. She was too busy yanking the almost dead bushes out of the ground.

Ted leaned in to check his target, then revved the chainsaw.

Whrr!

"What are you doing? Those plants aren't completely dead."

My wife spun around, streaks of dirt on her cheeks. A hungry Grellic clung to her neck like a baby primate. Its teeth nibbled on that soft spot I considered completely off limits to anyone not me, and that went doubly so to members of the Fairy family.

"Gah!

My wife wiped a hand across her forehead. "What? The stupid yard is dead. Might as well dig them up."

"No, wait, don't--"

Whrr!

Ted nodded at the pump, then wiped sweat from his face. "Yep, that's the spot. We're gonna get the back off this thing and fix those wires." He placed a barefoot on the pump casing and lined up the chainsaw.

"No, Ted!"

Thump!

One of my wife's favorite flowering bushes hit the ground in front of me, this one clearly still living. "Not enough flowers." Porter grumbled.

Triage, Gene.

"Ted!"

"Huh?" My neighbor paused. "It's cool, Gene. I've got it." Grellics clung to his neck and shoulders like vampire bats.

"Measure twice, cut once."

Ted frowned. My logic did little to stop the flood of Grellic-fueled frustration.

"Already done, neighbor."

Whrr!

"Hey, Moron!" Porter cried, tossing another prized bush on the ground. "Yeah, you, with the chainsaw. Why don't you make yourself useful and cut some of this up?"

Ted revved the saw over my rusty pump. "I've got the fix this first. Can't you see I'm working here?"

"Working? Working?!" My wife tossed another bush on the growing pile with her blood and dirt streaked hands. "Working would be actually getting something done. You appear to be just dancing around with that stupid saw. If you're going to cut something, then cut something. Don't just stand there like a moron."

Please don't...

With a primal yell, my neighbor rammed the chainsaw into what had been a reasonably functional irrigation pump. Sparks shot up like cheap fireworks, bathing a Grellic-covered Ted in a dusting of hot metal.

Well, at least he didn't hit the electrical li—

Pop!

It didn't sound like much but, judging by the look on my surprised neighbor's face, it felt a lot worse.

Ted landed on his backside, the still rumbling chainsaw narrowly avoiding removing his foot at the ankle by mere inches. Grellics scattered, jumping off his stunned body like fleas from a washed dog.

I raced to Ted's side and checked his pulse. My idiot neighbor was still alive. "Porter I need you to—Porter?"

Grellics covered her chest, their rubbery little feet sticking out of places no Fairy should be allowed.

"Porter?"

My wife picked up the saw. "This'll get the job done much faster."

"No, honey, don't—"

Whrr!

My wife revved the powerful motor and smiled, the blood on her face suddenly more akin to war paint. "Don't worry, sweetheart. I've got it."

* * *

"HONEY, PUT THE CHAINSAW DOWN."

My wife frowned and held the rumbling engine above her head like an expendable extra from some zombie movie. "Can't hear you. I've got a chainsaw."

Grellics nibbled at the nape of her neck, their poison sure to put Porter's frustration level through the roof. This was usually the point where seemingly good decisions went completely sideways. Sure, it's perfectly normal to remove some bushes from the yard. It wasn't perfectly normal to do it like you were making an ice sculpture blindfolded.

My wife tore into the closest bush. Dried leaves and small branches whipped into a frenzy of frustration-fueled destruction.

Think, Gene!

Grellics were related to Pixies, so they weren't high on the intelligence scale, but unlike their kleptomaniacal brethren they didn't give a damn about Magickal artifacts. Pixies could pick you clean of the good stuff in minutes, but Grellics were far more interested in hanging out and soaking up that tasty frustration—at least until you did something stupid enough to seriously injure yourself.

You couldn't put out much frustration incapacitated.

Whrr! Clunk!

More chunks of my wife's once-prized hedge hit the dirt, but not without doing a number on her bare arms. Grellics swarmed over them, their tiny rubbery bodies and oversized heads like malevolent hood-ornaments soaking up each drop of bloody frustration.

"Dad?"

Cathy!

My daughter popped her head out the back door. Her long hair resembled something you could only achieve with copious amounts of hair spray or if you happened to moon-light as the bride of Frankenstein. Cathy was a teenager and the sun had yet to reach mid-day. There was a really good chance she'd only just woken up.

"What's Mom doing?"

Porter swung around and caught sight of her daughter, then revved the saw a few times. "Mom's taking care of the yard."

"Dad..."

"No time, kiddo." My daughter couldn't see Grellics. Just like their hairy cousins, these tiny Fairies were some-thing only Magicians got to see. "You let all the rosemary die."

"No I didn't."

"Yes you did. The whole garden is dead. Completely dead. You didn't water it."

"I did. I watered it."

I pointed to the crusted remains of my raised bed. "Really, you watered that?"

"That's rosemary? I thought those were weeds."

Whrr!

Porter sliced through another bush, the saw blade catching on a thick branch just long enough to kick the entire machine back. The chainsaw missed her beautiful face by inches. "Argh!"

My wife's frustration rose and she sucked up Grellics by the dozens. Those tiny Fairies swarmed her legs like toddlers at feeding time.

You've got to stop this before she cuts a leg off, or worse.

I reached for my Magick, but hesitated. Anything I tried would put my wife in the crosshairs.

A lone Grellic shot past en route to Porter but hesitated seeing my teenage daughter hanging her head out the porch door.

"Don't even think about it," I said, pushing Cathy back inside and shooing away the Frustration Fairy with my foot.

"Dad!"

"Catherine, go back inside. I'll take care of your mom."

My daughter shook her head and pointed past me. "She's going after Kris's swingset."

"She's what?!"

I spun around to find my wife taking chunks out of the wooden play set I'd spent far too many hours building.

What the hell!

Honestly, I didn't really care that much about the bushes, but the swing set was sacred. That wobbly monstrosity represented the first time I'd actually followed instructions. Sure, I'd had to improvise when it came to the underlying structure. They'd been out of the proper-sized boards, and the deck screws weren't the best, but my son loved it, and I couldn't stand to see it turned to wood chips.

"I've got it. Get inside, Cathy. Now!"

"Why did you want rosemary?"

"Another time, Catherine. Inside!"

My daughter slammed the inner door shut, her face a mask of concern in the glass panes.

"Stop!" I shouted, waving my hands to get Porter's attention.

"It's a splinter factory, Gene."

"It is now."

Whrr!

Porter shrugged me off and went back to work on the quickly collapsing swings.

I'd had enough. Fairy or not, those little bastards needed to go before they destroyed something that couldn't be rebuilt.

I dropped to my knees in the formerly lush lawn and pushed aside enough leaves and dead grass to give myself a reasonably open spot. Working Magick around Fairies was always a crapshoot, so there was no way I was going to do it without a safety net. I needed a sigil to focus my power, but which one?

Clang! Clang! Clang!

Porter's chainsaw snagged on one of the swing chains and the spinning blade yanked her forward. My wife caught her footing, but not before narrowly missing losing those feet in the process.

Crap.

I didn't have time to think up some perfect sigil. I needed the Grellics off my wife and I needed it done yesterday.

My fingers traced frantic lines in the soft sand, circles within circles, and each one trapped inside a box.

Charlie's Corn Maze.

The Magick was oddly named. It really didn't have anything to do with corn, but it produced one hell of a complex trap. If I played my cards right it would lure those little bastards off my wife and straight to the sigil, where they'd get caught up in the confusing Magick that was the Corn Maze.

That was the theory at least. The old salt in Plant City I'd learned it from had a penchant for making and drinking his own hooch. At the time I think I could have set his breath on fire.

I closed up the last square in Charlie's sigil, then pressed my palms into the open spots. Magick, glorious Magick, rose up like a cresting wave in my chest only to pour into the complex creation beneath me. Cosmic energy danced between the lines and swelled in the tiny shapes. It filled out the sigil and in turn the simple design channeled the power's focus.

Whrr!

It wasn't a moment too soon, as Porter had turned her attention to the plastic slide.

Thump!

Thump!

Rubbery Grellics dropped off my wife, drawn by the old booze-hound's confusing Magick.

That's it, you little bastards. Come and get it.

I pumped more power into the sigil, sending bright light and complex twinkling sparks into the air. It was quite a light show, one I didn't remember when Charlie had shown it to me.

More Grellics climbed off swing-slaying Porter, enough to take her frustration from rage-induced yard demon to tired housewife and mother. That was a level of frustration I could deal with.

Like a flock of children swarming the neighborhood ice cream truck, the rubbery little monsters surrounded me.

I just needed a few more seconds and they'd be inside the swirling cloud of confusion. I didn't exactly have a plan for what happened after that, but that was a bridge I'd cross when I got to it. As of right now, there was no one swinging a chainsaw.

Progress!

Movement in what remained of the hedges drew my attention. There were a lot more Grellics. It appeared Ted had some in his yard, as did the neighbors on the other side. I did a little mental math and didn't like the numbers. There were now enough little devils to cover the ruined back yard, far more than I could capture in any confusion sigil.

Think, Gene...

I pumped more power into the sigil, which in turn only succeeded in bringing in more Grellics. How long had this infestation been going on?

Bulbous heads and sharp teeth edged closer.

Maybe I could adjust the sigil on the fly? Do something to trap what appeared to be the entire block's Frustration Fairies in a single pass.

I slowly raised a hand and examined the sigil. These things really weren't my style, and to change one of the fly was definitely not one of my smarter moves, but I really didn't have a choice. A couple dozen Grellics I could handle, but enough to cover my entire backyard was another story entirely.

I thought back to that old farmer. Charlie certainly hadn't put off the Master Magician vibe. If he could put this together then I could adjust it.

More Grellics swarmed the yard. They stopped briefly to sniff at Porter but when she didn't show much in the way of tasty frustration they moved on to the farmer's lightshow.

All right. You can do this, Gene. The Magick shouldn't be too hard. If you adjust the confining squares of Sil, then make sure you account for Circe's Circle diameter you ought to be able to—

Bang!

Cathy raced into the yard, a single sprig of rosemary in her hand.

"Cathy, don't—"

Too late, My well-meaning teenager put a foot in Charlie's Corn Maze, breaking the sigil and any control I had on the entire neighborhood's allotment of Frustration Fairies in a single motion.

"I found some rosemary."

Hungry Grellics shook off the Magickal lure, their teeth remarkably white in the late morning sun.

"That's great, honey."

* * *

CHARLIE'S CORN MAZE vanished like yesterday's news, and with it went the glorious confusion keeping a city block's worth of Grellics focused on something other than the four people in the backyard.

Crap.

Softball-like faces shook off the last Corn Maze's effects, their sharp teeth and beady eyes trained on a veritable feast of frustration—Ted was awake.

"I'm going to get that pump working neighbor," the heavy man said, completely unaware of the shifting horde of hungry Fairies around him. "Might not be the wiring. I'm thinking it's the well itself."

"Ted, don't—"

My neighbor pulled the broken pump off the ground and chucked it into what little remained of my bushes.

Too late.

"I've got it, Gene. Just need to get this stupid well to start producing water." Ted got on his hands and knees, and started digging at the exposed PVC pipe. All of this sent the Grellics into a tizzy. Frustration Fairies latched onto my neighbor's arms by the dozens, their tiny teeth chomping down and kicking off a heady rush of tasty emotions.

"What the hell are you doing?" My wife cried, coming to her senses long enough to have a few Grellics flock to her toned legs. Once again those little bastards were putting their mouths and tongues in places they didn't belong.

"Wait, Porter, don't—"

My wife tossed the chainsaw aside and muscled her way next to Ted. Her long brown hair streamed out behind her, as she ripped thick clumps of dirt out of our already ruined yard. "You're doing it all wrong. I'll show you how it's done."

"Oh yeah," Ted pushed her back, using his bulk to secure a better position in front of the tilted pipe that had been my irrigation well. "What do you know about shallow wells, woman?"

Oh, no.

Porter grew up around brothers, which meant that was exactly the wrong thing to say to her.

"*Woman?* You think because I'm a woman I don't know the proper way to dig a shallow well?"

"That's exactly what I'm saying." Grellics perched on Ted's shoulders and nibbled on his ears. "I'm saying maybe you should stick to the kitchen."

My wife cast deep fistfuls of dirt aside like a hopped-up Golden Retriever. "Is that why we never see Marcy? You've got her chained up in the kitchen so she can keep your fat ass just short of breaking the waistband on those boxers?"

"Oh, I break the waistband on my boxers because, unlike your husband, I actually have something between my—"

"Cathy, go inside," I said, cutting off my neighbor's words before my daughter could hear them.

Whrr!

Cathy was covered in Grellics, and she'd found the chainsaw.

Isn't that special?

My daughter revved the engine, which instantly grabbed everyone's attention.

"What are you doing?" Porter asked, flinging a wad of black earth and sending more Grellics racing up her petite backside in the process.

"Dad never made me a swing set." Cathy took an angry step toward what little remained of my son's play set.

Porter brushed her daughter off, but didn't knock free a single Grellic in the process. "He just doesn't like you as much."

Gah!

"Cathy, put the chainsaw down."

My daughter gunned the engine a few more times. The throaty roar brought even more Frustration Fairies surging up her young legs. "I'll put it down. I'll put it down right here!"

Not used to power tools or anything that resembled yard work, my daughter slammed the spinning blade awkwardly against the splintered remains of the swing's posts. Wood chips shot out in all directions, scattering Grellics only to have them surge forward again.

"Huh." Ted tossed another lump of dirt. "See, it's just like I told you. A woman's place is in the kitchen."

"Argh!" Porter launched herself at our neighbor, her hands finding his neck remarkably fast. "Take that back!"

"Never," Ted sputtered, his face mushed into the muck while even more Grellics scrambled over his ample body looking for a place to latch on.

"Dad?"

My son appeared at the back door, entirely confused and borderline crying. "What happened to my swing set?"

Grellic faces perked up at the sight of fresh meat.

"Nope," I said, kicking the closest one away and racing to shut the door. "Kris, stay inside."

"But my swing set..." Tear welled in his toddler eyes.

"I'll build you a new one."

"Of course you will," Cathy screamed, swinging the chainsaw around for another pass. "I knew you loved him more. Kris gets a swing set and what do I get?"

"I let you drive the car!"

A fresh batch of wood chips exploded in the air like confetti. "That's not a swing set!"

"Dad! Cathy's ruining my swing—"

I pushed the door closed and pressed my back against it, keeping my son inside and myself between him and a horde of hungry Grellics. "She's not ruining it. We're tearing it down to make room for a new one."

"She is?"

I nodded, kicking at another encroaching Fairy. "Totally. Why I think we should have one with—"

"With Dragons!"

"Dragons? Are you sure you want Dragons? I mean they're quite uppity and they have a reputation."

"Dragons, Dad. I want Dragons on the swing set."

"If I say yes, will you stay inside?"

No response.

"Kris?"

"I was nodding, Dad. That means yes."

"It does, but only if I'm looking at you."

"Oh."

As my young son contemplated this new piece of information, Cathy tore into what had been his swing set with renewed gusto. A pair of Grellic perched on her shoulders and sunk their teeth into her neck.

Porter and Ted weren't doing much better. My wife might have some serious passion, but Ted had bulk and he knew how to throw it around. The two of them banged against the shed just hard enough to dislodge a few Grellics, but those hungry monsters didn't stay detached for long.

"That's it," I said, rolling up my sleeves and reaching for my Magick. "I've had just about enough of your—Son of a!"

I looked down to find a Grellic clamped on my ankle.

Blood trickled from the tiny wound, and with it my own frustration hit the top of the scale. I kicked the rubbery little creature away, only to find four more scrambling up my legs to replace it.

Don't lose your cool, Gene!

The hell with that, you're a Magician, damn it. Magick something, you moron.

I dug into my power even as the Dance of the Frustration Fairies played out across my backyard. Cathy had almost finished destroying the last vestiges of the swing set, and appeared to be turning her attention to the shed. "You could build Kris a swing set and make yourself a shed but couldn't be bothered to make anything for your only daughter."

"Oh stop whining," Porter cried before Ted shoved her face in the dirt.

"How do you like that, woman?"

More Grellics bit down on my calves and nipped at my knees, and I kicked them away. This morning had started with so much promise. I'd just wanted to read my newspaper in peace, had that been too much to ask?

Cosmic power rippled in my chest, swirling like a whirlpool of terrible desires and frustration fueled decisions.

The tiny voice of modest reason in my head was drowned out by the Grellic's poison, and the rage-inducing whine of Ted's chainsaw.

Grellics crawled up my back and over my shoulders. Those little devils nipped at my bare neck and brought another trickle of blood running down my chest.

What to do?

Felgrim's Fog? Yes. The toxic mist would flay the skins from their bones.

"And yours," a tiny voice in my head reminded me. More Grellics chomped on my backside and I lost the voice in the haze of desperation.

No... I've got it! Jelker's Warmth. I'll make a fire big enough to consume the whole yard. Yes! That's the solution. Nothing can withstand a fire.

I dropped to my knees, vaguely aware of my wife and Ted taking turns slamming each other against our shed, the same shed my daughter had been skewering with the neighbor's chainsaw.

I pushed the broken branches and bits of swing set aside, then traced my fingers through the earth. I would have Jelker's Warmth, and it would be glorious.

My fingers completed the sigil and I leaned back to slam my hands into it and release all that Magick hungry for an escape, but right before I could, something green poked up from the edge of the design.

A single stalk of rosemary.

I picked it up to toss the offending greenery aside, then hesitated.

Porter wants a green yard, eh? Well, I'll give her a green yard.

I jammed the stalk into the ground and split apart Jelker's Warmth in the process.

"Choke on this greenery, sweetheart. Crescere!"

PORTER, Cathy, and I sat on the back step and admired the destruction, as well as the hundred or so rosemary bushes that peppered our yard now.

My daughter's shoulders slumped. "I'm so sorry I broke Kris's swing set."

"It was already ruined—by me." Porter frowned at her hands.

"I'm just glad neither of you got hurt," I said, looking past them to find Ted, black eye and all, glaring from the window of his house.

My wife stood up and put her hands on her hips. "What are we going to do with this much rosemary?"

"Make chicken," I said, before turning to go inside.

"Very funny, Gene. Where are you going?"

I didn't get to answer. My youngest son did it for me from just inside the house.

"Dad's going to make me a new swing set—a *Dragon* one."

MAGICIAN'S WEEKEND

I took a deep breath and tried to shake off the smell of Cathy's duffle bag in the back seat. My daughter had just wrapped up the week at a late October sleep-away camp in the mountains of northern Georgia. The poor kid was in a whirlwind this weekend—finishing camp, then meeting her mother and brother at the airport for a quick jaunt out to Kansas City and some time with the in-laws.

I reached down and turned up the radio, letting eighties music flood the Dad Wagon with the rich sounds of awesome.

Dad's Weekend!

I drummed on the steering wheel as the Mazda roared onto the highway. The family was safely at the airport and bound for the Midwest, which meant I was free: free to drink beer, ignore basic hygiene, and perhaps even take the weekend off from Magick.

My name is Eugene Law and I'm a Magician. I don't do card tricks or kid's birthday parties. I deal in real Magick, the cosmic powers of the universe, and all the crap that comes with.

An idiot stopped short in front of me, forcing me to throw on the breaks and bringing back a vivid reminder of the last week. I rubbed at my neck and the dull ache that had returned to roost between my shoulder blades. It wasn't unexpected—five nights of tracking a particularly malicious poltergeist, which had culminated in a complex and dangerous exorcism, had been an unpleasant way to spend the week.

But all that's behind me. It's Dad's Weekend!

I merged into traffic, my butt jiving along with righteous guitar riffs of my teenage anthem, while my sore shoulders did their best to rock out against the seat back—spirits be damned.

The wind whipped through my hair from an open window, and I let my open hand float on the breeze to the groove. There might have been a little more gray in my short locks than when I'd originally belted out the words to the song, but that didn't stop me from doing it again, or from ignoring the odd looks from passing motorists.

We need beer.

My brain reminded me that no Dad's Weekend was complete without a trip to my favorite brewery, so it was without hesitation that the Mazda and I pulled off the highway just outside of Ybor City north of Tampa to cruise in and pick up a little nectar of the gods.

* * *

"I'LL NEED a six pack of Unholy, please."

The young lady behind the bar was more than happy to take my cash and send me on my way with an icy cold package of the glorious Tampa Trippel. I set the beers next to

273

my daughter's duffle, the dirty bag's smell almost overpowering the joy of a free Magician's weekend. I smiled at the beer—well, almost.

Adult beverages secured the Mazda and I were back out on the surface streets, and navigating the narrow asphalt back to the Law estate, beer and the biohazard bag in tow.

I hit the button and pulled into the garage of a pale green bungalow Porter and I had lucked into early on in the marriage. After having two kids, we'd had to make a couple of additions to the place, but it still held a little of that old Tampa charm. The Dad Wagon safely back in its spot, I hopped out and practically danced my way around to the passenger door.

My wife's voice came back to me the instant I grabbed the handle of our teenage daughter's disgusting bag.

Don't forget to wash Cathy's clothes.

"No sense in doing today what you can put off for tomorrow," I said to the six pack dangling in my other hand. "These aren't going anywhere." I tossed the bag on the washing machine, letting it clang against the metal lid before promptly forgetting about it all together.

"Now, Mr. Beer, where were we?"

I lovingly carried the bottles into the house, and navigated my way around the toy trucks and blocks my son never seemed to get the hang of putting away until I reached the kitchen. I found a note from my wife on the counter.

Gene, by now you have forgotten about the bag. Put the beer down and wash Cathy's clothes. See you Sunday night. -P

I folded up the note and shoved it in my pocket. The clothes could wait; there were more important tasks ahead. I placed the beers in the fridge and pulled out my phone, my fingers dancing across the tiny glowing display.

"Mark's Pizza."

"Yeah, I'd like to get a..." I stopped, remembering there

was no family this weekend. "I'd like to get a large Man Pizza with double meat."

"Anything else, sir?"

"No, but is that sausage, pepperoni, steak, and—"

"And green peppers, sir," the young man said, his words mixed with the sounds of a busy pizza joint.

"Can you nix the rabbit food and add... I don't know, is there a meat left?"

"Ham, sir?"

"Perfect."

I wrapped up the order, then fished sufficient cash out of my wallet and placed it on the counter.

"Well, Mr. Beer," I said, checking the clock. "It's beverage-o'clock somewhere."

The hands of our large kitchen clock confirmed it was actually closer to seven, and given that it was mid-October, the sun was already quickly vanishing.

"Don't want to miss happy hour." I opened the fridge and let the cool air wash over me before selecting a single bottle to kick start the Dad Weekend.

Only heathens drink from the bottle.

"Ah ha!" I said, discovering a handful of dusty glasses in the cabinet behind an arm of kid's cups. "This'll do nicely."

It was right about this point then I realized that the dull ache between my shoulder blades had wormed its way up to my neck. I twisted my head from side to side a few times and tried to shrug it off, but that only exacerbated it further.

Pop. Fizz...

The beer poured gloriously, like majestic gold. The bright liquid filled my pint glass and left a narrow band of foamy head across the top.

You really should be hydrating if you have a headache.

Porter's voice in my head was right, but since when was my wife being right going to stop me?

"Beer is mostly water," I said to no one but myself.

I retreated to the living room, high-stepping over Kris's toys until I reached the couch, then unceremoniously deposited the kid junk that had consumed those cushions onto the floor and took a seat. I popped on the TV and let the mind-numbing laugh track of yet another recycled sitcom wash over me. We hadn't made it deep into the second act before the door bell rang.

Pizza!

I set the glass on the counter and scooped up the cash.

"Mark's Pizza," the young man on the door step said, holding the oversized box in his hands. "That'll be—"

"Here you go," I shoved the wad of cash into his hands. "Keep the change."

"Hey, thanks." The kid tucked the greenbacks in his jacket. "You got a cool cat, man."

"Huh?"

Sure enough, pressing against the young man's legs, was a black cat—its right ear torn like a cheap paperback and its nose clearly loving the smell of meat pizza.

"I don't have a cat."

"Oh," the kid said, not sure what to make of the stray pressing against his shins. "That's weird."

I shrugged my shoulders. "Cats."

The pain in my neck was ramping up, but I figured the pizza would help with that.

The feline made a motion toward the open door, and I pushed it back with my foot. "Nope, no cats in here."

Hiss!

The cat took a swipe at my shoe, but its claws didn't make it past the leather. "Go! Get out of here."

"You sure that's not your cat?"

"Positive," I said, frowning at the ornery animal sitting on my front porch.

"Odd."

"Whatever. Thanks for the pizza." I slammed the door and took my double-meat masterpiece back to the dining room table. For a second I contemplated getting a plate, but the blessed aroma of pizza and beer was too much. I opened the box and removed a slice.

"See this, Mr. Beer, this is double-meat—"

Meow!

The cat was perched at the sidelight window of my front door, its stupid clipped-ear face pressed up against the glass.

Meow!

"Go!" I shouted, putting the pizza down and feeling the full extent of the building headache. It had now solidly taken root at the base of my skull and was clamping down just behind the ears, constricting the blood flow to the important decision-making bits.

Meow!

"Damn cat." I banged on the glass. "Get out of here. Go!"

Chirp!

My cell phone chirped on the counter, pulling my attention away from the retreating tabby. It was Adam, my apprentice, an early thirty-something young man with a flair for Magick, but also a decidedly frustrating inability to grow up.

Gene, my Wizards and Warlocks group needs a place to game tonight. Mom kicked us out. Can we come in?

I had my fingers in motion drafting a resounding no when I noticed the second half of his message, then looked up to see the pudgy, bearded man waving through the same sidelight the cat had been in only moments before.

My headache immediately ramped up five notches.

* * *

"ADAM," I said, the door opening the moment after I remembered I'd given him a key and made sure all the protective incantations I'd placed on it would allow him through.

Damn it.

"What are you—"

My apprentice jingled a felt bag of what sounded like dice. "Gene, thank you so much for... Holy crap, is that double-meat Man Pizza?"

"Yes, I was going—"

"Hey everybody, Gene got us pizza!"

No, no, he most certainly didn't.

My apprentice gestured to a small group of equally ragtag individuals, introducing them one at a time and directing them into my house with what I hoped were their character names. "Okay, Gene, this is Amanderous the Flowing," he said directing my attention to the petite redhead.

She hid behind a pair of red and black horn-rimmed glasses and offered only a modest wave. "Hey."

"It's nice to meet you, but I'm not sure I have time to—"

"Amanderous is a sea-elf ranger. She's hella proficient with her Bow of Agility and Short Sword of Gleaming Might."

"Night," the young woman said, pulling out a seat at my kitchen table.

Adam tilted his head. "What's that?"

Amanderous pulled off her backpack and drew out a set of papers. "It's the Sword of Gleaming *Night.*"

That doesn't make any sense... Stop, Gene, you need to take control before this gets worse.

The redhead lifted the lid and snaked a piece of Man Pizza from the box. "Thanks for getting pizza."

Too late, it has officially gotten worse.

My headache jumped up a couple more notches. The

pounding at the base of my skull had now staked out new territory behind my ears. "I—"

Amanderous waved me off. "I don't need a plate, it's cool."

No, no it's not cool.

"Gene," my apprentice directed my attention back to the door. "This is Edvilandia."

The lanky young man stooped his shoulders to fit under the eve. "Hey."

"Uh, hi. Listen, Adam—"

"Edvilandia is a cleric of the dark gods."

"They have better spells." The young man slid my pizza box around and took a seat next to the redhead. "I mean, I get tired of healing all the time."

My scathing glare should have burned Adam to a crisp where he stood, but somehow my apprentice remained blissfully ignorant of the veins protruding from my neck.

"And last but not least, I want to introduce you to Jacster the…"

"Vengeful," the diminutive young man said, shucking his immense backpack on my floor like an overworked Sherpa. "I'm going with Jacster the Vengeful."

"Not the lawyerly?" Adam asked.

"No." The shorter man drew a few eye rolls from the rest of the pizza-eating party crashers. "Vengeful."

"Got it." My apprentice pointed to an open chair.

Jacster the Vengeful took his spot and immediately enacted his mighty vengeance on my Man Pizza, folding a particularly large slice and sticking the business end in his mouth.

"Adam." I fought back against the headache now crawling up the back of my head like a piton-driving mountaineer. "May I have a word with you?"

My bearded apprentice nodded, then placed his own backpack below the table and slid down the zipper of his hoodie to half-mast. "Sure thing. Let me get my Cavern Master's screen up and get things ready."

"Is he playing?" Amanderous pulled her hair back in a pony tail. "We need a rogue."

Edvilandia's lovestruck eyes glazed over. He was clearly a tad bit enamored with the sea elf sitting next to him. "That's a great idea."

"Yeah, that would be awesome. Gene, you don't mind taking a pre-made character, right?"

"I don't know what—"

"Pinkersty the Plucky." Jacster, the motley crew's bag man, removed a thick stack of books and papers from his pack. "Here you go."

Adam accepted the paper for me. "All right, I'll explain all of this, but for the moment you just have to get up to speed on the basics."

"Adam."

"This is Pinkersty the Plucky. He's a halfling rogue with a peg leg."

"Adam."

"I know what you're thinking, peg leg doesn't make sense for a thief, but I'm telling you, with a fifteen in agility and a sixteen in likability, Pinkersty is a force to be reckoned with."

"Adam!" I cried, grabbing the young man by his hoodie and dragging him into the kitchen. "Stop talking."

My apprentice's mouth hung open, his eyes as wide as the plates no one at my dining room table was presently using. "Okay."

I had a hundred things I wanted to say to him, but the lot of them couldn't decide which one would make it out my mouth first. It was like a checkout lane on Black Friday—all my choice words were too busy fighting each other rather than taking out their frustrations on the bearded kid directly in front of me. "Gah!"

Adam smiled and nodded, then placed a hand on my shoulder. "It's cool, man. I know you don't do role-playing games, but I can totally vouch for you. I'll keep it simple. Don't worry. In fact, I'll do the first few rolls for you."

I let go of his hoodie—I had to—the headache had made its way to the crown of my head, and I could feel each of my hairs. "Ugh."

"Gene's in," my apprentice cried, rejoining his band of merry misfits. "Anybody want a beer?"

No!

My apprentice opened the fridge and retrieved my Dad's Weekend five pack and placed it on the table. The bottles disappeared like puddles on a hot day, the resident sea elf providing a key-chain opener.

"So, where were we?" Adam pulled out the seat at the head of my table and set up a folded paper screen.

Jacster consulted the materials in front of him like my accountant at tax time. "Edvilandia was getting firewood and we were going to camp for the night. You had told him to roll for ingenuity."

Clunk!

The heavy plastic dice rolled across my table, the noise exacerbating the already throbbing pain between my ears.

"Fifteen," Edvilandia the Lanky slammed his palm on the table hard enough to rattle my already unhappy neurons. "Hot damn."

Adam's consulted his paper screen, his pudgy fingers running down a chart on the inside. "Success. The fire is lit and providing you warmth."

"I stand away from the flames," Amanderous said, clicking her pen in rapid-fire and highly grating fashion. "My sea elf doesn't want to risk drying out."

"Right." Adam nodded.

Jacster splayed out another book like he was field-gutting fresh game. "I use my perception and check the forest."

Perception? You failed, all of you failed.

"Roll," Adam said, his hands gripping the top of that paper screen.

"Sixteen." The small man's voice was giddy.

"You use your barbarian powers of perception to see deep into the forest and find something hiding in the brush."

"What is it?"

Adam turned to me. I was still leaning against the counter in the kitchen trying to fight through the darkening edges of my fading vision. "Let's let Pinkersty try. Would you like to roll?"

I'd like to roll all of you out my door.

"You can do it," I said, the sound of my words like a cheese grater against my cerebellum.

"Eighteen." Adam's cry elicited an excited table banging from the rest of the nerds and sent my head spinning. "You see... a troll!"

A hush descended over the table, only to be quickly replaced by Jacster's furious page turning. "I draw my Double-sided Battle Axe of Righteous Destruction and step in front of the fire."

"Amanderous, Edvilandia, what about you?" Adam the Cavern Master asked, rattling dice in his hand.

"Hey, Pinkersty." The young woman popped up and pointed to something by my door. "I think your cat wants inside." The sea-elf didn't let me finish before she slipped out of her seat and opened the door, letting the black ball of fur shoot past us into the living room.

Adam raised an eyebrow. "When did you get a cat, Gene?"

I wanted to respond, but the headache had made it to my temples, and had taken up jack hammering them like a teamster. "I..."

"I prepare a spell." Amanderous circled something on a paper in front of her.

"Which one?"

How about Leave House...

"I'm going to prepare to summon a Blade Mistress." The young woman rolled a few dice and totaled up the numbers. "It's going to take two rounds."

"The troll lets out a wild yell and smashes the closest tree," Adam cried, his words grating my already sensitive skull. "A piece of tree hits Pinkersty, knocking him to the ground and taking"—a die shot across the table—"five life points!"

Boom!

I hit the ground like I'd reached the end of a roller coaster and forgotten to put on my harness. Standing on the other side of the counter I'd just been leaning against and peeling back the broken drywall and shattered wall studs as if they were crepe paper was a very large, and very real Bridge Troll. Its round head and stucco-like skin were covered in tiny flecks of what had must have been a really nice part of the living room.

Adam rattled dice in his hand. "So, Pinkersty, you ready to roll for initiative?"

* * *

I CLUTCHED my head and tried to figure out how a Bridge Troll had made it past my Magickal defenses. "Adam, get down."

"You got it." My apprentice tossed a die across the table, oblivious to the troll tearing his way through what remained of the kitchen, "Pinkersty jabs his dagger at the troll's kneecap." The multi-faceted plastic rattled against the crumbly remains of what had been my Man Pizza. "Ten. That's a miss."

The Bridge Troll's massive body pushed past my sink, tearing the recently remodeled metal like a candy wrapper, before tossing it into the far wall where it crashed to the floor next to Edvilandia the Skinny.

"Is my champion summoned yet?" Amanderous doodled little swirls on her paper while a very real Bridge Troll grabbed my legs with both catcher's mitt hands.

Adam shook his head. "Nope, one more round. Jacster?"

The pint-sized bookbarian said something I couldn't make out against the backdrop of being dragged across the broken tile floor.

"Adam, snap out of it." I swung my arms and tried to get the bearded Cavern Master's attention.

"So you are going to try a Wild Yell Raging?" my apprentice asked, consulting his paper screen.

"Yeah."

The Troll had me by my shirt and inches from his oversized face. Its thick lay skin piled like badly poured concrete, holding two angry, deep-set eyes.

I tried to keep my pounding brain from oozing out my ears and spoke to the Troll in measured tones. "We don't have any issues. Just walk out that door and we'll call it even."

The Troll hesitated.

Please?

Jacster grabbed a handful of dice and shot them across the table. "Eight, plus my proficiency bonus and my magical Loin Cloth of Girding gives me fourteen."

"I'm sorry." Adam shook his head. "Your attempts to inspire strength and confidence in your party backfire and send the troll into a murderous rage."

Oh, hell.

The Bridge Troll's dark eyes flashed the instant before its

fist hit my chest. For the second time today, I hit the hard floor, this time expelling just about all the precious air that had been in my lungs.

"Edvilandia, it's your turn. Pinkersty is down five life points. Do you heal him?"

I coughed at the dust and did my best to suck air back into my lungs.

That would be nice.

"No, sorry, Pinkersty, I'm calling on the dark gods to bring their fury against the troll."

Of course you are.

Adam leaned over the cardboard shield like a kid at Christmas. "Roll."

"What the hell is wrong with you guys—"

"Fifteen." The string bean pumped his noodle arms in the air. "Yes!"

The lights flickered, and a swirling mass of unholy darkness appeared between me and the Troll. I squinted my eyes at the brilliant flashes of purple and green emanating from that cloud of hovering evil.

"Not so fast." The Cavern Master consulted his infernal chart, giving me time to back away from the malevolent black hole quickly filling the space between my kitchen and dining room. "The troll's natural magic resistance gives him an advantage against the dark gods." Adam rolled a die behind the cardboard cover. "Twenty!"

"Show me!" all three of the players shouted.

I might have wanted to see it too, but in that moment black tentacles had begun to reach out of the reality bending hole opening up in what had been my dining room. "Adam!"

"Damn." Jacster consulted his books. "Perfect strike. So what happens?"

"I can tell you what happens," I said, kicking back at the

vile octopus like appendages reaching for my legs. "You four get the hell out of my house and take whatever it is—"

"The dark gods turn on you. Their evil tentacles reach for you, hungry to crush your bones into dust."

"Whoops, sorry guys." Edvilandia's face fell.

"Son of a... That's it," I reached for my Magick. I'd had just about enough of all of this. It was time to hit back. I didn't know what sort of enchantment my apprentice was under, but I figured I'd swing first and ask questions later. "Ledo," I shouted, willing the well of cosmic power in my body to break the tentacle's grasp on my leg.

Nothing happened.

Oh, shit.

Adam shook his head. "Remember, you can't use magic. Pinkersty is a rogue. Sorry, Gene."

"What the—"

"Amanderous, it's your turn." The Cavern Master pointed to the redhead twirling her pen.

"Is my champion ready?"

Black and slimy tentacles reached for my legs. "Please no, guys! Just stop. I can't take much more of—"

Adam nodded. "You bet. The skies open and a beautiful Sword Maiden charges down on a moonbeam. She's the most stunning woman any of you have ever seen. Her armor shines with the brightness of the sun, and her sword glows with the righteous fire of the great warriors of old."

Amanderous scribbled something on her paper. "Kick ass. I tell her to attack the old gods and the Troll."

"You tell her what?"

Porter?!

Bedecked in shining armor that certainly was meant to attract the eye far more than protect its wearer from edged weapons, my wife stood behind me, broadsword in hand and flexing muscles I didn't remember her having. "What the hell?" she said, letting her sword dip so she could examine the undersized silver chest plate barely keeping a comically well-endowed bosom covered. "Is this how you see me?"

"Yes, but I'm far more concerned that this is how Adam sees you."

The valiant heroine removed her ornamental helmet, "Oh... now, that's just creepy."

The headache advanced past my forehead. It squeezed down on my eyes so much that I was fairly certain they'd pop out and roll across the floor if I made any sudden movements. Sadly, the dark gods didn't feel the same way. The black tentacles trapped my arms and legs, then dragged me across the floor. I rolled over the broken tile directly toward the yawning portal to madness. "Porter!"

"What do I do?" my wife cried, pushing the helmet back on her head.

"The sword. You swing the damn sword!"

"You don't have to yell at me."

More tentacles wrapped my legs, while somewhere behind the portal to insanity, the Bridge Troll had figured out how to take the long route back to me and smash his way through the other side of my kitchen.

"Just swing the—" My words were cut off by the slimy blackness of string bean's dark gods.

Slash!

My wife, the Sword Maiden, swung her blade in a wide arc, and sliced through the dark god's tentacles. The gleaming metal narrowly missed removing my leg in the process.

"Hey, this is kinda cool."

"Watch out," I cried, spitting the tentacle from my mouth.

"Huh?"

I was too late. The Bridge Troll's massive fist collided

with Porter's head, sending my heroine and her sword crashing into our coat rack.

"Your Sword Maiden takes twenty life points." Adam scribbled something on a sheet of paper. "How many does she have left?"

"Porter!"

"I'm okay." My wife pushed her gleaming, armored chest and bare legs out of the pile of broken wood and once-a-year winter coats.

Amanderous scrunched up her face. "Twenty? She's got three life points left."

Porter collapsed back into the splintered boards, blood suddenly flowing from newly discovered wounds, and her once shiny armor now laying bent and misshapen against her petite frame. I scrambled toward her, but Edvilandia the Lanky's dark gods and the Bridge Troll had other ideas. The former wrapped its tentacles around my neck, while the latter hooked my legs in its granite-crushing grip.

"Pinkersty," Adam said, looking up from his screen and twirling a pencil in his fingers. "It's your move."

I clawed at the tightening appendages of the inky black dark gods, while at the same time kicking out my feet in the hopes I could separate from the Bridge Troll—I wasn't making any headway with either.

"Do you want to use your dagger?" the Cavern Master asked, the rest of the motley crew leaning in to hear my response.

"I…"

The pain in my head had now come full circle, its vise-like pressure squeezing what brain cells I had left into an increasingly tighter space. If I still had my Magick, it had found a way to escape my every attempt to use it. The power I'd called upon to escape an almost countless number of scrapes was nowhere to be found, and Porter lay just beyond me, her once-gleaming sword faded and tarnished.

None of this made sense, but when Magick was involved things rarely did. Still, this entire experience was surreal even for me.

"Meow!"

Darkness encroached on the edges of my vision while that damn stray cat scratched at the door to my garage.

There's a cat in my house. Why is there a cat in my house?

"What do you want to do, Pinkersty? It's your move."

It might have been my move, but the dark gods and a very zealous Bridge Troll had already worked more than enough moves of their own—realigning my spine in unique and non-traditional ways.

"Meow!"

Why is there a cat in my house? And what does it want in the garage?

My head rolled to the side as the darkness closed in, leaving me with Adam's words and a view of Porter's sword.

It's your move...

* * *

THE SWORD, *just reach the sword.*

"Gene, I mean, Pinkersty it's your move. If you don't know what to do, I can help you."

Adam the Cavern Master was doing his best, but the blinding pain in my head was stronger. Flashes of light and starburst vision sparkled around the silvery blade.

Just a little closer.

My fingers grazed the sword's edge, even as I felt every one of my heartbeats.

Almost got it...

"Okay, I'll just have Pinkersty use his advanced rogue

subterfuge skills and escape detection," Adam rolled a few heavy plastic dice across my table. "Eighteen!"

"Nice work, Pinkersty." Jacster flipped through one of his many rulebooks. "It looks like he should be near undetectable for the current round unless his opponent succeeds in a thwarting throw of more than two times the current distance divided by the—"

"It works," the Cavern Master said, brushing off the pint-sized barbarian.

"But the—"

Adam leaned over his cardboard screen and made eye contact with the younger man. "It works."

"Well, that's not how the rules indicate, but I'll allow it." A clearly annoyed Jacster closed his book.

Thump.

I wasn't expecting to hit the ground, and for a moment I was sure I'd survived the impact—that was until the hot flash of pain lanced its way through my skull. "Ugh."

"Gene," Porter said, pushing herself up against the coat rack. Her skimpy armor splattered with blood. "Where are you?"

I sat up to find my wife's eyes searching the room frantically for me. "Here."

"I can't see you."

She might not see me, but the Bridge Troll could see her, and that was never a good thing.

"Look out!" I cried, but she didn't stand a chance. The living mountain of poorly laid concrete had her in its beady sights.

Porter raised a gauntleted wrist, but the Troll's fist was like taking a wrecking ball at close range. My Sword Maiden rocketed across the foyer and skid over the broken tile before slamming into the front door.

"Porter!"

"The troll takes"—Adam rolled a die—"one life point —lucky."

"Meow!" The feral cat continued to scrape its claws down the door to my garage. Her claws left faint marks in the white paint.

Amanderous pushed up her glasses and leafed through the papers in front of her, then paused to lean over and whisper something to Edvilandia. Based on the look on his face, she'd just inadvertently become the first woman not named mom to place her lips that close to his ears.

"Let's do it." Edvilandia grinned.

I was convinced she could have told him to clean the gutters and gotten the same reaction.

I grabbed Porter's sword. It was surprisingly heavy—but then again I'd never held a two-handed broadsword before today. Blinding flashes of pain lanced through my head. I tried to blink them back, but the room continued to pulse in time with the beating of my heart.

"Edvilandia and I are working together. I'm going to cast 'Bleeding Hearts of Inspiration' while the servant of the dark gods here is going to send the spirit of... who was it again?"

The string bean jumped up. "Morganus the Vile. I'm going to send the avenging demon Morganus the Vile into the Sword Maiden. That will boost her agility and her strength—"

"Life points go up by fifty," Jacster said, consulting one of the many volumes splayed out in front of him. "Nice work."

The Troll's back was to me. Just a few more feet and I'd be there. Porter's sword dragged along the tile, its blade too heavy for my tired shoulders.

Come on, you can do this!

"Sounds like a plan." Adam ran his fingers through an unkempt beard. "Roll."

"Sixteen," the duo said, excitement in the voices.

"It works!"

"Meow!"

The Troll's back was right in front of me. All I had to do was raise the sword and deliver a killing blow, but before I could get the silvery steel at the ready, a black and pulsing blade of pure evil tore through the Troll's thick hide.

"Porter?"

"Hardly," came a voice from my past on the other side of the dying monster.

"Morgan?"

Wearing dark, skintight armor laced with black roses and malevolent skulls, my ex-girlfriend's flaming black blade cut the Bridge Troll in two, and left a blue-blooded mess on my foyer floor.

"Gene, it's so good to see you," Morganus the Vile said, her eyes hungry with unholy malice. "I'm going to enjoy this."

Adam sat back behind his screen. "The troll is dead."

"Woohoo!"

"But." He leaned forward again, letting only his eyes peek above the screen. "Morganus the Vile summons an army of vampire zombies from the surrounding forest. Did you forget that this was the Dead Woods?"

The table plunged into silence, the excitement of defeating the troll vanishing instantly with this new revelation.

Crash!

Clawing undead hands shattered the sidelight of my front door and reached for us.

"Oh, for the love of all things—damn it, Adam," I fought to get Porter's sword off the ground. "Really?!"

The black flames of Morganus's cold steel cast a dark radiance against my wife's blade. "This is your end, Eugene Law."

Clang!

The black fire weapon cut the air in a wide arc and caught on the chandelier my wife had insisted on hanging when we first moved in. I'd been dead set against it at the time, but I hadn't counted on it being useful for edged weapon defense.

Adam checked the results of his last roll. "Morganus the Vile misses. Now, let's see how the vampiric zombie horde did."

I stumbled backward, trying to keep the sword maiden's blade between me and a heavily armed ex. "Son of a—are you serious?"

"Meow!"

Crash!

"The vampiric zombies attack"—our Cavern Master tossed a die across the table—"and get a... one?"

Pale white arms and bloody fangs broke through my front window, only to bunch up against the frame like overzealous preschoolers on free ice cream day.

"About damn time," I said, my back making contact with the door to the garage, the impact sending a fresh wave of pain through my skull. "Argh!"

"Meow!"

Boom.

Morganus the Vile's evil blade broke free of the chandelier and sent it crashing to the tile.

"Aw, hell."

My ex was on me in an instant, her dark armor flooding the house with an eerie purple light. "Now I'll end what you started all those years ago, Gene." She pressed the cold steel of her blade against my neck. "I'm going to enjoy watching you die."

Behind the demonic woman, the vampire zombie horde forced their way through the jagged remains of my front window. Pale white claws and bloody fangs filed into my house like spawning salmon.

"Meow!" The feral cat rammed its head against my knee, then resumed scratching at the door.

What the hell do you want?

"Morganus the Vile swings her sword to separate Pinkersty's head from his body—sorry, Gene, it's just a game." Adam shook the dice in his hand. "If she gets a sixteen or better, Pinkersty is toast."

Hatred, abject and pure boiled in the eyes of my ex. "It's finally over, Gene."

The plastic die rolled across the table, bouncing off the now empty pizza box and clanging against half-drunk beers.

Morganus's evil blade pressed against my neck, while something else squeezed my lower back.

The knob...

"She rolls a—"

"Meow!"

I dropped Porter's sword and closed my eyes. My fingers found the handle to the garage and gave it a turn.

"Fifteen!"

The door opened, and I fell backward, my demonic ex's blade missing me by scant inches as the garage floor raced up to greet the base of my skull.

Bright flashes of light erupted in my head, followed by gut-churning pain. Like a puma on the hunt, the cat leapt on to my workbench and sent half-repaired toys crashing to the ground along with an expertly sorted jars of screws. The room spun, the walls melting into a blurry watercolor of faded colors, but still the cat continued undaunted on her collision course with my daughter's faded bag.

Hiss! Scrape! Squeak!

The sound of claws on fabric and the high-pitched cry of a cornered animal were the last things I remembered before my world faded to white.

* * *

PURR...

I opened my eyes to find myself face to face with the bright golden eyes of that damn one-eared porch cat.

Thump.

She dropped one very dead and rather iridescent lump of wet flesh on my chest, then resumed her rather self-satisfied expression.

I pushed myself up, surprised to find my head no longer pounding.

"What's this... A Cerebellix?"

The now dead brain rat lay harmless on my chest. Native to the questionable decision-making states, the infuriating creatures possessed a penchant for causing hallucinations and, with enough exposure, madness. It must have made its way into Cathy's bag before she left Georgia.

I tossed the bloody lump aside and ran a hand over the cat's head. "Uh, thanks, buddy."

"Meow."

I dragged myself up and wandered back into the house, overjoyed to find it exactly the way I'd left it. There was no gaming group eating my rapidly cooling pizza, and the beers in my fridge were still unopened and waiting for what I hoped might be a salvageable Magician's weekend.

Knock! Knock!

My apprentice's face appeared in the sidelight, along with the faces of his buddies. "Hey, Gene, can we use your house for our—"

I immediately turned around and walked back into the garage.

"Hey, guys. I think he's going to open the garage door."

I opened the sprinkler box and turned them on, then

smiled to myself at the sound of Adam and his friends making a run for their car.

"So, cat," I said, returning to the house and finding my beer exactly where I'd left it. "How do you feel about Man Pizza?"

"Meow."

"I couldn't have said it better myself."

SHORT STOP

"*H*elp me, Scotty-wan-kenobi, you are my only hope."

That wasn't exactly true, but I needed the kid and he didn't appear exactly interested in offering assistance. I figured it would be best to appeal to his inner child-like sense of wonder.

I'd forgotten Scotty had no such thing.

"Scotty-wan-what?" The twelve-year-old scrunched up his face and tried to close the door on my foot a second time.

"You know, Star Wars? Come on. You've never seen Star Wars?"

"Star's fighting? It sounds lame. I have an early paper run in the morning. A paper I believe you still have yet to actually pay for."

The kid was right, but the Demon Hunting business had dried up as of late, and that meant cash was a rare commodity. In short, that meant I had none and could really use a paying gig before they turned off the power.

My name is Ed Lovely, and I hunt Demons. It's really

terribly dangerous and low-paying work, but I'll be damned if it isn't fun as hell.

The ginger-haired kid pushed at my sneaker with his own and tried to dislodge me from the door seam. "So have a good night, Ed."

"Night? It's barely nine. Come on, Scotland, where's your sense of adventure?"

"Getting ready to brush its teeth and go to bed. Do you have any idea how early the paper comes in the morning? Do you know how hard it is to get all of them delivered on time, to the appropriate location, bagged and sealed for safety?"

"Not directly, but having received—"

The kid sighed and slumped his shoulders with the same practiced precision I'd seen in men fifty years his senior. "Then you'll have to trust me when I say I need to go to bed now if you expect to get your paper in the morning."

Pop!

Scotty's foot dislodged mine and the door slammed shut, leaving me alone on the front porch.

"Scotty?"

Click!

The light above my head winked off. You'd almost have thought he wanted me to go.

"Scotty!" I pressed my face against a sidelight panel of dark glass beside the door making fish impressions. "It's important."

"Good night, Ed."

"It's a matter of life and death."

"That's nice. I'll see you in the morning."

"Fine. If you don't want to help the Sidewinders, then I'll find someone else."

I turned around and took a few pretend steps toward the stairs.

Three... Two...

Creak.

I turned around to find Scotty's face back in the door seam. "Did you say the Sidewinders?"

"Yes."

Scotty was a baseball fan. I can't say I cared much for sports one way or the other, but for the twelve-year-old, baseball was life. I think it appealed to his inner accountant. The kid got positively giddy filling out a box score during a game, pointing out the complex tracking needed to determine just what sort of 'out' had occurred. I tried to assure him at the time that there had to have been other people scoring the game, but that earned me nothing but an eye-roll and a long-winded speech on the benefits of understanding the game at a deeper level.

I'd left halfway through to get a hot dog.

"The Central Florida Sidewinders?"

I nodded, reeling in my catch like a practiced angler. "I don't know, are there other baseball teams in town?"

There weren't.

Bang!

The door closed and the light popped back on. It didn't take the kid more than sixty seconds to re-emerge from the house dressed in jeans and a Sidewinders t-shirt.

"So, I take it you are in?"

The ginger-headed baseball fanatic nodded. "What's the problem? Is it the batting? I figured there was something nefarious going on. The batting average has been dropping for weeks and after the last series against the Kinitsu Carp—"

"I'll explain on the way." I pointed to Scotty's bike locked up nicely on the porch. "I need you to drive."

Scotty hesitated, the kid's steely gaze returning quickly. "This isn't going to be like last time, is it?"

I frowned. "Last time?"

"When you almost got me eaten by a Mongolian Death Worm?"

I brushed his concern away. "You wouldn't have gotten eaten. Geez, so melodramatic, Scotland. Besides, that was a baby worm. It couldn't have been more than eight feet long. Plus, if I recall correctly, Mongol Mammas gave you a free side with your next order."

"I told you I'm never going back there."

"Really? That's a shame. I love their barbecue. I wonder if they'd let me use your coupon?"

Scotty frowned and turned toward the door. "On second thought maybe I should just stay home."

"Well, if you want. I just figured you wouldn't want to miss out on helping Clint Michael, but maybe I was wrong. Have a good night, Scotty. I'll do my best without you."

"Wait!" The delivery boy practically pounced on his bike to unlock it. "Clint? *The* Clint Michael?"

"I guess."

"Ed, the Sidewinder's three time MVP and home run derby champion?"

"Scotland, I have no idea what those words mean."

Thump.

Scotty tossed the bike chain in the corner and pointed to the handle bars. "I'll explain on the way. Do you think I can get an autograph?"

"I'm sure of it." I dropped my butt on the front of his bike as soon as it reached the sidewalk. "Just promise me you'll be cool about it."

"I will, totally. Clint Michael. Wow. Ed, this is the nicest thing anyone has ever done for me."

"You can thank me later. Tally ho, Scotland, danger awaits."

The kid pushed off and pedaled hard to overcome inertia,

then turned his bike toward the distant stadium. "This is going to be awesome."

"Sure is, Scotty, but we need to make a quick stop first. Tell me, did you bring any cash?"

* * *

WE PULLED up to the empty field a little past eleven. The joyous shine now rubbed completely off my favorite delivery boy. "Hot dogs and buns, Ed?"

"Don't forget the mustard," I said, the grocery bag bouncing in my lap. "You did yeoman's work back there. Really and truly. The way you complained to that old woman that the hot dogs came in a pack of eight, yet the buns were in a pack of ten? Genius."

"It's stupid. Why am I paying for buns I'm not going to eat?"

I hopped off the bike just outside the tiny stadium. "I ask myself this very same question every single day."

Scotty noticed the field was dark a good bit quicker than I expected him too. The kid was quite perceptive for his age.

"Why are the lights off? Where is Clint Michael?"

"Scotty, patience my good man, patience. Demon Hunting is an art."

"You said we were helping—"

I shoved the grocery bag into his hands. "We are helping. In fact, you are helping. I'm thinking there are going to be some free sides in your future, and no one is going to get eaten by a Mongolian Death Worm."

The ginger-haired kid leaned his bike against the closest tree. "Okay... If you say so." He ran a hand through his hair a few times. "Do I look okay? I want to look cool when I meet Clint."

"Totally." I pointed to the turnstiles outside the tiny baseball stadium. "Look, there he is now."

An old man, stooped over and leaning hard on the metal railing waved from the furthest gate.

"Ed, that's not Clint Michael."

I hooked an arm around the slippery delivery boy before he could change his mind and dragged him toward the waiting man. "Scotty, I would like to introduce you to Clinton Michael, groundskeeper for the Sidewinders and our client."

"Grounds keep—"

"It's a pleasure to meet you, young man." The wizened old salt extended a leathery hand. "The Sidewinders are lucky to have dedicated fans like you and Ed willing to help them when the chips are down. Speaking of chips, did you get any?" Clinton smacked his chapped lips.

I pulled a bag of the potato variety from the groceries and gave them a polite shake. "Yep, Scotland here found these on sale. I'm telling you, I don't know what I'd do without him. The boy is a miracle worker."

Clinton admired the bag briefly, then switched the turnstile open and unlocked the gate. "Good, because that's exactly what we need—a miracle."

"You hear that, Scotty?" I pushed a now very reluctant delivery boy into the darkened stadium. "They need you. The Sidewinders need you."

Clinton took a few steps, then stopped. "What size do you think he is?"

"Ed, what is he—"

"He's small, but wiry. I'd go with a petite."

"Petite?!"

Clinton hesitated. "I'm not sure we have a petite. Would a ladies small work?"

"I don't see why not."

Clinton nodded. "Excellent. We'll get you outfitted. It's almost feeding time."

"Ed!"

I brushed his concerns away with my hand and scooted him after the groundskeeper . "Miracles, Scotty. Miracles. The Sidewinders need you, but just in case, do you happen to have that free side coupon for Mongol Mammas?"

* * *

"You look great. Very form-fitting. You look fast just standing there."

Scotty tugged on the woefully undersized uniform and followed me toward the rubbery pentagon. "I don't know. I don't think it fits..."

"Bah! It fits great. Excellent. Superb. Why, you look like a baseball person."

"Player."

"What's that?"

Scotty frowned and swung his arms a few times trying to stretch out the stiff fabric. "Baseball player."

"Right, yes, that. Why, if I walked past you on the street I'd say there's a guy that can score goals. Lots of goals."

Scotty opened his mouth as if to correct me, but instead just slumped his shoulders. "What are we doing here, Ed?"

Pop! Pop!

Bright-white light flooded the orange clay and green grass. Clinton must have turned on the field lights.

"Huh, it's diamond shaped..." I found the geometric shape of the field oddly satisfying.

"That's why they call it a baseball diamond, Ed. Do you really know nothing about baseball?"

Scotty asked this question with a tone that had me

thinking he found my lack of knowledge strangely off-putting.

"I could ask you the same thing. Tell me, Mr. Junior Assistant Demon Hunter. How much do you know about Lelvicks and luck wrangling in our nation's oldest pastime?"

Scotty frowned. "You just made that up."

"I most certainly did not. Latin name Fortunam Timere Vermis, the Lelvick comes from the same genus as the—"

"Hey, Ed!" groundskeeper Clinton waved from an open gate by the side of the chalk-painted diamond, a small black grill in his hands. "I'm going to set up on the third base line."

"What's that mean?" I whispered to Scotty.

The kid sighed and pointed down the painted diamond to a spot off to our left. "He's going to put the Hibachi over there."

"The what?"

"The tiny grill. It's Japanese."

"Huh. That makes a lot of sense," I said, surprised at the kismet of Clinton's Japanese grill. "Okay, Scotland. Here's the deal. I need you to stand on that white pentagon there."

"You mean home plate?"

I rolled my eyes. "Sure, if that's what you want to call it. The point is I need you to stand on it."

Scotty didn't budge, and instead stared intently at the rubbery off-white platform. "What's it going to do to me?"

The sharp smell of kerosene filled the evening air as Clinton dumped lighter fluid on the tiny grill.

"What's it going to do—It's not going to do anything to you." I put a foot on the pentagon and took it off again, then repeated this maneuver a few times until I was reasonably certain Scotty believed me. The kid was still frowning, but that was sort of his default position, so it was hard to be sure. "Hop on."

The ginger-headed delivery boy shook his head. "No."

Whoosh!

The sound of lighter fluid erupting into flames got both of our attention, but Clinton was a pro, and certainly appeared to still be in possession of both eyebrows.

"What do you mean no? The Sidewinders need you."

Scotty took a step back. "Ever since I've known you I've almost lost my soul on at least five occasions, and I've lost count of how many times something has tried to eat me."

"Really?" I scrunched up my face. "I would have figured you kept a spreadsheet or something."

"That's it. I'm out of here."

"Wait." I grabbed his arm. "The Sidewinders need you."

"What, Ed? What do they need me to do?"

The smell of burning charcoal wafted up from Clinton's grill.

"All right, Scotland. I'll level with you."

"Finally."

I nodded slowly and looped an arm around the boy's shoulder, gently directing him toward the pentagon. "It's luck, Scotty."

"Luck?"

"The Kinitsu Carp—"

"I hate those guys," Scotty said, a hint of venom in his voice.

"Yeah, terrible baseball peop—players. Just terrible. But they left something behind."

Scotty hesitated. "What did they leave behind?"

I frowned and swept my hand over the field. "Bad luck."

Scotty stomped his foot. "I knew it."

"Wait, you what?"

The kid slipped out from under my arm and started counting off incidents with his fingers. "Unforced errors, wild pitches, a batting average that's tanking like a boat anchor."

"Exactly! See unforced pitches and boat anchor errors are exactly why they need you."

"What can I do?"

I pointed to the rubbery pentagon. "Hop on and I'll tell you."

The delivery boy jumped on with both feet. The instant he did, the first tremors started.

"What was that?" Scotty asked, all the color immediately draining from his face.

"Fortuna Timere Vermis, Scotty, a whole lot of them, but we've got you."

Sizzle!

The distant groundskeeper threw a hot dog on the tiny grill. "Ready when you are, Ed!"

"Thanks, Clinton. They're stirring. Should be good to go any minute."

Scotty went to step off, but I stopped him. "Nope. You have to run the squares."

"It's bases, and no way."

The bright orange clay rippled as something moved underneath it, many somethings by the look of it.

"That's odd, I figured there'd just be two. They come in pairs most of the time."

The clay shifted like a herd of migrating gophers had set up shop just below the surface.

"Ed—"

"Hey, Clinton. We're gonna need more hot dogs."

The groundskeeper nodded and pulled out the plastic package. "How many?"

Clay rolled in from the distant bases like waves at the shore. "All of them."

Sizzle!

"You got it."

I gave him a thumbs up then turned my attention back to

the shaking delivery boy. "All right, Scotland. Are you ready to fix the Sidewinder's luck problem?"

"No."

"That's the spirit! We're going to show those Kinistu Carp we look out for the home squad."

"Team."

I nodded. "Right. Go team!"

The clay in front of Scotland rolled like boiling pasta.

"Ed?!"

"Yeah, look at all that bad luck. It's no surprise they called me. I'm just glad I had a baseball person, err, player I could count on to help."

"Hey, kid. What do you like on your hot dogs?" Clinton asked, waving to get Scotty's attention.

"Uhh…" was all the kid could manage, his eyes fixed on the churning orange soil.

"He likes mustard." I leaned in. "Right? You look like a mustard man."

Clay splashed up on the rubbery pentagon and Scotty jumped up to get out of the way.

"I'll take that as a yes. He wants mustard, Clinton!"

Another thumbs-up from the old man.

"Okay, Scotland." I put my hands on his shoulders and surveyed the churning ground. "You've got them all wound-up. It's time to run the squ—bases."

"What?!"

"Yeah, you just run like hell and suck up that bad luck like a shammy. It's not hard."

"Why can't you—"

"Why can't I do it? Easy, I'm not a baseball person. Are you sure it's not person? Baseball person sounds much better."

"What does being a baseball player have to do with

anything?" Scotty hopped from foot to foot to avoid the churning clay.

"Scotland, I don't make the rules."

"What rules?"

"Now, now, you of all people know life is full of rules. I've heard you rattle off axioms of newspaper delivery. You know as well as I do that anything good and proper has rules. Dealing with Oriental Luck Worms is no different."

"Worms?!"

Bang!

The serrated maw of a juvenile luck worm slammed into home plate, narrowly missing Scotty's foot by inches.

"I know, it's so odd isn't it? I mean, first it was Mongolian Death Worms, and now Oriental Luck Worms. What are the chances? Uncanny."

More segmented bodies flailed in the churned up clay, their circular mouths full of sharp teeth that shined in the bright lights.

"Ed, get me out of here!"

A smaller worm shot just past Scotty's shoe and sent the mass into a frenzy.

"No can do. They've got your scent now. Only option is to run the bases, fast."

"What are you going to do?" Scotty asked, abject terror in his eyes.

"Me?"

"Yes, you."

I stepped onto the pentagon behind him and used my hands to point the shaking kid toward what I guessed was the first square. "I'm going to cheer you on."

"What?!"

"Well, that and suck up the wave of bad luck you're going to generate with this." I pulled a scuffed up baseball out of my pocket. "Been holding onto this beauty for a long time.

Somebody named Buckner missed this bad boy in a baseball game. People got really ticked."

"The curse of the Bambino?"

"No, that's a kids' movie. Even I know that. It's got a rabbit and a deer. Everybody cries when his mom dies."

"Not Bambi!"

"You got it, Scotland, whatever it is you baseball people say." I pushed him toward the first square. "Not Bambi! Not Bambi!"

The kid took off like a bullet, with a surging horde of Luck Worms right behind him. They chewed up the clay like the rabid mass of blood-thirsty monsters they were.

"Clinton, that's a lot more than you told me there were."

"Yeah, and we haven't even seen the big ones yet."

"I'm sorry, I could have sworn you said big ones?"

* * *

THE KID PUMPED his legs and raced down the first square line. You'd almost think he had experience with this given just how fast he was moving. Then again, one couldn't discount the motivation sharp teeth provided.

"Doing a great job, Scotty. Excellent work! Really. I can feel the luck swelling."

That was a lie. I couldn't feel anything yet, but sometimes people need a little push, even baseball people.

Rumble!

The ground in front of Scotty split like beach sand falling away in the heavy surf.

"Ed!"

"Right. So there might be a few larger ones, but it's nothing an Assistant Demon Hunter can't handle."

A great segmented head erupted from the soft clay. Rows of teeth shined in the bright light, while clumps of dirt and saliva splattered the ground. Sightless eyes searched for the tasty delivery boy.

"Ah. That's a mature female. Nothing to worry about, just keep running and we'll suck all that bad luck right up."

Scotty kept running all right, just not where I wanted him to go. The kid screamed and made a break for the gate, leaving the clay behind him.

"No! You can't do that. You have to stay on the dirt. You're going to get that bad luck everywhere!"

Bzzt!

An electrical wire popped free from its overhead lines and landed on the chain-link gate. Sparks showered the ground and Scotty panicked.

"Right. You see? Bad luck. Get back on those squares."

"He's not listening, Ed." The groundskeeper turned over nicely roasting hot dogs with a pair of tongs. "Looks like he's headed into the outfield."

"What?!"

Scotty had swung a hard left and was now screaming his way into the grassy part.

Sigh.

Sometimes you have to do it yourself.

"Deputize me, Clint."

The old salt looked up from his grill. "Say what?"

"Deputize me. I need to be a groundskeeper, now."

Clinton snapped his tongs a few times as if rolling the idea over in his head. "I don't know, Ed. You haven't been trained. You didn't grow up in the long standing tradition of grounds keeping. It's not something you just do. It's a calling."

Scotty's scream echoed off the back wall, his ginger hair and wild hands all I could make out beyond the writhing bodies of hungry luck worms.

"You could always help him yourself," I said, rolling up my sleeves.

Clinton frowned. "Fine, fine. I'm getting too old for this stuff anyway. I, Clinton Michaels, hereby deputize you, Edwin Lovely as a Junior Assistant groundskeeper. May the turf grow green beneath your toes and the lines you chalk remain forever straight."

"Works for me." I raced past the old man and got my hands on the chalk line machine. It looked more like a wheelbarrow full of white powder than anything else.

"Hey, don't go ruining my—"

"Too late, Clint. I'm a groundskeeper now."

"Junior Assistant grounds—"

"Whatever. I'm coming, Scotland!"

I shot across the churned up clay. The line machine bounced in front of me, spilling chalk and leaving broken white marks on the orange earth.

"Gah! Ed, you're making a mess of my field!"

"Just have those hot dogs ready for him. We're going to have just one shot at this."

Clinton frowned but went back to his grill.

I found Scotty near the far end of the field. He'd made it to the back wall, but it was too tall for him to climb.

"Hang on, little buddy, I'm coming!"

"Ed!"

The female launched herself at Scotty.

"Duck!"

Scotland hit the deck just in time. The massive Lelvick's jagged teeth tore into the padded wall the young man had been standing in front of like it was cotton candy.

"Nobody's leaving the field of play tonight." I squeezed the chalk machine's handles and sent a wide white line spilling out across the torn up sod. "Scotty, get on the other side of the line."

The Junior Demon Hunter and self-proclaimed baseball

person's head popped up from beneath the worm's churning maw. "Ed!"

"I'm a groundskeeper now. It's fine." I expected that new found bit of knowledge to inspire him, but it didn't seem to make a dent in his panic.

"Help me!"

"What do you think I'm trying to do." I kicked away juvenile luck worms that appeared to have developed an interest in snacking on my feet. "You need to get back on the squares. I'm here to help you do that. Get on the other side of the line."

"I don't understand."

The large female ripped herself free of the padded wall and turned those sightless eyes on Scotty.

"Damn it, son. It's simple. I've been deputized as a member of the holy order of groundskeepers. They're a fraternity of luck wranglers going back hundreds of years. Now, get behind the line and let's wrap this thing up. I hope you're hungry." I swung by the kid dropping chalk like a mad fool. "Come on."

Together Scotty and I booked it for the bright orange clay, the two of us doing our best to keep to the right of that glorious white line of luck wrangling chalk. The Lelvicks surged behind us, frustrated at being penned, they picked up speed. "Run the squares, Scotty!"

My assistant's face was bright red, and it looked for all the world like a heart attack was imminent.

"Don't do it for me." I switched off the chalk just in time to give the kid an opening. "Do it for Clint Michael. Do it for the holy order of luck wranglers. Do it for the Sidewinders!"

"I... hate... you..." Scotty slammed a foot down on the first square.

"Whatever helps you do it, Scotland. I'll take it. Just run those squares!"

My favorite delivery boy found his second wind and gunned it for the next white lump, which was basically the same time the rest of the luck worms turned their attention to me.

Crap.

I switched the chalk dropping lever back on and took off after him. "Wait for me!"

Lelvicks nipped at our heels, their sharp teeth tearing off chunks of shoe in the process.

Scotty hit the second square and had only begun to round the corner when the large female erupted from the chewed-up ground and blocked his path.

"Look out, Scotland!"

It was a thing of beauty to behold. She snapped and he slid. That baseball person made all baseball people proud. He slid right past the monster, and right into the third square.

"Hot damn, kid. I knew you could do it! Now just back to the pentagon and we can close this up."

A clay-smeared Scotty struggled to his feet, the once-white uniform now a mess of grass stains and orange streaks.

"You can do it, kid! Go! I'll handle the grounds keeping."

Scotty limped down the line while I turned my attention to the female.

"It's time to get grounded." I switched the chalk back on and shot past the massive worm. "Let's see you get out of this!"

The luck worm shrieked as the first white line cut off her pursuit.

"Yeah, no fun is it?" I switched off the chalk, then swung the machine around and skipped over a few more aggressive babies. The worm tried to beat me to the edge, but I switched the chalk back on, sealed off her escape, and pinned the massive beast against the third base line.

This elicited a smile and a wave from Clinton. "Not bad, Ed. You've got a future in grounds keeping."

"Thanks." I dumped a final bit of chalk to make sure the hungry monster was secured, then turned my attention to Scotty. He was only a few feet from the pentagon.

We're gonna do it!

Chomp!

Baby luck worm teeth bit into my foot and I yelped.

Scotty slowed to look back.

"Go! Finish it. I'll be fine. It's just a flesh wound." I tore the squirming beast off.

But Scotty didn't move. The poor kid was frozen, his eyes wide and completely focused on something behind me.

Rumble!

"I don't want to look, do I, Clinton?"

The groundskeeper removed hot dogs from the grill and placed them on waiting buns. "Nope."

A hot and decidedly stinky breeze rolled over my back.

Sigh.

"It's the male, isn't it?"

The old man nodded. "Yep."

"Ed, behind you!" Scotty cried, fear in his eyes.

"Yeah, that's the bull worm. Get to pentagon, Scotty."

"But..."

"Do it, kid! Now!"

I spun around just in time to dive out of the way of a sedan-sized mouth full of serrated teeth.

"Ed!"

I scrambled backwards, on my butt, baby luck worms nipping at my hands. "Go!"

Thump!

Scotty's feet pounded on the rubbery pentagon. "I did it, Ed. I ran the squa—bases. I ran the bases!"

"Great job!" I kicked at hungry juveniles while the bull worm's bulk blotted out the lights. "We're almost there."

"Huh? What do you mean almost there?"

Gooey globs of saliva dripped like heavy Florida rain on the churned up clay.

"Hot dogs are done." Clinton pointed to a stack of paper plates piled high with mustard-smeared sausages.

"Ed, I don't—"

"Eat up, Scotland. Eat up like my life depends on it, because it does."

"What?!"

* * *

HOT DOG EATING contests have been around since there were hot dogs to eat. The prevailing wisdom was that they were created by the hot dog companies in an effort to sell more hot dogs. Maybe that's a tangential reason. It's certainly what the holy order of groundskeepers would have you believe. They were a secretive cabal keeping track of the relative luck in the world, and if that meant finding expert hot dog eaters, then who was I to question them?

I just hoped Scotty could eat those hot dogs faster than the bull worm could eat me.

Life goals.

Clinton shoved the first mustard-smeared dog into Scotty's trembling hand. "Here you go."

The delivery boy blanched. "No, we've got to save Ed!"

The wily old salt nodded. "That's what we're doing. Luck, like all things that are important, prefers sacrifice. Seeing as you bought the cheap dogs I'm smelling one hell of a sacrifice. You should have seen it the time we used tofu... Kicked off the last big stock market run."

The bull worm's deafening shriek rolled over Scotty's

response, but I thought it had something to do with a relaxed monetary policy or something else equally inane.

"Just eat the hot dogs, Scotland!"

A clearly confused delivery boy shoved the first sausage into his mouth and started chewing.

I didn't have time to watch the spectacle and had to settle for diving out of the way of the bull worm's massive jaws. By the time I was on my feet again I found Scotty still working on the same bite. "Chewing?! Really, Scotty?"

My assistant turned his chipmunk-like cheeks toward me, confusion in his eyes. "Mmrph?"

Scotty still had half a dog in hand when Clinton presented the next one. "Ed's right. You need to cut back on the whole chewing process if you're going to get these done in time."

Baby worms swarmed around my feet, their tiny teeth slicing up my shoes and nicking at the tasty Ed-flesh underneath.

"Crap!" I lunged out of the way of yet another biting attack from the massive male. Juveniles shrieked in protest before being snuffed out by the much larger beast. "Come on, Scotty. Pick up the pace, man."

The delivery boy dropped an empty paper plate and accepted the next one from Clinton. At this rate I'd be worm food three times over before he reached the fifth dog, let alone the eighth.

I need to buy myself some time, and fast. I'd met denture wearers with more hot dog consuming speed than Scotty appeared capable of.

Mom can pound hot dogs faster than... That's it, Mom!

The mature female appeared massively pissed at being penned in by the sacred chalk, but she also appeared even more angry at the number of babies getting crushed or inadvertently eaten by the much larger male in his attempt to get to me.

"Go, go, go!" I chanted, running past the painfully slow-eating delivery boy. "What number is he on, Clinton?"

"Two."

"Two?!"

The angry female hissed and shrieked from inside her chalk prison.

"Did you give him the speech?"

"Ed, I'm getting too old for all this. If the kid can't eat eight hot dogs before the Lelvicks consume you, then what kind of luck winner is he? I mean, really? Show a little appreciation for the institution."

I reached the chalk jail and took a deep breath before I broke it and unleashed even more danger in a crowded field of problems.

"Tell him you'll introduce him to your nephew."

The old salt frowned. "You think that'll make a difference?"

I kicked my torn up shoe through the lump of white line and released the female luck worm, then immediately ran for the first open stretch of clay I could find. "Don't care. Just do it."

Scotty pushed down the second hot dog and accepted the third, his face a particularly unpleasant shade of green. "I'm eating as fast as I can."

"That's the problem, son," Clinton said, another dog in his hand. "You're eating. This is a battle. A show of strength. It's you versus the universe."

Scotty opened his mouth to say something, but the groundskeeper only pushed Scotty's half-eaten dog closer. "No time for that. You've got a mission. A sacred duty."

Scotland's eyes bugged out, but he kept chewing. The question was, would he be fast enough?

Lelvicks shrieked behind me, and for a few brief moments I felt like I had a decent chance. That female was quite unhappy, and being me I had plenty of experience with unhappy females—worm-like or otherwise. Given that knowledge, I had a pretty good feeling the bull was going to get an earful.

Do worms have ears?

I pondered that as I scrambled over the second square.

Scotty wasn't the best of Demon Hunting assistants, but he was right about this whole baseball thing. Running the squares was actually kind of fun.

Shriek!

I turned around in time to see the familiar frustration play out in giant worm-like living color. There were a few lunging bites, some shrieks, and then a very off-putting rubbing dance that made me wonder if I just witnessed something that should have come after wine and chocolates.

"Great work, kid. You're halfway there." The groundskeeper shoved another dog in Scotty's visibly deflated fingers.

"Good work, Scotland!"

The Lelvicks separated and turned their attention to me. They were like twin maws of churning teeth, with segmented bodies now coated in a layer of slime I got the distinct feeling I really didn't want to touch. They shrieked again, then exploded off the mark like purebred racehorses.

Funny, when I do that I'm always really tired afterwards.

"Go faster, Scotty!" I jumped off the square and led the hungry worms into the grassy field beyond the clay. They were moving a good bit faster now that sexy-time slime had given them a nice boost in speed.

That's just swell.

"Nice work, kid! Now that's how we eat a dog!" Clinton shouted. I couldn't see them anymore, but I figured Scotty must have gotten the hang of it to illicit that sort of response. I jumped the closest chewed-up chalk line, but it was too ruined to even slow down the Lelvicks at my heels. "He's only got one left, Ed!"

I wanted to respond, but I couldn't get out much more than a wave before the bull worm slammed into the turf behind me.

"Ed, the kid says you have the ball."

The ball!

In the commotion I'd forgotten about that cursed baseball in my pocket.

"The luck winner needs his ball if he's gonna wrap this up!" the groundskeeper shouted, reminding me of the first rule of luck winning.

Don't forget the ball.

I'd forgotten the ball.

The mature female swung into view, the two Lelvicks trapping me in a pincher-like move. Baby worms snapped at my feet, while their parents opened serrated mouths wide.

"Ed!" Scotty's grey-green face appeared along the distant chalk line, bits of bun and mustard smearing his puffy cheeks. "Throw it."

"Huh?"

"Throw the ball!"

Lelvicks writhed around me. The kid was right, there was no other way.

"It's a cursed ball. Don't miss it."

"I won't."

I reared back to throw, the male's monstrous maw crashing down at me the moment the ball left my fingers. That scuffed up wad of string and leather tumbled end over end in the air. It wasn't going to make it. The throw was short, but that didn't stop Scotty. Maybe the kid really was a decent baseball person. I didn't know, as the last thing I saw were the sharp teeth of a sexually-satisfied bull worm blotting out the stadium's bright lights.

* * *

A VERY QUEASY delivery boy leaned on the bleachers, his belt drooping like a dog's tongue in the summer heat.

"Nice work, Scotland" I turned over the luck-soaked ball in my fingers.

Clinton handed me an open bag of potato chips and nodded. The three of us admired the torn up field. "I'd say. You two have a real future in luck wrangling if you want it. I haven't seen that sort of tandem work in years, not since Sarasota Statesmen in fifty-five. Now those boys were luck wranglers."

Scotty tried over to vomit, but nothing came up. "Ed, I feel terrible."

"That's the luck." Clinton dug his hands into the bag. "You're gonna need to get rid of that ball."

"Any suggestions?" I asked between mouthfuls of chips.

The groundskeeper wiped grease on his pants. "It needs to go to a team. Someone that deserves—"

Scotty snapped the ball out of my fingers. "The Kinitstu Carp are playing in Jacksonville tomorrow."

The old man smiled. "I like this one, Ed."

I nodded, pointing the chip bag at my assistant.

Scotty turned a vile shade of green, then promptly vomited. I patted the kid on the back a few times, then returned into the chips.

"I do too. He's got a bright future in Demon Hunting. Now, can we get a ride to Jacksonville?"

SLEEP TO DREAM HER

"*I*s that kid ever going to get up?"

I folded the paper over to stare at my wife, even though I knew exactly which of our kids she was talking about. "Cathy's a teenager. Sleep is basically their national pastime."

Porter frowned at her empty coffee cup. "Well, I could think of a lot better pastimes."

"I'm sure you could."

My wife left the kitchen table to pour herself the last bits of black tar from the pot. I'd made the coffee this morning which meant it was Magician grade.

That was just a fancy word for paint remover.

"I'm serious, Gene. She won't go run with me, or ride a bike, or anything. I swear she spends her entire life in that room."

"Again, very much teenager."

Porter put the mug down to hunt for creamer, or basically anything capable of cutting the cauldron of caustic. "Well, it's not healthy."

"Also, teenager."

My wife grunted out something in Angry Porter and I smiled behind the newly unfolded paper. They both had a zest for life, but neither of them could see it.

I spent half the evening trying to get Cathy to actually go to bed, whereas Porter was comatose when the sun hadn't completely set. The morning was the exact opposite, with my wife up in the dark and ready to run a damn marathon, and Cathy dead to the world until at least noon if you let her.

This created a very volatile weekend morning routine, one I was neck deep in trying to avoid right now.

Kris, our son and the youngest member of the family, was up, but he might as well have been asleep. He had become a cartoon zombie. We'd see him, and the list of things he wanted from the toy store, in a few hours.

Porter closed the fridge in a huff. Her long dark hair was already in a ponytail, much like the predators from most nature shows. This meant danger, or in Porter's world, high-intensity exercise.

She banged a hand on the counter, the uncut coffee still black as graveyard dirt, and just as flavorful. "We're out of creamer."

"I see."

"I'm going for a run. Please make sure Cathy is up by the time I get back."

I glanced at the clock and tried to do the mental math as to how long I could wait before waking the teenage undead. Porter was a fast runner, but I had procrastination on my side.

"You got it."

My wife retreated to our bedroom only to return a few minutes later spandexed for battle with the demons of sloth. As much as I wanted to, this was not the time to comment on her butt. I needed to save that for some other time. Right now, she had that whole steely-eyed death stare going. She got that way before a run, like life and death would be decided by whether she beat the sun to rising.

While it could be maddening at times, I liked that fiery personality. It was one of the many things I'd fallen for when we were in college, and it was the same thing I admired now, even if there was no way in hell she was going to get me running without something monstrous chasing me.

We were fresh out of bears. I checked.

Porter paused briefly at the door to slip on fancy running shoes and queue up music on her phone. She'd be thumping to the beat by the time she reached the first corner, and hopefully feeling much better about life by the time she hit the last.

That was always the hope, and why I made the coffee strong enough to peel paint.

It got Porter out the door and gave me a little more time to enjoy the quiet morning.

It only took me a decade of marriage to figure that out.

Satisfied she was loaded for departure, but before she could get her engines roaring, my wife paused just outside the open door. "Oh, I meant to tell you. I paid Jimmy— you know, the Anderson's kid—to pressure wash the house yesterday."

"You what?"

Porter picked at the chipped paint on the door. "Yeah, I figured you might not have noticed when you got home last night. He did a decent job, but I think he got the nozzle too close to the paint or something."

"They let Jimmy use gas-powered tools?"

"Gene, he's in college."

"Are they teaching him how to not saw his arm off?"

The Anderson's kid had a penchant for wrecking manual labor jobs, and doubly so when they required the use of anything beyond a shovel. When I'd first met the kid, I'd thought he was some sort of latent Magician, a moron savant if you will. A few sigils and a lot of investigation later I confirmed otherwise.

Jimmy wasn't Magickal. He was just amazingly clumsy.

"Anyway. I told him not to spray them, but I think he peeled off some of your Magick doodles."

"He did what?"

True to form, Porter popped her headphones in and gave a thumbs-up, then hit the road, leaving not much more than a pleasant-smelling vapor trail in her wake.

I left the paper and checked the door.

Jimmy had done a lot more than ruin a handful of sigils —he'd blasted through essentially my entire protective series with what amounted to a high-pressure garden hose.

My name is Eugene Law, and when I'm not making ingestible paint remover, I'm a Magician. I don't make national monuments disappear, nor am I much for pulling doves out of my sleeves. I deal in real Magick, the cosmic powers of the universe, and all the terrible things that come with.

Right now, that meant figuring out just how bad a number the Anderson kid did to my house. Normally, the sigils wouldn't have budged, but Porter had nullified all that by asking the kid to blast the bejesus out of the paint. Consent was important, both in marriages, and in Magick.

My wife had unknowingly consented to removing the complex designs keeping us safe from all manner of evil things in the holy name of curb appeal, and too many hours of home improvement television.

Without knowing it, she's served us up like roast turkey to whatever might want to take a late night crack at a Magician and his family.

I turned back to the kitchen and grabbed a marker out of the junk drawer, then made sure my young son was still comfortably ensconced behind the glowing box and accepting his toy demands from the forces of commerce. Once I was convinced it would take a literal bomb to pull his attention away from the tube, I grabbed a flashlight and slipped out the front door.

"Jimmy, what are you doing to me?"

The Magickal designs were a mess. Porter had been right. The kid must have pushed the pressure washer directly against the paint judging by how much of it—and the complex symbols it had held—was now on the ground.

I gave the marker a couple good shakes and set to work fixing the designs. This was *exactly* what I wanted to be doing in the dark on a Saturday morning, but without these things we were basically exposed. It was like I had the Magickal equivalent of a backed-up toilet running non-stop and threatening to swamp the house.

This was not the time to go back and enjoy the paper. This was the time to fix Jimmy's job, and be the Dad.

"Being the Dad sucks," I said to no one but the marker in my hand.

The tiny ink slinger agreed, and together we fought the forces of Jimmy at each window.

By the time we'd rounded the back of the house and made it to Cathy's room, my valiant marker had almost given up its ghost.

"Come on, just a few more and you're done."

The pen grudgingly spit out enough ink to get the start of a sigil going, but I'd only just put my fingers on the sill when I knew we had a problem.

It wasn't just the marker that smelled.

Figments.

I traced the seam with my hand, but there was no denying it. My daughter's window was covered in Figment stink.

Crap.

Figments were the trash pandas of the dream world. Wildly inventive and cunning as foxes, they loved to sneak through windows and past sliding glass doors to make their way into your dreams. They thrived on that heady mixture of fear, panic, and doubt so common in well-conceived nightmares. If that was it, then that would have been bad enough, but that was rarely all they did. If you got enough of them together, they'd make a nest in that head, and then you'd have real problems.

The sigils were there to keep things like Figments out, and the Anderson kid had pressure washed them to Kingdom Come.

I rushed back to the front door and pushed it open to find my son still watching television and basking in its blue-grey glow.

Cathy!

I gently opened the door to my daughter's bedroom.

It took a second for my eyes to adjust, and to remember that this was a teenager's room. It resembled a war zone, just a decidedly young woman sort of war zone, complete with unwashed clothes, hair product, and posters of boys that looked like they abstained from showering.

It would have been nice if that was all there was.

Multi-color like soap bubbles, but long and stringy like walking pole beans, a small group of Figments had set up shop on her head.

We made eye contact for only a second before they wiggled up her nose and down her ears like roaches diving for cover when you turn the lights on.

* * *

FIGMENTS.

Of all the things to get in after Jimmy pressure washed the hell out of my sigils, I got Figments.

Nasty little creatures, they were related to Fairies, but only so much. The best way to think of them was to imagine self-propelled mental backwash from a series of increasingly bad dreams. They were living nightmare fungus, with slippery little bean-pole bodies, sticky hands, and bad times written all over them.

And now they were in my daughter.

Great.

I tossed the flashlight and flipped the bedroom lamp on just in time to watch the last of them squirm its way up her nose.

There was no sense waking her up. Figments secrete a barely detectable knock-out juice from their pores. Besides, Cathy was a teenager, so I didn't exactly need the Figments to render her comatose.

There were a couple of ways to get dream demons out of someone's head, but none of them were pretty.

In the old days, you'd shove hot pokers up the nose. Most of the time the victim died, but every so often the Figment would come out stuck to the brain-boiling metal.

Nope. I would not be giving Cathy a lobotomy. That option was off the table.

What else?

There was an exorcism of sorts, but I needed far more mundanity than I could safely exist around. We'd need weaponized boredom—the sort of thing only a veteran accountant or practically retired lawyer can produce in volume, and good luck finding one of them before the sun was up.

There was only one option left.

I had to go inside and kick them out.

This is gonna hurt.

"Kris!"

True to the zombification of modern cartoons, my son did not answer me.

"Kristopher Law!"

Unlike demons, using his full name had zero effect on my son, but walking up and turning off the TV did.

"Dad!"

"You can watch Cowboy Keen and the rest of the Horse Head Nebula after—"

My young son crossed his arms. "I don't watch little kids shows."

"But you were so into that last Christmas and I... I mean Santa got you that action figure that—"

"I gave it to the poor kids."

Of course you did.

"Great, that's very noble of you. Somewhere one of Santa's helpers is crying in his candy cane beer, but right now I need your help."

Kris tilted his head. He was still in pajamas, but it would have appeared I said the magic words. At that age he wanted to help with anything. Sadly, all I had to do was wait for him to get to his teenage years, then all of this helpfulness would disappear to make room for the sudden acquisition of knowledge that comes from turning thirteen.

"Okay. What do I do?"

"Go to your room and get that dart gun your mother doesn't know I bought you."

Kris' little eyes went wide. That was a secret gift he only got to play with when Mom wasn't around. She knew about it, but this meant he didn't terrorize all of us with darts twenty-four seven. "Is Mom..."

"She's out running. So we've got a little time. Hop to it, little man. Get the gun and all your darts from the secret spot under your bed and meet me in your sister's room."

It was as if I'd thrown wide the gates to the Forbidden City. My son didn't appear to know how to handle this newfound level of access to hitherto strictly off limits items and locations. His eyes were wide and legs spastic. "Cathy's room?"

I got a hand behind his crazy bed-head hair. "Yes, unless you have another sister I don't know about."

"I have another sister!"

Whoops.

I wasn't sure if you could have a heart attack at his age, but I was positive I took a few years off his young life with that one. "No! Not unless your mother... You know what, no. Just no. You have one sister. I think that's enough sisters. Don't you?"

"Yes!"

I nodded. "Good. Now. Dart gun, Mister. Get your dart gun and all the darts you can carry, then meet me in Cathy's room on the double."

I was positive he didn't understand that last part, but being a kid he nodded just the same and shot off for his room.

The darts were important, but I needed something from the garage if I was going to have any chance of success.

I stumbled into the concrete Florida walk-in humidor and immediately started pulling boxes off the shelves. Christmas trinkets, Halloween decor, and a series of bins that must have held every single softball mitt Porter had ever owned in her entire life came crashing down in the process. As interesting as all that was, it wasn't what I needed.

"It's got to be here," I said to myself as I sifted through the contents of a ratty-looking old VCR box. "I know I saved it."

Back in my college days I'd collected a fair share of Magickal junk, most of it coming from my old roommate, Ed Lovely. He had a flair for finding all manner of odd artifacts that found their way to the Sunshine State. He kept most of the good ones, but somehow he'd let me hang onto this one.

"Ah ha!"

I pulled the broken dream catcher out of underneath a tape rewinder I had no idea why I was keeping.

I set the funny racquet-looking thing on the workbench and carefully started unwinding the string. The Magick wasn't in the dream catcher. Those things were a dime-a-dozen at flea markets. The Magick was in the string.

Nuffer hair.

Creatures of the lower dream plains, Nuffers were like the bison of the dreamlands, big, tough, and responsible for every dream you've ever had that involved roaming in green fields.

Their fur didn't look like much, but spun into twine it was hella tough to cut, springy, and enough to pull me back when I needed it.

The downside?

Figments were known to pick a Nuffer clean in seconds, fur and all.

I tied the Nuffer string around my wrist. Even after years in the garage stuck under a VHS rewinder from the eighties, it still had enough Magick in it to do what I wanted.

I just really hoped I knew what the hell that was, and whether it was remotely the right thing to do.

Kris was waiting for me in his sister's room. He'd even gone so far as to get lots of extra army men and set them up in strategic locations or her desk, her dresser, and the shelves of her closet.

I had to admire his willingness to go all in for the cause.

"Good work, soldier." I unraveled the string in my hands.

"It's me, Dad. It's Kris."

"Right. I knew that, but right now I need you to be a soldier."

"Okay!"

What are you doing, Gene?

I'm covering my six.

He's just a kid!

I gave his elaborate strap of darts that crisscrossed his chest a once-over.

On second thought, proceed.

I placed a hand on his shoulder and whispered the Magick into place. I didn't need much. Outside the body, Figments couldn't go far, and a well-placed dart would surely do them in, especially after I charged up those darts with a little "Elmer's Aim."

"What do I do, Dad?"

I walked him to the foot of Cathy's bed, then got down to the little man's level.

Kris stole a glance over my shoulder at his sister. "She's sleeping."

"She is."

"You don't want to wake up Cathy, Dad." There was more than a little trepidation in his voice.

He knew we were in the lion's den.

I tied the opposite end of the Nuffer string to the bed post, effectively tethering myself.

"Okay, little man. I'm going to disappear."

"You mean like when you go to the potty for a really long time? Mom says you disappear then."

Cute.

"Yeah, sort of. Here's what's going to happen. There are bugs in Cathy's bed."

"Bed bugs!" He said the words in hushed tones, keeping one eye on the sheets and his sleeping sister.

"Right, but they look like green beans with feet."

"I hate green beans."

If I hadn't heard the venom in his voice I wouldn't have

known it was possible to harbor that much hate for a vegetable at such a tender age, but that was why he was here.

"Good, cause you are going to shoot them."

All my son needed was a serape and a wide-brimmed hat. He had the rest of Eastwood's look down pat, steely eyes and all. "I can do it."

"Good." I patted him on the back and took a few steps toward the door to get a running start. "Oh, Kris?"

"Yeah."

"Don't tell your Mom."

He cocked his head. "Tell her what?"

"Exactly."

I ran toward Cathy's bed, jumping at the last second and willing my Magick into the Nuffer cord. I was about to do the unthinkable.

I was going to enter a teenager's dreams.

* * *

DREAMS WERE SQUIRRELLY THINGS, and I avoided them like the plague for a reason. First, they rarely made sense; and second, the longer you stayed in one, the more likely you were to accept that shared illusion as fact, and that's where things could become dangerous—really dangerous.

'Are you the dreamer? Or merely part of someone else's dream?'

Poetic, but also terrifying, because that was pretty much what I was risking on the inside. Listen, there were Magicians that knew this stuff. They knew it like the back of their hands. They didn't keep Nuffer cords in their garage. In fact, they used things much more grounding than herd animal fur, but I wasn't one of them, and I didn't have time to track one down.

I had a teenager with three Figments running wild in her

head. I had to boot them the hell out and not get lost in this shifting landscape in the process.

Bang!

A locker door slammed shut, startling me out of my mental haze. Cathy leaned against the wall of muted green metal boxes next to me, a modest stack of books under her arm. "That skirt looks good on you."

"Huh?"

"It's a good color, Darcy."

Darcy?

She was one of Cathy's friends from the neighborhood. A sort of on-again-off-again troublemaker we grudgingly put up with, and also, it would appear, my role to play in this shared hallucination.

Nearest I could tell, I didn't look like her, at least not yet. I was still me, hairy legs and all, but I did have a skirt on.

That was troubling on a lot of levels, none of which had anything to do with how it matched my eyes.

Cathy nodded, as if confirming her words through gestures. My daughter wasn't tall, but she wasn't the smallest one either. She had that same dirty blond hair her mother used to when she was younger, and the same casual charm Porter rocked in his youth. Unlike her Mom, though, she wasn't athletic, and instead spent her time focused on academics.

"Hey, Cathy..."

A skinny boy shot by, his sexually-charged tone jarring to my paternal ears. "You ditching?"

My daughter is not skipping any classes, she's—

"Yeah. Back lot, Tristan?"

The lanky troublemaker ran a hand through his thick, if poorly groomed, hair. "Yeah, Senior lot."

My daughter waited until he was out of earshot to grab my arm. "Darcy!"

"Uh..."

"It's happening!"

My heart almost exploded inside my chest.

It's all a dream, Gene. This is just a dream. She's not ditching classes to do whatever with...him.

The teenager with far too much interest in my daughter's butt for any self-respecting parent cruised around the corner, his eyes going soap bubble swirly for a second in the process.

Figment!

There was one. Now to find the rest of them and boot these things the hell out of my daughter's head.

"Cathy, I don't think you should skip this class."

My daughter frowned and tilted her head. "Huh? You're the one that's always trying to get me *to* skip."

"That makes sense on so many levels, but this time I mean it. I don't think you should."

"It's just Algebra II. You said you'd give me your notes, and we can copy off each other's tests."

"I... We... What are you—"

A swift, powerful, and far too grabby hand to my butt launched me a solid few inches into the air.

"Whoa, Darcy. Chill, girl."

"Hey, Brian," Cathy said, a hint of annoyance in her voice.

The muscly teenager put a hand on my wrist. "What's this?" His fingers played under the rough edges of the Nuffer string pressed gently against my skin.

"Hey! I need that, don't—"

Strong fingers stretched out the knot and slid it off my wrist with ease. "Smells good." He pressed it to his nose. "Smells like you. Can I keep it?"

"Sure."

Brian's hand found my butt again, and he guided me gently away from Cathy. "Let's go."

"Wait..." I hesitated, my legs cold beneath the blowing A/C. "Cathy?"

"Yeah?"

"Have fun and don't get caught!"

"You got it, Darc."

Cathy rounded the corner and slipped out the side door, while Brian and his butt-pilot hand herded me the other way. He pushed the steel door open with those impressive muscles and directed me toward a car that just happened to be idling in the drop-off lane. We got close enough to the glass for me to check my hair, and make sure my top was showing off just enough, but not too much. I had to make him work for it.

Brian pulled open the back seat door and ushered me inside. Where my backpack went I didn't know. In fact, I wasn't sure where the books I was holding had gone either. The back seat was spacious, so much so that it felt more like a long and cushioned tunnel than the back of the sporty car it was.

The big man leaned in close, his eyes swirling with colors like abstract art. His mouth opened to kiss me, at first the normal size, and then wider. He was like a snake when their jaws unlock, his taffy skin stretching to obscene lengths.

For some reason, it didn't bother me. All I could focus on was those eyes, and the mesmerizing colors swirling inside them.

I wanted to be lost in those eyes, in their colors, and in lies.

Thump!

A twisted piece of twine dropped out of his pocket and landed on my skirt.

The string...

It seemed important, but he grabbed my hand before I could get a finger on those ratty threads.

"Darcy, come to me..."

He leaned in for the kiss, but I couldn't shake the string. It was there for something—something important. I just couldn't remember what.

My face was almost inside his swelling head, when the door behind Brian swung open, and a pair of strong hands yanked him clean out of the car.

"Hey, we were—" I didn't get to finish my words before those same hands returned for me.

I stumbled out of the car only to find myself in what looked like a conference room. The walls were lined with pictures of kids, the wholesome kind that made you want to send yours here, even if you didn't have a choice in the matter.

Where there weren't pictures, there was a single sheet of glass, like a window to the outside hallway.

Brian and some older man argued in that hallway. Their eyes were both full of those shifting colors. They gesticulated like mad, pointing at the glass, and at me on the other side.

At first, I got the impression Brian was sticking up for me, but before long it looked like they'd worked out a deal and cooler heads had prevailed.

Would we be allowed to leave?

Maybe we'd pick back up where we left off?

The door opened and the two of them filed in. I found that silly string dangling out of the older man's pocket.

The string! What was it about string? Think, Darcy. Think about that string.

Ugh.

I didn't want to think. Thinking hurt. Trying to make sense of anything was too hard. They moved closer, those same eyes shining while their mouths swelled like hot air balloons.

Balloons...

I liked balloons. Balloons were fun.

I should get some.

I reached out a hand to touch their comically large heads, but it was slapped away.

That was rude.

The small of my back found the conference room table. They were like parade balloons on steroids, comical faces full of oddly waving teeth. I reached out again, this time hoping to poke those cheeks, but my hands never made it.

Strong arms pushed them aside, then yanked the table away. In seconds, I was up against the wall, the balloon people consuming all the space in front of me. They'd sucked the air out of the room, and the thoughts out of my head.

I drifted, nothing making sense, but at the same time being perfectly normal. I admired the jaws, and the tongues tucked inside them.

I wonder if it'll hurt?

I dropped to my butt and waited for the end I was so very sure was coming.

That was when I found the string sticking out of Brian's pocket.

* * *

I GOT my fingers around the twine, and got a solid helping of dream bison, with all its plodding glory. Nuffers weren't much for conversation, but they had one hell of a memory, and were pretty lethal with a head butt.

That was something I could get behind.

I rammed into Brian, the closest Figment, smashing his swollen face with a forehead that would have made Nuffers everywhere swish their long tails in happiness.

I wasn't Darcy anymore, even if I was still wearing her

woefully risqué and under-sized clothes. I was Gene Law, adult, father, and generally pissed off Magician.

Brian struggled to regain his balance, but I couldn't get to him before the administration looking dude had those skinny arms draped around my back.

I tried turning the tables on him, but I'd lost the element of surprise. Figments might be small and easy to deal with in the real world, but in here they were anything but. My spinning fist never made contact, because the person I was targeting sprung out of the way before I could reach her.

Her?!

The Figment pulled and stretched like taffy until it was someone far more familiar, my wife. Still, it wasn't exactly like Porter, because this was Cathy's head, so this was how she perceived her mom.

I would not be speaking of this to the real Porter, because this one looked like she could bend steel with her teeth. It was as if my wife had been guzzling steroids and sneaking to the gym basically around the clock.

"You're not her. Just because you look like Porter doesn't mean I won't swing on—"

The Figment hit me hard enough to knock a tooth out. It was like taking a side swipe from an industrial tractor.

I hit the floor, hard, and almost lost my Nuffer cord in the process.

Beefcake Porter was on me in an instant, her muscled hips pinning me to the ground. I was going to take the beating to end all beatings if I didn't come up with something fast.

Magick might work in here, but I'd need to concentrate for that, and feeling that missing tooth spot with my tongue was totally throwing anything in the way of concentration.

I needed a distraction and I needed it now. So I decided to go for broke.

"Cathy left her towel on the bathroom floor again!"

My illusionary wife reared her hand back to leave a foot-deep dent in my skull, then paused. "She did?"

"Totally. Wet towel. Floor. Terrible."

I could tell the Figment was trying to overcome Cathy's mental mother construct, but having a hell of a time doing it. This was part of the challenge one deals with when dream-hopping. Just ask the guy stuck wearing one very short mini-skirt.

"Yeah, and we've got company coming over. You know, Marcy from up the street? The one we think is secretly judging your homemaking skills."

Porter peeled herself off me and made for the door, the multi-colored bean-pole Figment inside her trying to pry itself free.

I had him right where I wanted him. Confused, disoriented, and trying to climb out of my terrifying bone-crusher of a dream wife.

"Gotcha!"

I ripped the Figment out and squeezed the tiny monster in my fingers. "Tell Kris I said hi!"

The Technicolor pole bean squirmed but couldn't escape my fingers, or the pleasing sound they made when he popped between them.

Kris would be filling him with hot darts on the other side. At least, I hoped that was what my son was doing. I had left a rather pivotal part of the plan up to a kid easily distracted by cartoons.

Speaking of easily distracted, where was Brian?

I followed Hulk Porter into the hallway, not surprised to be back with the lockers. Dreams didn't make sense, and I figured teenage girl dreams doubly so.

Brian!

I found what I assumed was Darcy's terrible taste in men

along with what looked like a posse of athletic youths. There were certainly enough of them to be intimidating, but I had two hundred pounds of skull-crushing she-babe in my corner. All I had to do was convince beefcake Porter these guys thought she had terrible taste in paint or couldn't bake her way out of a paper bag and I'd be golden.

"Hey, Porter, these guys think you're a bad mom."

Nothing.

I turned around. "Porter?"

My wife was gone.

Dreams can turn on you so fast.

Something else that moves fast? Athletic teenagers.

Before I could assemble much in the way of a plan, I was surrounded.

The Figment appeared rather full of itself and made sure Brian was smiling.

I smiled too, but that was just because I'd seen the rest of these guys on their posters a few million times. Up close I realized these weren't high school boys from Cathy's classes. They were members of the band whose poster she'd had on her wall for years.

I couldn't begin to tell you how many hours driving to school I'd spent listening to their music, or hearing about their antics. For a time, my daughter had been a one woman fan club all to herself.

It pays to listen to your kids.

"Timmy, Billy, Bobby, Scotty, and Big Joe?"

The band members nodded. "Hey, this guy knows who we are!"

"You bet I do."

Brian the Figment tried to back away.

Not on my watch, buddy.

"I love your last album, Baby, my Baby, Baby."

"Right on!"

"I was really sorry to hear about your manager."

Big Joe pounded the locker. "Damn straight. If he were here right now, I'd lay him out."

Figments were stretchy, and so were dreams. It didn't take much Magick to stretch Brian into a weasely boy band manager.

"Isn't that him?"

I'd never seen a boy band attack someone before, but after watching Manager Brian take the beating of a lifetime I decided there was something to coordinated dance moves, and it was damn scary on a host of different levels.

A bent and limping Figment slipped out of the boy band beatdown. He didn't make it two feet before I scooped him up.

"Incoming, Kris! Look alive."

The Figment tried to escape, but I ripped him in two and tossed the still wriggling ends away, then left my daughter's imaginary dude posse to finish enacting righteous vengeance and bolted for the door, almost toppling over more than once in these stupid heels.

I had no idea where the Senior lot was, or how long it would take to get there, but that was when I remembered this was all a dream and it didn't matter.

Time and space were relative here. I just needed to imagine where I wanted to be. It didn't have to be perfect, it just had to be.

"I'm coming, Cathy!"

I slammed two hands on the push bar and swung the steel door open, only to be surrounded by cars far nicer than the Dad Wagon.

"Get off of me!"

"Cathy!"

My daughter pressed her face up against the glass of a

sleek black sports car briefly, then disappeared beneath a swirl of water color motion.

"I'm coming!"

I grabbed the handle and ripped it open, only to find the stupid Figment had been waiting for me. It sprung over my daughter and slammed me against the pavement.

The string snapped, and with it went my focus.

"Darcy!" Cathy scrambled out of the car. "He's my boyfriend. I told you to stop trying to steal him."

Darcy?

"I'm sorry. I just… I thought he was hurting you."

Skinny Tristan's multi-colored eyes bore holes right through me. I couldn't look away.

"We're fine. I think you should leave." Cathy stepped out of the car and pulled Tristan off me.

It was clear he wasn't pleased about it, but listened to her just the same.

Cathy pulled me to my feet. "Now, go. Get out of here."

"But…"

She shook her head and pushed me back. "I said go, and take your stupid bracelet with you."

She picked up the broken string and froze.

"Dad? Why are you wearing a skirt?"

Dad?

Shit, that's me!

"Long story." I pushed her out of the way, then returned the favor and drove that stupid Figment into the ground. He squirmed, but couldn't escape my grasp.

"What is that, Dad?"

I pulled the wriggling chili pepper-looking jerk right out of Cathy's boyfriend. The teenager promptly vanished, leaving me with the last remaining Figment. "It's just a dream, Cathy." I popped the little bastard between my fingers. "I need that string."

Cathy stared at it, and at me. "This is just a dream, right?"

"Yes, but if you skip classes, all of this will come true, and you'll never get the sight of your dad in a mini-skirt out of your head... ever."

Cathy's face went snow white.

"Exactly."

She handed me the Nuffer twine and I took it with both hands. "I'm watching you."

My daughter visibly gulped.

"I thought so. Oh, and clean your room, and tell Darcy to wear something that doesn't show off her butt."

I pulled the twine taunt and left my daughter completely confused and most likely a little emotionally scarred.

* * *

"NICE SHOOTING, TEX." I pointed to the three dart covered Figments twitching on the floor.

"Who's Tex?" my son asked, scrunching up his face.

"You are."

"No. I'm Kris."

Sigh.

"I tell you what." I scooped up the Figments, then patted my son on the shoulder. "You keep this up, and I can clearly see a new, much bigger, higher-capacity dart gun in your future."

"Really?" It was clear Kris had no idea what those words meant, but 'new' and 'dart gun' appeared to stick.

One of the Figments twitched, and I snapped it like a pole bean.

"Really."

MESOZOIC MAGICK

"*J*ust hold those two pieces together while the glue dries." I pointed to the two blocks of wood in my young son's hands.

"Okay." He mashed them together with all the aesthetic detail a five-year-old master wood craftsman could muster, which was basically none.

"No, Kris. Not like that, like this." I adjusted the pieces in his hands. "The glue is on *this* side, not the other one. Wait..."

My son held up his glue-covered palm. "No. It's here."

"Crap."

"Yeah, crap!"

I shook my head. "No, don't say crap. Your mom's going to kill me."

"Oh, no. Crap!"

"Kris!"

My son dropped the wood on the workbench and beat a path for the living room. "Mom! Don't hurt Dad. He got crap on my hands."

"Gene!"

"Kris!"

My son slammed the door behind him, and for the next few minutes all I could do was clean up glue and adjust the little wooden project. The entire stack of wood pieces, miniature bottle of adhesive and still—largely—folded instructions had been a gift from Porter's dad.

Grandpa mailed it down, along with a subtle jab at me when he'd noted that there were instructions in the box—just in case Gene needs them.

Thanks, Grandpa.

That's not to say I *didn't* need the instructions, but now there was no way my fatherly pride was going to let me open them up and actually read them. Besides, they looked like Chinese.

With the glue cleaned off, I took a few minutes to line up the pieces again. They really didn't fit together remotely like the box. In fact, if the box were to be believed, we were building a tiny wooden dinosaur.

It looked more like a stack of oddly-shaped poker chips and some nice splinters just raring to end up in my hands rather than any sort of prehistoric monster.

Still, dinosaurs were my son's thing now, so dinos were what his grandparents sent. We had plastic dinos, big ones, little ones, the kind that fly, and the kind that hide in the carpet waiting for bare feet. Lately, there'd been a lot of those. They had sharp teeth and spiky tails. They had leathery wings and angry beaks. If it was part of the dinosaur family, it got its mail delivered here.

Porter opened the garage door slowly, so as to not upset the tiny paleontology reconstruction. "Are you still working on that?"

"Yes." I had my eyes down at the workbench level trying to line up the pieces yet another way.

"You do know there are instructions, right?"

"I'm aware of this, yes."

Porter frowned. "And you do know they are right there on the workbench?"

I picked up the accordion-folded stack of complex diagrams and Chinese characters and used it as a tent to lean an offending wood piece against. "Yep. Very helpful. Thank you."

"Uh huh. Well, you aren't going to like this, but Cathy taught Kris how to use the tablet and call Grandpa."

"Porter, I don't need your old man telling—"

Kris pushed the door open like only a five-year-old could. "So this is Dad."

"Hey, Gene." Porter's father waved from the screen. As was typical with my wife's family, only half of his head was in the frame; the rest of it was mercifully missing. My in-laws were not great with the techno-gadgets. "How's that dinosaur coming?"

"It's crap." Kris volunteered only to elicit a stern look from his mother.

"It's great, Dad. Thank you so much for sending it to him." Ever the mother, Porter slipped the tablet out of her son's hand and put it on the workbench next to me.

I got to have my father-in-law's chin pointed at my face, and at the stack of wood bits that were supposed to be a dinosaur.

"Hmm, did you look at the instructions, Gene?"

"Yeah."

Kris's head popped up on the screen from beneath my arms. "Dad said instructions are for dum—"

"Thanks, Kris. Yeah. I'll get it figured out. Just taking my time to make sure I get it right. You know, projects like this..."

The old man's chin slipped out of view, only to be replaced with a resplendent dinosaur, right down to the perfectly assembled skeleton. That jerk had bought two kits. He'd made one in his workshop, and the other he'd sent me.

"Wow, Grandpa!"

"Isn't it amazing? Look." My father-in-law's hands popped into the frame and tugged on one of the wooden bones, and I'll be damned if the stupid thing's mouth didn't open and close.

Son of a...

"Wow, Dad. That's really great. Gene, do you think ours will do that?"

"I'm not su—"

"It should. It's the same kit."

Thanks, Grandpa.

"Grandpa." Kris grabbed the tablet off the workbench and knocked over my poorly constructed pieces in the process. "I want to show you my tyran... tyranas... I want to show you my T-Rex!"

"Sure thing. I'd love to see it. Let's give your dad some space to get that project going. I'm sure he'll appreciate it."

Damn straight he will...

"Thanks." I waved to Grandpa's chin as Kris, tablet-in-law, and Porter returned to the house.

It was just me and a stack of wooden toy bits which were supposed to be a pretty amazing-looking dinosaur.

Yeah, like that's magically going to happen.

I picked up a few of the pieces, then hesitated.

Well, it could Magickally happen...

My name is Eugene Law and I'm a Magician. I don't pull rabbits out of hats, or saw women in half. I deal in real Magick, the cosmic powers of the universe, and I'm really not great with crafts.

Maybe there was some Magick I could use?

I shook that thought away and made for the garage refrigerator to grab some thinking juice. I must have been having a number of pontification sessions as of late, as there were only a few cans of premium inspiration in the largely empty appliance.

Well, that, and the fridge hated us.

We put it in the garage a few months ago to make room for the fancy new one Porter had wanted, and ever since that time the old fridge had made everything we put in it taste like hell. Oddly enough, it never bothered the adult beverages.

Go figure.

I popped the top on a sweaty can and slipped it into the koozie I kept in the workbench just for these occasions.

Now to figure out how to build a wood-o-saur and make it do neat moving head things.

An empty can later, and I was in exactly the same spot I'd been at the start. I had a nice pile of wood bits, some glue, and the beginnings of a headache.

Somewhere inside Kris continued to talk his grandfather through the complete collection of plastic dinosaur toys that roamed free on his floor.

Grandpa was never going to let me live this one down. He'd get a subtle dig in at Christmas, or over Thanksgiving. In fact, I could imagine him handing me instructions before pointing at the bird and asking if I needed time to practice carving.

Nope. That wasn't happening to this dad.

I was going to assemble a wooden dinosaur and make his mouth move if it killed me.

By the time I finished the second beer I was pretty much convinced it would do me in and was already working on my overly-elaborate headstone.

Here lies Eugene Law, Husband, Father, Man unable to assemble a wooden toy. See his father-in-law for the completed project. Yes, the mouth moves.

I pulled open the drawer and grabbed a permanent marker.

What are you doing, Gene?

I knew exactly what I was doing, just a little Magick, nothing too fancy.

That's cheating.

I squinted at the tiny wooden ribs. "No it's not. It's not cheating if *I* do it."

That logic didn't make sense. But, after a few beers, arguing with yourself rarely did.

I popped the top off the marker and set to work on the proper sigil. I didn't actually have a design for assembling complex wooden dinosaurs, but I figured I could work something together.

The pen met wood and I danced it across the piece, drawing lines, completing curves, and whistling to myself the entire time. I just needed to put together a few different concepts. It wasn't rocket science. I needed Mortimer's Mechanical Magnificence, and I'd just couple that with a hint of Telli-Toe-Tims Temporal Tempering. That should have been exactly what the good doctor ordered.

I held the piece up to the light and smiled. It wasn't my finest work, but it would do.

I contemplated adding something from Payton's Pyros series, but then I remembered dinosaurs didn't breathe fire.

Who says?

"Right, who says dinosaurs didn't breathe fire?"

Scientists, Gene.

I shook my head. "Yeah, like they've ever seen one in real life. How would they know?"

My marker added just a touch for Payton's Pyro. Not enough to take your eyebrows off, but we'd get a good show out of it.

Satisfied I had a workable sigil, I took a sip from my beer and pushed Magick into the newly constructed design.

Nothing happened.

"Huh, I wonder if…" I reached for the toy and knocked over the can."Shit!"

The little bit left in the bottom blurred my design.

"No. No. No!" I yanked the offending can off the work-bench, and slipped, my back hitting the fridge.

Magick swirled through the ruined design, me, and the stupid appliance.

That was right about the point when the garage disappeared.

"Crap."

* * *

IT TOOK me a few seconds to come to grips with the fact the garage was gone, but the fridge was still there. The hulking monstrosity sat tilted in the muck, not quite upright, but also not completely toppled over.

Wait, *muck*?

As hard as the fridge was to make sense of, the muck was worse. This was old fashioned muck: the kind that eats shoes and burbles about it later. I was up to my knees in it, but the fridge? Nope, that jerk had landed on a relatively dry patch, and was practically flaunting that fact.

I rubbed my head for a moment and realized I was still holding the pen and my beer. The latter was disappointingly empty, and the former was missing a cap, but they were something.

It was the rest of what had been my garage that was troubling.

See, there was no garage and there was no house either.

That went for the cars, too, and thankfully the wooden dinosaur toy that Grandpa had sent.

It was me, the fridge, a lot of muck, and what resembled the middle of the state at late day.

In other words, I was in a swamp. This wasn't just any swamp either. This was the mother of all swamps. Thick tropical fronds sucked up the sky like overzealous fans, while the ground slurped and grumbled its way beneath me. There was a mist in the air, an almost palpable humidity that made the normal Florida summer seem tame by comparison.

I crumpled up the beer can and got ready to drop it, then thought better of that and yanked open the fridge to toss it inside.

That was a really bad move.

The appliance door opened and upset the fragile balance of power between the world's surliest appliance and the ground beneath it.

The bastard toppled forward, its door jamming into the muck, and a couple of empty shelves sliding out to hit me in both the gut and face at almost the exact same time.

"Son of a bitch!" I rammed the shelves back in and tried to push the thing closed, but that only made it want to flop backward, with me still holding on to it.

Splash!

The fridge hit the watery muck, and I lost a shoe as I was pulled on top of it. Thankfully I was large enough to not actually get stuck inside. I would have had to have lost a bunch of pounds for anything remotely that dangerous to actually happen.

Basically, I was in a swamp, standing awkwardly in an old garage fridge that hated me, and straddling the cheap shelves I'd just put back in there.

I dropped the beer can inside and waited for the entire thing to sink further into the muddy water.

It didn't.

I accepted this modest reward and tried to figure out what had happened. The details were hazy, but I had the general idea that Magick and a modified sigil were involved.

Based on my general location, I must have accidentally done something with Tiggy's Telemetry. It wasn't an easy one to screw up, but I'd had a couple of beers and was pretty ticked at Porter's dad, so some mistakes might have been made.

The simple solution was to work out where in the state the fridge and I had ended up, then go from there.

Magicking myself back would have been a heck of a task, but there was always a rental car.

I put a hand to my back pocket.

Strike that. You couldn't rent a car on good looks and charm, especially if I really didn't have either.

I'll just call Porter. She'll get a chuckle out of this, and she'll even appreciate the fact that I got rid of the fridge.

I patted the off-white behemoth on the side. "Sorry, buddy, but there's just no way we can haul you out of here. I'm not exactly sure how I'm going to haul *me* out of here."

I put my hand in my other pocket, only to remember I didn't have my phone either.

I'd been neck deep in 'family time,' so by my own decree devices had been off limits.

That's a stupid rule.

Somewhere my daughter was agreeing with me.

Okay, now this meant we were in a bit of a bind, but nothing I couldn't work out.

I brushed away a very large and inquisitive dragonfly and focused my attention on the plain white surface on the inside of the fridge. It was like a whiteboard of epic proportions. All I needed to do was put together a little bit of relativity Magick and we'd be in business.

I wiped away a bit of mud that had besmirched the inside of the door and readied the marker.

The overall design shouldn't be too hard. I just needed to be back in Tampa. Seeing as there was a really good chance I was already in the state—given the swamp-like conditions, greenery, and bugs—I figured it wouldn't take long to get something functional together.

That was the thing with repositioning Magick. It wasn't overly tricky, but it helped to have a solid feel for where you were going. I knew Tampa, and I knew my garage.

I contemplated bringing the fridge with me. There were pros and cons to this, but the thought of hearing from my daughter about the environmental impact of this old appliance rotting in the swamp somewhere overpowered the rest of them.

"Yeah, you're coming with me."

The muck beneath us grumbled in assent.

"All right. Now I just have to complete the Lines of Linearity and the Pins Popping Points..." I danced the marker in a complex set of lines and dots that to any normal person would have looked like very poorly done graffiti. "There we go. That should do it."

Satisfied with my work, I shoved the marker behind my ear and gave my handiwork a final once over. It wouldn't have done to get this far and end up in Lutz or something.

I shuddered at the thought.

"Okay, Mr. Fridge, it's time to head home. Don't worry, you still have many more days of keeping adult beverages cold in front of you. No appliances left behind."

I pressed my hand against the seal and dipped into the cosmic power that made its home inside my chest. I didn't need much. I wasn't moving heaven and earth, just me and an old fridge.

Another one of those absurdly large dragonflies landed on my hand. "Hey, shoo!"

The insect rubbed its legs together and didn't budge. That gave me an idea. If I adjusted for this bug, I could bring it back and impress Kris. Who needs a wooden dinosaur when you have a foot long dragonfly?

Works for me.

I closed my eyes and poured Magick into the seal, making sure to account for the monster dragonfly, as well as the fridge and myself. I got the distinct impression of my molecules pulling themselves apart. This hurt like hell, but virtually guaranteed we were on the right track.

I imagined the garage, our cars, and Porter standing in the door with her arms crossed.

When the Magick cleared, I opened my eyes to find we'd moved a whopping three feet.

The dragonfly was not amused. It fluttered its wings a few times before lifting into the late afternoon sky.

"What the hell?"

I checked the seal again and confirmed each line's accuracy. This was the right layout to get me back to Tampa, and my garage, but nothing here resembled either.

I'd let the yard go before, but never like this.

The insect returned, followed by another one, and then another. Before I knew it I had a sizable multi-eyed peanut gallery perched on the side of the fridge.

"What are you looking at?"

Being insects, they didn't respond, but the muck beneath us did.

It let out a sizable burp and dropped the fridge a few inches.

Crap.

I scrambled to check the door again, brushing aside the annoying bugs in the process. It was completely accurate. I wasn't a pro at these sorts of things, but I knew how to move through spacetime.

Spacetime...

The muck burped again, and the fridge rocked with it, but it wasn't just the mud making room for our least favorite garage appliance; something else shook the ground, something big.

That was right about the same time the dragonflies scattered and the thick tropical fronds bent over sideways. Thick rows of teeth, too many to count, and very much brown from use, pressed through the damaged leaves. Those teeth were attached to a head that was more than big enough to swallow me whole if it wanted to. I didn't really know why, but right at that moment I understood exactly what part of my son's dinosaur puzzle I had wrong.

All of it.

* * *

GROWING UP, I'd watched a lot of Twilight Zone on late night TV. Of course, like any fan of the after-hours creepy, I had my favorite episode.

And right now, I just happened to be living in it.

I scrambled away from the fridge before the door got ripped off and tossed aside by hungry jaws and steel-shredding teeth.

I wasn't an expert on dinosaurs, but I got the impression appliances weren't nearly as flavorful as pink and squishy Magicians.

Run!

That proved a good bit harder than it looked. The muck and muddy water made for painfully slow going, but the massive lizard's claws weren't much better.

I hit dry land and picked up my pace, shooting over the

sandy ground with its tall fronds and dangling branches. I slowed down once to look behind me and caught my foot in the process, falling forward to land in a hollowed out mound.

Those are called nests, Gene.

Yes, I'd put myself in a dinosaur egg nest, complete with very large pre-omelets and a few pint-sized versions of the original one behind me.

They were cute, but also hungry, and it stung like hell when they bit into my arms.

I shook off the squeaking monsters and bolted for the trees, my brain on overdrive trying to figure out exactly how this happened, and exactly what I needed to do to get back.

The beer must have smudged the seal and given me something else entirely.

"Oh yes, another poor decision compounded by alcohol."

I could almost hear Porter's voice in my head. She wasn't wrong, but head-wife wasn't helping me either. I needed to focus and try to remember what I'd done so I could undo it.

Time Magick...

Of all the monumentally stupid things to do.

I ducked behind a massive palm and held my breath while I waited for scaly and the chompers to find me, and snack on the only living human being.

The only...

I held up a hand and turned it over. My skin was still intact, but for how long? There was a reason why no Magician ever tried something this stupid.

Paradoxical erasure was a thing, a very painful and well-documented thing. Back in the thirties there'd been a few ill-fated attempts to avoid the Great Depression. At the time, we hadn't figured out just how much of it had been created by a species of greed-eating goblins. It wasn't until the eighties that we uncovered those bastards. But still, during the Great Depression the few Magicians that took notes tried to go back to the Roaring Twenties and stop the inexorable march of time.

Yeah, that hadn't ended well for many reasons. Time was pretty damn resilient. It finds a way to self-correct. Kill the person responsible for something terrible, a new person would crop up to take their place. Kill the replacement? Hello person number three. This could go on indefinitely, but that wasn't the bad part.

I stared at my hand again and frowned. There was the pins-and-needles feeling I'd been dreading.

I couldn't see them, but they were there.

Temporal Weevils.

At least that's what the notes called them. There was only one woman who made it back, and she'd lost most of her flesh in the process.

Even grainy, the pictures had been terrifying to me as a young Magician.

Temporal Weevils, like the modern day counterparts, were vicious little bastards that craved a nice bit of paradoxical goodness. That Magician had gone back to a time when she hadn't existed. That meant she was a living paradox, and those metaphysical insects loved that sort of thing.

They'd cleaned through her skin at a molecular level so they could feed on the juicy organs underneath.

Just like they wanted to chew on *my* organs.

I shook my hand a few times to push away the increasing loss of sensation.

Plan, Gene.

I needed a plan, and I needed it quickly. Sitting around waiting to become paradox pill bug chow wasn't high on my list of options.

The trees rustled above me as something large settled in the branches.

Shit.

What had she done? How had that woman gotten back to her time?

I'd never been great at staying on top of some of the old stories. See, my brain would have looked at the few surviving pictures of Temporal Weevils and noped right out. Even in black and white it was hard to not get squeamish when the insides were rapidly becoming outsides.

What had it been? Was there a seal?

Branches cracked and popped above me. Whatever was in the tree was certainly not interested in sitting there quietly while I contemplated how not to become time-bug feed.

A long, narrow, and very reptilian head poked out from the thick branches. Inquisitive eyes stared down at me from the back side of a snout designed like a pair of hedge clippers. I'd stepped on one of these going into my son's room, but somehow seeing it in person and being on the business end of those jaws left me with a very different impression.

Run?

I tossed that thought the instant a second head appeared. There were two of those things, and basically no chance I'd outrun them both. They had wings—at least I thought they did. I hadn't hung around to study their two-inch tall rubber counterparts after they'd stabbed the bottom of my foot.

Magick?

I frowned and pressed my back harder against the tree. Magick was part of what brought the Weevils. In fact, being a moron back there and trying to adjust my location had been like spraying myself down with sugar water before rolling around on an anthill.

Using more Magick now was really not smart, but neither was getting snapped in half by flying hedge clippers.

I needed something quick, something simple, something that wouldn't cause me to end up with pureed skin or be left holding my spleen.

Felgrim's Fog? The Fires of Fillandrum?

No, and very much no. I needed something mundane, simple, and not flashy. The crazier the Magick, the better the chance I had of speeding up the time it took before I ended up a pool of liquefied Magician bits.

I wracked my brain for options even as the tree-dwelling creatures crawled closer. They weren't exactly like Kris' rubber dinosaurs, but they were pretty close. Close enough that I couldn't help but be impressed with the tiny toys' accuracy.

My son loved those toys, and his dinosaurs. Plus, for a kid his age, he was really good at remembering all the details.

"No, Dad. That one is a plant eater," he'd said when I'd pretended to have one of the big ones attack these bird-like things.

"It is?"

"Uh huh."

I remembered turning the rubber lizard over in my hands. "So, he eats his vegetables?"

"Yes."

"And why don't you?"

My young son picked up yet another brightly colored, prehistoric floor monster and handed it to me. "Because I'm a meat eater, like this one."

Bingo.

Sometimes the best Magick was the stuff that didn't seem like Magick at all. The things that could have happened by happenstance, random luck, or chance.

Maybe it could be just bad luck for the scaly hedge-clippers climbing out of the tree to investigate me if a larger, hungrier, and decidedly more dinosaur-eating monster were to show up.

The question was how to do that?

There weren't a lot of Magickal seals for summoning

dinosaurs. In fact, there really weren't any. Nearest I could tell, I was the first idiot to end up here.

Or did all the rest die a horrible death?

That was a cheery thought.

I shook out my hand again, trying very hard not to notice the fact that it had picked up a decent shade of red.

You don't need the circle, or a seal. You just need the Magick. This is prehistory: the cosmic power back here was off the charts.

I just needed to dip into that and tell the universe what I wanted.

I slowly stepped away from the tree, my eyes on the rapidly closing flying monsters and their serrated jaws.

Here goes nothing...

I thought of Kris' toys, the plastic rubber menagerie that lived on our living room floor. I imagined the ones he said were meat-eaters, their jaws, and their claws.

Magick bubbled up and danced across those images, catching them up like a massive wave.

I just needed one. Something to spook these things and get them on the run.

The power swelled and then stopped, popping like a party balloon.

I blinked my eyes and tasted iron. I wiped a hand across my face and it came back red.

Shit.

I was standing there, bleeding from my eyes and trying very hard not to panic when the tree line filled with the toothy faces of half-a-dozen of my son's favorite meat-eaters.

I got what I wanted, sort of.

Crap.

* * *

SURROUNDED by hungry dinosaurs wasn't the best of times to contemplate life's decisions, but you went with what you had.

I'd really screwed the pooch on this one. The tree line held more teeth than a dentures convention, and unlike those falsies, *these* were connected to strong jaws and sharp enough to slice me to ribbons, if the Weevils didn't do it first.

Warm blood trickled down my cheek.

Yeah, the Weevils might do it first.

Not to be outdone by invisible paradox eaters, the newcomer dinos pushed their way into the clearing.

These were definitely part of the meat-eating family, and appeared more than happy to enjoy a nice rack of Magician without hesitation.

Great.

I took a few steps backward, only to be nipped at by the flying versions of what was shaping up to be Gene's greatest nightmare.

Magick?

Judging by the blood seeping out from under my nails, Magick was only making me more enticing to the Weevils.

At most I had enough left for a single push to get home, provided I could figure out a way to do that.

Standing in the middle of a dinosaur stand-off wasn't doing anything to help see that goal to fruition.

Run!

I bolted for the nearest biped, going for the legs in the hopes I could comically slip under them. That worked about as well as I figured, in other words, not at all.

The great lizard snapped its head and powerful jaws out and I narrowly avoided losing my head in the process.

I ended up in dirt, staring up at what very much looked like the scaly end of a life moderately well-lived.

'Local husband and father vanishes, takes beer fridge with him.'

It had a very Florida ring to it.

The towering dino's jaws made for my chest, but before they could add a new cavity, one of its partners grabbed the beast's neck. It appeared dinosaurs were as good at sharing a snack as my own kids.

Who knew?

Claws flashed and in an instant we had a full melee in process. The meat-eating dinosaurs decided they all wanted a piece of me, which meant they had to go through each other. The tree-hugging, flappy ones joined the fray and in short order it became an insane free-for-all.

It was a little like Thanksgiving Dinner at the Law house, with me playing the role of the turkey.

I scrambled to my feet and made a break for the trees, but a wide tail hit me broadside and put the whole world on its side.

My back hit a patch of ferns and wide bushes. I rolled end-over-end once, then twice, and finally a third time before banging my head against something hard.

Bong!

That was metal. Even in my highly confused state, I knew there shouldn't be any metal here.

Dinosaurs weren't known for their ironworking skills.

Safely hidden behind the ferns, I took a few seconds to wait for the world to stop spinning before I turned over to see what had stopped my inane tumble.

The fridge door.

Beat up, scratched to hell, and barely recognizable in the muck, it was all that remained of my trusty beer fridge.

It had landed face up, giving me a view of the few magnet-stuck pictures my kids had deposited on it over the years. Most of them were ruined by the elements, faded, and now torn to bits by dinosaur teeth, but it wasn't the stick figures or their crooked smiles that got my attention. It was the magnet. Kris hadn't been in school long. He was at that age where it was colors, numbers, letters, and tons of macaroni art. My son was a dried pasta savant, or at least that's what his teachers said. I wasn't convinced he didn't enjoy the medium for its snackable qualities.

That boy was always hungry and could eat basically anything. Dried pasta was certainly on his menu.

I pried the tiny noodle art off the door and held it in my bloody hand. I had to admire the shape selection and judicious amount of glue, as well as the way he sculpted dad with only one backwards letter. I did consider myself one bad dad just the same. It was nice of him to immortalize that in pasta.

Still, none of that mattered, because just like my fingers, my eyes, and any other place the Weevils could get to, the pasta was crumbling. It wasn't the pasta, it was the magnet.

Science and Magick have a very challenging relationship that goes back an untold number of years. They get along, but not much better than my in-laws at family gatherings. You had to have a Porter there to keep her brothers and parents in line.

For science and Magick, you needed a magnet. They were sort of the peacemakers in that forever cold war.

This cheap strip of black material gave me an idea.

The magnet, just like me, was from a different time. A time when dinosaurs were two inches tall, made of rubber, and roamed free on the living room floor.

It, just like me, wanted to get back to that time. The difference was that magnet had pull, and a sense of direction.

It was primed to go home. I just had to supply it with the right Magick. But what *was* the right Magick?

I brushed the fading pasta away with my fingers, only to discover more blood. The Weevils were moving faster. I blinked away the red tint to my vision.

If I didn't hurry up, I'd end up just like those still frames, a gooey pile of organic tissue, and back here that meant I'd be a human-tasting Jell-O shot.

Nice visual, Gene.

Wait... There was something to that visual. Not the part about turning into a pile of pulp. That I was distinctly not interested in, but the way those Weevils worked meant they'd eventually tear through the magnet, and as they did it would give up the weird mix of science and Magick trapped inside it, and when it did, I could harvest it for a one way trip home. The magnet wanted to go home, and so did I.

Bits of magnetic dust brushed off on my fingers.

Those little bastards were moving fast. I had to hurry.

I used my foot to clear a spot on the dirty ground and immediately set to work on the seal. My fingers stung with each pass through the mud. I was risking the world's worst infection, but it wouldn't matter if I stayed here much longer.

I had to get home.

Satisfied with the design, I set the magnet in the center of it and wiped my face one last time. The Magick swirled around in my chest, excited at the prospect of going home, but also concerned about the fact I appeared to be moving from solid to liquid quite rapidly.

I blinked away the red, my vision fading into a blur of colors and shapes.

Those shapes moved.

Shit!

I heard the claws in the muck before the dinosaur hit me. It was a smaller one, something from the house-cat sized family, but it had plenty of teeth, claws, and friends.

The magnet was still there, but it was fading fast. The Weevils had already chewed through the bulk of it, and they'd chew through me if these scaly monsters didn't beat them to it.

I extended a hand trying to feel for the tiny strip of power, and for the love my son had poured into it.

It was there, but barely hanging on.

Something bit down on my hand and I was proud to say I got the other hand around its scaly neck.

The lizard thing clawed at my arm, even as more of its family showed up for a Magician feast, but I'd found the magnet, my son, and my way home.

I pounded my bloody hand into the dirt and let the Magick go.

Let's see how you like the twenty-first century!

* * *

THE MAGICK FADED, taking with it my pain, and the prehistoric swamp. Never had I been so happy to be lying on the hard garage floor clutching a wriggling dinosaur in my hand.

The dino!

I let the creature go, only to watch him melt away before my eyes. Temporal Weevils existed in all times, and they knew I was the only dinosaur that belonged in my garage.

The cat-sized creature managed to cover a few spastic steps before its skin peeled away. That was followed shortly after by a slurry organs and connective tissue.

The resulting mass of jelly continued boiling down until only the bones remained, clean, white, and practically fossilized.

* * *

"HE GOT YOU *REAL* DINOSAUR BONES?!" Grandpa leaned into the screen and squinted at the pristine skull in my son's hands.

"Yeah! They are so cool. I have so many of them. Do you

want to see them all?" Kris proceeded to direct his attention to the pile of polished awesome from his dad's worst trip ever.

The old man frowned ever so slightly on the tablet. "They are. I had no idea you could even do that. How did your dad..."

I popped my head into the frame and winked at my father-in-law, enjoying his frustration probably more than I should have.

"Magick."

THANK YOU FOR READING

Thank you for reading. Books take time to write, but they also take time to read. Your time is valuable, and I very much appreciate you spending it with me.

If it's not too much to ask, we authors live on caffeine, panic, and reviews. If you'd be so kind as to leave one for this book, I'd be grateful.

Feel free to use the following link to go to Amazon and get started.

Leave a review at Amazon.

MARTIN SHANNON'S WEIRD FLORIDA

Tales of Weird Florida (The Eugene Law Cycle)

Complete Omnibus - Boxed Set Books 1-5

1 - Dead Set

2 - Gathering Gloom

3 - Beaten Path

4 -Bloody Deed

5 - No Fury

Black Tar Souls

I - Crazy

2 - Son of a Gun

3 - Sweetwater

4 - Midnight Riders

5 - The Infinite Pain

6 - Undone

Viburna

1 - Blood and Lies

2 - Last Call

3 - Arms and Iron

4 - Saving Grace

5 - Knife's Edge

6 - The Tigress of Ybor

Discarded Arcana

1 - Careless Wishes

2 - Black Ribbon

3 - Girls and Gun Smoke

Short Stories

0 - Danderous Delivery (Newsletter Subscribers Only)

1 - Hook, Line, and Slinker

2 - Ballroom and Chain

3 - Bahama Blues

4 - Plasma Pistols

5 - Lights Out

6 - Mourning Paper

7 - Ignorance and Unleaded

8 - Black Valentine

9 - Soulless

10 - Ten Turns

11 - Irrigated

12 - Magician's Weekend

13 - Short Stop

14 - Sleep to Dream Her

15 - Mesozoic Magick

ABOUT THE AUTHOR

Martin Shannon's been using his imagination to avoid weeding since he was in short pants. His first series, *Tales of Weird Florida*, is an homage to the Sunshine State he knows and loves, and spent countless hours riding his bike through as a kid. It's got mystery, mayhem, and more than a little Magick. He hopes you enjoy the supernatural side of the upside down state, but if not, he's got a banjo, and he knows how to use it. You can find out more at www.martin-shannon.com.